# FALLOUT

"Jones is unflinching as she plots the course of fallout with no shelter, of wounded lives undone by desperation in love and art." —*New York Times*

"I can't help but feel that if she had been born Samuel Jones she would already be considered on a par with the Barneses and McEwans of this parish. . . . Jones's gift—like all great writers—is to leave us wanting so desperately to believe that the story will continue without us once the scenery has been cleared away."
—*Observer*

"The novel is at its best when the characters quietly seek an audience for their pleasures, their pains, and the 'more permanent wounds of their longer lives waiting, undiscovered.'"
—*The New Yorker*

"Jones highlights beautifully the energetic, naive, cheap red-wine fug of the Seventies start-up, and its decadent antithesis, the emptiness of fatally compromised success."
—*The Sunday Telegraph*

"The strength of *Fallout* is the insistent thread of hope that runs through all the humiliation and bad behavior. The result is . . . a fuller, more emotionally satisfying story."
—*Wall Street Journal*

"An intelligent, pacy tale of pretty, talented people, striving for recognition but held back by their past. . . . Every summer needs a *One Day*–style read; this book is a contender for that crown."
—*The Times*

"Jones's intricate, complex plot, sympathetically drawn characters, and authentic depictions of damaged genius make an unassailable claim for the power of a writer's detailed observation in the face of formula fiction."
—*Library Journal*

# FALLOUT

Also by Sadie Jones

*The Outcast*
*Small Wars*
*The Uninvited Guests*

# FALLOUT

A Novel

## Sadie Jones

HARPER ● PERENNIAL

NEW YORK ● LONDON ● TORONTO ● SYDNEY ● NEW DELHI ● AUCKLAND

HARPER ⬤ PERENNIAL

First published in Great Britain in 2014 by Chatto & Windus.

FIRST HARPER PERENNIAL EDITION PUBLISHED 2015.

The Library of Congress has catalogued the hardcover edition as follows:

Jones, Sadie.
 Fallout : a novel / Sadie Jones.——First edition.
     pages cm
 First published in Great Britain in 2014 by Chatto & Windus.
    ISBN 978-0-06-229281-0 (hardback)——ISBN 978-0-06-229282-7 (paperback)——ISBN 978-0-06-229283-4 (ebook)
    1. Theater——England——London——Fiction. 2. Adultery——Fiction. I. Title.
 PR6110.O638F35 2014
 823'.92——dc23

2013036944

15  16  17  18  19   OFF/RRD   10  9  8  7  6  5  4  3  2  1

Dedicated with love to EJ and JJ

## Afterwards – New York – 1975

New York was not his city and this was not his life. He bought postcards and wrote them to the people he loved but he did not send them. At night he dreamed the ache of human kindness and every stranger's face he saw reminded him of home. The title of his play and the name that was not his real name, and other names on other theatres on the crowded billboards of the street, shone on canopies ringed by lights. It was every Broadway film imagining made humble by the rubbish-blowing poverty of the world; nostalgia torn down in the grey afternoon – this is what it feels like, not that, but *this*.

They did not need him at rehearsal so he walked the streets he had become familiar with, then further, to the unknown maze beyond. In the afternoon he went back to the hotel apartment and looking out at the distant heights of the city he thought of her. He did not think that she would come.

Lucasz Kanowski broke his mother out of the insane asylum the quiet way; they went through the back gate. He sprang the padlock with a piece of bent wire, a skill maintained despite grammar school's refining influence. He brought her some clothes stuffed into his school satchel: a woollen scarf – worried, absurdly, that she would hang herself with it – a cardigan with daisies at the neck and an old coat. He had a pair of wellingtons for her. He had wanted to bring real shoes, ladies' shoes, but he had not been able to find any. It was possible his father had thrown them all away but that seemed such a decisive step Luke did not think his slow and inward father would have taken it. Wellingtons were not elegant but they would do for his mother's escape. The grounds of the asylum were large; they would not be missed for a while.

He pulled the iron gate open, crushing the long grass.

'*Allez-y*,' he said and she stepped through, lifting her chin and shivering.

They stood together by the road as finches hopped and darted in the hedge. Luke saw that his mother was frightened. She stood quite still, hugging herself, small inside her cardigan.

'We can catch the bus,' he said, as if everything were normal, but his thirteen-year-old voice was breaking and nothing sounded normal.

'*Maman?* Let's go.'

Looking into her eyes he saw the chasm. People were scared of the insane and thought it was because of what they might do, but Luke knew really they were scared of that gap behind their eyes. Luke wasn't frightened; it was she who had to live there. He would have done anything to save her. And he still prayed for her, even though his arguments disproving God's existence were louder these days than the prayers. He prayed, and couldn't help believing that if he did something right – perfectly right – she might get better.

'*Maman? On y va?*'

She glanced at him and smiled. Her skin had a pinkness, the flush of sunlight, as if the blood had begun to flow, and Luke felt the power of rescue. They crossed the road to the bus stop. When the bus came they climbed onto it and sat in silence as it took them away.

Three days before, they had sat together on Seston Asylum's bare patchy lawn in their splintering chairs among the dandelions, with the tangle of pipes crawling down the walls behind them and the chimneys crowded on the Victorian Gothic roofs above. Hélène had given him one of her most assured looks and said, 'I read in *The Times* that the National Gallery in London is to make an exhibition of French painting. Cézannes. Renoir. *J'aimerais te le montrer, Luc.*'

Luke's first thought was that to see paintings if you wanted to, to read books, listen to music, was the very minimum for a tolerable life. Even his father listened to music. Later, when they said goodbye and she left him to go back to the dayroom and do whatever it was she did when he was not there, he said quietly, 'Shall we go to Lincoln? Look at pictures in a gallery?'

But his mother was a Parisienne and a snob.

'*Lincoln? So provincial.*' She leaned close to his ear. '*Londres.*'

'*Londres?*' Luke could not help half-laughing; bested by a woman, and a feeble one at that.

'*Chut!*'

Her hair was absurdly messy. She was standing in her slippers on the lino by Rose Ward, her candlewick dressing gown gaping and scorch-marked bruises on her temples from the electroshock therapy. Soft slippered footfalls defined the patients at Seston. The nurses, orderlies, doctors, all had shoes in which they might leave, that tapped or slapped the lino. The patients' feet were all but silent. Their voices might be loud – sometimes they were very loud – but they were not grounded, and could not be heard.

'*En train ce n'est pas très loin.*'

She was right, by train it was not far at all.

The nurses at the reception desk did not look up as he left through the mesh cage at the entrance, or as the door banged behind him and the catches locked. He had been visiting his mother at Seston since he was five years old, he came and went as he pleased.

Even as he collected the timetables at the library for his mother's escape Luke felt the weight of the odds stacked against him. He made schedules, lists –

*Leave Seston 10 a.m. London train, 11.07.*

He had contingency plans –

*Event of police, lie.*

But he knew that the greatest danger was not the authorities but his mother herself. Taking her away from the hospital, and her medication, she would be jolted from the familiar and vulnerable to a thousand horrors. As the day approached he didn't dare remind her of their plan in case she let it slip to one of the nurses. It was his alone, his dreadful secret, but Luke believed that if one had the blessing of sanity then self-doubt was cowardly, and so great as his fear of disaster was, in outrage his resolve responded.

Now they emerged from King's Cross Station, tiny against the vastness of brick and concrete. Thin sooty air. She in her wellingtons and wrapped-round cardigan like a gypsy; he with his home-cut hair, humiliated all at once by context. Mother and son held hands so tightly their bones dug into one another. People passed them by, a man shoving Hélène's shoulder as he overtook. She shrank away with a mumbled sound through closed lips. Luke knew the sound and recognised danger.

'*Je ne suis jamais venue ici* —' She formed the words as if with an unfamiliar mouth. '*Tu comprends?*'

Luke hadn't ever been to London before either but he said nothing.

'*I say!*' shouted a woman nearby. '*Taxi!*' His mother ducked, as if avoiding the swipe of a monster's paw. Her eyes were all at once wild. Another mumbled sound, this one guttural — *yu* — as she brought her shoulders up and cringed. He realised he could not rely on her for human company, not for the moment. The day ahead was huge and unfettered. He decided to see her as a zoo animal; not less than human, simply other. She was a rare and unpredictable creature; he was a professional, armed with tranquilliser darts. He was ashamed to find himself wishing the tranquilliser darts were real.

'Don't worry, I have all the information we need,' he said, reaching into his pocket and taking out his bus timetables.

She withdrew into herself on the bus, and they were nearly hit by a taxi on the Strand. Once, she began to talk to somebody he couldn't see, so Luke held her hand and told her what he'd had for dinner the night before. After that — his fault — they went the wrong way down Whitehall, but she had calmed down by then and looked around very happily as they walked back.

Trafalgar Square felt as wide and steady as a field, Nelson's Column towering in its centre like a talisman.

Once they were inside the gallery itself an exotic normality overtook. And so it happened. For half an hour — more even than that — they walked and looked at pictures and were happy. He had the privilege of her uncluttered brain; her senses wide open, her mind working. He was old enough to know there was danger in imagining God punished or rewarded the people going about the unpatterned world, but he could not help but feel, just this once, that the unjust chaos of his mother's truncated life had been noticed, and that He had been kind.

'Close your eyes,' she said, when they were standing almost alone in a big room, surrounded by Cézannes and Monets. 'You can *feel* the paintings, no?'

Luke closed his eyes.

'Or do you think, Luc, if the walls were empty, the air would feel just the same?'

Luke waited with his eyes closed and felt the life of the work around him. It shifted the atmosphere. He thought about genius consolidated by time and the immeasurable charisma of fame. He didn't know how to put these things into words, only that the paintings seemed to breathe.

'It's like being in the room with people,' he said, and opened his eyes.

They stood, with the quiet pictures framed in gold. Sunlit water. Flowers. Bright southern cliffs.

His mother shrugged. 'Perhaps you don't want to believe all *this* is for nothing,' she said.

He felt embarrassed, caught out, but as they walked on she glanced at him and smiled, and he knew it wasn't for nothing. They were in the company of greatness and they both knew it and were raised up. He looked over his shoulder as they left, and thanked the pictures in his mind, as his mother took his arm.

Eleven-year-old Nina Hollings gazed up at the two painted sisters, and with glad, moneyed smiles they gazed back down at her. Looking in awe at their linked arms, their velvet and silk, Nina felt exactly what she was: uncompleted by love or beauty.

Behind her, her mother's voice, clear and strong –

'Only men can paint women.' She placed her hands lightly on Nina's shoulders. 'Only men make really good *coiffeurs*, and only men can cut clothes properly.'

'Why?' Nina did not take her eyes from Singer Sargent's rendering of the sisters' tiny waists beneath their party dresses, the dewy life shining from their eyes. 'Why only men?'

'Because men desire women, and can create them – even homosexual men. Women hairdressers have no idea at all. Very often they're jealous and *want* you to look ordinary.'

'Are there *any* lady artists?' asked Nina.

'There are, but they are concerned with ugliness for the most part – as for *couture!*'

Marianne gave a tiny snort and took her green leather gloves from her bag. She began to put them on. Her mother couldn't run away while she was putting on her gloves so Nina leaned on one leg and performed heel-toe exercises with the rested foot. She looked around the room at the tweedy ladies murmuring in pairs and two students in sweaters, kissing. The girl was in a baggy skirt and flat shoes and the boy's arm was wrapped around her body.

After a moment Nina said, 'What about Coco Chanel?'

Marianne chopped the crevices between her fingers.

'Chanel is a *terrible* couturière. All her good cutters are men,' she said. 'Come along now.'

She took her daughter's hand and they went. Nina stared at the kissing students as they passed. The girl leaned over her boyfriend's shoulder and gave her a mascara-laden wink.

As they reached the long central gallery, and Trafalgar Square could be seen beyond the doors, Nina said, 'Look, French Painting. A special exhibition!'

'Perhaps next time.'

'One more room?'

'Just one.' Marianne sighed, as if another moment with her daughter was a great burden.

Standing before Uccello's *St George and the Dragon* Nina looked at the long-necked maiden, daintily bound, and the lavishly armoured St George thrusting his lance through the dragon's eye.

'It doesn't say who the princess is,' she said. 'And she doesn't look very frightened, does she?'

Marianne looked at her watch.

'She's being saved,' she said.

And that was that. They left the gallery under a white sky. They were meeting Aunt Mat by the lions.

Some children with tins of birdseed were throwing it for the pigeons swooping low in the air and jostling together on the ground. A little girl was standing like a scarecrow with pigeons perching up and down her arms. She was laughing through her nose, and spluttering. Seed dripped from the folds of her coat. Nina watched enviously as the girl's father knelt to take a photograph.

'Disgusting,' said Marianne, pulling her away.

Aunt Mat was waiting sturdily by the plinth, a giant black lion's paw behind her head and a carrier over her arm as well as her handbag, the crocodile depths of which held toffees and Player's No.6. She gave a cheery wave.

'There you are,' she said. 'Did you have fun?'

Nina stared at Aunt Mat's sensible shoes.

'Hello, Matilda,' said her mother, standing like a thoroughbred, one leg extended. She wore a moss-green suit, belted, that stood out like a jewel against the grey.

'Marianne,' said Aunt Mat, coolly. She smiled down at Nina, her eyes creasing her powder-soft cheeks. Nina couldn't smile back.

When her mother smiled her face was not disturbed. Nina had tried it in the mirror but she, like Aunt Mat, was distorted by her smile, like an ape. She didn't think she would be a beauty.

'I have an interview,' said Marianne.

'Much on at the moment?' asked Aunt Mat.

'Oh, you know, it's dreadfully slow.'

'You said you were busy last week. Auditions?'

'I am busy!'

'Mummy . . . please,' said Nina in a tiny voice as her hand, despite herself, crept back into her mother's.

'Nina . . .' Marianne knelt as deeply as her skirt would allow and looked into her face.

'Darling. Please be brave. It upsets Mummy so much when you cry.'

There was a sharp movement beside them as Aunt Mat ground her low-heels into the paving.

'I adore you,' whispered Marianne to her daughter. 'When I am away from you I have a pain in my heart.'

Nina felt her own chest tighten as if a belt was crushing it.

'Say *goodbye*, darling. Kiss Mummy.'

Last time Nina had begged and clung, crushed her mother's clothes. She had caused a public scene. There had been ecstasy in the abandon; to have no control, to be abject. Part of her believed it would bind her mother to her, but it had driven her away. Who would want such a desperate creature? She was determined not to cry this time.

'Goodbye, my darling,' said her mother, tears shining. But Nina gripped her fingers tightly, not letting go.

'For God's sake, Marianne!' said Aunt Mat. 'Stop it!'

But Marianne did not stop. 'My love,' she said, 'let me go.' It was too much. Nina began to cry, falling fast into it.

'Darling,' said her mother, 'I *must* go—'

'*Why?*' sobbed Nina, tears and spit and snot.

'Please, darling—'

'Just go!' exclaimed Aunt Mat.

'How can you say that? My daughter is *crying*!' said Marianne.

Aunt Mat was powerless. Nina could not control herself; Marianne would not leave until she did. It was hopelessness, not will, that made her give up and finally let go of her.

Marianne walked slowly away, turning every few seconds to wave. She had gone.

'Come along,' said Aunt Mat briskly, taking Nina's hand.

Pulled along roughly, Nina tried to keep up – tripped – her aunt stopped. She did not kneel or take Nina in her arms.

'I'm sorry, dear,' she said. 'It's not your fault.' She rearranged her bags on her arm, an habitual regrouping.

'Did you have a nice time? . . . Would you like a cup of tea and a nice bun?'

Nina didn't answer. Aunt Mat sighed and surrendered for a moment the effort of being something for Nina. She looked sadly around at the pigeons and the crouching lions. A cold breeze moved the dirt on the ground into swirls about the plinths. She looked back at her niece's desolate face.

'Would you like to feed the pigeons?'

'. . . No,' whispered Nina, 'they're disgusting.'

'What did you say, dear?'

Nina was about to answer when she saw that on the steps of the gallery ahead of them there was a woman in wellington boots.

'What's that lady doing?' she asked, distracted.

Aunt Mat looked.

'She's sitting down.'

'Why is she sitting on the steps? They're dirty. And why is she wearing boots? And what is that boy doing?'

'He's trying to make her come along, I should think, which is what we should be doing.'

'Is she crying?'

'Don't stare.'

'She can't see me.'

'It's rude.'

'We're miles away. Oh look, there's a policeman!'

Aunt Mat couldn't help but look too. A uniformed man, talking emphatically, was trying to approach the lanky boy who seemed to be shielding the woman, holding out his arms in a gesture of defence.

'That's not a policeman,' said Aunt Mat, 'that's a guard from the gallery.'

'What does he guard?'

'The paintings — and he makes sure people behave sensibly.'

'*She* isn't behaving sensibly.'

The woman on the steps was rocking back and forth, pulling at her cardigan, and the boy and the guard seemed to be arguing. Aunt Mat took Nina's hand again.

'They're probably tramps. Let's go inside and see if we can't find a cup of tea.'

They began to walk towards the steps, just to one side so as to avoid the scene rising in pitch between the guard, the boy and the woman in the wellington boots. Passers-by had become bystanders; bystanders developed into an uncertain crowd as the woman began to wail, a stream of sounds punctuated by words and phrases.

'. . . there were *seven hundred of them*,' she was saying, '*sept cents, vous voyez*? Not all of them *were* alive. You're not a policeman . . .' And she shied away, as if she were being assaulted.

'Where do you live? What's your name?' asked the guard as the boy went from one foot to the other, glancing anxiously between them.

'She's all right,' he kept saying, white-faced. 'Please — you're making it worse.'

'Come with me, Nina,' said Aunt Mat. 'It's none of our business.' And she pulled Nina through the doors.

Inside the gallery were muted echoes, lowered voices, and the soft *shush* of the tall heavy doors brushing the floors as they opened and closed. Nina twisted her head to look, but the woman and strange boy were out of sight. Her mouth felt dry. She had been frightened going past them, as well as fascinated.

There was something else. Everyone had looked at the woman – her distress, her pallor. She was so fragile, with the scruffy boy who was too young to look after anybody standing over her, resolute and protective. Nina realised what she felt; it was envy.

She tugged Aunt Mat's hand. 'She was very pretty, wasn't she?' she said.

'I can't say I noticed. French, possibly.'

'Like Mummy.'

'Like your grandmother. Your mother is as English as I am, nearly.'

'What will happen to her?'

'They'll take her away, poor thing,' said Aunt Mat.

'Where will they take her?'

'Never you mind.'

'Poor lady,' murmured Nina.

She imagined her, wrapped in soft ropes like the painted maiden and taken by soldiers to an unseen salvation. It seemed to her a wonderful thing to be so helpless; to be taken up, and saved.

———————

It was long after midnight when Tomasz Kanowski opened the door to his son and the two policemen. There was an orange shade over the dim bulb in the hall – fabric with flowers on it – and Tomasz was a dark bulk in the doorway. A smell of stewed onion, cigarette smoke and, faintly, sour fish floated round him from the inside of the house. The policemen took off their helmets to show that this was a family matter.

'Mr Kanowski?'

'Yes,' he said. 'Come into the house, Lucasz.'

His voice seemed to struggle from his throat, the accent thickened by drink and feeling.

Luke went sideways past his father and looked at the two pasty-faced constables from behind his shoulder. The policemen exchanged looks. Tomasz stared at them in odd and passive challenge; it was decidedly un-English. They waited for him to say something else but he did not speak.

When they had gone, he closed the door slowly. Luke hung his head, weaving with tiredness, weak with relief to be home safe in their solid, stinking little prison. His father held the back of his neck and drew him towards the bulk of his chest until Luke's forehead rested against the thick collarbone beneath his father's shirt.

'This was a brave and very stupid thing to do,' he said softly, his big fingers pressing Luke's skull.

Luke nodded, burning with sorrow. His father's smell of beer and sweat was in his nostrils.

'I think you must have frightened your mother very much.'

'I don't care,' said Luke, urgent through gritted teeth. 'She loved it. She wanted it, and she was happy. Some of the time. Why won't you see her? You should visit her.'

Tomasz pressed his son's head against his chest.

'Stop, Lukasz.'

They stayed in the fierce lock of their embrace until Tomasz nodded and Luke felt his hot breath on his neck as he exhaled. Tomasz pushed his son slowly away, gripping his face in both hands. If his mother's eyes fronted a void, his father's, complicated and sodden, were spilling over. He kissed Luke's forehead, hard, and released him.

'Go to bed now,' he said.

Luke sat on his bed, shivering in the luxury of his solitude. The evening passed across his memory: the succession of vehicles that had transported them along strange dark roads; the police officers who had questioned him, first with sympathy and suspicion, then pity, as his small crime was discovered and the fact that his mother had never been anywhere else in his lifetime but an asylum. *Nowhere else until today*, thought Luke. He pressed his hands to his eyes to shut out the inhuman subjugation it had taken to separate her from him, and his own shameful relief when she had gone.

He lay down, surrendering more than deciding, and stared at the dark-wood and gold crucifix on the wall opposite the end of his bed. Sometimes he laughed at the idea of God, other times he quaked in fear. Often he crossed himself unthinkingly, or bowed his head, or felt rage well up like blood at the blind patriarchal hand that held him down. Now he gazed upon the cheap crucifix hanging on its one nail and prayed. He could hear his father's slow footfalls. His eyes drifted to the ceiling. The footsteps faded. His focus blurred.

*'Zdrowas Maryjo, łaski pełna, Pan z Toba . . .'*

*Hail Mary, full of grace. Our Lord is with thee. Blessed art thou among women, and blessed is the fruit of thy womb, Jesus. Holy Mary, Mother of God, pray for us sinners, now and at the hour of our death . . .*

A stream of Hurricane bombers flew silently above him.

His father, as he had never known him but knew he once had been, in a scarf and gauntlet gloves, waved a cheery salute as he flew by — and Luke slept.

Above his head, cheaply framed, the Virgin wearing powder-blue and unlikely lipstick, smiled down on him.


## 1965

In the September of 1965 Luke Kanowski in Lincolnshire was beginning his lower-sixth year at Seston Grammar, while in London Nina Hollings had just left school.

'I want Nina to come with me to Paris,' Marianne said, on the telephone to Aunt Mat.

There was a battle for territory being fought. Aunt Mat was a mild person but her sister-in-law enraged her.

'Paris isn't suitable,' she said and straightened the rug with her toe, her heart beating hard against the things she must not say.

Marianne's voice came down the line like an over-tightened violin string. 'She's fifteen! Paris isn't suitable for *what*? Put her on!'

It was her *glad mother* tone, the one that said *my darling, I missed you* when she hadn't called for three months; when she forgot another birthday; when she arrived with an armful of presents — sugar mice. Aunt Mat did not have that trump card to play. She had only Horlicks, bedtimes and the solace of a good book against sporadic joy, fugitive love. However much *sensible* she instilled, one word from her mother sent Nina reeling towards the ridiculous.

'All right,' she said. 'I'll get her.'

Nina was upstairs, listening to her dreadful records. Aunt Mat called her down and Nina spoke to her mother, wrapping the telephone cord around her fingers, as she murmured like a lover to her parent. Aunt Mat sat on the sofa in the sitting room like a bad fairy, watching through the open door, with the fat marmalade cat purring aggressively behind her on the sill, the net curtain hitched on his unknowing ear.

'. . . really Mummy? Really?' her niece whispered.

Aunt Mat felt familiar vile jealousy mixing with fear for Nina's future. Paris with Marianne – the woman had no morals, no talent, no money. Nina put the receiver down and waited, her narrow shoulders eloquent.

'How was your mother?' asked Aunt Mat, levelly.

Nina turned; thickly kholled eyes, spiky triumph and guilt –

'I thought I'd go to Paris next week,' she said airily; the febrile shadow of Marianne, without the steel, without the acid.

'I see. How will you get there?' said Aunt Mat tightly.

'On the train, I should think.'

'What on earth for?' burst out Aunt Mat, uncharacteristic, and Nina blazed, '*Because my mother wants me!*' so violently, so ringing with righteous, operatic gratitude, that Aunt Mat crumpled. She wanted to cry. Nina thrust out her face and widened her eyes in silent demand – the whites so bright against the massed lashes and dark pupils the effect would have thrown them back against their seats in the circle.

'Save the theatrics, dear. If Marianne wants to take you to Paris there's nothing I can do about it. You'll always have a home here, if it goes to the bad.'

'*Lucky me!*' Nina turned away with a hair-flick, ruining her exit by stepping over the telephone cord in an awkward sideways knee-lift, like a stork on the mudflats.

One hand on the newel post, jumping the first three stairs, she ran to her room and slammed the door so that the overhead light shook down a drift of plaster-dust. These were the sounds of Aunt Mat's guardianship: the running feet, the door slam, the record player starting up. *Be my, be my baby — be my — be my little baby, be my baby now-ow-ow* . . . And Aunt Mat, loving her, whispered along — *be my, be my baby* — and pulled the ugly cat onto her lap where he settled, resentful and content.

Nina was amazed how simple it was to leave home. She packed a case, and said *goodbye* and walked to the tube station. Aunt Mat, who avoided scenes, barely acknowledged their parting. It hurt but did not surprise Nina. She had not recognised Aunt Mat's care as love. For Nina, love was longing. She thought Aunt Mat must not love her at all, and did not know that she cried when Nina left.

The few tube stops from Fulham Broadway felt like an ocean voyage, then her mother's street lay before her, curving away from the Cromwell Road to end in a square of sooty laurels held in by railings. The houses were tall and flaking white with electrical wires stapled loosely down the fronts and different sets of curtains at each of the windows. Nina walked quickly, checking the numbers, then stood on the top step with her case. Perhaps her mother had bought them a cake to celebrate. Aunt Mat often bought Victoria sponges, gritty with sugar, for tea. Her finger hovering over the bell. **Jacobs**. Not Hollings, her unknown father's name. Jacobs. She pressed it, firmly.

Marianne's flat was up five flights. *Marvellously good for the figure but they really must do something about the common parts.* The stairs had shredding carpets and smelled of budgie cages despite more than one sign stating pets were strictly not allowed. *I don't know who they could be, these poor souls with their pets, best not to dwell.* The top-floor flats were cramped and asymmetrical, corners filled out with boxed-in pipes seeping welcome heat.

Nina put her toothbrush by the basin in the bedroom and unpacked into the bottom drawer of the wardrobe. She put her shampoo and hairbrush in the clothes drawer too. Marianne had found three wire hangers and Nina hung her blouses and skirts on top of one another while her mother watched, smoking.

'It turns out we aren't going to Paris after all,' she said.

'Oh!' Nina turned. She was holding her pyjamas and the smell of home rose up from them. 'Why not?'

Her mother glanced around the room, restlessly.

'I've got a part. Isn't it marvellous?'

'Marvellous! What in?'

'Oh, it's nothing much. I'm doing the director a favour, really.'

Marianne slipped off her heels and walked in stockinged feet to the kitchen part of the room, where a Baby Belling stood propped on a tile, put out her cigarette and filled the kettle.

'How long are you staying?'

*Staying?*

'I don't know.'

Marianne slammed the kettle onto the hob in arbitrary temper but then turned, smiling.

'I should think Matilda was *livid*,' she said. '*Was* she?'

Aunt Mat had helped Nina pack, taught her to fold her

blouses and offered tissue paper, but Nina was determined to please.

'You'd think I was running away to join the circus!'

Marianne smiled and cast her eye across her daughter's small frame.

'God, Nina, you look dreadful,' she said, like a casual kick to the stomach, and then she went to the sofa and sat down. 'Here —' She patted the seat.

Nina sat, settling the pyjamas on her lap.

'Darling, are you really serious about drama school?'

Nina was still watching the Paris apartment fade in her imagining.

'. . . Nina?'

Drama school was something they had talked about. Nina had photographs of film stars on her walls, but apart from the occasional thrill of seeing her mother in a play her life had been Aunt Mat's front room and school uniforms; baked eggs and the pictures on Saturday afternoons.

'Do you have any idea what it costs? Look at me.'

Nina was embarrassed at her age to look anybody full in the face.

'You have a look of Natalie Wood . . . an unspoilt look. We're too dark to be the girl-next-door — it's because we're French . . .' Her eyes lit with anger. 'This *ridiculous* play. They want me to be somebody's *mother*! Not a young wife with a baby! A *mother*. I come on. I'm shocked about something. I give people tea. I go off again. They'll probably have me in a pinny.'

Nina didn't know what to say.

'Don't look so dreary.' Marianne was cheerful again. 'One must face reality.'

According to Aunt Mat Marianne never faced reality so this was cheering.

'Yes,' she said.

'And the reality *is*, darling, that *you* have all the chances that were taken from me when—' She stopped. 'You're old enough to hear it – when I got preggers.'

'When did you get pregnant?'

'Nina! Don't be dense. With *you*!'

Nina's mind was racing to keep up.

'Those cows from drama school married directors,' continued Marianne, oblivious. 'Some of them married *casting* directors! But more than half of those were queer, so I shouldn't think *that* was a walk in the park. I don't mind admitting, darling, meeting your father was a disaster. But he *was* so romantic. He used to drive extremely fast. *Angel*—'

She took Nina's cold hands, and held them. Nina gazed at her, full of love.

'Get the kettle. It will boil dry without singing.'

The play came and went, and there wasn't another. Marianne coached her daughter in monologues for auditions they had not yet applied for and bemoaned their poverty. She told Nina what she was, what she wasn't and what she might be – if only they had the money – and Nina, as she had always done, struggled to gain her praise. *We won't be here for ever, it's just a stopgap,* said Marianne and Nina agreed, and remained small, doing her best to please. When she failed to impress Marianne would lose her temper.

*Come along, you're behaving like a child!*

*Don't you know how to speak on the telephone?*

*Go into a shop.*

*Hail a taxi.*

*Smoke without looking like somebody's maid.*

Then: *You're what I might have been*, she would say, adjusting Nina's hair, lovingly.

Late at night, over small, cheap brandies, she tearfully confessed how it had hurt to give her baby daughter up to her sister-in-law's guardianship, how every day without her it had felt as though her heart were breaking. She forgave Nina the past and Nina, in gratitude, took on the yoke of the future.

Nina visited Aunt Mat every few weeks for tea that she had not made herself and Victoria sponge. She saw the house, and her relative, through her mother's eyes and felt like a cuckoo trying to return to its borrowed nest; not unwelcome but disapproved of.

'Not in Paris, yet?' Aunt Mat would say, and Nina felt attacked by it, until she realised one afternoon – it was an edge of anxiety, not criticism. Aunt Mat did not want her to go away.

Hugging goodbye on the step, Nina felt as though she were leaving her for the first time. She clung for a moment, but Aunt Mat did not give away a tear.

When she returned home her mother was lying on the sofa with an ice pack on her brow. Nina began to tiptoe to her room, but then she stopped.

'Mummy?' she said, approaching.

'What is it?' said Marianne, behind closed lids.

'Mummy . . .' Nina sat down. 'I think Aunt Mat will pay for drama school and – things – if it means we're staying in London.'

She waited to see the effect of her words.

Marianne's head lifted on her long neck as she removed the ice pack. She turned until her eyes rested on her daughter.

'Ah,' she said. 'Do you?'

So Nina, for whom exposure was agony, was to make a career of it.

----

Luke Kanowski went from school to home to the hospital, and could not raise his head to the future. He did his homework in his bedroom with Christ and the Virgin's sorrowful, silent approval and trained for the cross-country mile around the Seston Asylum grounds; *dodging loonies*, he and his mother called it.

Seston Grammar, like the mental asylum, was red-brick, but where the asylum was gargantuan the school was a size too small, like a tight pair of shoes. The cheesy corridors were packed with boys. The hall doubled as a gymnasium and tripled as a theatre, mildewed and dispiriting. It was better than the minor public school a few miles away but snobbishly despised, and the grammar schoolboys' hair was neater than the public schoolboys ever bothered to make theirs. There was just one goal – university. Seston boys had their eyes on a clean escape. Oxford. Cambridge. London. The day in September the head-master made his speech to the upper-sixth *inspiring them to aspire*, Luke's classmates went into town to the newly opened coffee shop to discuss their keen ambitions and Luke went to visit his mother.

The headmaster had said, *Some of you boys will be invited to stay on for the Oxbridge term . . .*

Luke knew that he was one of them. That despite his poverty, his questionable background, foreign parentage and suspected Judaism; despite his excess energy and chaotic attention, his facility had been greedily noted.

*Difficult though it is to believe that you boys might yet achieve the heights of excellence, experience tells me they are not beyond your reach.*

Luke climbed the asylum railings, cut across the ragged lawn towards the entrance and rang the bell.

Maudy, a young nurse with a big bust and brown teeth, who liked him, opened the door.

'Hiya, Luke, y'all right?'

They waited in the mesh cage while the other nurse, Lynne, who was in her sixties, unlocked the second door.

As they went through Lynne said comfortably, 'She had a very good night, your mum.'

'Good,' said Luke. He didn't want to stop – never wanted to stop, he often had the urge to click at people like cows to hurry them up.

'But she wasn't at her best this afternoon, I'm afraid. She was in Hawthorn for a couple of hours, calming herself down.'

He did stop then. Hawthorn meant his mother would have been restrained; either straitjacketed or else with her wrists and ankles strapped to the bars of a bed. He was used to distress. He had learned to manage it and to forget, to push it from his mind and carry on. It didn't make it all right. She had been alone. She had suffered. He pushed his hands into his pockets, squinted, chewed something imaginary with his front teeth, looked around the ceiling, pressed the feeling back down into himself and when he could, he asked, 'What happened?'

'Nothing to worry about, pet. Just Dr Herrick didn't want her hurting herself,' said Lynne. 'She's all better now, love. You might find her a bit sleepy. You can cheer her up.'

The dayroom was huge, with randomly placed chairs, a piano and primeval-looking potted plants leaning against the tall panes of limescaled glass. There were a few rugs scattered over the lino and finned iron radiators. Luke stood in the doorway with the corridor stretching away behind him. There were the normal sounds of people talking or humming to themselves; doors banged and clattered as patients were taken from one place to another and a radio somewhere played classical music – of a kind – relentless, cheerful; the sort of music you would march to.

He could not see his mother. He forced himself to look more calmly. There. She was in a chair near the piano. Very often relief was worse than crisis. He wished he were more defended. His hands shook as he fetched the piano stool, carried it to her side and sat down.

The corner of her mouth was shining with saliva and her hair had not been brushed. She took a moment to register his arrival, and her speech was slurred.

'Oh, I thought you were Dr Herrick,' she said.

Then she smiled for him.

'No,' said Luke. He handed her the hairbrush from the bag at her side. She took it and held it loosely.

'I got another detention yesterday,' he said.

She began to brush her hair, slowly.

'I forgot my French book,' said Luke, 'and then didn't listen.'

The silence dragged. But then she said, 'You should teach

*him* French, silly man.' And, after searching her mind, 'Mr *Gordon*.'

Luke let out his breath. He hadn't realised he was holding it.

'Yes,' he said, quietly, 'Mr Gordon.'

When he left, Maudy winked at him. 'See? She was all right, your mam?' she said.

He should have liked to grab her and kiss her, brown teeth and all, and forgot everything that had just happened, picturing it. He liked the way the buttons gaped over her bust. He hoped he wouldn't have a lifelong obsession with girls in nurses' uniforms because of Seston Asylum. It wasn't exactly original; not the sort of sexual neurosis you could stand behind. It didn't help that the well-thumbed magazines boys smuggled into school were so preoccupied with them.

'See you Wednesday then,' said Lynne as he went.

'See ya,' he said.

He didn't pause. He needed to get home.

He got off the bus in the high street, pulled a string bag out of his satchel, found money in the bottom – mixed up with fluff and pencils – and bought fish for tea. Mr Bradley in the off-licence sold Luke vodka despite his school uniform because if he didn't his father came down and shouted at him in Polish. Neither Luke nor Mr Bradley wanted that particular embarrassment again.

The headmaster had said, *The Oxbridge term is a rigorous one, and many of you will not be suited to it. Discuss it with your parents . . .*

He walked home with his satchel and the string bag bumping and passed an hour's joyful immersion in the French Revolution at the kitchen table before frying the fish and cutting bread to go with it. His father came in as Luke put down their plates and sat, leaving his half-smoked cigarette on a saucer next to his place.

*Some of your parents may have questions. Any boy whose mother or father would like to speak to me should make an appointment with the secretary.*

'Thank you, Lucasz. Good boy,' said Tomasz as he wiped his plate clean with a piece of bread. He stood up, slowly pushing his chair back, took his cigarette, vodka bottle and glass, and left the room. Luke cleared up and waited for his father to use the toilet outside and go upstairs then he followed him, washed, and went up himself.

In his room, he stood by his bed and said his rosary. For years Tomasz had insisted Luke attend mass, but had stopped going to church and now never spoke of his faith, or its lack. Nor would he talk about the past, never spoke of his former comrades, or his wartime experience. When he first came to England Hélène had been left behind in France, in the soup kitchen queue that stretched from Calais to Paris, and it was a year before she was allowed to join him. His squadron had been billeted outside Seston, at the asylum – the same building where almost ten years later she was to become a permanent patient. The irony and oddity of the hospital being sometime home to both his parents did not escape Luke. The irony could not escape him, but it was his home, too.

*You may come to me or Mr Whiteson before half-term regarding your applications, which are in a special box in alphabetical order in Miss Higson's office. Don't forget to collect, please. And don't slack off now, boys, it isn't the time.*

He had gleaned only the numbers of his mother's life. One son; one husband; one stillbirth; two miscarriages; two suicide attempts . . . His birth had been fierce proof to her of unquenchable life, she said, and she had given him a name to span three countries. Lucas. Lucasz. Luke. She had named him for luck and light, but he could not see beyond the present. His invalid parents. The tiny house. The labyrinthine hospital; he was made up of these parts. Tomasz would not visit his mother and she had nobody else but Luke.

He stood listening to his thoughts and then he nodded, because he had told himself he wouldn't be going to university, and smiled, because it was sort of funny that he had ever thought he might.

So Luke chose the paper mill over the colliery and his childhood ended.

He was a junior assistant clerk making £2/10 shillings a week. He worked from 8.30 until 5.30 and visited Hélène every other day.

At school he had been punished for his energy, set to do sports and extra work, and had embraced it as a distraction and challenge. The exercise had helped him sleep. Now he was older the night-times were vaguer and darker but the world was too dark a place already, and agony easily come by, and so he would put the light on and write. He had no axe to grind, no wound to pick at; he found, had always found, an intense joy in blissful escape. He was a scientist of the imagination; he could travel. He wrote poems and plays, hiding them under his bed from his own critical eyes, kept a diary and learned to play a second-hand EKO guitar. He read newspapers, the *NME* and *Melody Maker*, all the way through and through again, even the ads at the back, and stored them, with the poems, under his bed.

He had a shilling pay rise.

He obsessed about chord changes, key changes, rhyme schemes and Shakespeare; reading three or four books a week, exhausting the library's parochial shelves. He enjoyed the librarian's girlish thrill at the arrival of the new Agatha Christie or James Bond, and chatted to her about the characters and plot-twists. He read Plato, Proust — to see what the fuss was all about — and *The Collector*, three times. *Raise High the Roof Beam*, over and over. *A Clockwork Orange*, twice. *The Loneliness of the Long Distance Runner*. He read anything, everything, and then his Shakespeare again. And again.

He was promoted to assistant clerk.

Believing he had grown out of religion but fascinated by what he saw as the Catholic fetish of suffering, he built a crucifix in the middle of his bedroom out of broken glass from the bottles his father threw away. He used the pieces of glass with the labels for the Christ figure and in his youth thought himself ironic.

He went to the pictures every week, in Seston or on the bus to Lincoln — *Bonnie and Clyde*, *Blow-Up*, *Belle de Jour*, *Cul-de-sac* — films that were like visitations from exotic gods; shocking, beautiful glimpses of other minds, and evidence that it wasn't just his eye that was a distorted, highly coloured lens. He sat through them three and four times, until he lost the narrative and just counted the beats of the shots, saw patterns in the cuts and felt the shape of the story like music. Then he would watch them again. The physical world shrank. His inner horizon took scale. He bought a television and his father, at first suspicious, quite soon became attached to it; falling asleep to the national anthem each night and waking to the high-pitched closedown shriek. Luke caught him staring at it after he switched it off, sucking the last of the life from the fading white dot as the screen went black.

When Luke watched the television he sat with his knees to his chest, as close to the flickering static-furred glass as he could get. He watched all the plays on the BBC, wrote down the names of the playwrights and transposed the dialogue in a high-speed scrawl, not looking at the page.

And the songs, the songs – there was a party going on somewhere and he wasn't at it. He ran down the batteries on his radio late at night, looking for anything that had even half the energy that he had. Every week he heard something that broke the week before into pieces, music that was splitting its skin with every hour; growing up and getting younger. The Who, Them, The Stones, The Kinks, Aretha Franklin, James Brown, Bob Dylan. Bob Dylan. He hadn't known pop music could grow up like that. He hadn't known there was a mind so big in it. He bought all the records he could afford, watching the vinyl and the labels, the spinning words the right way up – angled – upside down. All the way round at 45rpm. The life inside him was tearing him up; writing himself inside out in lined-paper notebooks, rushing and looking and working and moving but knowing all the time that he was just staying still.

He wore a narrow black tie and white shirt. He greased his hair back, he let it grow, he grew sideburns, he shaved them off, he washed the grease out, he cut his hair, he grew it again. He got a job on Saturday nights at the working men's club that had bands play once a week between the bingo and the comic, fighting off every would-be pop star and Romeo in Seston to get it and, when he did, he felt as if God's hand had pointed down and His great voice had said, *Yes, Lucasz*

*Kanowski, you will work behind a bar and you will meet girls and there will be music . . .* And he did. And there was. Most of the music was very bad because Seston wasn't exactly a major stop-off on the touring circuit; it even knew itself that it was a pathetic, half-dead place. But if the music wasn't up to much the girls were easy harmony. Almost all girls had something about them that sang. They smelled the same – hairspray and mentholated cigarettes, thick perfumed lipstick. Jill, Sheila, Sandra, Mavis; tough girls who took care of themselves, made sure he knew he mustn't *do anything*, but then always made sure he did; wanting the heat of what they ought not do – and no babies. Christ knew Luke didn't want babies either and he found ways of doing everything but the one thing they both wanted, taking Catholic pleasure in the ache of holding back. He had to be ingenious. He was. He used his imagination in the toilets of the club, in the alley behind his house, at the bus stop near theirs, in front gardens, back gardens, on buses and on benches, and discovered that the thrill of female pleasure, like a blessing, was enough to still the constant seeking frenzy of his mind so there was no mill office next day, no asylum, no father, no mother, just that girl, her heat and smiling whispered refusals – could he get this far, this, this – until it was over and he was left alone; satisfied if she was brave enough to touch him back or frustrated if she wasn't and, like a cold rain falling, the truth of his life would return to him.

He got another pay rise.

He went through a phase of switching his accent at work every day to see if anyone in the mill office would notice. He jumped from French to Polish to Lincolnshire to extreme upper class but the only nickname that stuck was the Frog.

He was working as an assistant clerk in a paper mill and being called the Frog. He was going mad.

## April – 1968

London's spring was wet and harsh. Bitter rain fell on the metal, the mud and building sites and the towers that broke the soft stone skyline. With cheery brutality, in hail and chasing sun, the Post Office Tower had risen sky-high. Beneath it and around it, bowler hats and suede hats and miniskirts, shop-fronts and hairdressers, tourists and tat, music in bars, rattled through the gentility, the fresh sharp concrete, the chipped plaster of the scrabbling city. Soho's basements burst, revealed and revelling, into the cross-currents of the seedy raincoated old guard; the jazz, the up-yours sex and post-war boozing, fag-ash dusted filth pouring life and dirt into the new plastic streets. Kensington's invaded little shopping parades jostled greengrocers with boutiques. The city strained against the rich belt of its suburbs. Housewives, old at twenty-five, hired nannies and faced their decline, and commuters, smudgy fingered on the train, read newspaper stories of debauch.

Nina Jacobs, in her third year at LAMDA, was emerging into the world with the others. Groups of students would make forays into London like little herds of deer exploring the forest; the theatres of the West End, the boutiques of the King's Road. Nina made friends with a girl called Chrissie Southey, who had a mane of amber hair and a crisp, knowing sexuality. Her parents lived in a house in Chelsea and Nina and Chrissie would go there and try on clothes in her bedroom, giggling over magazines, experimenting with their eye make-up and then setting forth for the delights of Carnaby Street.

'I'm the little lamb who never gets caught!' cried Chrissie as they both bolted one day along the pavement away from some stringy boys who told them they were photographers.

'Leches!' shouted Nina, careering into a postcard stand and they both fell into the shop, laughing, and bought French cigarettes with the last of their money.

She dreamed of high success; the blessed release of approval. The dusty shell of the school had nourished her, brain and spirit, plumping her up. She had played there, worked hard like a child but now, she knew, she was for the market.

'Chop chop,' her mother would say every morning, hurrying her out of the door, and as the days flipped towards her final term she seemed to see an axe teetering above her. Equity card. Repertory. Auditions. Agents.

The third-year productions turned the stage on which she had practised into a shop-front. Producers and agents sat in the cramped auction house of the dark auditorium, marking one-sheet cast-lists with biro hieroglyphs. Nina's year group, who had studied together in honest brotherhood, now pretended it to cover their envy. The end of the race was too close for better feelings. National unemployment may have been at record lows, but for actors it still held its eternal majority. Proven friendships broke and reformed with sudden loyalty and unclear motivations. Students thrown into a character role where they felt themselves to be a lead or tossed a meagre two lines where a rival had speeches were bitter – bitter with fear of the oblivious world beyond their playpen. Nina had loved the exercise of self and psyche, the studying of texts, but the stage terrified her, and her mother, for all her personal dissembling, never once allowed the laziness of false praise to pass her lips.

*Nina, free your voice, you sound like Princess Margaret. Where is your voice?*

A guest director, Richard Weymouth, was announced to work with them. The students approached the auditions with affected professionalism, a guessed-at approximation of their future lives. Nina, nervous and proud, was given the youngest of Chekhov's *Three Sisters*, Irina, to play.

'Oh, Nina,' said Marianne, and clutched her tightly. 'Well done, well done.' And she whispered into her hair, 'I always wanted to play that part and never did, I'm thrilled for you.'

Nina had loved *The Three Sisters* when they studied it in her first year. She was determined to overcome her fear and do it justice. Irina was childlike, and had the child in her destroyed; she yearned for love's escape but instead found her salvation in hard work. Nina's soul recognised Irina blindly, as if she herself were a paper cut-out, and the written character was the flesh.

'I'm terrified,' she said to Chrissie in the coffee shop on the Earls Court Road after school.

They were pouring white sugar onto their cappuccinos and spooning the froth into their mouths. Skinny as they were, they were both always trying to lose weight – the lipstick and coffee diet, they called it. This was their lunch.

'Richard Weymouth will look after you, he fancies you rotten.'

'Don't be silly, he's forty,' said Nina, not missing the implication she had been given the role for the wrong reasons. In *The Three Sisters* Chrissie was to be the ancient maid, Anfisa.

34

She had played Juliet in February – rather badly, Nina thought – and didn't feel sorry for her at all.

The boy cast as Tuzenbach was called Jeremy Elton. He was a year or two older than most of the others, smoked Sobranies, had silvery-blond hair and wore a long, narrow black coat. He was very much desired. In each year there were the happy few that everybody knew – or thought they knew – would have big careers, ready-made stars, untested, and he was one of them; film-actor-to-be, Jeremy Elton. Nina could not help but love him. It was easy to flirt; Tuzenbach was in love with Irina. Nina felt prettier when Jeremy was there and forgot her nerves in the thrill of their scenes together. Off the stage she was charged with joy, able to find Irina's sadness because her own emotions had been unstopped by infatuation. *This is a crush*, thought one, cool corner of her mind, as she wrote *Mrs Jeremy Elton* on her notebooks and, *We are pleased to announce the wedding of Jeremy Elton and Nina Jacobs . . .*

A week and a half into rehearsals, he asked her out. She waited until after dinner to tell her mother. She couldn't keep the secret any longer than that.

Marianne was making her a dress, kneeling on the ground, pinning the hem as Nina stood on a low stool and turned in slow circles like a dancer on a music box.

'Your legs are very good,' said Marianne as she took up more pins. 'Your knees aren't wonderful, but your ankles and thighs are perfect. What did you eat today?'

'Just breakfast.'

'Good girl! There, get down. I'll finish it tonight.'

Nina climbed from the stool.

'Mummy, Jeremy Elton has asked me out.'

Marianne stopped in the middle of the room, her hands to her breast.

'I told you.'

'He says Saturday.'

'He'll have to come here first, I'm not having you go out and meet him just anywhere.'

So on Saturday Jeremy climbed the five flights to collect Nina from her mother's flat. They went to an Italian restaurant in Kensington that he told her was fashionable. It was very noisy, the sound of voices and scraping chairs bouncing off the black and white tiled floors, and Nina had no appetite. None of the food was familiar to her. There were people at the next table Jeremy knew, friends of his parents, and he chatted to them and barely addressed to her. She sat, silent in her shyness and increasing misery, and couldn't think what to say or do to draw his attention.

When he brought her home they paused on the pavement by the steps. Nina, who had seen all the films, waited to be kissed but Jeremy glanced up at the lit windows of the fifth floor.

'Shall I walk you up?' he said.

'If you like.'

Marianne was waiting. She was not ready for bed, but fully made-up, as if she had not moved since they left.

'Jeremy!', she said, rising, 'can I offer you a drink?'

He looked much younger, standing there next to her mother, Nina noticed, and his chin was somewhat small in relation to his forehead.

'Oh yes, thanks awfully,' he said.

'Gin and tonic all right?'

'Super.'

He stroked his hair forwards and followed Marianne further inside.

'I'm afraid we haven't any ice and please, do forgive the humble horror of your surroundings. It's so convenient for LAMDA and of course I can't take any work while Nina needs me.'

'It's very nice,' he said politely. 'You're an actress?'

'*Resting* . . .' A hollow laugh. 'No G and T for you, Nina.' She turned to Jeremy again. 'You're not related to James Elton, the director, are you?'

'He's my uncle.'

'No, honestly?'

'Fraid so.'

'Don't be *afraid*, what a funny thing! He's the most charming man I have almost ever met.'

Nina looked from one to the other.

'So they say,' he said.

'Has he passed it on?'

'I've no idea, but he's hell to work with.'

'You've worked with him?'

She handed him his drink and Nina stood in the middle of the floor with the bow at her waist, like an unwrapped present, the smile fixed on her face never fading.

The three of them sat. Jeremy and her mother talked; nothing Nina could contribute to, nothing she knew about. She did not question that her mother outshone her, the fact of it was an absolute; it almost comforted her. But she had liked Jeremy so much, and he had stopped even glancing at her now, as if she were a coat left on the back of a chair.

Her mother tucked her legs up and leaned her elbow on the back of the sofa with her chin on her hand as she listened to him talk. Nina sat rigidly upright in the only other chair, raging against herself and her gaucheness. Jealously she stared at her mother's grace; the easy way her fingers rested on her cheek, her collarbone, her hair, drawing attention from one to the other like a sales assistant in a jeweller's. Is this to your liking? And this? And this?

After a long time, Marianne said, 'Nina, aren't you exhausted? Off you go to bed, darling, I'll see Jeremy out.'

Nina stared at her. She knew she mustn't make a fuss.

'Darling? Bed?'

It would be more childish to argue than to go, and so she pretended relief, taking pride in hiding her feelings.

'Goodnight, Jeremy,' she said, getting up. 'Goodnight, Mummy.'

Jeremy did not meet her eye.

'I'll see you tomorrow,' he said.

'Thank you for a lovely evening,' said Nina; 'it was marvellous.'

As she left them she heard her mother say, 'The *darling* . . .'

She had to come out of her room again to go to the bathroom on the landing and they pretended they hadn't seen her because she was carrying her sponge bag.

When she was finally in bed, when the light was out, she turned her face into the pillow and she cried, biting her fingers until they hurt to stop it. It was pathetic to cry. She should grow up. She lay trembling, listening to her mother's laughter, and the low hum of Jeremy's voice.

She was not near sleep. She waited for the sound of the front door but it did not come. Straining, she thought she heard footsteps tiptoe past the door and her mother laughed again, very quietly. He had not gone. He had not left. He was in her mother's bedroom.

She closed her eyes . . . *Be my, be my baby* . . .

That night she had a dream – a dream or a vision, afterwards she couldn't tell. A man was coming up the stairs of her mother's house, striding up, two at a time, with benign strength. He knew where to find her. He was coming to save her. She could not see his clothes – her eighteen-year-old mind stopped short of armour and a sword – but he didn't seem imaginary. She was sure he was not pretend. She sensed him, and though she could not see his face at all she knew that he loved her, and he would set her free.

---

The clerk immediately above Luke at Seston Paper was a spare young man called Eric Trimble. He and Luke had a mismatched friendship born on Luke's first day, three years before, when Eric, showing him the mill, office, kitchenette and toilets, had said that his mother believed he'd always have a future in paper because people needed it for both their eyes and their arses. Disappointingly, Seston Mill didn't make paper for books or toilet rolls, but tissue-paper of exotic colours, to be shipped off to other happier locations for prettier things than could ever be found locally. Sometimes Eric Trimble came to the club and Luke gave him free drinks for whichever girl he was trying to impress. He tried not to covet and steal Eric's girl-friends. He tried not to covet and steal Eric's *mother*, and luckily Eric's father had a knack of creeping in his slippers from the front room if she ever made an offer of tea.

Eric would stay behind with him at the club if he needed to lock up or they had both failed in the girl-hunt, and they would walk home past the Trimbles' house and drop him off,

Luke rattling away about whatever currently preoccupied him and Eric laughing or thinking about something else or, Luke suspected, quite often nothing at all.

They were standing together outside Eric's house at eight o'clock on a Tuesday night in the pouring rain. Eric was finishing a fag. His mother always insisted he carry an umbrella, it was huge and they were sharing it as the rain pattered down around them. Luke was talking about *2001: A Space Odyssey*, which he had seen the night before.

'Sounds mental,' said Eric flatly when Luke drew breath, and he stamped out the tiny damp end of his cigarette.

'See ya.' And he was off up his path, leaving Luke in the rain.

It may as well have been three o'clock in the morning. Seston was empty. Luke put up his collar and started home. The pavements were bright with rain, and the gutters brimming. Then, with the discordant sound of broken-winded brakes and a sluice of filthy water that fanned up in front of him like an ocean wave, a car drew up.

It was a Mini, the wipers banging back and forth helplessly.

The driver's window squeaked down an inch. Luke looked down to see a pair of female, Cleopatra eyes between the top of the glass and a heavy dark-brown fringe.

'Excuse me . . .'

'Hiya,' said Luke.

A male voice came from the dark interior, loud, northern – slightly – but not local: 'We're completely fucking lost.'

Luke bent down to peer into the car. The window squeaked down another inch.

'You're letting the bloody rain in!' shouted the passenger, a young man, pale face, past the girl in the tiny car.

'Well, he's the one standing in it!' she retorted. She sounded like a girl off the telly, clipped.

'Get in then,' barked the man, who couldn't have been more than Luke's age.

He got out, chin tucked down into his collar, and Luke ran round the car before he could change his mind and folded himself into the back, fighting with the lever for the front seat and dripping everywhere.

The man climbed back in, slammed the door, turned to Luke and held out a hand.

'Paul Driscoll,' he said. He was sandy, with short, forward-combed hair.

'Luke Kanowski,' said Luke and he had the impression, oddly, that someone was taking a photograph of them shaking hands, like Kennedy and Hoover, a flashbulb moment of a meeting, saying their names in the dry bubble of the car surrounded by the driving rain.

'I'm Leigh Radley,' said the girl rather crossly, not turning, so Luke couldn't see her face just the memory of her eyes above the window. She put a hand over her shoulder and he held it for a moment and then drew his back, but not more quickly than she did.

'Can we get on now?' said Paul.

'Don't be so bossy,' said the girl.

'Where are you trying to get to?' asked Luke.

'A pub called the Bell Inn. D'you know it?'

Luke did know it: an old man's pub known locally as the Bell End. It had none of the gathering feeling of the working men's club; a disparately populated, dying place. Paul Driscoll pulled out a huge sodden map that had plainly been their unhelpful passenger; an enemy, torn and wrinkled.

'HELL!' he shouted and tried to fold it.

'That's a 1:25000 Ordnance Survey,' said Luke.

'What did you say?' Paul looked round, surprised and aggressive.

'You aren't going to find your way around a town with a 1:25000 Ordnance Survey, are you?'

'You can get out now,' said Paul but didn't mean it.

The girl said, 'I told him,' grumpy and quiet.

Paul rocked back and forth, moaning a bit. Luke laughed.

'You're well out of your way,' he said, jiggling his foot up and down and beginning to enjoy himself.

'Not exactly well lit, is it, your town?' said Paul. 'Like being down a bloody mine.'

'Well, yeah,' said Luke, 'it's better unseen.'

The girl revved the engine.

'Sterling Moss,' said Paul. 'So, please, in your own time, Luke whatever-it-was, where is this pub or don't you know?'

The girl's hand flicked the indicator.

'Go down here and turn right,' said Luke, who liked them both. 'Where have you come from?'

The girl, Leigh, started to drive.

'Staying in Sheffield tonight, but up from London,' said Paul, crushing up the map and shoving it down past his legs.

'Why?' asked Luke.

'To meet someone.'

'Who?' asked Luke.

'Why?' said the girl, and Luke caught a glimpse of her eyes in the mirror.

'Why what?' said Luke. 'Left.'

'Why'd you ask who?' she responded, turning and accelerating at the same time.

'Left again at the end here. I was just wondering who you were going to meet at the Bell End. I wouldn't come from Nottingham for it.'

'The Bell End?' Paul gave a snort of laughter but recovered his bad mood as soon as he could.

'Which way?' asked Leigh, easing slightly off the gas as the Mini careered towards a wall.

Luke wound down the window and put his face out into the rain to see. 'Right,' he said. 'There's Market Street at the end there, see? It's past there. I can tell you the way. You can let me out here if you want.'

The girl jammed on the brakes and they skidded into the kerb. Luke banged his cheekbone on the window frame, metal and loose rubber.

'Jesus Christ,' said Paul.

'Or you can come with us, if you like,' she said, still without turning. Her hair long and thick – dark – inches from Luke's eyes.

'Can he?' said Paul, looking at her.

'If he likes,' said Leigh, looking straight ahead.

'Well, it's your bloody car.'

'Thanks,' said Luke, 'I will.'

She started the car again and Paul shrugged. 'I suppose he might still be there.'

'Who?' asked Luke.

'Don't bloody start that again.'

There was a slight movement in front and Luke thought that it was possible Leigh was laughing.

\*

The Bell End was chilly and stank of sour beer. The three of them, fresh from the rain, stood in the doorway; the youngest people in the imaginable universe, straightening their limbs out from the Mini. The talk, such as it was, had stopped when they came in. The barman was very short, peering at them through the beer taps, and apart from an old man sitting at the black piano and hitting the same three sharp notes on and off between sips of his beer, it was very quiet.

'Jumpin',' said Paul, pulling a packet of Strands from his pocket and going over to the bar as he lit one.

'Evening,' said the barman, expressionless.

Leigh stalked over to a table in the corner, ringed with glass-marks and a cut-glass ashtray heaped with fag-ends, and sat down. She didn't look approachable so Luke hovered busily in the doorway for a while, until Paul said over his shoulder, 'Drink?'

'All right.'

'Leigh?'

She shrugged. Paul, unable to interpret this, waited.

She glared at him. 'No. Thanks.'

Luke went and sat with her at the table. Rocking slightly and rubbing his palms on his knees, he watched her as she pulled a piece of paper out of her pocket. She looked up.

'What?' she said, interrupted by his staring at her.

'Who are we meeting?' he asked.

Grudgingly, she held out the paper. It was very crumpled. Luke took it. It was warm from her pocket. It said in pencil, *Joe Furst, 7p.m., Bell Inn, Seston.* He handed it back as Paul came over with two pints and a small glass of something cloudy-looking for Leigh. He put the drinks down.

'I got you a gin and tonic.'

She looked nonplussed. 'But I didn't want anything. Thanks.'

She had a strong face with wide cheekbones, high up, right under her eyes that reminded him of somebody, but he didn't know who.

'Well, he's not bloody here, if that's what you were wondering,' said Paul.

'Joe Furst?' said Luke.

Paul jerked a thumb at Luke. 'How does he know?' he said to Leigh.

'But who is Joe Furst?' asked Luke.

'He's a writer.'

Luke hadn't thought they were seeing a man about a dog but still he was shocked. The word *writer* coming out of Paul's mouth. It was as if he were having a conversation he had dreamed, a moment he had lived, but forgotten. He had never, he realised, in his life heard anyone referred to as a *writer* before. He grew sharper, quickening, and tried to cover it, knowing he was sharp enough at the best of times for most people.

'He's a what?'

Leigh glanced at him briefly, sipping her drink.

Paul said, 'A *writer*. Heard of him?'

His sarcasm bounced off Luke who smiled. 'No. What are you meeting him about?'

'A play he's written.'

'For what?'

'For what? For the theatre. For fun. For money. I don't bloody know. It's a play.'

Luke's mind was buzzing, too fast for comfort. He looked around the Bell End — took in the black piano, the peeling carpet, the derelict fireplace, the yellow walls and fake flowers in an earthenware pot . . . What would Joe Furst, *playwright*, be doing here? What in God's name would he be doing in Seston and, if he was, why didn't Luke know about it? Joe Furst. A bloody writer.

'Why'd you want to meet him?' he asked Paul. 'What's his play got to do with you?'

'I'm a producer.'

At this bold statement Leigh cast Paul a look and then her eyes went down again to her lap.

Luke had an instinct for thin ice. The ground beneath his own feet was too fragile not to have a good sense of other people's weaknesses. He could tell Paul didn't want to say anything else.

'Are you an actress, then?' he said to Leigh instead.

'No.' She looked bored, angry to be asked, and Luke was surprised; most girls were pleased if you asked them that. Paul looked at him as if to say, *See what I put up with?* And shook his head. Luke couldn't work out if they were together or not.

'So what's in Nottingham, then?' he asked Paul. 'Been to the Playhouse? Did you see *The Resistible Rise? The Resistible Rise of Arturo Ui?*'

'Yeah,' said Paul.

'Was it good?'

'What you asking me for?'

'I didn't see it,' said Luke.

'Right.' Paul squinted, trying to get the measure of him.

'*Othello?*' Luke ploughed on. 'Last year?'

'I thought they fucked it up.'

'Did you?'

'Yes, Robert Ryan's just a movie star,' said Paul. 'What did you think?'

'Didn't see it. Read it.'

He could feel Leigh's eyes on him.

'*Oedipus?*' Paul asked him.

'Didn't see it,' said Luke. 'Read it.'

'Read it?'

'*Oedipus Rex?* Yeah. A few times . . .'

'It's *Nottingham*,' said Paul, gesturing over his shoulder as if the city were just there in the street outside, 'it's not Broadway.'

'Well, I – I'm busy.'

'Busy doing what?'

'I work in the office at the paper mill.'

Paul nodded, respectfully. 'Ah.' He picked up his drink.

'And nights in a place up the road sometimes.'

Paul nodded again, and sipped his pint.

'I mean, it's not all that easy to get away.' There was silence. 'I've got the programmes,' Luke said, unable to stop himself.

Leigh's eyes, again, flicked up at Luke and away. Paul said, 'You what?'

'I've got the programmes. From the last two seasons at the Playhouse.'

'Serious?'

'Yeah. And I've got the reviews. I save them. I sent off for the programmes. The plays too, if I can.'

'You never,' Paul said softly, but without mockery.

'I do. They're bringing back *Volpone*,' said Luke. He cleared his throat. 'I heard.'

Paul smiled slightly. 'It's *Volpone*,' he corrected him, 'like pony.'

'Is it? Thanks. I've only ever seen it written.'

'Excuse me.' Leigh got up, suddenly, and went off towards the Ladies.

'I don't think our Mr Furst is probably coming,' said Paul. 'Or else he's been and gone. There's a phone over there; I'll try his number.' He began to search his pockets for change.

'*Thebes, city of death,*' said Luke and Paul, startled, looked up.

'*One long cortège,*' said Luke, warming to his performance, and the shrivelled man at the piano ceased his one-finger playing to turn and watch him with rheumy eyes '. . . *and the suffering rises. Wails for mercy rise, and the wild hymn for the Healer blazes out, clashing with our sobs.*'

Paul stared.

'Seston!' said Luke, more loudly. '*City of death! One long cortège. And the suffering rises. Wails for mercy rise, clashing with our sobs.*' He stopped. He could have gone on – he could have done it in Greek – but he checked himself with an effort that made him blink.

There was a silence. Luke tapped his foot. *Oedipus* running across his mind, biting his tongue to stay quiet.

'Someone said Pink Floyd played a gig in Seston,' said Paul; 'it can't be that bad.'

'It was at the club where I work. I was there.'

Paul's face broke into a huge grin. The solidity of his face, prematurely manly, relaxed into boyishness. 'Seriously?' he said. 'You were there?'

'Last March. They probably fired their manager after, for booking them there. Syd Barrett probably *left* because of Seston.'

'Bloody hell!' said Paul. 'And all that *moaning*. Thebes my arse. Hang on a minute.' He got up.

He went to the telephone, pulling coins from his pockets. Leigh came out of the toilet and stood next to Paul as he dialled.

Luke looked at the two of them. *I know you*, he thought, *you're my friends.*

Paul listened for a while as Leigh stood, her hands in her pockets, reading a bill posted next to the phone on the wall; something about a circus, a broad fan of red and orange, and then he put the receiver down and shook his head.

'No answer,' he said, and they came back to the table.

Paul downed the rest of his pint. 'We thought we might get something to eat, if there is anything. Want to come?'

Luke nodded and got up fast. 'There's chips up the road,' he said, 'or we could go to Parker's.'

'Parker's?'

'Parker's Pies,' said Luke, as if they should have known, and they left the pub together.


Earlier that evening, before the three of them met for the first time, Leigh Radley and Paul Driscoll in her Mini had chased the rain clouds towards Seston.

Paul busied himself with the map, wondering how to please this quiet and apparently assured young woman as she sped heedlessly past the factories and chimneys and into the dank and blackening landscape, making no effort to please him, as far as he could see, except the fact of her presence.

Paul owned a three-year-old Ford Anglia that up until then had not let him down. Leigh was doing the props on a student production that he had just seen and they met in the Union bar afterwards. He had Joe Furst's typed manuscript in his pocket and gave it to her for a second opinion, and to pay her the compliment of asking.

She left it two days before she rang him at his bed and breakfast and pronounced it, 'Not bad.'

'That's what I thought,' he said and asked her out for a drink.

When they met at the bar, she asked for a pint. Paul had nearly fallen over in shock and had to stop himself from laughing at her as she drank it. It just looked unnatural to him, her woman's hand around the glass. And she seemed so bad tempered.

'Like bitter, do you?' he asked and she glared at him. 'Much of a beer drinker?'

'Shouldn't I be?'

'Do what you like,' he said, shrugging.

'Thanks very much.'

But then she smiled and he found himself telling her his car had packed it in – which was true – and would she happen to know of anyone who might be able to give him a lift to Seston to meet the playwright? He had seen her parking over the road in a bright blue Mini Cooper, noticed her bottom as she got out of it and took his chances.

'I'll take you, if you like,' she'd said, and he felt such warmth that he smiled right into her frighteningly direct gaze, and she smiled back.

Leigh's hands gripped the wheel, pleased that she was driving and not Paul. Producer, know-all-seen-everything Paul Driscoll.

She didn't know how someone could be her age, and so sure of his place and his plan. Where she fitted in, Leigh had no idea. She was quite clear about the great many things that made her angry. Being called a *bird*, *chick*, *love*, *darling*, *poppet*, *dear*, *darling*, *baby* made her angry. Being called *posh*, *soft*, *southern*, *blue-stocking*, and asked if she'd like a sweet sherry and if she were an actress or a model made her furious. She didn't like to be persuaded. She knew the things she loved. She was reading History, English Literature and French at Sheffield and loved all three of those. She loved Sheffield even though it had been very hard on her at first; the whole of the first year had felt like being in a boxing ring, on the ropes with her gloves up. She loved to write stories but she never told a single soul about that. She drank bitter although she hated it and left to herself it would be port and lemon every time. And she was shy. She was painfully shy; an unlikely affliction given her warrior heart. Guarded and untried, she was terrified of falling in love. The very term summed it up: *falling in love*, as if it were tripping over a brick into a chasm. Romantic love felt to her like the cheapest fairground con around; being dragged along for a ride on a wobbly circus bicycle and then falling flat on your face in a pie to the laughter of the cynical universe. Her childhood had been full of her mother's tears over her father's relentless faithlessness. She had seen clever girls turned into bleating sheep and reasonable boys unmanned by love, her own parents reduced to children. So Leigh decided a muscular intellect was the best defence against baseless weeping over someone you'd grow out of in a year anyway – someone like Paul Driscoll, apparently so impressive with his neat hair and man's strong face, peering uselessly at the map in his hands.

'Are you getting anywhere at all with that?' she asked. 'I think we should stop if you can't manage.'

She had the idea Paul took her for an idiot. She did not see that he quaked and had a suspicion she was a lesbian.

'If you'd stop driving like a maniac I might have a chance.'

'I don't see how it makes any difference what speed I go. If you can't read the thing, you can't read it.'

They had bickered the whole journey, quite easily. Paul came from a big bickering family, Leigh from a small bickering family; both felt quite at home.

When the rain began to fall she pulled sharply into a sliding muddy track, switched off the engine and the headlights and turned on the light inside the car, above the rear-view mirror.

'I have to turn the headlights off, the battery is a bit dicky,' she said, 'so don't be too long. Apparently it's the alternator.'

He was hugely impressed by her casual use of the word alternator but did not show it. 'Thanks.'

He lit a cigarette, offered her one, and studied the map. The rain drummed on the car roof. Leigh flexed her chilled hands, smiling at the thrill of going into the unknown on bona fide theatrical business, but—

'Seston? It's the back of bloody beyond,' said Paul, so Leigh kept her naïve delight to herself.

'You should let me drive.'

'It's my car. And I hate being driven.'

'I'm a good driver.'

She glanced at his profile, outlined by the dim little bulb. She liked his shoulders, which were broad, the taciturn presence he had, and that he didn't flirt with her. He seemed reliable. She liked reliable. She pressed her thighs more closely together and rolled down the window.

'Don't let the rain in,' he said, not raising his eyes.

'Don't bloody smoke then!' she retorted.

He reached across her to flick the burning fag-end out of the car, his arm, shoulder, then his head and clean short hair, all inches from her face. She had never been that close to a man without him trying to kiss her before.

He returned to his side of the car. 'I think we missed the turn,' he said. 'The one you said. Three or four miles back.'

'Oh.' She smiled at him, forgiving. 'We're so late.'

'Where did you get those cheekbones?' he asked, almost before he'd thought it. 'Your face is lovely.'

'Woolworths,' she said. 'Special offer.' And she started the car.

They found Seston and drove round it and through it and back across it with increasing speed and irritation as the rain poured down, their squabbling increasing with their lateness and Leigh's rising resentment following the cheekbones remark. Now she knew. The great Paul Driscoll had only asked her because he fancied her and needed a lift in her Mini Cooper. It wasn't that she didn't like men, she thought, with rage – as he popped Polos and argued with her – it was that she didn't like being cajoled and persuaded, tricked as if she were a seven-year-old. However many papers she wrote, rallies she attended, opinions she formed, here she was again, chased down in the absurd game of How Will I Get Into Her Knickers. She gave a snort, and laughed.

'Hello?' he said, drily.

'We should just ASK somebody!'

'We're fine.'

'Fine. We're fine. *Fine*.'

'All right, we're lost.'

'Thank you!'

'No bloody thanks to you.'

'Me? I'm just the taxi driver! You're the one who's lost.'

'Well, ask someone then!'

She sped down the dark and narrow road, overtook a bus, violently, and through the driving rain saw the back of someone with a too-big greatcoat and no umbrella – walking.

She slammed the brakes on in a two-pedal skid, and stopped, next to him, on the wrong side of the road.

She wound down the window just an inch.

She looked up and she saw Luke Kanowski.

'Excuse me.'

'Hiya,' he said.

*I know you*, she thought – except she almost didn't think it, so small a thing was it, so delicate, that as soon as the words formed in her head they were gone. She didn't know him. He was a stranger to her. His hair was dripping rain and he looked very alive, as if he were happily interrupted in the middle of something. She looked up at him through the gap in the window.

'We're completely bloody lost—' shouted Paul.

And Luke had got into the car behind her with a rush of cold air and the almost imperceptible fresh scent of another human being – the skin, flesh and bones of a new creature.

They all introduced themselves. Leigh held her hand behind her and he took it. And it was then, when he was unseen and close to her – exactly then – that she would always remember.

She drove on. Paul spoke and the boy, man – Luke – answered. Leigh, straining her eyes to see the road through the wet night ahead of her, had only the impression of him, bright with rain – no picture, nothing literal, just her own jolted recognising stop at seeing him.

He was giving them directions. His intonations were odd,

almost as if he were speaking in translation. Not foreign exactly, no accent, but – Luke K . . . ? She hadn't caught it. What sort of a name was it? They talked. It was funny the way he wanted to know their business and didn't care what they thought, and she couldn't fathom his lack of self-consciousness; his downright, open-wide *friendliness* – open but to her still unreadable.

They found the pub. Paul left her alone with him to go to the bar, bought her the drink, made his call, and Leigh took comfort in the acceptable silence of women.

When Luke asked her about the playwright, he had smiled at her and she had offered him the little piece of paper knowing it was warm, as if she were showing him a part of her self. Then Paul mocked him, feeling him out, making it funny that he hadn't ever got out of Seston and hadn't been to the stupid Playhouse – and her discomfort was so intense that she couldn't watch, she'd had to leave. He was too guileless. His honesty was laid out to be picked at. It had felt as though she were watching herself, not him, put upon a table and dissected.

There was no sentiment, no softness in her feelings for him. It ought to have been laughable, pleasurable, but it was so frightening. She was invaded. Undone. And it was exactly as she had feared; it was like falling. A lurching tumble into the dark. She had left them at the table and stood in the dingy pub toilet not moving, too scared to look at her face in the mirror and have the change in herself confirmed. Wanting to cry. There was no reason to care this much, no reason at all. She didn't even know him.

They left the pub, piled back into the stale, smoked-drenched Mini and Luke took them to Parker's Pies, at the top of Market Street.

'Is it always like this here? You'd think they'd dropped the bomb,' said Paul.

There wasn't a single soul about, just the driving rain and the wind blowing some wet chip-paper against a lamp-post outside as they pushed open the door, making the little lace curtain tremble and the bell ring.

'Not always.' Luke was a little defensive. 'It's Tuesday,' he said, pushing his hands into his coat pockets and pacing up and down the shiny wooden counter.

He jumped onto it, leaning on his forearms with his feet off the ground, craning to peer into the back, while Paul and Leigh stood in the doorway.

'*Thebes, city of death . . .*' said Paul.

'Shut up,' hissed Leigh, and turned to look outside at the street. She had just seen that Luke wore odd socks, one black and one grey, showing between his trousers and shoes as he hung off the counter.

'Hel-lo?' said Luke, just as a waitress emerged from the back, stuffing a frilly apron into a carrier bag, looking up at Luke and blushing.

'Hiya,' she said, flatly, then looked over at Paul and Leigh, suspicious.

'Hiya, Mandy – serving?'

'Closing,' she said.

Leigh saw Paul was trying not to laugh. She took his hand and gripped the little finger viciously, to stop him. It stopped him all right; it hurt, he looked at her in startled confusion.

The round-faced pimply girl stared at Luke. Leigh had the idea they knew one another well – or that the girl thought they did.

'I'm just off,' she said. 'Jim's closing up.'

'It's not nine.'

'It's too late!'

And with that she marched past them on short legs and left, slamming the door.

Luke faced Paul and Leigh with his hands jammed into his trouser pockets, bouncing a bit from side to side, and gave them a sideways smile. 'Not looking like pies, then.'

They looked regretfully at the tables, neatly wiped; empty tucked-in chairs on which they would not sit. Leigh and Paul paused in the doorway of the squeaky-clean dead-as-night restaurant, then Paul seemed to make a decision. He clapped his hands together and rubbed them.

'Right, then. That's that. We'd best get back anyway.'

'We could try Rousham's . . .' said Luke. 'But it's dear.'

'We should go. Leigh?'

Leigh felt panic. Luke felt it too, seeing that it was over; they wouldn't be staying or talking more about theatre to him, telling him where they had come from and what they knew.

'I could . . .'

What could he do? Invite them back to his for a vodka with his dad? Rustle up a roast dinner and seduce them both into staying in Seston for ever? Show them his collection of theatre programmes, his records, the four-foot glass crucifix in his bedroom, now complete and completely sodding mental-looking?

'I'll tell you the way,' he finished. 'It's easy to get out of Seston.'

Now that was just a flat-out lie.


They said goodbye on the pavement in front of the curved Parker's Pies glass-front, all three feeling there ought to be some reason to meet again, knowing there wasn't. They shook hands, awkwardly, getting wet with standing there. Luke opened the car door for Leigh and she got in without looking up.

'Thanks,' she said.

'We'll give you a lift back to yours, if you like,' said Paul.

Luke shook his head. 'I'll walk.'

'If you see Joe Furst, tell him he can give me a ring if he likes,' said Paul.

'What if I see Joe last?' said Luke, for something to say.

'Yeah, funny.'

'Where'll you be?' asked Luke, too sharp, too keen. 'Where do you stay?'

'I'll be back in London. I'm in the book.' And he got into the car.

Leigh's door was still open with the rain falling onto the steering wheel and her legs. She was shivering.

'Bye, then,' said Luke.

'Bye.'

And she slammed the car door on the whole wet ugly street, and him, and all of it.

---

In the weeks that followed his meeting with Paul Driscoll and the girl, Luke cast round for something to fix on about them that had meant so much to him. Back and forth from work, to home, to the asylum, he thought about that night, and all the things he did not do. He pulled out his books of plays, programmes from Sheffield and Manchester, London and the Playhouse – everything he was missing, the things he had not seen, and was angry with himself. Paul was right, it was a matter of an hour, less, there were buses, trains, there were ways. People did these things. It wasn't as if he needed to make his world so bound, so closed, so idiotically, frenziedly, obsessively, monomaniacally – face it, he told himself, so *insanely* closed as he did. He had made himself a prison.

Leaving work in the spring twilight, thoughts spinning in his head, he found he was unable to turn into the streets that would take him home and was walking around in small circles on the corner near the closed-down Chinese restaurant. He made himself stop. And breathe. And think. The silent town lay stagnant around him and Luke Kanowski realised that his life was harming him.

The next morning he did not go into work.

Stepping off the bus onto the lumpy verge outside the asylum the grass was frozen and the mud beneath as stiff as toffee. The sound of the bus and the burnt diesel smell disappeared. He was alone. He climbed the fence and started across the grounds, around the side of the chapel, past the mortuary, and then the long wall of Rose Ward to the front door. He had often wondered, had often asked his father, which of the wards he had slept in when he was billeted there but – *These places were not called Rose or Hazel when I was there*, Tomasz would answer so Luke had long since stopped asking.

The patients had just finished their breakfast. The smell of it was in the air, toast and the hot-metal of the urns. Luke walked through the familiar corridors and waited in the dayroom as people began to come in. Nearly all of them were known to him, some saying hello, others not. He rehearsed sentences, forgot them – pacing just to do something – and then his mother came in and he stopped. She was wearing a skirt and blouse and a cardigan – clothes she had owned as long as he could remember, clothes that had never been outside this place – and pale green slippers over her woollen tights. She stood in the doorway, unaware of him, and for that moment she was anonymous, the patient she was when he was not there to make her a mother. Putting it from his mind, he went to her quickly and she frowned, confused at the sight of him. Her confusion had increased with age; distress replaced by a growing bewilderment.

'It's not the weekend,' he said, to save her asking. 'It's Wednesday. I took the day off.'

They kissed. She was dressed and carrying some sewing and a book.

The chair she liked best, by the window, was occupied by a tiny old woman in a shawl.

'*Ooph!*' exclaimed his mother, showing him her sewing and the book she was carrying, her planned morning, ruined.

She had called this same ancient woman a *salope* before, Luke didn't want to get involved in an argument.

'Never mind. Shall we go for a walk?' he said.

She shrugged, staring viciously at the old lady in her place.

Luke touched her arm to get her attention. 'Leave these here. Walk.'

'No! I must put them away – someone will take them.'

He took her arm. 'All right, leave them in your room and we can get your coat. It's cold.'

He waited for her by the door to her bedroom, respecting her privacy, and then longer, while she fumbled slowly with the buttons of her coat. Helplessly, he imagined other people's departures, happy, reasoned mothers waving them off. Eric Trimble's parents constantly urging him to marry and leave them in peace. Brave would be the girl to marry Eric and live up to his mother's exacting standards.

'Ready now,' she said, smiling up at him.

'Good,' said Luke, but could not smile back. He wished he was either more or less of a coward, that he could do this thing well or not at all.

Hélène held his arm as they walked the paths. The frost had melted, leaving the grass wet, spring sunshine washing everything. He must speak; it blanked his mind to do it, like the moment's grace between the impact of a blow and the pain. He took a breath.

'I'm leaving home,' he said and stopped walking. She did not – she just let go of his arm and carried on. He was going to have to say it again.

'*Luc?*' she said, over her shoulder.

'Did you hear me?'

Sometimes she did this – this performance of stubborn feyness that took in nobody – because she didn't want to hear. He closed the distance between them, reached her and she took his arm again and looked up at him brightly.

'Will you send me postcards?' she said.

He glanced down at her but she just started to walk again, slowly.

'Postcards, *Luc?*' she said again.

'Of course.'

'From what place?' she asked. 'Where are you going?'

'London.'

At that, she stopped again and they stood, the two of them, with the birds singing and the distant hum of the generator the only sounds.

'What a beautiful day,' she said, lifting her chin, breathing in.

He looked around. There was not much beauty in it to him.

'Now, off you go,' said his mother.

'Now?' Luke was surprised. 'I'll take you in.'

'No,' she said, dismissing him. It was the only power she had. 'I'll go in alone.'

She kissed his cheek, pressing hers against his.

'Live well for me, Luc. Don't say goodbye when you go.'

And then she walked away. She did not turn back to look at him; she did not mark the moment, make it harder, make it hurt. She just walked away. Luke watched her go. He thought that she was a good mother, and had always been. He wanted to tell her but he did not know how and she would not have believed him.

After that it was quick. He gave his notice at the mill office and withdrew all his savings from the bank with fugitive delight.

'You should visit my mother,' he told his father, but he knew Tomasz would not. Tomasz had cried when he told him he was going; but then, he cried a great deal anyway, Luke observed.

He took his cold money, his familiar clothes and his record player – with the catches sellotaped over for safety. He took as many of the things he loved as would fit into his bags, and left for the station. He imagined carrying the glass crucifix to London on his back and almost did it, just because the idea made him laugh.

———

Friday. Five o'clock. Darkness falling. Luke had only been to King's Cross once before, for the National Gallery with his mother and now, bent under the weight of his belongings, the pigeon-seething arches high above him, he walked through the crowds with the ghost of her at his side, and fear for her. The distance between them stretched from his back like sinew.

He crossed the street to a newsagent and bought a stack of postcards – Buckingham Palace, Beefeaters – and digging into his pocket for a pencil, wrote two of them there in the shop, leaning on the counter.

*In London. Safe. Luke.*

Both the same. He addressed one to the asylum and one to his father's house and then he went out and posted them immediately in the box on the corner. He couldn't hear them drop, they just disappeared, two small gestures towards redemption. The line was cut. The noose, the hook, the web had gone. He was free-falling and newborn. All he could see was grey and black. Lines of cars and noise covering everything and the crowds of blind strangers. Then, all at once, the long line of streetlamps came on. Nobody else looked up but Luke. He turned his face to the celebration parade of lights. The streetlamps greeted his release in silent chorus. The short burst of a car horn brought him back.

He had one plan and no back-up.

He looked around for a phone box, pushed through the people and hauled open the door. He set down his bags and record player on the ground but they didn't fit and stayed wedged half in and half out, rain spreading in dark stains on the canvas. The phone box smelled of piss, glass panels scratched with initials from coins or knives, cigarette burns on the chipped paint divides. Luke pulled up the A–D phone book from its metal casing and ruffled the thin pages. *D for Driscoll. Paul Driscoll.* Producer. *D . . .*

\*

63

And Paul Driscoll, all unknowing, just a few tube stops away, shaved before the dripping mirror of his flat in Barons Court.

Paul almost didn't hear the telephone ringing over the running tap but when he did he wiped the soap from his face and turned off the water. It had stopped. He waited, looking at himself emerging from the mirror that dripped as the air cooled, then turned on the tap again. He knew the phone would start if he did. And there it was. Insistent and bogey-coloured, it stood on a small table near the front door. Paul went to it and picked it up.

'Paul Driscoll.'

'Hiya, Paul, it's Luke.'

'Who?'

'Luke Kanowski.'

'Have you got the right number?'

'I hope so. There are five in the book and you're the last.'

'Do I know you?' Paul could hear noise behind, traffic.

'I'm Luke Kanowski from Seston. You were in a Mini with Leigh, I think she was called. Joe Furst?'

'Bloody hell. What are you doing in London?'

'I was hoping you might have some ideas.'

Evening had darkened the room while he was bathing. Paul switched on the overhead. Sudden brightness. He remembered ghostly Seston, the pub, the bizarre young man spouting *Oedipus*, and beautiful, curvaceous Leigh Radley whom he hadn't seen since.

'Hello?' said the crackly voice of Luke Kanowski. 'You busy, then?'

'Yeah, hold on,' said Paul. He thought some more. Then, 'I was just on my way out — want to meet up for a coffee or something?'

'Coffee?' said Luke, as if the word were golden. 'Yes.'

They met at the tube station; Paul, short hair, workman's jacket; Luke, leaner, in his father's air force greatcoat, three feet apart from one another and appraising. Paul took in Luke's duffel bag and holdall.

'Off somewhere?'

'Just got here.'

'Oh, right . . .'

'What are you doing?' asked Luke, keenly.

'What am I doing?' *Standing on the pavement by Barons Court tube in the drizzle and the dark . . .*

'I mean are you busy?'

'I was going to see a play.'

'In the West End?'

'No, in fact, at a drama school. LAMDA. Students.'

'What is it?'

'*Three Sisters.*'

'I love that. Can I come?'

Paul laughed. 'What are you going to do with all that?' He nodded towards Luke's luggage.

Luke looked down with surprise at his two lumpy bags slumped on the pavement beside him, the record player propped against them.

'Where are you staying?' asked Paul, and Luke rubbed the back of his neck vigorously. He gave a shudder that seemed to go through his whole body and laughed.

'Not sure,' he said.

'There's a coffee shop on the corner. I've not much at home.'


They walked to the theatre in Logan Place in the damp chill, Luke bounced along, craning his head from left to right, looking up at the houses, down at the cracks in the pavement, into windows and backs of cars, firing questions at Paul and trying to shut himself up, itching with the blood rushing through him and his thoughts, topped up with life – too full, too tight. Very often he welcomed this familiar singing charge in himself but out of Seston, like a patient on day release, he had an unusual desire to be normal. Paul appeared to be indulging him, head down against the rain and smoking; taciturn and friendly.

The small foyer was cramped and crowded with people shaking off raincoats, pushing together in one movement towards the interior. Over their heads, beyond the double doors to the studio, was blackness. They went inside. Voices dropped as people took their seats. Luke willed himself to stay still and not to say he had never been to the theatre before in his life. Paul was ignoring him, greeting one or two people he knew. Luke sensed a well-controlled tension in his affability. He realised Paul wanted to impress.

'Who are they?' Luke's eyes switched from face to face, from black-framed glasses to long hair trailing over the back of a seat. He could smell scent mixed with stale smoke and the singed dust on the lenses of the lights in the rig above him.

'Agents. Producers. Friends and family of the students. They're third years.'

'Who, the students?'

'Yes, the *students* . . .' And Paul's eyes flicked over him, briefly sardonic.

Luke shut up.


The dressing-room air was charged with fear and thrill as each girl followed rituals according to her personality; chatter or

66

steadying breaths, warm-up or silence, like athletes drawing focus from within.

The others hurried into their costumes but Nina took her time. The sisters went on first; her entrance wasn't for twenty minutes or more.

After the night that her mother and Jeremy had— Nina could not think what they had done, and thought of it now only as *leaving her out*. After that night, Nina had lost the fragile hold she'd had on the part of Irina. She couldn't look at Jeremy, lost her lines, and stumbled through a week's humiliation before Richard Weymouth had taken the part away from her. He had swapped Nina and Chrissie's roles; Chrissie was Irina now and Nina was demoted to Anfisa, the servant. Jeremy's performance was unaffected. If anything, it had improved.

*Anfisa!* her mother had said as Nina lay on the sofa crying. *In a grey wig and some ghastly padding! You'll never be seen!* She never referred to Jeremy again, nor gave any sign that her failure might stem from anything but her daughter's own weakness. It was a yoke beneath which Nina easily bent; not Marianne's fault, but her own. And anyway, she forgot it quite fast. She had to. She had been left out. She had deserved it.

From her corner, she watched Chrissie put on her make-up as if nothing else existed in the world but her own face.

The knock at the door.

'Five minutes. Full house.'

A brief silence, a smothered explosion of whispers. Laughter. Hope. *Five minutes.*

Chrissie turned to her, a hairpin in her mouth. 'Nina, are you all right?'

'Fine. Good luck.'

And Chrissie smiled and turned away. Nina climbed into her clumsy stiff costume and was grateful for its black disguise. She hid behind her make-up, the shell of years, and envied Anfisa her station; the limited desires of the servant in Chekhov's fragile stage-house.

The lights came up on an almost bare set, a few pieces of polished nineteenth-century furniture, out of place in the modern square, suggesting a large drawing room. Upstage and centre was a square opening, brightly lit, through which shone white sunlight on silver trunks, a dream exterior. Three young women were seated on the stage. Luke felt a stab of recognition as they began to talk because he knew the play so well. Hearing it spoken gave him a rush of emotion, as words that he had felt existed only in the limited contract between his eye and the page were given life.

For three hours he alternated between Chekhov and sex. Thinking too hard, feeling too much, the thrill of new experience always jolted him to raw desire. Intensely focused, he studied the actresses. The men interested him less and looked silly in their false moustaches. It was a woman's play and he had thought it funnier when he read it – not comedy, but treading the path of its story more lightly. This *Three Sisters* seemed all-out tragedy. The maid, Anfisa, came on after some time, and Luke pitied her her thankless task, eighteen playing eighty and not much to say. He mentally de-wigged and stripped her of her apron before turning back to the amber-haired girl who was complaining about her life. Her voice was limited. And it saddened him, having read her, that Irina should be belittled by this girlish telling.

Marianne waited for Nina in the emptying foyer.

'You were forever!'

'I had to get my make-up off. I looked like a hag.'

'Come on,' hissed her mother, furious.

'Was I all right?'

'This is hopeless.'

Marianne pushed ahead through the crowd, stopping once to kiss a man's cheek and introduce Nina, who didn't catch his name and felt only shame and embarrassment that they were running out as others stayed to talk and meet, names and glances exchanged, compliments, the happy thrill of afterwards that she, for some reason, was being denied.

'Your Chrissie Southey is a pill,' said her mother.

'Shh! She's just there. Shouldn't we stay?' Nina leaned closer and whispered, 'Mummy! Agents!'

Her mother laughed, shortly. 'Not for you, darling, not this time. Would you mind if we just got out of here? It's dreadful . . .'

Nina realised her mother was embarrassed to be her mother and not somebody else's. Then her arm was grabbed by Tad Lambert. The thinning crowd threw them together.

'Nina!' he laughed, inches from her face. 'Come to the pub with us.'

'Congratulations, you were marvellous,' said Marianne warmly. 'You *all* were.'

'Thanks.' He let go of Nina, grinned and met her eye. 'Can I kidnap your daughter?'

Nina could have hugged him, there was something to be

salvaged from the evening; with only months to go before they were all parted, she had friends.

'Mummy?'

'Not too late . . .'

Just behind him, Paul and Luke left the theatre. Nina registered them as they crossed the edge of her vision; two young men, one dark, one fair, arresting her attention for a moment before she looked back at Tad, and smiled, and let go of her mother's arm.

'See you later, Mummy,' she said, and watched her leave with rebellious delight.

Paul put up his collar in the doorway and Luke, as had been his habit in Seston, a town too small to dominate the sky, looked for stars but saw only the glow of the city's lights diffused.

'Pub?' said Paul and Luke nodded. 'The Hansom Cab, up the road.'

'Brilliant,' Luke said and nodded.

And the people all moved out into the night.

The pub was seething with locals and the sudden influx of Friday-night crowd. Twenty minutes to last orders, a rush on the bar. Luke, trying not to trip people up with his holdalls and record player, glimpsed the bottles on the far wall gleaming in the false Victorian lamplight, flock wallpaper behind them like a jungle. It was a moment before he realised Paul was not with him, but still outside on the pavement, with a cigarette in his mouth and his hands shoved deeply into his pockets. Luke hovered on the edge of the crowd.

'What?'

'Sod it, let's go back to mine.'

So he joined Paul on the pavement, London girls and city noise denied him.

'There's no sodding point,' said Paul.

He began to walk and Luke followed, while inside, crushed up against the bar, Nina, drinking a gin and tonic, kept her back to Jeremy Elton and took comfort in the fact that she had perfected, over time, a mask. Hardly anybody ever knew what she was feeling. She fended off Tad's after-show euphoric flirtation and endured Chrissie's wide-eyed surprise at having not one but three agents interested in signing her. As the high relief of coming off stage drained she felt only disappointment with herself. She looked around what seemed to her the uniformly bright and sure faces of her classmates and felt her own talent, her will, too weak and uncertain. It was Chrissie who had won the prize that night, not she.

'I think you're the sexiest old lady in London,' said Tad in a cod Russian accent, breathing beerily into her face. 'Won't you lift up your apron and let me see your samovar?'

Nina laughed, matching his accent.

'I'll show you my samovar if you take me to Moscow,' she said, 'and buy me a drink.'


Paul didn't speak during the short walk back to his flat and trudged morosely up the stairs ahead of Luke, who kept silent, an unwelcome guest weighed down by bags, trying not to think about what he would do if he were thrown out. Inside, Paul slammed the door behind them both, swiped at the switch and the room was flooded with light so bright it seemed to ring. He fetched a bottle of whisky from the fake-wooden sideboard and held it up.

'Thanks,' said Luke and Paul fetched two tumblers from the kitchen.

He sloshed the whisky into them, cigarette in mouth, and handed one to Luke, going over to stare out of the window into the street below. Luke held his full glass and winced and fidgeted and wondered what to do. His bags were heaped like a pair of bulging corpses in the middle of the room, the record player leaning damply against them.

Without turning, Paul barked, 'What did you think of the play?'

Luke hadn't moved or taken off his coat and was just holding his glass of whisky like a prop.

'I imagined them real when I read it,' he said, quickly, 'but two of them were like schoolgirls, and I thought it was sad. The words have everything. Masha was the best of them. That redhead just did a face.'

Paul turned round to face him.

'I don't know what I'm *sodding* doing,' he said.

'Right,' said Luke, nonplussed.

'I don't want to be an engineer. I'm an engineer. I want to be a –' he stumbled, '– producer . . . but I don't *do* bloody anything except go to the theatre and read and ring people up and not get rung back and I haven't a blind sodding clue what to do about it. I hate my job. I'll be twenty-three in a month! I spent all my money from my dad on this flat and now I don't have anything else to get started and—' He stopped and drained his whisky. Luke had the impression he wasn't normally a drinker. It was a lot of whisky all for one time and afterwards he recovered, obviously embarrassed by needing to choke and having made a speech and revealed himself.

'You're an engineer?' said Luke.

Paul nodded, red faced, and then shouted, 'NO!'

Luke knew he was going to laugh – and it burst out suddenly from him in a kind of explosive *HA* sound, making Paul's head spasm up to look at him.

'What's so bloody funny?' he said, but before finishing saying it, laughed too, still half-choking on the whisky. He stopped laughing and visibly relaxed, exhaling and exhausted like a man twice his age. He sat on the edge of the sofa and looked into his empty glass.

'Sod it,' he said, with relative cheeriness.

Luke handed him his still-full glass. Paul said 'yeah' and put his empty one on the floor.

'What's in those, then?' He nodded towards Luke's bags, gratefully moving away from the discomfort of confession.

'Clothes. Books. Things.'

'Quite a lot of things, isn't it?' said Paul.

Luke knelt on the ground and unzipped a holdall. He held up a book.

'*Three Sisters*, see? And it's got –' he checked the tattered cover, '*The Cherry Orchard* and *Uncle Vanya* in there, too.'

'Grand,' said Paul.

'Brought my Fitzgerald and my Brecht, cause you can't do without, can you?' said Luke, showing him another. 'And my Shakespeare – Kafka . . . and then . . . some other things. Couldn't leave my records.'

He opened up the other bag and showed him as if they were private photographs. *The Freewheelin' Bob Dylan*, The Velvet Underground, Leonard Cohen . . .

'And what's that?' said Paul, pointing to notebooks underneath the records, drawing-covered and filthy with dust and ink.

'Just writing. You know.'

There were at least ten of them, dark blue cloth-covered notebooks. The doodling on the outside was a pattern of geometric and snakelike shapes.

'You draw, too?' said Paul.

'Not that much just now,' said Luke, thinking of the crucifix, that he supposed he had chosen words and wondering what that meant.

He sat up and put his legs up in front of him, resting his forearms on his knees and looking at his belongings spilling from the bags like guts with something approaching a father's love. Or a mother's. Paul put down the second whisky, barely touched. He was warmed and softened by drink already and he got up, opened the window a little, lit a cigarette and sat down again.

'There's so much to do,' he said to Luke with hunger, the urgency of somebody hearing the clock tick – taking the moments away from him.

Luke looked up at him, open, as if he knew what Paul was going to say as if he spoke for both of them. Paul took a long drag on his cigarette, talking quietly through the smoke, not meeting Luke's eye.

'I'm not talented. I don't mind. I like it. Talent is . . .' He frowned, unable to articulate what he did not miss. 'But I want to be *part of things*. I know what's good. I'm sick of pressing my nose up against the fucking window. There's so much happening – I want to be in there but I don't know how to get in.'

Luke nodded.

'My dad is a structural engineer. He's a successful man. Worked on the Post Office Tower.' He jerked his thumb in its general direction. 'He knows what he is. Came down from Yorkshire. Builds. Thinks I should do the same. I *did* what he wanted. I got my degree. I thought I could please him *and* myself but I can't. I'm going mad just *acting* as if I'm someone, when I'm not.'

'You said you were a producer,' Luke pressed him, wanting truth.

Paul got up and went to a cupboard in the corner. He opened it and took out a pristine rectangular box with an address label on the top. He handed it to Luke and sat down again. It was surprisingly heavy. Luke took off the lid. The box was full, a stack of letter-headed paper, still in its paper-band seal, unused: *Paul Driscoll Management*.

'I had those done a year ago. Longer. *Producer?* No. I'm an engineer who goes to the theatre, as it turns out.' He gave a half-smile.

'I gave notice on my job in Seston last month,' said Luke. 'I've got about a hundred and fifty pounds. I'm hoping it will let me stay away for long enough.'

'From?'

'Seston. And.' Luke didn't trail off, he stopped.

Paul leaned back against the brown sofa with the ashtray on his stomach and looked up at the overhead's unforgiving glare. The box of a room and the two of them in it were lit like an interrogation. Luke expected a white-coated lab technician to lift the ceiling off and poke them with a giant pencil. The silence waited for him, demanding his confession in return for Paul's. He did not know what he would say, but knew that it might define him. He wanted to convey himself, the path of his hopes, but those were not the words that came.

'My mother's in a mental hospital,' he said. 'She's been in it since I was five. She's not coming out.'

It was dug out of him like a wound. He never wanted to have to say it again.

Paul did not speak. He looked down in either embarrassment or respect and, finally, 'What's your father like?' he asked.

'He's Polish.' Luke didn't feel the need to add to this.

'Isn't your name Jewish?'

'Everyone thinks that. Polish. Kanowski.'

'Stay away long enough – for what?'

There was silence.

'Don't know.'

The future was a blank presence in the room, like fear.

Paul was still looking up at the ceiling. Luke, on the floor, glanced down at the pristine box of writing paper. He slipped four fingers under the loose paper band and closed his hand. It gave a snap as it broke. He picked up a sheet of the letterhead, turning it in the light. Not another word was spoken. Whatever it was they were looking for, they were in it together.

## Now – London – 1972

They called their company Graft. After more than four years working in touring theatre they knew the meaning of the word. Graft's home was a 150-seat space above a pub in the City called the Lord Grafton. They liked the counterpoint of it: up front the Lord Grafton, while behind was the dark space where the work took place, *Graft*.

Paul had met Jack Payne when he and Luke were in Liverpool

with the Playhouse. Jack had come from rep and had been a staff director in Cardiff. He was thirty-seven, bearded, and smoked a pipe. They all shared socialist convictions and the hope of shaking up the status quo, and Paul was impressed by Jack's experience. Together with Luke they dreamed up their small company over late-night red wine and the spark of new friendship. Graft would find serious, current work and place it in the heart of the establishment, they would carve their ideas, welcome or unwelcome, into the City.

They had two plays and would alternate them each for a month while rehearsing another two – which they hadn't yet found. Their first production was a play called *Deaf Hill*, written by a fifty-five-year-old Yorkshireman, Mike Wall. It was a short piece; a violent, bestial hour about mines and miners. None of them could agree on much about it except that it was 'important' and it needed a lot of work. Jack Payne, sucking on his pipe, world-weary, seemed confident the many wrinkles could be ironed out under his direction and, as the writer was willing, they were pushing on. They scheduled a tentative three weeks rehearsal, to open the play at the end of the month.

The lease was signed, the permit was given, and the Arts Council grant was enough to get started. So Paul and Luke painted the upstairs windows at the Grafton black on the inside and fixed roller blinds over them. The floorboards of the two-hundred-year-old pub bumped and sloped, creaking, so that the stage didn't lie exactly flat and had wedges – corks and doorstops – filling the gaps. The seating was benches: pine boxes with oval holes for handles, that doubled as steps and could be bolted together. They installed a rudimentary lighting rig; heavy, deep-black dusty tabs on hinged poles and a brand-new cyc, white and pristine at the back of the stage. Two fire extinguishers, a red fire bucket full of sand and fag-ends, and nothing but black paint on the walls. They were made children again by their delight in the thrill of ownership, or else they weren't yet fully grown. They would sit downstairs in the Lord Grafton proper, an unlikely band of players in the old City drinking hole, and not real customers to the landlord, Ron; he always served them last. The corner table was their office. They didn't wear suits like the City gents, coming in for their pies and pints with their briefcases, secretaries on their arms, pinstripe three-pieces and sideburns. Graft were like infiltrators. Astrakhan collars. Suede. Coloured socks, cheesecloth and black polo necks. Gitanes and roll-ups. Graft were:

Paul Driscoll, artistic director.
Jack Payne, co-artistic director, director.
Patrick Orange, lighting/set design.
Tanya Cook, stage manager/costume design.
Luke Kanowski, ASM/props.

Luke was part time because he was working for Hammersmith and Fulham Council as a dustman three days a week in the mornings and wasn't free until lunch. He had needed a job that would free his days and wanted one that wasn't in an office. He'd had enough of offices to last a lifetime. He was up at four, and on the dustcart from a quarter to five. Their route was a square mile of Hammersmith that took in neat river-view terraces and council flats, office blocks and the hospital. The other men, the lifers in Luke's mind, were bent by the grind, heavier on top than below from the carrying and tipping of metal bins for twenty years or more, and oblivious to the smell. They were second and third generation, some of them – bodies invisible beneath heavy jackets, hands like thickened leather. They didn't think Luke would last – laughed at someone like him taking it on – and he agreed with them and didn't mind being laughed at. He didn't want to last, and was grateful for the work. He didn't care about the dirt and stench because the job gave him the streets; it gave him London, all of it, from top to bottom, an endless supply of humanity, the living and dead-heaped detritus of everyday life. He would finish his shift, get back to Paul's flat, wash, and arrive at the Grafton with the sandwiches at one or two, in time to hear the latest round of arguments.

*Deaf Hill* was not near ready. They were casting female roles for *The Duchess of Malfi* that afternoon, and then the men for both plays the following day. They were eating ham sandwiches from the paper they'd been wrapped in and drinking beer. Ron, behind the bar, pretended they weren't there, pulling pints for the City gents and sherry for the ladies.

'I'm interested to see Trevor Albert for Tel,' said Paul.

Jack Payne lit his pipe and sat back, legs wide, a man whose silence was like a knock on the table – *I'm the director, listen to me.*

'We don't need *telly* actors.'

Paul caught Luke's eye. 'If Trevor Albert wants to take a punt on a new play in pub theatre who are we to turn up our noses?' he said.

'I'm not chasing sales to fill some Arts Council balance sheet.' Jack sucked his pipe, intractable.

'Yes. We agree. Although it would be nice to sell some tickets.'

Paul looked to Luke again for support, but Luke had his

own problems; Tanya Cook was edging towards him with the look of a girl who might climb onto his lap.

Tanya was a tiny blonde girl from Bristol. She had studied at the Old Vic and was homesick for her family in Temple Meads. She chain-smoked and had pockets full of tissues and shadows under her eyes. She leaned forward, biting her lip.

'Luke?' she murmured, two drawn-out syllables, and Paul saw Luke smile at her, then wince, hoist up his left foot over his right knee and rub his ankle, glancing around the pub urgently as if he were looking for something. Tanya sat back, lit another cigarette and turned her face away from him. *Hello*, thought Paul.

'What time is Mike coming in?' asked Patrick Orange. He was a big-nosed young man, with longish fair hair, who smilingly underlined stage directions in his coloured biros and climbed ladders to fix gels over the lights with tiny crocodile clips. His place within Graft had become the peacemaker, beatific.

'He should be here any minute with the new draft,' said Jack. 'We'll have an hour or two before the birds start coming in.'

'Which is the other thing . . .' Paul didn't finish the sentence.

They all knew they had only one play, the *Duchess*, with any female roles.

'We can't *shove* women into Mike's play just to satisfy your casting rules,' said Jack. 'Wives and daughters making Yorkshire pudding for the menfolk just because we need them in corsets for the *Duchess* in the evening?'

'I know that, Jack,' said Paul, noticing that Tanya had begun to cry and was having her hand held by Patrick. Luke rustled a newspaper, hunched up over the foreign news as if his life depended on it.

'Here's the man himself,' said Paul as Mike, the writer, came into the pub.

'Hello, you lot,' he said, grizzled, grey-haired, and more ancient to them even than his fifty-five years, one wrinkled manuscript stuffed in the pocket of his overcoat and another poking out of the string bag he carried his Heinz tomato soup about in.

'Just the two drafts with you today, Mike?' said Paul and grinned at him.

'The two latest,' said Mike. 'Gentlemen. Lady.' He looked around for a chair.

Tanya stood up, quivering inside her scrappy suede coat, nose red and clutching her cigarette and tissue.

'You can have my seat, I'm off.'

They all looked up – except Luke, studying the tiny newsprint, deaf.

'Look, I think this is really shitty of you, after yesterday. You're a right shit, Luke. I'm off.'

Paul started up. 'Hey, Tanya, can I—'

'No, Paul! It's all right. I'll see you. I suppose.' And she left, her swinging shoulder-bag bumping against the backs of businessmen as she went.

The men of Graft shifted in their seats, raised their eyebrows. Luke looked at Paul, but Paul refused to smile.

'Great,' he said. 'Marvellous, Luke. Are you going to go after our stage management and costume department, or just let her go?'

'Bit late,' said Luke. 'Probably.'

They all absorbed the new reality. Graft minus one.

'So what now?' said Paul. 'No bloody stage manager. It's a shambles.'

Patrick smiled and shook his head. 'Not to worry, fellas,' he said. 'I'm sure we'll sort something out. I might ring this girl I know, she's really nice.'

'What girl? Just any girl?' asked Paul, looking at Luke pointedly.

'She was ASM at The Basement.'

'Still might be.'

'I'll call her.'

'You call her,' said Jack. 'Mike and me will adjourn upstairs. Paul can come if he likes, and Luke can have a cold shower.'

'Yes, Jack, of course I'm coming. Casting birds at four,' said Paul. 'And one of us will have to read with them now Tanya's gone.'

He, Mike and Jack trooped off through the flock wallpapered door that had a sheet of A4 taped to it that said 'Graft Upstairs' in Tanya's black marker, Patrick went to the payphone and Luke was left in disgrace. He moved to a chair against the wall, pulled a notebook from his pocket and began to write.

Leigh Radley left her bedsit in Camden for the Lord Grafton as soon as she got Patrick's call. She had been out of work for three weeks, just helping out and hoping, writing her diaries and stories she hated immediately they were finished, and eating too much, and she didn't want to be late.

Another day without electric light. A power cut was scheduled between two in the afternoon and eleven that night. Winter dark was already falling faster and more completely than usual as people hurried home to their houses in an atmosphere of endurance and perverse excitement at facing the long hours ahead with no electricity.

Leigh caught the bus and sat upstairs in the smoky fug, poring over her *Duchess of Malfi* beneath the yellow bulbs and counting the stops.

'Smithfield Street, Snow Hill!' shouted the bus conductor from the lower deck and then the *ting-ting* of the bell as they moved on.

Two old ladies in headscarves complained to one another about the government as the bus bounced along.

'I'd like to see Mr Heath wash his smalls by candlelight; it's all right for some.'

Leigh rested her forehead against the glass, watching the blind-black shop windows and a supermarket lit like a cathedral full of tins and cigarettes. They passed St Barts, the windows blazing above the city that was gradually fading away into shadows around it.

'That's the place to be, Dor,' said one of the old ladies and they clutched their handbags, laughing their Monty Python laughs and Leigh bit her lip to stop from laughing with them.

'Newgate Street!'

She hurried down the steep spiral as the bus leaned, and waited, clinging to the barley-sugar plastic-wrapped pole in the cold air, past the emptying offices to her stop. She got off, dragging her *A–Z* from her bag, striking up her lighter to read it, and set off through the unlike-themselves streets.

She found the Lord Grafton, closed and locked, and knocked on the glass. She looked up and down the street and checked the sign above her; a rough painting of a coat of arms: a sword, a shield.

Inside, Luke was lighting cheap, white candles from a box under his arm and waiting for Leigh. The moment Patrick

Orange said her name he had remembered her: the wet night in Seston four years before. The Mini throwing up a dirty wave as it left him. He hadn't told Paul yet that Patrick's ASM friend was Leigh Radley. They had never talked about her, he might not remember as perfectly as Luke did. It was so long ago.

Through the frosted patterned glass, Leigh could see a shadow-figure inside, moving around with lights. Thinking it was Patrick, she smiled. She knocked again, straightened up and tucked her hair behind her ears as the figure came towards her.

He had a candle on a saucer that threw a flickering light up onto his face as the bolts were slid back. He opened the door. It wasn't Patrick. She knew him immediately. Luke.

'Come in,' he said.

He stepped aside. She went past him into the pub. On the bar an oil lamp and candles pooled light along the shiny wood. Luke held up the flickering candle-stump on the saucer. She felt spotlit. She couldn't think what to say. The soft light held them close.

'I love power cuts,' he said. 'Don't you?'

'Am I in the right place?' she asked.

'You don't remember me,' said Luke, smiling at her.

'Yes, I do,' she said, an admission. 'Luke.'

The small flame blew sideways and went out. He closed the door.

There was silence. It was cold.

'Patrick's just gone for more candles,' he said. 'The landlord has loads but he's that mean with them. Come over here.'

She followed him, trying not to bump into the chairs, to

84

three more candles on saucers on the corner table and a notebook, open, with a pen lying across the pages. Luke closed it.

'Y'all right then?' he asked.

'It's like the Blitz or something.'

'Good, isn't it?'

She nodded. Luke just kept looking at her.

'Is this where Graft are?' she prompted.

'They're all upstairs. I'll take you up if you like. What have you been up to?'

'Since . . . ?'

'Since back then.'

'Four years.'

'Yeah.'

She shrugged. 'Working in rep. Here and there . . . I should probably go up.'

'Oh, yeah. Come with me. Take one of these. I've finished anyway.'

She took the candle he offered and followed him to a door in the wall. He opened it.

'So the director is Jack Payne?' she asked.

'Yes, do you know him?'

The stairs went up ahead of them in darkness. She could hear voices.

'We met once, I think.'

They didn't say anything else, but started to go up. She could smell lamp-oil. The stairs were narrow, the walls close on each side of them. Her candle shrank and sputtered in the draught. Then she felt him put his hand onto her wrist where her coat met the back of her hand. He put her hand onto the rail and withdrew his.

On the landing at the top of the stairs were three doors and Luke opened one. Leigh was dazzled momentarily, even though, as she adjusted, the glare was only lanterns, haloing in the gloom of the black paint and curtains all around.

'You remember Paul Driscoll?'

Three faces looked up at her; Paul, who she remembered – the same but different – and two others, both bearded; one the director, Jack, and one older.

'I'm Leigh,' she said.

'Are you an actress?' asked the older one.

Before she could answer Luke said, 'No.' And he laughed, inexplicably. Leigh ignored him.

Paul stood up and came towards her. His handshake was a welcome harbour, like an old friend.

'I remember you – Leigh . . . ?'

'Radley.'

'Right!' He continued to shake her hand for a moment before releasing her. 'This is Jack, our director, this is Mike, the writer.'

'We've met,' said Leigh to Jack, who gave her a noncommittal nod.

'I don't know how much Patrick told you,' Paul said. 'I'm sorry about all this.' He gestured around but it was too dark to see anything, only the pale faces and suggested clothes of the five of them and the presence of Luke, in black, just behind her shoulder. 'We get light tomorrow,' said Paul. 'Then out again on Friday.'

'Bloody miners,' said Mike, who had a strong Yorkshire accent, and all three laughed, very loudly, at a mutual joke. Leigh smiled, to be polite, and Luke said, 'Mike used to work the mines. The play is about all of this. All of that.'

'The play is about too bloody much, as it turns out,' said Mike and sat down again.

Paul began to say something, but then a muffled knocking came from below.

'Bugger it, Patrick,' said Luke and went, suddenly.

She heard him running down the stairs, bumping off the walls, and the bang of the door at the bottom. She felt tremendous relief he had gone, breathing again.

'You'll have to catch me up,' she said, briskly, taking off her coat. 'Patrick said you're casting today?'

Downstairs, hurrying to let Patrick in, Luke thought of Tanya Cook and how he mustn't make passes at the stage management. He realised that already he couldn't remember what Tanya looked like.

All afternoon, Leigh read in the other parts for the actresses; a parade of femininity in winding scarves, layers, shoulder-bags; some confident, perky, others quiet or businesslike, all attempting to occupy the space with their presence. There were fifteen of them, chosen from *Spotlight*, met at parties, friends or strangers. There was some cursory chat then Paul, Patrick, Mike, Jack and Luke sat on the big stepped seating, with Leigh reading in as Antonio, the young man seduced. When the actress was reading badly the men just looked at Leigh.

'Principal boy,' whispered Mike, 'dead sexy.'

Once, when a girl trying out for the Duchess made a mistake – twisting up the words – and she and Leigh laughed, Luke glanced across at Paul and saw that he was watching her closely. He wondered what had been between them, if anything, the night four years ago when the three of them met. He saw the way Paul met her eye; how he seemed to grow a little when they spoke.

'No Newcastle Brown for you then, Leigh?' said Paul downstairs, as Luke stood ready to get the drinks in and they went over their notes.

Leigh smiled. 'I gave it up.'

'Sherry then, is it?'

'Not sherry. Gin and tonic please.' Leigh smiled again.

She had a dimple, Luke saw, enjoying the little sign of fragility, that she could be sweet. Paul obviously liked it too.

'Off you go, Luke,' he said, 'you heard.'

Luke went.

They talked about the actresses they had seen. The drink went straight to their empty stomachs and exhaustion made them all slow, sleepy.

'Joanna Harris, Rebecca Rose, Amanda Larch . . .' said Jack, scribbling biro onto his list.

It was after ten. Ron the landlord's counter-wiping was resentful.

'They were the best,' said Paul. 'Let's sleep on it. In at nine.'

'Still driving that Mini, Leigh?' said Paul, out on the pavement.

It was just the three of them. The others had gone – Jack Payne giving a lift to Mike and ignoring everyone else.

'It died a noble death,' said Leigh. 'Did your Ford Anglia make a recovery?'

'Full. It's doddery though. It's round the corner – can we give you a lift anywhere?'

*We.* Leigh looked from Luke to Paul.

'I'm in Camden,' she said.

'We're in Fulham. Not much of a detour,' said Paul, and they laughed, because of course it was.

They were revived. They had a late-night wakefulness, like morning. They could stay out. They didn't have to sleep.

'Camden it is, then,' said Paul. 'On my way.'

The streets were totally empty and dark as a mine.

'Remember when we met?' said Luke, from the back of the car. 'It was just like this.'

Just as he said it the power came back, windows appearing in the dark, revealing the buildings above them; ambient light where there had been none.

Paul laughed. 'Just like magic,' he said, trying for dryness but expressing only wonder.

Leigh's bedsit was tiny. The bed took up most of the floor and there was a lino vestibule for a kitchen on one side of the door and a single sash window hard up against the corner. She shared a bathroom on the landing.

The two men came up with her and the three of them stood squashed all together by the front door, Luke and Paul not presuming to go into the bedroom part of the room. Leigh went in, by the bed, and spread her arms out.

'Well. This is me,' she said.

Luke and Paul nodded and Leigh kicked some clothes under the bed. She had painted the walls white, green and brown, in geometric patterns, hand-drawn, and the lampshade was hooped paper. A plant sagged by the window. She made coffee, and then all three sat on the bed – there was nowhere else – but still bundled in their coats, partly because it was cold and partly because they didn't want it to look as if they were undressing at all.

'I've got a two-bar,' she said.

'Crank it up,' said Paul.

Leigh put the electric heater onto the pine table because if it went on the ground it singed the sheets. She got into a tangle with the flex tying around her legs and then knocked over some leaflets from a museum onto the floor, and she began to laugh. They all three laughed for a second but Leigh had a giggling fit coming on; a rising hysterical surge of gasping laughter, for no reason but that there were two men in their dark coats sitting on her lonely bed and staring at her fighting with the two-bar heater. She couldn't stop.

'Sorry,' she managed, horrified, unable to control herself. She was crying with laughter. 'Someone slap me,' she said.

Paul and Luke exchanged a look.

'It's probably hysterical hysteria,' wept Leigh, 'like Freud said, it's a sort of mad sex thing, you know – repressed virgin needs or – God, I have to stop – I'm a woman . . .'

And she slithered onto the floor between the bed and the wall, laughing more, the giggling bumping up against sorrow, threatening to release something from her, weak sadness or abandon. Her legs were feeble. She could not breathe for laughing.

Paul found that he was blushing. His cheeks were burning. It wasn't the two-bar, that had begun to glow furiously; it was the words *sex*, *Freud* and, mostly, *virgin*. He averted his eyes as if Leigh were doing something lewd, and looked at her bookshelf instead: Simone de Beauvoir, Jung, Anaïs Nin, Marx, Greer. *Oh God*, he thought. He noticed Luke was smiling; he didn't seem embarrassed at all. He was smiling at Leigh as if she were doing a special trick all for him.

Leigh was invisible behind the bed now, on the ground. Both men stared at the gap and, after a while, with just the sounds of her breathing, she emerged, red faced, but not giggling any more. She wiped her eyes.

'I could have died,' she said, matter-of-factly. 'I promise you, I'm not like this normally.'

'You've got Karl Marx,' said Luke, easily, who must have been looking at her books too. 'I haven't read it. Can I borrow it?'

And the evening began again. A new night. A fresh thing. All the books came out. Records were played on Leigh's record player on the pine table next to the two-bar. The Maxwell House was finished. None of them were hungry. It was one o'clock. It was two o'clock. The three of them, cross-legged on the bed, and the record sleeves scattered around them.

At about half past two Paul fell asleep, with his face on his arm, and Luke and Leigh, whose voices had been easy, over-lapping until then, noticed him sleeping, and fell silent.

The song carried on. It was 'Homeward Bound'. They had been talking about their visions of America, where neither had ever been, and if England's cramped spaces could ever offer such romantic loneliness as the railway stations and Greyhounds and endless roads of there; of New York and Greenwich Village, if those places really were what they seemed, or just constructs in the minds of the artists, the troubadours, the vagabonds.

Leigh changed the record. 'Corrina Corrina' . . .

She got back onto the bed and glanced at Paul, then her and Luke's eyes met, frighteningly alone but at the same time in thrilling danger of being witnessed. They had been talking quickly before, finishing one another's thoughts; meeting in recognition and play, forgetting – a little – how closely they were sitting and that they were on a bed. Now, with no conversation, and the record playing on, there was only the awareness that they were not touching, and that they wanted to touch. Now, the wanting one another was in the room so quickly it was like vertigo.

Leigh did not look directly at Luke but she put her hand, slowly, into the charged territory of the space between them. She hadn't known she was going to do it.

Luke's hand was resting on his knee – and, under his leg, Bob Dylan, young, his arm linked with the woman in the suede coat as they walked towards the camera in the New York winter, parked cars and fire escapes.

Leigh glanced up at him, fearful, and smiled. He looked at her quietly, his eyes were serious, the unselfconscious looking at her that she could not hide from. Their fingertips touched and then their hands, moving over each other, light and deliberate, finding the spaces in between, the sides of their fingers. It was as if hands never did ordinary things, they felt so new. Then Luke closed his fingers around hers and reached his other hand to the back of her neck, warm under her hair – she looked quickly at Paul, and Luke took his hand away.

They both laughed – almost – quietly. There was nowhere to go with it.

They sat and looked at each other. Paul gave a small snore. Leigh bit her lip, felt giggling rising again in her chest, but then Luke took hold of both her wrists in his hands. His fingertips pressing against her pulse stopped her. It steadied her, but lost her, too. She hadn't felt this before — she had known it on her own, with her own imaginings, but this was so fast, getting away from her. She thought, *I always knew I'd see you again.*

'When we met the first time I thought I knew you already,' he said. It was the truth. 'Do you ever get that?'

She was embarrassed, and looked away, just as he got up — shocking her.

'Here,' he said and held out his hand.

Leigh glanced back at Paul.

'He's asleep,' he said. 'It's all right.'

He had none of the movement he normally did, no nerves, just quiet and focused, knowing what he wanted. She got up. She'd have followed him anywhere. He took her hand and they went around the corner, just out of sight, the only place to go, where the wall went to the front door. He put his hands onto her shoulders, her collarbones, and pressed her back, gently, against the wall, and he kissed her. His hands moved up her neck, until he held her face between both of them, the fingers pressing into her neck, and the cold hard wall behind her back. They kissed. Revealed and encircled. Her arms were around him, across his back, pulling him into her as they kissed. Breathless.

He was still in his coat, she had taken hers off hours before and had a dress underneath, short over her jeans, with thin corduroy and tiny buttons that didn't open. She wanted him to try to open them so that she could tell him they didn't open and he could find some other way into her.

'I'm not really a virgin,' she said.

This gave him pause; he backed off a little — his face coming into focus — and frowned at her.

'Are you?' he said.

'No, I said I'm not.'

'Why would you say you're not?'

'Because I said I was before.'

'Did you?'

'Yes, when I was laughing. It was a figure of speech.'

'It was a – being a virgin was a figure of speech?'

'I think I said "virginal", not virgin.'

He laughed – a great sort of guffaw, suddenly and very loud.

'*Shh!*'

They both looked around the corner – Paul was sleeping peacefully.

Luke kissed her again, sweet, but then stopped, putting his mouth to her ear.

'What's the difference?' he whispered, very close, keeping quiet for her. 'What's the difference between virgin and virginal when virgin is a figure of speech?'

She smiled but thought she might cry. The talking and then kissing – the reality of him, too close, too human, too honest for her to bear. She didn't know why it should hurt so much, being so perfect.

'Just – I feel as if I'm untouched, but I'm not. I've had boyfriends – I just – you're . . . I feel untouched,' she said again.

Luke saw that she had tears in her eyes. It was awful. He took both her hands and held them up between their faces, double fists, like a promise. Blinkered, they were safe in the tiny space of their hands, their eyes the biggest thing in the world, so close up. And there, in the very briefest of moments, there was love.

Then he stepped back from her, and shook his head, and laughed.

'Don't chat up the stage management,' he said, and left.

Leigh lay next to Paul in her clothes, slept hardly at all and waking first, watched him for a while. The early-morning light showed his paleness and the silver gleam of his hair, which was brown in the shadows. He needed to shave. The stubble was sandy; not so much a shadow as a burnishing, a softening of his jaw.

The night before was at her back like a dream or fever. She felt Luke wrenched from her; his painful absence. He had not liked her enough to stay. She refused to countenance humiliation but it had its way with her anyway. *Don't chat up the stage management.* His mouth and hands on her face and neck. She had been assaulted by her reaction to him — had plainly imagined something quite different to his experience. Foolish. Trusting. She settled against the pillow, against the wall. Set her jaw. Shut her eyes, was grateful Paul was sleeping and could not see her. It would take time and careful sense to push Luke from her mind. *He is one of those men,* she thought, to fix him in her controllable universe, *just one of those men — that cause pain and don't think.* Her father had been one. Charisma and blind hunger; she had never known what her mother meant by it but now she saw. Now she had felt it. Just because her mother had fallen in love with a man like that, it didn't mean she must. She would be well-guarded. She would. Slowly, she came back to herself.

Paul was a quiet sleeper, kindly and untroubled. The morning light touched them.

95

At seven she got up and went to make tea.

'Where did Luke get to?' asked Paul as soon as he sat up, disorientated and disarranged. He scratched and shuffled his clothes about when he knew she had her back turned.

'He left,' said Leigh. 'At about three.'

'He's on his rounds, Thursdays,' said Paul. He shook his head to wake up, like a cartoon character recovering from a punch.

They went into the Lord Grafton together for nine o'clock sharp, through the cold stale smoke of the pub in the morning light and up to the theatre. They were casting the men from ten. Mike and Jack hadn't arrived yet, it was just the two of them.

'They'll be here soon,' said Paul.

They should have been talking about the day, making sure they had the pages ready, but they sat in silence, each on a separate step, a few feet apart. Leigh's mind felt thin with sleeplessness and drained of feeling.

Paul was examining his hands, front and back, turning them. They were big hands, broad, with short square nails and no visible veins. He looked at them as if he were assessing his soul, the maleness of himself, and then, joining them together in resolution, he looked straight up and at her and said, 'Will you come out with me one night?'

Leigh knew that it was a serious question. She wanted him to hold her in his arms. She imagined telling him about Luke. *Don't chat up the stage management.*

'You don't have to,' said Paul, 'it's not part of the job or anything.' And he smiled grimly, anticipating rejection.

'Yes, please,' she answered.

They heard Mike Wall's coal-dust smoker's cough as he came up the stairs.

'Beautiful morning,' he said.

Luke had no sleep at all. He walked the five miles from Camden to the depot in Hammersmith and had to make do with his ordinary clothes, and getting the stink of rotting bins on himself. He borrowed boots and gloves, which stank themselves.

He could only think, in febrile sleepless repetition, that Paul wanted Leigh and that she was just the girl for him. She was as nice as he was, and strong like him. He thought of Jack Payne, leching about her being a principal boy. But she wasn't Peter Pan, she was Saint Joan. She ought to have armour and a sword. Leigh had nothing wrong with her the way Paul had nothing wrong. They were of good stock, with no shadows cast over them from behind. They were not like him, they were not contaminated.

It was hard physical work catching up to the cart as it crawled; lifting the dented metal bins from a standstill; shouting to each other, keeping it going. Normally, Luke gained energy from rising above the shit as all of them did; businesslike absurdity, dirty jokes. But that morning he did not speak. He just thought about Leigh and that he must not want her.

Then home, coated in the stench, broken glass in the soles of his boots, hair stinking of the air that breathed from the back of the dustcart. He cleaned up, scrubbed – nails, arms, back of neck – covered himself in Pears soap like washing socks out in a basin. He did not feel the lack of sleep. He hoped Paul had got up the nerve to ask Leigh out. Paul didn't mess about with women any more, not for a couple of years, and even when he had he was half-hearted about it. He was serious, looking for a girl he could really like.

Good luck to them; it was not for him. He needed the drug of sex, not that, not the tiny sharp thing he felt last night with Leigh, the prospect of raw, sweet kindness. He didn't recognise it and it couldn't draw him.

When he got to the theatre he ran up the stairs and stopped, getting his breath, before opening the door. An older actor was reading, obviously uncomfortable, and there was a feeling of awful endurance in the room. Luke slipped inside, against the wall, and looked at the tableau of the others on the steps.

They all, in their way, greeted him — a nod, a raised hand — except Leigh. She kept her eyes down on the page, her thick, dark hair hiding her face. Paul, just past her, smiled at him and went back to watching the actor, but he moved his hand — not onto Leigh's shoulder or arm, but to rest on her jacket, thrown onto the step behind. It was enough.

Luke saw them together and despite himself, despite all his certainty, he felt nothing but loss; the breaking of something precious in the heart of him that he had not known how to keep safe. Frightened, he shuddered the feeling from his skin. He pushed his coat sleeve up his arm, rubbed his neck — restored himself. He was pleased for Paul. He was. He smiled as a familiar restlessness overtook; he felt the habitual painful joy of searching and the lack, the lack, the distance from love that was his moulded shape, the fallout that had warped his heart.

---

On the morning of Nina's twenty-third birthday she was washing out her tights in the basin of a boarding house in Cambridge, squeezing the gritty water from the toes and soaping them again, with a bar of Lux. Lynsey de Paul was singing 'Sugar Me' on the radio by the bed where her mother was lying, wearing a towelling dressing gown over her old silk one.

At breakfast that morning Marianne had reached over the doily and teapot to hand her a red lipstick, unwrapped.

'Happy Birthday, my darling,' she said. 'By the time I was your age I had had you, and your father had disappeared off to Australia . . . but then I also had something of a film career. You're not as young as you think you are.'

Nina had imagined when she left drama school she would have to fend for herself, but in all the towns they went to, all the theatres, rehearsal rooms, bedsits and boarding houses, Marianne had been her constant shadow. She altered Nina's costumes and fixed her face, took her part in rows with directors, fought for her with her agent.

They had been in Cambridge for ten days. Before that it had been Worthing. Before that, London. In London the job had been a subversive pantomime that Marianne condemned as pornography. Nina had been the front end of an angry camel stitched from sack-cloth, released from her normal inhibition by the anarchy of the production and giggling with the rest of the camel, a down-to-earth girl named Suzy. Suzy had stocky legs for a camel and didn't care if she ever worked again because she was in love with the lighting designer. The writer and director said the piece was about the absurdity of Christianity. The Church had been publicly and gratifyingly offended, but the dwindling audiences remained largely mystified.

Suddenly, though, in the past weeks, there had been a change. When Nina was galloping about the London stage as a camel, Marianne met a theatrical producer named Tony Moore. The Worthing run was fraught with telephone messages and stage-door notes. Immediately they moved into their Cambridge digs Marianne had slipped away; train tickets and a small suitcase, taxis throbbing by the rehearsal-room door. For the first time in her professional career Nina had been alone. She presented herself at rehearsals without her mother; went to the pub afterwards unchaperoned. It irked her that her new freedom was stalked by fear, as if she depended upon her mother's tight harness for safety. She had dreamed of kicking over the traces, but she had missed her company.

The birthday lipstick, unfashionably scarlet, sat on the glass shelf over the basin on the opposite wall from the bed. Nina ran the cold tap over the tights again, her reddened hands kneading the flesh-coloured nylon.

'*Oh dear, I feel so sad,*' said Marianne behind her, reading the script she was holding.

'*Bored, dear, bored. Not sad,*' recited Nina back, wringing out the tights and hanging them on the radiator. '*Call things by their right names.*'

She dried her hands on the balding towel that hung beneath the basin.

'. . . blah blah . . .' said Marianne. '*I can see the snow falling.* Is this what passes for drama these days?'

'That's not helpful. *It has snowed. It will snow . . .*'

'. . . *Yawn. Zithern.*'

Nina yawned, obediently, and mimed playing a zithern. Marianne laughed.

'I can't imagine that's accurate. Have they *found* you this rumoured zithern yet?'

'Not yet. We have a lute.'

'Darling, they're not going to black you up for this?'

'Japanese people aren't black.'

'You know what I mean. Slitty eyes. Wigs.' Marianne riffled through the pages. 'It's like a ghastly intellectual *Mikado*.'

'It's a very exciting piece,' said Nina, who was trying to convince herself. 'Iris Murdoch, Mummy?'

'She isn't even a dramatist, she's just dabbling. Aren't you glad I wouldn't let you cut your hair? I should think that's the reason they cast you.'

Nina went to the end of the bed and sat, pulling a corner of the blanket over her feet.

'*Such* a drag.' Marianne put the script down. She leaned forward and cupped Nina's face in her hands. 'You're so pale. You should make more of an effort. I'm going to have a bath.'

She got up, shedding the two dressing gowns like a skin despite the cold, and collecting her sponge bag and towel from the chest of drawers.

Nina picked up the script again, but Marianne paused at the door, her body beneath her nightdress taut and ready.

'Darling, I want you to meet Tony,' she said.

Nina looked up. 'Why?'

'He's a very nice man.'

Nina felt her heart jump uncomfortably. Inexplicably she abhorred the mention of her mother's lover's name, dreaded the closeness of the association.

She paused before she said, 'Mummy, he's *your* very nice man.'

'Don't be silly. He's a producer. He's casting.'

'Oh.'

'*Now* you're interested.' Marianne's tone was lascivious.

'I'm actually not – I've got rehearsals.'

'Not until Monday. Come tonight. It's your birthday.'

It wasn't an invitation; it was an order.


And so Nina and Marianne dressed for Saturday-night dinner-after-the-theatre in London at five o'clock in the afternoon in Cambridge. Marianne, in a wide-legged silk trouser-suit with a knotted plaited belt, lounged on the bed back-combing her hair and smoking, as Nina tried first her maxi-skirt and printed blouse, then her mini-dress over the same blouse, then her hot-pants, then her denim skirt, her waistcoat, her deep-necked pale blue party dress – until the floor was awash with wrinkled rejection. Finally she unearthed a tiny, rather old, navy-blue mini-dress with a white round collar.

'This. Yes. And lots of eye make-up,' Marianne instructed. 'There's a difference between pure and dowdy. Thank God for your legs.'

'Why?' Nina was hot and frantic, and close to tears after an hour of her mother's constant assessment of her anatomy. 'What does it *matter*? *God*.'

'Believe me, it matters.' Marianne put out her cigarette. 'It's too late for my legs now.'

'They help you walk about, don't they?'

'Very droll. My knees have dropped. No more miniskirts for me.'

Nina finished putting on her shoes, damping down her impatience, and then turned to look down at her mother on the bed. She looked mournful; not her usual unassailable self, but small. Nina, standing above her, felt the power of youth against her parent's slow diminishing.

'You're so beautiful, Mummy. You always have been.'

'No, darling,' said Marianne, and met her eye. 'My time is over.'

They took the train, make-up glaring in the unforgiving light. Nina read, while Marianne sat, barely moving. Her expression – and Nina hesitated to look – was set and her lips closed tight, calculating something beyond her sight.

They took a taxi to the Strand and arrived at 10.30 exactly.

Nina had never been to the Savoy before. The taxi turned in and approached the hotel, deeply recessed off the street, like a backdrop on a stage, and stopped at the entrance. Stepping out, Nina waited while her mother paid the driver. The hotel was the most glamorous thing she had ever seen. She stared up at the 1930s lettering. Marianne turned to her daughter with her handbag over her arm. The liveried doormen did not look at them as, with her cigarette in her mouth, narrowing her eyes against the smoke, she adjusted Nina's shiny hair over her shoulders.

'I have a good instinct for luck, my darling,' she said when she had finished, 'and tonight feels lucky. Don't you think so?'

Nina did not know why Marianne's eyes were bright. She did not think it was for her, but seeing her excitement, she could not help her heart reaching out.

'Shall we go in?' said Marianne.

Inside, they crossed the marble floor, leaving the vastness of the hotel behind to enter the Grill. It was like stepping back in time; formality that Nina, in her youth – her Equity-minimum adventuring – had never before encountered or desired. She pulled down her miniskirt.

They were greeted by the head waiter, a small man who

gave the impression he had been hoping they would come, and was delighted with them.

'Yes. Tony Moore,' said Marianne airily, and then, over her shoulder to Nina, 'He has a regular table.'

The room was crowded, high, square and dark; tablecloths bright white against the panelling and a wall of conversation and laughter that dipped and paused as they entered and everyone, quite subtly, looked up to see who had arrived.

'Madame . . .' The waiter gestured across the room and they went with him.

Nina followed her mother like a child, trying not to study the people they passed for well-known faces, suddenly grateful and filled with love for her parent, who was so beautiful, walking carelessly into this secret, celebratory world. The people – men in dark suits, women, some jewelled, some shockingly blasé in their casual modernity against the background – were eating, talking and looking up to watch at the same time, giving the impression of people in a pavement café watching the evening promenade. It reminded her of young delight, some dream of theatre she had never actually known but might never leave her free; pictures she had seen in old magazines as a child of Olivier and Vivien Leigh – he in black tie, she in organza and pearls – dining in that very room. She had lain on her childhood bed at Aunt Mat's and dreamed, and hoped she might see her mother in the pictures, too. And then she had grown up and realised that of course her mother's life was very different.

Waiters moved with speed in silence. They had arrived at a corner table.

'Ah!' cried Marianne.

She opened her arms wide, her sleeve fluttering across a

tray of martinis, kissing the rims of the glasses but not dislodging them. The material swept aside like a curtain, revealing a group of people looking up at her exclamation. The table was round, half-full; the wall behind a severe backdrop to their frivolity. The man facing her, Nina knew immediately, was Tony Moore.

'Darling,' he said, and stood up. He embraced her mother, kissed both cheeks, all the time keeping his eyes on Nina.

'Tony – my daughter, Nina Jacobs,' said Marianne. 'It's her birthday.'

'Happy birthday, you precious, gorgeous thing,' said Tony, and took her hand. His fingers did not grip hers, but simply laid over them, briefly. 'I so loved your work in the Feydeau last year. So fresh. How marvellous you are to come all this way in this ghastly weather. Do you loathe your mother for dragging you?'

Nina felt washed with affection. His approval was a delight to her. She had expected somebody frowsy, with a pipe and thick black glasses – a producer. The ones she had known left snail-trails of cigarette packets and sweet-wrappers. This man was slender, pale-haired, delicate, and yet she was struck by him so strongly, intrigued by his confidence so completely, that she could not speak. He didn't notice.

'Darlings – Chrissie, you know Marianne? David? Marianne and Nina Jacobs. Sit, both of you. What will you have? We're waiting for the Garrick to come out – Honor Lamb and Jerry are coming. We're dead with boredom. Sit. Sit. Marianne, gorgeous – how Fitzgerald you look.'

The Chrissie he introduced to her she already knew – Chrissie Southey from drama school. Prettiness undimmed. A great deal more hair. Now a starlet.

'Hello, Nina! I wondered where you had got to!' she cried in delight and immediately turned away. The man, David, smiled and shook her hand. She didn't recognise him. She felt she should.

A waiter pulled out her chair, surprising her, and Nina had to side-step not to trip on his toes, gauche and blushing.

'No, no, darling,' said her mother, quick as a whip. 'You sit here.' She gestured the seat next to Tony.

Tony smiled. 'I'd love it,' he said, and Nina felt beautiful.

Drinks were ordered. She glanced at him as he talked to her mother. He was younger than Marianne; closer to her own age. He could only be thirty – in his thirties – she turned to look around the room and noticed that people looked away when she caught them watching. She realised, with a halting thrill of power, that the people at the other tables were looking at *her* – not wanting to be caught. It was not she looking at them as it had always been. She noticed suddenly that Tony's upper arm was resting ever so lightly against hers. There was plenty of space at the table. He didn't need to be touching her. The feeling of power moved in her like sex – no, she felt the current clearly, it *was* sex – the blood rushed through her. Shocked at herself, she looked with quick guilt towards her mother to see if she had noticed. She had. She was looking at her.

Nina moved her arm away from Tony's, but then she realised that her mother was smiling. In a tiny movement Marianne raised her glass to her and gave her the warmest – the truly kindest  smile that Nina had ever had from her. She smiled at her daughter with sadness and with love and then she looked away. Nina felt the heat of Tony's arm once more as it moved towards hers. This evening was different, this was her future.

There was pale-pink and green apple blossom over London; a gleam on the black railings; sunshine over the cracks.

Tony Moore, it transpired, was producing and co-writing a sex-comedy revue called *Wot, Not Married?!* He carried a number of poster-sized sheets under his arm as he led Nina inside, and up the stairs of his Chelsea house.

'It's ridiculous, I admit,' he was saying over his shoulder, 'and there's nothing in it for you, you'll be relieved to hear – unless you want to bare your breasts and brandish a duster?'

Nina laughed but the allusion to nudity didn't help her nerves; alone in the tall narrow house with Tony, seeing him on a professional footing when two months had passed since their first meeting.

In that time her mother had ceased mentioning him as her 'friend' and referred to him simply as Tony. To nobody's surprise the Iris Murdoch in Cambridge had not transferred. The cast scattered to other projects and Nina and Marianne had returned somewhat gratefully to another temporary stopgap, this one of two years' standing, a maisonette in Pimlico.

Tony Moore lived just off the King's Road in a tall, narrow red-brick house he had yet to do up, although his plans for it were ambitious. It was guessed that he may have inherited the house, but nobody knew from whom. Nobody really knew where he came from. He was well-connected but hadn't started in Footlights or OUDS, he had been something in rep. He had an occasional iconoclastic column in the *Evening Standard*, a sharp tongue and a good nose for talent. He seemed to have a bit of money but he hadn't had a big hit. All the head waiters knew him and the agents took his calls and he had a regular Sunday-night soirée – he called it that – but the jury was as yet firmly out and sequestered on Tony Moore.

The walls above the chipped dado rail in the hall were painted dark red like raw aged steak. The floorboards were stained a dusty aubergine and covered in rush matting runners. Theatre playbills lined the stairs on both the way up to the drawing room and down into the basement kitchen. They weren't all his own productions but he'd had something to do with most of them, and if challenged could plead nostalgia. He had also hung, filling up the gaps, posters and prints: Magritte, Gaudi, Lichtenstein, Picasso, so that all in all there was a broad enough palette for anybody. *See anything you like?* the house seemed to say, *let's talk about it.*

Tony had his study on the second floor at the back, looking out at the plane trees and holly bushes of the courtyard gardens. As she reached the top of the stairs Nina, joining him on the landing, glimpsed what she guessed was his bedroom, curtains closed against the day. It seemed she could smell the air breathing from the room, but it wasn't that, it just had an atmosphere. Perhaps being unlit.

'Not there,' he said. 'Here we are.' And he gestured the open door to the sunny study.

Nina went in and stood looking out at the mess of windows in the big houses and mansion flats behind.

'What do we think?' he asked, and she turned.

He was laying out the posters on the neat desk, weighing down the corners with paperweights and a desk-lighter. They were variations on a theme: a selection of French maids, bananas, exclamation marks, and startled-looking red-faced men in suits – sometimes with their trousers down, sometimes looking up the girls' skirts – all in a seaside postcard style. The *Wot, Not Married?!* was in a variety of fonts and sizes; hand-drawn, sketchy artwork and rubbings out. Nina stared.

'Yes, yes,' said Tony, self-deprecating, 'but bums on seats, you know.'

'Bums everywhere,' she said, and he laughed.

'Would it disappoint you to know it's not nearly as risqué as *Oh! Calcutta!*?'

'Isn't it?'

'No, darling, it's rather cosier. And I'm *not* ashamed to say it also lacks Tynan's pretension. Broad and bawdy, that's our motto. The thinnest of plots. My *Not Married* is more Restoration than revolution.'

'More *Carry On* than *Country Wife?*' said Nina and was thrilled to see he was tickled by the allusion.

'Oh, very good! Yes, it's *indefensibly* silly,' he said, 'and lots of flesh. But Lord knows the world's grim enough, we need a bit of that. A bit of *the other*.' He laughed. 'So sorry. It's contagious. Sit down.'

Nina sat in the black leather swivel chair by the desk. Tony stood against the wall, one leg crossed over the other at the ankle, his sharp elbow resting on his hand above the shiny steel buckle of his narrow belt.

'You think I have something in mind for you but I don't,' he stated.

Nina wasn't sure what to say.

'*Mea culpa*,' he said. 'There's no new play. There's no Chekhov – however it is you see yourself . . . . How *do* you see yourself?'

'How do you see me?' she asked, blank. It was her stock

response, when challenged — throw the ball back, let the producer, the director, the *man* — juggle it.

Tony blinked, twice, rapidly. His eyes were pale grey. 'Clever girl,' he said. 'Do you worry you've missed the boat? Twenty . . . ?'

That hurt; he was as bad as her mother.

'Three.'

'Twenty-three. Well into your best years. What about film work?'

She shrugged. 'I've done a little. I was cut from *Daytrippers* — I had a scene with Albert Finney—'

'I'm not interested in that.' He cut her off.

'What *are* you interested in?'

'Talent. Whipping it into shape. Making something intelligent, challenging, big enough to be worth the price of the ticket.'

Nina couldn't help but glance at the myriad *Wot, Not Married?!* images splashed across the desk. Tony raised his eyebrows.

'And money.' He smiled.

'Money's nice,' allowed Nina.

'Was your mother ever any good? She talks a good career but I've a feeling she was rather poor. Walk-ons and fairly tawdry rep. What do you think?'

Nina was shocked; as if Marianne were crouched in the cupboard, under the desk, listening, but at the same time she was delighted — he was so dismissive.

'Well, she's . . . I don't *think* she was,' she almost whispered and, seeing his eyes gleam, giggled.

'My God, she's a tough old bitch, isn't she?' he said.

Nina stared, and had to remember to close her mouth.

'Bet you can't wait to be shot of her. What would it take?'

This was too far. This was awful. She wanted to run to Marianne and hold her. Was this the world's view of them both?

'I've shocked you. I'm sorry. I'm very fond of your dear old mum. We had a lot of fun and she's a knockout to look at, just like you.'

Nina, confused, couldn't help warming to the praise.

'Look,' he said, and he went over to her, leaning on the desk so that his hips – as narrow as hers – were at a level with her eye. 'When your agent asks about this meeting, Nina, I don't want you to have anything to hide. Jo's a mate of mine. She's not stupid. And I don't want you to have to lie to your mother.'

He stopped, and stared at her until she was so uncomfortable she couldn't breathe. He leaned forward, whispering a secret.

'Nobody knows about me, yet. Nobody knows me at all.' He was fixing her with intensity, thoughts crossing his face like fast clouds across the sky. 'My mother was a – I won't say it again, but maybe she was something like yours. Not physically. God, no. She was a bog-Irish harpy, elbow deep in filth all her life despite turning petit-bourgeois in bloody Bournemouth. My dad was an old soak and wife-beater. He hit us all. Belts. Sticks.'

Nina saw his nerve fail – infant-like sadness, like a toddler who had scraped his knee stopping himself from crying – and she looked away from him so that he could gather himself back. There was a pause, then he said, 'I know something of you. I don't want you to think that I want *you* –' he sat up and waved his hand casually over the posters across the desk

'— for this. In any way. Understand? I'm here to stay. I think you are, too. I can't give you a job. Yet. But I can give you a nice juicy steak at San Fred's — coming?'

He went across the room and, collecting keys from a hook behind the door, checking his wallet, outlined clearly through the fabric of his back pocket.

Nina leapt from her chair, and they went to lunch at San Frediano's.

Nina was between jobs. *Wot, Not Married?!* was opening in May at the Comedy, and during the last days at the rehearsal rooms in Waterloo, Tony's struggles with finance, hasty rewrites and then faltering tech runs when they had at last moved in to the theatre itself, she saw him often. She sat by him as he argued with the director in cafés and pubs. She brought him drinks as he scoured angry lines through the script. He hated her to sleep if he was not and relied on her presence and silent acquiescence. She forgot it was just *Not Married*. It became Molière. She argued there was not so much difference between them. But still, it was hard to imagine *Not Married* revived in two hundred years.

She came to know the house on Tite Street very well; friends and acquaintances wandering in and out bringing or taking wine, stacks of records, books, hash. Tony's was a curious world of demi-success; parties that were work meetings; friendships that were professional liaisons. Nina felt privileged to be let in on some of his secrets but knew that most of him was hidden from her. Marianne slipped into the wings of her life as if she, too, were resting, observing with pleasure her daughter's absorption into Tony's world. Being unemployed had never been so comfortable.

The Sunday-night gatherings were performances in themselves. Tony would snap and quarrel with nerves, the languor that had so taken her in was a veneer. He did not fear failure, only that nobody would witness his magnificence.

In London as in New York, Tony knew, the play was – as one might say – the thing. Nina was impressed by him, perched on his lily pad at the centre of his little pond, croaking his confidence to the world, but from his vantage point Tony himself felt no satisfaction. He could only see the other ponds: Olivier at the Old Vic, splashing about with Diana Rigg, Tom Stoppard, Michael Horden, spotlit on their glistening, well-loved lily pads; Nottingham, Liverpool, Sheffield, where talent grew like multifarious spawn, admired and revered from hungry London: Ian McKellen, Trevor Griffiths. And then, painfully close and most jealously observed, the Royal Court's waters reflected his bright green envy, hopping with William Gaskill, Lindsay Anderson, George Devine. Tony shook hands and remembered credits, chatted up agents and spun his network of friendships, but he was not *there*. His was as yet murky water, awaiting talent's oxygen that it might teem with the right sort of life.

Nina was unofficial hostess at Tite Street, part maid, part girlfriend, but he never made a pass at her. She began to wonder if he were homosexual, at which her mother, with strange relish, laughed,

'Nina, you're so naïve.'

Tony had a horror of the bourgeois. Nina once suggested vol-au-vents and his outrage was comical and comfortingly acute.

'If you think I want to make a housewife out of you, you're wrong,' he said.

Part of her questioned whether the idea of *wife* – sans curlers and canapés – was as abhorrent.

He took her shopping. She was so pleasingly decorative, he said. The women in the boutiques knew him – sometimes murmured discussions about cheques and light persuasions took place at the till that Nina would embarrassedly ignore. He preferred her to wear trousers, tight-fitting, with waist-coats, translucent ruffled shirts. He liked her skinny and watched what she ate, waspishly. Often he would come to her flat and bring her shoes or necklaces as she dressed, drinking gin and tonic with Marianne as they debated what would suit her and lay on the bed together, laughing, as she turned around for them.

The night of the first preview of *Not Married* they had arranged to meet at the theatre at six. She was dressing when she got his call.

'Nina, come to the house. We'll go together.'

When she arrived she found the front door on the latch. She shut it behind her. Noise from below drew her down the steep stair to the kitchen where a little party had made themselves at home. A couple of unemployed actors, a model she had met before and the teenage son of a well-known Irish novelist Tony was cultivating were sitting at the table. Halfway down, seeing Tony was not there, Nina withdrew and went upstairs. She looked into the big drawing room, where the empty furniture and full drinks trolley stood undisturbed. She paused, and then climbed the last flight to the landing. The bedroom door was open. She had never been inside.

'Tony?'

'In here.'

He had laid out upon the bed a selection of shirts and ties

and was standing in the middle of the room in only his slim black trousers and bare feet. His chest was white and startlingly thin. Nina had never seen him undressed before.

'Come here.'

He stared at her – not her face, but her chest as she stood before him.

Without saying a word he undid the buttons on her blouse, precisely, one by one, and pushed the half-transparent silk from her shoulders with his fingertips. Nina did not move. Withdrawn and appraising, he gazed at her naked stomach, her small breasts inside her bra and fast-shallow breath moving her chest. Then he took her hands and gripped her fingers, hard.

'I'm going to be a laughing stock,' he hissed. '*What have I done?*'

Nina sensed the gape of the wide-open door behind her, heard the footsteps of the people below, and voices. She felt acutely isolated, far from her mother, and aware of the two of them standing there, their vulnerability and the fact he was not kissing her – did not seem about to kiss her.

'It will be fine,' she said mechanically.

'I promise I'll find you something,' he said. 'Better than this. A real play. We'll find a good play.'

'It's all right.'

'I'm just extremely . . .' His eyelids fluttered, his lips seemed to disobey him. 'Frightened,' he said at last.

Unable to sustain eye-contact Nina took in the clothes on the bed, the bottle of vodka on the bedside table, drawn blinds and crumpled curtains. She couldn't tell if he should start drinking or stop.

'You are so good,' he said. Then stepped away abruptly and with his normal irritation said, 'I just can't fucking decide at *all* what to wear. Not at all.'

Nina fumbled with her task and looked at the crisp, virtually identical white shirts, and the narrow ties in lemon yellow, pale blue, black. 'I think that black one is the best,' she offered. 'Smart.'

He took the tie from the bed and looped it between his hands.

'Yes, you're right,' he announced. He picked up a shirt and began to remove the pins.

'Cover up, Nina,' he said.

————————

The critics despised it, but *Not Married* was an unashamed success. Where first the tribal youth-invasion of the musical *Hair* and then *Oh! Calcutta!* had trampled three centuries' legal veto on stage nudity, *Not Married* made capital of freedom's gain without even so much as a nod to the avant-garde. There were naked or semi-naked shower scenes, bedroom scenes, even a naked card game — strip-poker, naturally — and audiences deserted the BBC in the corner and Dick Francis on the bedside table to revel in the slamming doors and bare behinds; the cosy, naughty, empty-headed girls with fully dressed apologetic men pursuing them. For a few weeks after it opened the theatre was picketed by an uneasy alliance of feminists and Christians, and once the revue was perceived by the press as a slice of the country's moral decline the public gobbled it up.

At the Savoy Grill after the opening night, celebrating with the financiers and the lead actors, Tony praised the cast, dismissed the still uncertain future of the show and, without pausing in his conversation, slipped his butter knife from the plate in front of him. Reaching under the damask tablecloth, he ran the cool blade lightly up Nina's inner thigh. She felt the shock of the metal against her warm skin, sensing its edge. For twenty minutes he stroked her with the steel, high enough for danger, up and down. And Nina gripped his other hand with hers while, helpless and shocked, she lost herself to it; trying not to move in her chair, terrified they would be noticed, disturbed and almost tearful — silent. She excused herself and went to the lavatory, leaning against the cubicle wall and masturbating, silently, viciously, with her eyes screwed shut, not thinking of anything but the feeling of need he pulled out from her.

Afterwards, washing her hands, she did not have her handbag and could not leave a tip for the tiny old lady attendant who politely handed her a towel.

When she got back to the table she didn't look up for some time and Tony did not acknowledge her. The plates had been cleared, she noticed, and a fresh martini placed in front of her. She took an icy sip of it — and then another.

'No,' she heard Tony saying quietly to the actress sitting on his other side, 'my mother was rather grand. She married my father in secret because her family wouldn't have stood it despite his wealth. She was from Scotland; a wonderful but cold-hearted woman.'

Nina put her glass down not seeing the napkin bunched beneath it, and the glass tipped and fell. The vodka pooled across the cloth and was absorbed.

'Silly girl,' said Tony to her, *sotto voce*.

*

A few miles from the Comedy in lowly, proud, pub theatre, Graft, with more compromises than they could ever have anticipated, pulled and pushed Mike Wall's mining play, *Deaf Hill*, to its opening.

Leigh's invaluable contribution had been the concept: that the mine, the house, the whole set, were bright white. Instead of trying to show the blackness of the coalmines, the darkness of the lives of the characters in shadow – and very often without electricity – she had the idea that filth, physical and emotional, was best played out against a spotless backdrop. It had been the one thing the company could agree about. Halfway through rehearsals Jack Payne had decided the parts should be played by non-actors, real miners, whose authenticity would make something fresh of a play creaking beneath the weight of its politics. The irony of breaking Equity rules to tell a story of the moral stronghold of the NUM did not escape the rest of them and the corner table at the Lord Grafton became more Speakers' Corner than pub. In the end Jack lost the argument and the working men of Wakefield were spared the discomfort. But *Deaf Hill*, which had seemed so truthful, brutal, on the page, in rehearsal beat a weary, grinding rhythm.

'You know what the problem is, don't you?' Luke said to Paul as they walked home through another inky, powerless night.

'Mm?' Paul said, through the damp end of his roll-up.

'The play,' said Luke, 'is terrible.'

'Helpful,' said Paul, and laughed.

'Paul! The scenes don't work because the polemic is like a bloody sledgehammer.'

'If you say agitprop again I'll lay you out,' said Paul grimly.

'Mike thinks he's fucking Bertolt Brecht and Jack agrees with him.'

'Well, he's not Arthur Miller. He reminds me of this old man used to shout at us from the corner by the paper mill in Seston every day. And the interval kills what drama there is stone dead. Paul, we want to cut it right down; you know I'm right.'

Paul laughed again. 'Tell Mike that—'

'I will if you like,' said Luke. 'I *hate* bad work. The characters are stereotypes,' he gestured, hugely, 'the dialogue is as stilted as a giraffe with a false leg.'

'Well, you can sort it tomorrow on your own. I can't come in.'

This was so unlike Paul that Luke stopped dead in the street. Paul turned.

'What?'

'We open in a week and a half – or are bloody meant to – and you can't come in tomorrow morning? Why?'

'Leigh,' said Paul, shortly, and flashed a smile that was so innocent and irrepressible he looked like a boy. 'She won't be there either.'

Luke's eyebrows went up as he absorbed the fact of Paul's new priority. He made a performance of taking off his greatcoat and hooking it over his shoulder.

'What d'you want to bunk off tomorrow for?' he asked.

'Her mother is in London and we're going to the zoo.'

Luke laughed – and then stopped, realising this was no laughing matter.

'Oh,' he said slowly; kind. 'Gotcha.'

They walked on for a bit.

'Where does her mother live normally?' he asked.

'Left Highgate for Manhattan.'

'All right for some.'

'Yep.'

And so the next day while Paul and Leigh went to the zoo with her mother from New York, Luke met the appalled actors, the already murderous Jack and the outraged Mike with his proposed cuts. The play limped to its grim opening and ran for three weeks, a qualified success, punctuated somehow fatuously by the ill-chosen *Duchess of Malfi*. Afterwards, Mike Wall returned to Wakefield, the actors to unemployment and Graft were left with a few boxes full of stinking costumes the Arts Council grant had been too tight to have cleaned.

'You could have lit the air in that theatre like a fart,' said Luke succinctly.

————

Following *Deaf Hill* — with Paul and Jack Payne unable to agree on a new play — Graft took refuge in Shakespeare, alternating a surreal *Tempest* with a virtually two-handed *Macbeth*, heavily influenced by Brook's *A Midsummer Night's Dream* but without his magic or the budget with which to realise it. They cast a talented young actor and actress straight out of drama school. The speeches and exchanges came almost back to back barely punctuated by other characters, as if the cues were merely stage directions for the marriage. Paul, Luke, Leigh and Jack text-cut and set-built in a frenzy of broken deadlines, late nights and long mornings. Luke could see that the others were exhausted but for him Graft was a vital engine. Its successes inspired him; its failures provided counterpoints. In any gap, with any opportunity, he wrote, controlling his own work as he could not control the collaboration.

During the days Paul was old-fashioned in his coolness towards Leigh. They were only alone when he gave her a lift home at night. Luke would wait in the car while Paul saw Leigh to her door, and kissed her. Murmured conversations.

'You looked nice today.'

'So did you.'

'I want to take you out properly.'

Then he would say goodnight, run down the steps and drive home talking to Luke about the plays, Jack, anything, but really – Luke recognised – talking about Leigh. Fifteen minutes in the hallway of Leigh's flat standing on old envelopes and listening out for the neighbours made Paul happy all the way, and happy through the night, knowing he would see her again in the morning.

For Leigh, being with Paul alone in the night-time hallway was more peaceful than erotic. Beautiful, easeful, calm; the precious pause between work and sleep, away from the others. Away from Luke. Because even when she was alone in her bed she did not have any rest from Luke. The stretch of empty wall by her front door was now only the place where they had kissed. Where he had whispered to her about her suspected or figurative virginity. He had backed her up against that cold wall. They had held hands. Beginning to love Paul as she was, Leigh could not face in herself that he was the one thing that gave her safety from Luke.

'I want to buy you dinner,' Paul told her, and they went to a trattoria in Soho, early on a Saturday, far from the cold office buildings and lifeless streets around the Lord Grafton. Leigh ate spaghetti alle vongole and didn't worry about the garlic.

He didn't make her nervous about things like that. They had made a rule not to talk about Graft but the funny thing was, all Paul did was talk about Luke.

'If he doesn't show me what he's writing, I'll kill him. I think it's plays,' he said and, 'Did you know his father was in the RAF?' and 'He sends a postcard home every week. *Every* week, Leigh.'

Leigh twirled the wet spaghetti on her fork, chased the little tinned clams about the plate and Paul poured more red wine. The tiny restaurant was half-full. A table of Australians were throwing some far-gone joke back and forth, and Leigh watched them jealously. For months her world had been Jack Payne's relentless speechifying, the black upstairs room at the Lord Grafton and frantic last-minute searches across London for the right sort of coal sacks, or a leather-bound book, or begging fake blood from friends at the Old Vic, where they had a budget and a proper props department. Saved bus receipts for petty cash. Fingers needle-pricked until they were swollen. Words from plays going around her head like songs.

'Neither of us has had a night off since *Deaf Hill* finished,' said Paul, as if she had spoken.

She put her chin in her hands and smiled at him.

'*Is this a dagger which I see before me . . .*'

'God,' he said, 'you've got it stuck, too.'

'Drives me mad.'

'Here.' He held his hand out to her across the table and she put down her fork and took it.

'Look at the state of you,' he said, his father's Yorkshire accent creeping in, as it did when he was affectionate or angry.

Her fingers were paint-stained. She had a blister from

hammering nails through the blackout blinds. Paul took his napkin and dipped it into his water glass, dabbing the paint and scratches.

'*I washed my face and hands before I came, I did,*' she said.

'You're not a proper girl at all.'

'What about you? Pansying about in theatre. Your dad despairs of you.'

'Not despairing,' said Paul. 'But nearly.'

'You want *a proper job with a good living wage.*'

'Can't get married without a good wage.'

The word *married*. Like a great flag, waving at her. *Silly*, she thought.

'Wants you married, does he?' she said, just to prove she too could say it weightlessly.

He held her hand in both of his.

'Have you had enough to eat?' he asked. 'Would you like to go?'

They left the restaurant and walked along Shaftesbury Avenue. The theatres were coming out, pouring onto the pavements beneath the canopies, names and titles lit-up hugely above them. They walked slowly, holding hands and laughing at people, reading what plays they had come out of by their clothes.

'Glasses, polo neck – Robert Bolt, Nicholls.'

'Long flowery skirt – Bolt, Stoppard.'

'Fur coat – Ayckbourn.'

They had reached the charmless broken round of Piccadilly Circus. It was emptying already, red buses and cars dreamily traversing the unmarked tarmac. A bouncer outside a peep show was talking to a policeman and lighting his cigarette for him.

'I was counting the digs I've stayed in the other day,' said Leigh.

'Thrilling.'

'Shh — instead of counting sheep. You know: Birmingham, Liverpool, Sheffield, Doncaster, Cardiff, Bournemouth . . .'

'Ah me, happy Bournemouth, paved with gold.'

'I must have stayed in twenty places.'

'More.'

'And glamour!'

'So much glamour.'

They turned down Haymarket and walked on, past a taxi stopped on the corner of Panton Street by heaps of rubbish bags, open-doored and grumbling to itself as a man in black tie stepped over it to lean in and pay.

'When you were in Worthing,' she said, 'did you ever stay with Mrs Mac?'

Paul gave a laugh. '*Mrs Mac in Worthing.*'

'With her signed pictures?'

'*They've all stayed here, dear . . .*'

To their left they could see the giant-looming glare of the Comedy. Leigh stopped and looked. She began to walk towards it. Her face was lit by the bulbs surrounding the bent-over French maid and red-faced butler and the flapper behind them, whose mouth formed the scarlet, suggestive O of the 'WOT', her hands held up in comic surprise.

'Suit, fur coat — *Not Married*,' said Paul.

'Bloody look at them,' spat Leigh. 'And they all are married too. I bet they hope it makes their wives randy.'

'Shh! They'll hear.'

The scented smoky crowd came out, opening like a fan from the hot theatre, waving down taxis, patting rigid hair.

'I don't care,' said Leigh, and Paul saw she was furious.

'Enjoy that, did you?' she said, loudly, to a man walking towards them. He looked startled, not sure if she was talking to him.

'Leigh,' said Paul, hovering.

'How would you like to train for three years to play Lady Macbeth and then run around in your knickers for two hours and get paid less than half what the men do?' she demanded.

The man, embarrassed, moved his mouth in such a way as to look as if he were responding but turned away, wordlessly. He took the arm of the woman next to him, who had an embroidered evening coat and diamonds, and they hurried off.

'Prick!' she shouted.

'Leigh? Are you pissed?' said Paul.

He hadn't thought she was drunk.

Leigh glared at him and pulled away, going up the steps of the theatre until she had a vantage point. Nobody had seen or noticed her. She took a huge breath

'YOU ARE ALL GUILTY OF PERPETUATING THE DEGRADATION OF WOMEN!' she shouted.

A few heads turned and then looked away in distaste, hoping there wasn't going to be a row.

'*I SAID, YOU'RE SEXIST PIGS!*' shouted Leigh.

'And you're a lesbian,' came an invisible little voice from the crowd.

There was laughter. Somebody clapped. Nobody looked at Leigh. They all pretended she wasn't there.

'DO YOU WANT TO SEE MY TITS?' she shouted.

A few people turned then − startled − but immediately away again in embarrassment. This was very nasty indeed.

'I'LL SHOW YOU MY TITS IF YOU LIKE!' she shouted again, full of wild joy, and she glimpsed Paul, red-faced, backing away towards the kerb. He looked terrified.

'SEE?' she screamed, ignoring him. 'YOU ONLY WANT TO SEE THEM IF THEY'RE BOUGHT AND PAID FOR! IT'S NOT SEX – IT'S COMMERCE! THIS SHOW DEGRADES WOMEN!'

A small angry man in a frilly shirt suddenly appeared at her shoulder, a little group of ushers and usherettes watching wide-eyed from the foyer. He wore a bow tie and had a moustache. He grabbed Leigh's arm.

'Now look here,' he said, 'we've had enough of your lot. I shall call the police if you carry on with this. Just clear off.'

'Let go of my arm!' shouted Leigh, furiously. 'LET GO OF ME!'

All at once, she was aware of a couple at the other end of the steps. They were watching her from beneath the brightly lit canopy. The man was slim and fair and the young woman on his arm had long brown hair and a mysteriously veiled, blank expression. The man, even from fifteen yards away, had a presence – ownership or power – and he was smiling at Leigh indulgently. He looked pleased that she was there. She registered it all in one quick moment and then was distracted by the pain in her arm, where the theatre manager was gripping it.

'You're causing a disturbance,' he hissed.

'Good!' said Leigh. 'You should be ashamed of yourself.'

'*Policeman!*' called the man, sharply, holding his hand up in the air as if he wanted to speak out in class.

Leigh looked about wildly, wriggling away, but the man was holding her arm in a pincer grip.

'Hey! Police!' shouted a portly usher in the foyer behind, and waved.

'Let go!' said Leigh.

People were happy to watch now; now that she was captive. Stopping and staring, talking about her.

Paul appeared at her shoulder, barging up to the manager, aggressively crowding him.

'Let go of my girlfriend,' he said. 'Now.'

The manager let go of her, quickly, just as a policeman's helmet came bobbing towards them through the gawping crowd.

'Your girlfriend?' said the theatre manager. 'Well, I suggest you control her.'

'How dare you!' said Leigh. 'How dare you speak to me like that?'

'I wasn't speaking to you, young lady,' said the manager, with distaste.

'I am not a "lady",' said Leigh.

'That much is plain,' he sniffed.

'Fuck off,' said Leigh, distinctly.

'Leigh, for God's sake,' said Paul, looking towards the policeman, and he put his hand on her arm.

'Get off me!' She turned with angry tears. '*Your* girlfriend — I'm not *yours*!'

And she pushed past him, and into the clear night, away from the glare of the canopy, and out into the welcoming dark.

The policeman had arrived, anxious beneath his helmet. 'Everything all right, sir?' He held his whistle poised, and the manager opened his mouth — Paul didn't wait to hear.

'I'm sorry,' he said and ran after Leigh.

She had almost disappeared from view. He didn't want to lose her. 'Shit!' he said, catching her up. 'Are you all right?'

'*Him*? You were just as bad,' she was choked with anger and storming. He had to chase her to keep up. '*Worse!*'

'Me? What did I do?'

'Nothing! "Oh excuse *my* girlfriend, she's mad" . . .' She was tearful with rage.

'I was just trying to help.'

'Using their language. *My* girlfriend . . . P-possessive,' she was hiccuping the letters in her distress, 'p-personal pronoun . . .'

'I'm sorry. I was just – I was surprised.'

'Oh really?' She had stopped walking to rail at him. 'You haven't read all about that horrible show in the papers? The outcry from all *thinking* people? You haven't heard a million times what I think of it? Do you think I'm just going to walk past, and laugh and smile when I'm being dragged by my hair back to the bloody Dark Ages by this demeaning crap—'

'Shh – calm down.'

'No! They changed the law for *freedom* in 'sixty-eight – and now people who hate women use it to make fucking money!' Leigh had stopped crying.

'I'm sorry,' he said, 'it's okay—'

'It's not okay! I hate it. I hate them all, with the way they look at us and the way they talk to us and do what they want with us, and we're supposed to just take it – and you bloody apologised for me!'

They stood on the pavement as the cars passed by, blind.

'I'm sorry,' said Paul. 'I was just surprised, that's all.'

'Shocked.'

'Not shocked. Surprised. Maybe a bit shocked.'

She smiled at him, damply. 'You think I'm a harpy, too.'

'What do you care? I'm only a man,' he dared.

And he leaned down quickly, and kissed her.

A car honked at them.

They stopped kissing but stayed together, cheek to cheek.

'All the fun of the fair with me,' she whispered.

'Beats arguing with Jack,' he said. 'He wouldn't taste so nice. We should do this more often. There's some porno cinemas on Wardour Street we could hit next time. I'll make a placard.'

'Shut up.' She held him close to her. 'If you tease me, I'll punch you. I'm not a lady, you know.'

They drove out of Soho, west along Oxford Street. Paul put a cassette into the portable tape-deck they kept in the car and Leigh repaired her eye make-up in the vanity mirror while Al Green sang. Then she looked out at the people at the bus stops, the tube stations closing.

'Will you spend the night?' asked Paul. They had turned onto the Edgware Road.

'With you?' she said.

'No, Mrs Mac in Worthing – yes, me.'

She leaned over towards him across the car and put her cheek against his shoulder. She lifted her lips to his ear. 'You'd better come to me instead,' she said softly.

Paul swerved the car violently, over the white line and back again.

'Sorry.'

She sat up, sharply. 'Glad I excite you.'

'You do. Lost control of myself.'

'I can tell.'

'I can't come to you, though,' he said, and his voice was nervous, more nervous than she'd ever heard him.

It touched her that he should be anxious about her, when they liked each other so much and she'd already said yes.

'We'll have to go to Fulham,' he said. 'I've got my script notes at home, and there's stuff I need.'

She looked out of the car. They were already driving the wrong way for Camden, out of control. 'Your place? What — about Luke?' It was too late.

'He'll be all right.'

'Really?' She felt panicky.

'He might not be there.'

'Where would he be?'

'With Lady Macbeth.'

'Oh.' Leigh had seen Luke and their Lady Macbeth. She had not thought it had got so far.

'Or someone else might be there,' said Paul.

'Well, let's leave it.' *Someone else?*

'But he might not.' Paul was hasty now, scared of losing her. 'It's not as if he *always* does.'

Her hands had begun to sweat. She didn't want to be talking about what Luke did or didn't do with girls. Not now. 'That's restrained of him,' she said.

'Restrained,' said Paul, shortly. 'Well, he's not, is he? But he does all the cooking so I can't turf him out.'

'I just wish we could go to my place,' she said miserably.

Paul checked the mirror very deliberately, indicated, slowed and stopped the car on a yellow line. He turned the music down. 'I need my things,' he said. 'If you like, we could stop off at mine and then go to you.'

'No,' she said, 'it's late. That would be mad. It's fine.'

'Are you upset?'

'Why would I be?'

'It's not very romantic.'

The word sounded odd coming from him – generous, as if he was making himself say it for her, because he wanted to be clear what he wanted them to be like together.

'It doesn't matter,' she said.

He leaned awkwardly over and kissed her. Then he took her hands and kissed them, too.

'We'll make it romantic,' he said.


Luke was in bed but not sleeping, just lying in the dark thinking about a problem he was having with the latest play he was writing and not planning to show to anybody. He was not expecting sleep. He heard Paul opening the front door noisily. He wasn't being careful. It was as if he wanted to let Luke know he was there.

Voices.

Paul saying, 'All right?'

And then a woman whispered, 'Yes.'

She said it very quietly but Luke recognised Leigh immediately.

He closed his eyes in his dark room and listened to them walking about, murmured conversation, the bathroom light going on and off, water, doors. He kept his eyes closed as the floorboards of the flat creaked, and Paul's bedroom door shut for the last time. He realised with strange release that he felt happy that Leigh was there. It felt right to him that she should be there with them. He went to sleep quite quickly after that, and his sleep was dreamless.

\*

'THIS SHOW DEGRADES WOMEN!'

Nina watched the other dark-haired girl making the scene on the steps with a mixture of envy and embarrassment; caught in the moment of her rage without vanity, without fear. Nina couldn't imagine feeling so strongly about anything that it would free her from herself. Her mother always said that women's libbers were the ugly girls, just jealous, but this girl wasn't ugly. In fact – this once – Nina forgot to judge whether she was pretty or not, and saw only her actions, heard only her words; unsexed by rage.

All Tony said was, 'Pity there were no press here.'

*XXX Cinema Club. Peepshow. Girls. Models. Paradise Club.* The red and pink neon flashed, streaming past Nina's unfocused eyes from behind the thick glass of the taxi taking them home from dinner. Tony always locked the doors of taxis when they got into them. The cab bumped down Old Compton Street. The signs floated past her vision – *Raymond's Revuebar. Triple X-Rated Striptease. Massage.* The women stood in pairs by open doors, red-glow behind them, piled-up hair.

Nina felt the cool weight of something sliding onto her lap. She looked down. It was a manuscript.

Tony eyed her with satisfaction. 'It might do very well for us. Let me know what you think of it.'

The play was in several stapled sections, paper-clipped and well-thumbed. Nina read the title.

*En Custodia/In Custody* by Hector Romero.

'What's it about?'

'Argentina. Lanusse. It's a two-hander. Very shocking. Quite new. It's set in a prison and I believe it's based on the experiences of Hector Romero's wife – or his sister. The part of the woman made me think of you.'

Nina looked up from the page and across at Tony. 'Why?'

'I'm always looking for roles for you. Didn't you know?'

Nina felt honoured. 'No,' she said softly, 'I didn't. Thank you.'

'It just takes the right part. Yours is a very delicate soul,' said Tony, and smiled at her. 'And *that* is an extraordinary piece of work.'

As Nina switched on the reading light the degraded world she had been contemplating outside the taxi disappeared. It was the two of them, and the play.

She turned to page one.

*ACT ONE. Scene One. An unknown country. A bare stage representing a prison*, she read. *The sounds of metal doors. Tortured cries, echo. A woman enters, Elena. She is gagged and blindfolded.*

Luke was making breakfast when Leigh came out of Paul's room to go to the bathroom. She was wrapped in a sheet, like a Greek statue, thick hair curling down her back. He glimpsed her going down the hall.

'Morning,' he said, turning round with the frying pan full of sloppy bacon.

She stopped, turned – smudgy eye make-up, messy hair. 'Hello . . .'

'Do you want some tea?'

He was in jeans and a T-shirt – socks. Not his working self, intimate.

'Yes, please.'

'Is Paul awake?'

'No.'

'I'll make a pot.'

'Okay.'

'Don't look like that.'

'Like what?' she said.

'All . . .' He shrugged and made a face.

She smiled, backed away into the bathroom and closed the door.

In the end, it wasn't at all as strange as she had feared, having Luke there. She bathed, and dressed, and the three of them ate breakfast together at the kitchen table and talked about rehearsals and the days ahead. There was no need to hide, just the peculiar natural comfort of the three of them together, made stronger by her sharing of Paul's bed. March. April. May. June. July. The summer days were long and exquisitely balanced, as if happiness were so strong it could not leave them, but perhaps sharpened by the unexamined sense of something hidden; the more permanent wounds of their longer lives waiting, undiscovered. Sundays were peace. Shops shut. Empty streets. If they had found time the day before, and had enough money and had remembered to go to the shops, they would give Luke the day off cooking and roast a chicken at Paul's flat.

'We're playing house,' Leigh said once, and Paul kissed her neck underneath her ear.

Luke often slept for twelve or fourteen hours after the show on Saturday night, catching up after his week. When he woke he was quiet. He would eat and write his postcard to Seston Asylum then spend the day reading or typing up the hand-written work in his notebooks. He would curl up in his corner out of the way, with the typewriter on the floor and his knees to his chest, not minding the record player or if Paul and Leigh kissed, or talked. They comforted him with their company, and because Luke never spoke about himself the other two did more easily. The simple fact of him made them appreciate the blessing of a past that could bear examination, the luxury of memories. Leigh would tell of the slow realisation in childhood of her father's infidelities, her mother's growing unhappiness, and then the shock of their divorce. Paul had decided his family were dull enough to make an exaggerated satire of middle-class drabness, and made her and Luke laugh with 'The Day My Dad Announced My Mother Should Learn To Drive' or 'I Had Measles Once'. It was so exotic it delighted Luke, but then –

'What about you, Luke?' would be met with –

'I don't remember.'

Or he would just turn the tables with –

'What's your mum doing now, is she proud of you?' because storyteller as he was he could not articulate his own self.

Paul did not ask because he knew Luke didn't want him to, and Leigh learned not to either. He was like a jigsaw with pieces missing, she thought. She noted the postcards he bought and posted with mechanical regularity. She knew he went home each Christmas. He received letters which he took to his room to read and did not talk about. Sometimes she was repelled by the extent of his abnormality and welcomed the feeling, shoring it up against him as proof to herself he was not right. She did not want him to be worth her pain.

Paul stayed nights at Leigh's flat less often. They told one another they relished it when it was just the two of them but it wasn't true; they were better together when Luke was with them. Paul felt reassured that Leigh was a girl Luke could be near without making a pass. She was a balancer, a small offering towards keeping his friend whole.

For Luke it was more simple; Leigh and Paul were home to him. Late at night when the music was turned off and radiators cold, deep in the dark, he would go off to sleep with the security of them both next door to him and feel — at last, just a little — at ease. He loved the three of them together and he thought they did too. Sometimes, when he was having his bedtime wank before sleeping, he would know that Paul and Leigh were making love at the same time, on the other side of the wall. They weren't noisy about it, but he could tell. It wasn't exciting or disgusting to him, and he didn't picture them or imagine it, but in that half-sleeping state there was a certain companionship to it, to be doing the same thing they were. Having no experience or understanding of intimacy, it was to him a safe sort of loving.

Graft found a rhythm of rehearsal and production, and each cycle of plays was stronger. Theirs was a risky public training ground. In July, they had a new piece called *Cartwright's Army* about to open and were rehearsing an adaptation of Kafka's *The Penal Colony* at the same time. A very young writer with no agent had pressed it into Leigh's hand on the pavement one night when the audience for *Macbeth* was coming out. He was insecure, and *The Penal Colony*, gripped in Jack Payne's iron fist, could not breathe. Exploration of the text was stamped out by Jack's stifling certainty.

The only thing they could all be enthusiastic about was the centrepiece of the play, the torture machine. Described in Kafka's text, it was interpreted by Luke with such painstaking care it looked fit for horrible purpose. He and Patrick built it in a friend's garage, over weeks, with spare parts and rubbish-dump findings, and Luke was obsessed by it.

'It's a fucking *crucifixion bed*,' he'd say. 'Isn't that perfect? You'd think Kafka was Catholic. You learn the lesson of society because it's *written* into your body as you die – by the harrow, see?'

The machine took a day to install, had to be dismantled to get it up the narrow steps and then rebuilt – Luke welding the rusty iron back together recklessly, setting fire to the floor. And it was extraordinary: a magical, miserable monument to distress around which the four characters moved as its cruel justice was gradually revealed.

At Leigh's insistence they had cast women in two of the four roles and Jack, as revenge, made the actress playing The Soldier cry every day, like a ritual.

'It's after eleven,' Paul would whisper to Leigh, 'she's not gone yet – oh, there she goes.'

The other actress, who played The Condemned, cried because Luke had slept with her the week she was cast but now had forgotten and didn't watch her rehearse. Then Luke slept with The Soldier, so she cried more, and then The Soldier found out about The Condemned, and *she* cried even more.

'He's sabotaging the company and upsetting the cast,' said Paul, shocked at the disparity between Luke's vast humanity and the way he consumed girls like a drunk with a bottle. There was nothing happy in it.

He tried to talk to him but Luke just blamed their Soviet-style uniforms.

'They look so good dressed up like that,' he said.

It got so that if any actress was late or blowing her nose everyone looked at Luke. Luke himself was oblivious; frenetic – there was no anger to be found against him because he did not understand the rules he was breaking. And as he spread chaos with distracted abandon Leigh was there, but she held Paul's hand. She comforted weeping young women and tried not to watch. She could see it coming; the look he had, noticing them, and then the sweet, interested way he spoke to them. The rapt attention they gave him; the way he could move in close, very quickly, without making the girl back off. She saw, and she knew how it felt. He had done it to her. Watching him, she felt freshly how he had hurt her, as if he were opening her up again. So she turned her face away, and looked back only when he was satisfied, and was returned to them – to her and Paul – and the kind sureness of their lives together, the three of them.

On 14 July, *Cartwright's Army* opened. From the first night they knew it was different to everything they had done before. And it sold out every night; the pub was packed, queues out onto the pavement for stand-bys five nights in a row. Normally, audiences were a simple crowd of separate people; for *Cartwright's Army* they became one person. The audience, the production, the actors, the words, all were part of a single mechanism, connected, and the life of it charged the air. Even Jack and Paul forgot their disagreements. The actors proudly told their friends what they were doing at the moment; not *something in a pub over in the City*, but *a play for Graft, they're new*. *Cartwright's Army* was reviewed – not only in *The Stage* and *Time Out* – but written up in the broadsheets. Critics travelled to see it, felt the ripples of its impact touch them. On the pages of the invisible Domesday Book of works, sensed but never precisely defined – sometimes called success, respect, even fame – Graft had made their mark.

'*George Myers has written an acerbic but still heartfelt diatribe against the smug inertia of the suburban classes,*' read Leigh, with her scissors, cutting out clippings to send to her mother in New York.

She was on the sofa. Luke was lying on his back on the floor with his feet up next to her and Paul was in the armchair, smiling like a man after a three-course dinner.

'He has, bless his little cotton socks,' said Paul.

'*Judith Hallaway shines as the neurotic, desperate woman driven to desert her child.*'

'She does,' said Paul. 'I like that one.'

'Look, there it is again,' said Leigh. 'This play Malcolm Dewberry is directing at the Nag's Head.'

'Argentine playwright, Hector Romero,' said Luke to the ceiling. 'Lanusse locking everyone up. Can't go back to Argentina or they'd shoot him. And the pies are rubbish over there, too, so he's stopping here.'

Leigh looked up and smiled. 'That's the one,' she said. 'I can't bloody go, can I? Nobody cares if the producers are there, but I actually have a job to do.'

'If me and Paul can go tomorrow night I'll cover for you on Tuesday,' said Luke.

'Good,' said Paul. 'What's it called?'

'*In Custody.*' Leigh studied the review. '*New actress* — they always say that, probably been at it for years — *inspired.*'

'Who is she?' asked Luke.

'Nina Jacobs.'

'Never heard of her,' said Paul. 'Let's go.'

———

'Busman's holiday,' said Paul, the next night as they stood in the heated crush of the Nag's Head bar, five minutes to curtain. 'Did you hear from Flowers?'

Eric Flowers was a West End manager who had been to see

*Cartwright* twice, and Paul had called his office since but had no reply.

'He's probably here,' said Paul, looking around and lighting a cigarette, his big shoulders hunched. 'The bastard.'

'This will transfer.'

'Probably, yeah.'

The crowd had begun to move towards the door to the upstairs theatre. They drained their glasses and went with them. 'But it might not be as good as they say. Might be shit.'

'I hope it's not,' said Luke. 'We could be at the Grafton.'

Paul crushed his cigarette out in a fire bucket as they passed. 'Right, yeah, we don't spend enough time there.'

Luke smiled but he would have spent every night at the Grafton, even with Jack Payne as counterpoint to the harmony. He would have slept there.

They kept seeing people they knew, and a group sitting in front — four girls together — flicking their shiny hair from their eyes, were glancing over their shoulders at them both.

'You've probably shagged about half the chicks in here,' Paul whispered to Luke as the lights dropped into blackout and Luke choked on his laugh to stop it.

There was murmuring, and then quiet. The house-lights went to black. They sat in darkness for what seemed like a long time. Long enough for the audience to fall silent, and throat-clearing to stop, then just long enough again for discomfort to settle over them. The waiting stopped being collective, and became each person's private thoughts, vulnerable.

They waited. The silence grew heavier. It stretched to its tightest, most dangerous moment. Then, making them jump, there sounded a muffled clanging noise.

At first it seemed like a distant bell, rhythmic, but it became clear that it was a succession of metal gates, closing, nearer and nearer to them in the pitch dark.

Luke felt the tension of the audience around him. Part of his mind enjoyed the stagecraft but more deeply, unsettled, the ancient, animal part hated it. Feared it. He did not think, *I know this, I've been here*, and yet he was flooded with sadness; pain unlocked and alarming. And still – darkness. Abandonment. Then a distant scream and the physical walls of the auditorium were dissolved by the echoing sound that came as if from a corridor, or a cell, and now Luke knew what he was remembering. He had heard too many screams like that in his life to have to try to place this. This was Seston Asylum. This sound was his. He looked about him; told himself he had a choice, he wasn't forced to stay there with the doors closing on him. He could get away. He would have shut his eyes to it but he was in the dark already. He felt Paul move beside him but he didn't think he had made a sound. He didn't think he had forgotten himself, it was only his breathing that had changed. No one would know he was not all right. The shutting metal doors approached, louder, one by one, and then – the opposite sound: the slow squeak of thick hinges as a door, offstage, was opened and cold light came from the direction of the sound. Bleak though it was, it was respite, bringing him back to the present. And in that grateful bliss of reason a woman walked onto the stage.

He almost laughed. She was just a girl – too young. This couldn't hurt. But then he began to look at her.

She was blindfolded and she wore a grey dress of thick cotton. Another piece of material was around her mouth, both that and the blindfold were tied at the back, and her arms were also bound behind her, also with material, or rags. Her feet were bare. Blindly, she inched towards the middle of the stage. Her hair was long and dark, separated into wettish strands by sweat or blood. The light was harsh and dust in tiny particles floated all around her.

Reaching centre-stage she felt around, tentatively, carefully, with her bare feet, and then knelt, facing out. For long moments her chest rose and fell beneath her gown as she struggled, sightless, to stay balanced. Luke felt ashamed that he could see her, but she could not see him.

Then there was the sound of heavy footsteps in the imagined corridor and she turned fearfully. Luke felt the audience waiting. A dark, bearded man in fatigues came onto the stage. He went to stand behind her. She waited, trembling. The man stood close behind her, seeming to enjoy the waiting. With a smile he reached out a hand and eased the gag from her mouth as if with love. Then with both hands he undid the blindfold and removed it. Nina's face was revealed. She looked out at Luke.

---

The steep North London alleyway behind the Nag's Head glistened with wet cobbles. Luke paced up and down waiting for the stage door to open and Paul stood apart, watching him.

'Wish we had a stage door at the Grafton,' Paul said. 'Classy, this is.'

He was embarrassed to be waiting by a stage door. He hadn't done that since he was twelve and went to see *The Mousetrap* for his birthday, clutching an autograph book in his chocolate-smudged hands.

'What can you say to her anyway?' he asked.

Luke jerked his head, twitching off the intrusion.

'Seriously, Luke—'

'I know!' Luke stopped, facing him.

Paul didn't think he'd seen him so – he looked for the word – *upset*, before.

'What are you doing, man?' he asked gently, with a feeling something bad was happening to his friend, or going to happen.

'I just want to meet this girl,' said Luke.

'Yeah, but there are lots of girls . . .' That was an understatement. Paul shrugged. Gave up. There was nothing to be done.

'I just think, I just want – she seemed unhappy.'

'Of course she was unhappy. Not a barrel of laughs these Argentine prisons.'

'She needed help.'

Paul turned away from his illogical pain.

'I'm going. This is nuts,' he said, feeling suddenly like his own mother drawing the line at a tantrum. The yawning world of a grown-up future before him. He realised he was scared.

He started down the alley towards the busy street and the traffic and then stopped.

He smiled at Luke, reassuring. 'You coming, or what?'

'I'll stop here,' said Luke, avoiding him.

There was the banging sound of a kick on metal and the stage door opened, clattering. Nina Jacobs, with the actor who had played the interrogator, Henry Fidele, and another man came out into the alley.

Luke stopped still and stared at her.

She glanced at him.

The man they didn't know was a slight figure in a

camel-hair coat. He took in Luke, then Paul, with a glance, raised his eyebrows and the three of them walked away up the steep alleyway towards a single street light.

As she went, Nina turned and looked over her shoulder at Luke, who was staring at her. She kept looking and he kept watching her. Then she turned away.

The three of them walked into the spotlit pool of the street light, and then disappeared into the dark beyond. Laughter. Footsteps. Silence.

Paul and Luke were alone.

'You didn't speak to her,' said Paul.

Luke shook his head. He looked down to the ground, diminished.

'Let's go,' he said.

———————

Tony and Nina said goodbye to Henry on Upper Street. He took her straight home.

'Aren't we going out?'

'Not tonight. Did you know those two?'

'Who?'

'At the stage door.'

'I had a feeling I'd seen one of them before . . .'

'He was very handsome,' said Tony.

'Which one?'

'The dark one – both, actually,' he said lightly. 'But the one you were staring at, he was particularly handsome, in that Jewish way.'

Nina was shocked at the phrase. 'That Jewish way?'

When they got back to Tite Street, Tony turned on the hall

lights and swivelled slowly to face Nina. He took her face in his hands, closed the door with his foot, shrugged off his coat, and kissed her. It was their first kiss. He held her gently and his lips were soft.

'You were absolutely marvellous tonight,' he said.

Nina observed the moment curiously. The months of seduction, the bullying rehearsals, the teasing; all of it had led to this predictable kiss. She felt distant from him, still defined by her working self. He kissed her again, his tongue parting her lips.

She wondered if she wanted to leave or if she ought to stay and go up to his room. What her mother would say, if she did. He was stroking her head, like the soothing of an animal. Then his hand gathered the long clean hair into a ponytail at the base of her neck, and tightened. He was holding her by her hair.

'What is it?' he said, noticing she had frozen with surprise. Her heart had begun to beat rapidly. He was breathless, she noticed. His eyes were shining, half-closed, as he watched her.

'You're holding my hair,' she said clearly.

He tightened his grip.

'I've got a surprise for you,' he said, as if to a child.

Nina felt him tug her hair all together in his fist. It wasn't at all painful. She realised he was leading her slowly towards the stairs.

'Come with me,' he said.

They went up the stairs like that, awkwardly, two flights. Her neck ached from being held sideways. At the bedroom door he released her. She straightened, jittery with freedom, and he laughed.

'What?'

'It's funny,' he said. 'The way you always do what I want.'

He went to the drinks tray he kept in the corner, between the window and the wardrobe.

'Sit on the bed,' he said, busying himself with glasses and bottles.

She sat on the edge of the bed and took off her coat, leaving it heaped around her for comfort.

He came over with a Martini glass, bright with gin, and knelt down in front of her. He held out the glass. The icy gin tipped and glinted. In the bottom of it was a diamond ring.

'Will you marry me?' he said.

Nina stared at him. She looked down at the ring under the inches of alcohol like sunken treasure, the large stone clutched in the platinum claw.

'You seem surprised,' he said.

'Of course I'm surprised.'

He put his finger into the gin and scooped up the ring on his index finger. He held it out to her, dripping, and she opened her mouth automatically. He slipped the gin-wet finger and the spiky diamond ring into her mouth and she closed her lips around him.

'Suck,' he said.

She sucked the gin from the ring as Tony drained the glass and swallowed, with a grimace of distaste.

He removed his finger from her mouth, the ring still wedged on the end of it, and put down the glass on the carpet. He smiled very warmly at her.

'Darling,' he said.

She realised he was on one knee to her.

'You are so beautiful and you are so talented. Isn't this romantic? Do you like my surprise?'

'I don't know,' she said slowly. 'I don't think I know what romantic is.'

'You'll see with me, beautiful Nina, I promise,' he said.

He embraced her. He held her very tightly, with his lips to her ear.

'Say yes,' he whispered. 'Say yes. Say yes. Say yes.'

She felt the warmth of his hug. She felt beautiful.

'Yes,' she said.

He released her and taking her slim hand in his, he slipped the still-wet ring onto her finger.


Paul and Luke took the last tube home and didn't mention the play. Usually they deconstructed everything they saw exhaustively, but not this. Paul talked about rehearsals and Luke listened, and tried to get himself back, and pretend. At Barons Court they bought some stale chips for half price by the tube station just as the chip shop was closing.

At three o'clock in the morning Paul and Leigh were woken from deep sleep by Luke shouting. It was an incoherent cry from some far-off place. They lay rigidly, waiting, but there wasn't another sound.

In his room, Luke had sat up in bed to be sure he wouldn't risk returning to the terror of his dream. He was sweating. Cold. Imprisoned. He thought of Nina Jacobs kneeling blind and bound. The play had cut him open and there she'd been, offering herself up to be saved. He had been stripped to nothingness and then the pretty sight of her, like an answer. She had seemed so right to him. She seemed to call out.

\*

Kafka's *The Penal Colony* was about to open and it felt inconceivable it would be ready. Jack had taken to bringing a half-bottle of whisky with him to rehearsals and rebuffed the actors' appeals for help, distancing himself from the seemingly unavoidable approach of failure.

'This is horrible,' Leigh whispered urgently to Paul as the cast stumbled through the first act of the dress rehearsal. 'They have to go out there tomorrow.'

Luke held himself back with difficulty – watching sideways from the back of the room. He knew what he would have done with the play but he wasn't the writer, he wasn't Jack. The afternoon was a cold failure.


Because of *Cartwright's Army*'s success on opening night the house was full but there was no gratifying buzz, no delight, and the actors' mutual congratulations afterwards were only to comfort one another. Jack blamed Kafka. The rest of them blamed Jack. *The Penal Colony* had been reduced to a heartless fable.

The audience had gone. The seats were empty. Patrick turned out his lights upstairs and left, his big nose bunged up with a cold and the smell of defeat. The rest of Graft sat glumly around two tables downstairs. Jack had insisted they all stay, and sat, feet planted wide, glaring morosely. The actors were looking at their watches, resentful at having been the messengers to deliver such poor work. Leigh was pretending to read a manuscript from the collection she carried in her sack-like shoulder-bag and Paul was leaning back against the wall, chair tipped on two legs, staring at the brass light-fitting above his head.

'All right,' Jack said, looking around the waiting faces.

Luke sat astride his backwards chair with his legs sticking out, bent forward over the table and making patterns in the wet beer-rings with his finger, forehead resting on the back of his other hand as he listened.

Graham, the writer, took out the script and sat surrounded by pages, biro and type mingling miserably on the lines, and waited, pen poised.

'I know what's wrong here,' Jack announced, looking from face to face. 'It's the bloody torture machine. It has to go.'

'What?' said Graham.

The actors exchanged glances.

'*The Penal Colony* is a play of ideas, not gimmicks,' said Jack. 'What fantasy world are we trying to conjure here? We need to remove the machine. We'll take it down tomorrow.'

Paul, weary, appalled, looked at Luke but Luke didn't raise his head. He had been distracted ever since *In Custody* and Paul didn't know if he was even listening.

Jack turned to the cast. 'And again, folks,' he growled, 'can we take down the *feeling*? We know we're in a theatre, we're not children, don't patronise us.'

'Jack,' said Paul, 'this can all wait until tomorrow—'

'How can we lose the machine, Jack?' Graham interrupted, ignoring him. 'It *is* the play. And we've opened.'

'Work in progress, Graham,' said Jack; it was one of his catchphrases. 'Work in progress.'

'But The Explorer examines the machine,' said Graham. 'How will he do that if it's not there? It's miraculous, what Luke did – it's what I imagined. It's straight off the page.'

Jack took the bottle from his pocket, unscrewed it and slopped whisky into his glass, ignoring him.

'My play worked before,' said Graham shakily. 'It doesn't now.'

'It's true,' said Leigh; 'it was a good play.'

'No fucking machine!' Jack shouted suddenly. 'Why can't you all see?' He stared from one to the other. 'We'll come in early tomorrow. Eight o'clock. Spend the day. We'll chuck out the bloody machine. We'll sort it out.'

'Excuse me,' said The Condemned, 'I'm supposed to be at my aunt's wedding.'

'For Christ's sake!' barked Jack, slamming his glass down onto the table. 'Is this a nursery school?'

There was a silence, and then —

'Okay. Right,' Graham said, cramming the script back into his canvas bag with trembling fingers. 'Fine. Fuck off.'

And he stood up and left, slamming the door behind him so that the remaining few customers in the pub jumped and stared.

'Jesus Christ,' said Jack. '*Writers.*'

The Prisoner, The Explorer, The Soldier and The Condemned looked at one another.

'Er, Jack,' said The Prisoner. 'Actually you can't call us before ten.'

'Sod Equity,' said Jack.

'Well, sod you,' said The Prisoner, 'I'm going home.' And he did.

The other actors followed, without a word, leaving only Luke, Paul and Leigh.

'Thank you, Jack,' said Paul. 'Super. *Marvellous.*'

There was a silence. Ron, behind the bar, glared at them.

'We're not called Graft because it sounded good to you lads,' said Jack, speaking more slowly the more vitriolic he became.

'I want to do *significant work*, not just an alternative to the goggle-box. If this play *is* a dud, it's an honourable dud.'

'If you say so,' said Paul evenly, staring up at the ceiling.

'*The Colony* falls between two stools because you can't get over your bourgeois hang-ups. You three, you're just *playing*.' He knocked back his whisky, saw that his half-bottle was empty, and patted his pockets for change.

'Jack!' said Luke, animatedly, looking up. 'You're talking out of your arse.'

Paul tipped his chair forward abruptly, suddenly alert.

Luke was smiling. 'They call them plays because they are fucking plays, Jack. You've got it backwards.'

'Have I, Luke?'

'You're denying the muse.'

'Am I? *Denying the muse.*'

People could react like that to Luke, Leigh thought, because he was unafraid of mockery. He didn't mind what he said.

'Yes,' said Luke. 'You see a dead world, and you're wrong. It's a miracle you didn't fuck up *Cartwright's Army*, and that was mainly because Paul didn't let you and the script was watertight.'

Leigh was leaning forward in her chair; she could not stop looking at him – so was Paul, with a particular, humorous pleasure.

Jack stared.

'Listen,' said Luke, in the spirit of somebody generously explaining a thing, 'who are you to say there is no value in the construct when the construct is all we have? The play should *play*. Look at the semantics: art. What is *artful*, full of art, artfully done? You think *art* is bourgeois and *beauty* is bourgeois. Form – the crafting of drama as if it were a quartet, a painting.

You say we're just playing, but we *have* to. Playful and artful. See? I don't get why you want to make theatre when you think the world is flat like you do. It's round. You're trying to regress to some touring Bible-lecture in the fourteenth century, and no breath of life in it. But even those were called *mystery* plays. You don't even *want* to ascend the brightest heaven of invention.'

Jack laughed his rage out. 'He's quoting *Shakespeare* to me! Jesus Christ—'

'Yes, Jack, because clearly you've overlooked the Renaissance. You have to *not make things flat*. You want to make Graft flat. But I don't want that. Do you, Paul? Do you want that?'

Paul was startled. 'Me? No.'

'Leigh?'

Leigh swallowed. 'No,' she said.

There was a silence.

Luke went back to making shapes with the beer-rings on the table.

'Jesus fucking Christ,' said Jack.

Paul stood up portentously, but instead of speaking, he left the table.

'He's gone to the Gents,' said Leigh, helpfully.

Then Luke looked up at her and smiled. He put out his hand and nudged her face – her jaw – with his thumb, as if to say, *Hello, just saw you there.* Leigh smiled back and then looked away from him, and down as her heart contracted. Sweet. She closed her eyes. Pain. Ridiculous he didn't know. He wouldn't care if he did.

Jack coughed, loudly, picked up his glass and stared into its emptiness.

Paul returned from the toilet and sat down, heavily. 'Well,' he said. 'All right then.' He looked from one to the other of them. 'It is a shame. But I think it's time we called it a day. Leigh?'

She nodded.

'Luke?'

Luke stared, entirely surprised at this turn of events, trying to take it in.

'Too fucking right,' said Jack.

'We've had a fair run,' said Paul. 'And the lease is up next month. Jack?'

'The name is *mine*,' said Jack. 'Graft.'

Luke frowned in confusion. 'The name?'

But Paul shrugged. 'If you like. I'm off home. Coming?' he said to the other two, and the three of them got up.

Leigh went over to Jack and embraced him, awkwardly, her bag slipping heavily off her shoulder.

'Goodbye, Jack,' she said.

Jack didn't move. 'You children fuck off and play, then,' he said.

And with that their company was over.

They walked to the car in silence, separate. Paul got into the driver's seat and Leigh got in next to him. It was a moment before Luke got into the back.

'I can't believe this has happened,' said Leigh.

Paul glanced at her then put the key in the ignition. He turned it but there was no sound from the engine, just the empty click of no connection.

'Shit,' he said.

They sat in the silent car. Paul turned the key again. And again.

'It's dead,' he said. 'Damn.'

They sat staring at inertia.

'Oh bloody hell,' Leigh said, in utter misery, but did not cry.

'It's all right,' Paul said as she leaned over into his arms. 'We'll get the bus.'

It was after midnight. Luke stood in the middle of the sitting room while Leigh made tea and Paul rolled a joint and put on a record. None of them wanted to end the night badly.

'It's too bright in here,' said Leigh, turning off the overhead light with her elbow as she came back in. She put the tea on the table and lit some candles, then she sat next to Paul on the sofa. Luke hadn't moved from where he was standing.

'I'm sorry,' he said. 'I didn't mean that to happen.'

'You don't have to keep saying it. It wasn't really you,' said Paul. 'Things end. Things change.'

Luke supposed that was true, he knew it was, but he had not thought this would end. His endings had been about survival; this felt like a death.

'Okay?' said Paul.

'Yeah, of course,' he answered, automatically, and stopped himself from saying he was sorry again. He leaned back against the armchair and put his head down on his arms. He thought about loss and that he was powerless.

Paul and Leigh never got high if they were working, only at parties, or together in bed sometimes. Now seemed as good a time as any. Neil Young was singing about dreams and lies – slow, fearful melancholy – and they passed the joint between them.

Luke didn't smoke hash; he never had. He had an instinct he ought not. But now he felt the strong need to join with the other two. They were toasting one another over the grave of their shared work. They didn't want to cry over it, they wanted to laugh. He reached out for it and Leigh handed him the joint and leaned back against Paul, waiting to feel better, or different.

Because Luke didn't smoke at all it hit the back of his throat in a solid burning mass and he coughed, violently, leaning forward and disgusted by it.

'Oh God, Luke – no, you'll throw up,' said Leigh, laughing at him. 'Give it here.'

Luke shook his head and said, 'Shit. God. Awful.'

'Blow-back,' said Paul.

Leigh looked at him, quizzically.

'If he wants it,' said Paul. 'I'm not doing it,' shuddering at the idea of man-to-man smoke exchange.

'Blow-back, Luke?' said Leigh, coolly, with an eyebrow slightly raised.

Luke knew what that was, he'd seen her and Paul a hundred times, their lips coming close together like a kiss and the smoke blown gently into the other's mouth. Then usually they did kiss.

'Will I cough?' he said.

'Not so much,' said Paul, laughing at him.

Leigh came down off the sofa to the floor opposite him.

'Here,' she said. She took a drag, very ladylike, not like she did when it was for herself, but politely, because it was for Luke.

Paul watched smilingly from the sofa as Leigh leaned towards Luke. He came forward to meet her, closing the gap between them halfway each, slightly embarrassed. Closer. She looked into his eyes, trying not to smile with the smoke in her mouth.

Luke thought how kind she looked, as if she were giving him medicine, or blessing him. They came together. Luke allowed his lips to open and Leigh blew. She blew the smoke coolly, slowly, in a steady, narrow stream into his mouth as he breathed in. It didn't burn. He exhaled.

'It's really strong stuff,' said Paul.

Luke looked at her. 'Yeah, go on. Again,' he said.

She took another drag, deeper, and when they came together they could feel the warmth of their lips, faces so close, not touching. He breathed in, trying not to get turned on by her and not succeeding.

And then she did it again to him, the third breath, and this time he was dizzy just from that.

Afterwards Leigh moved away abruptly and didn't look at him. She handed the joint back to Paul and got up to turn the record over. She kept the needle hovering for a long time to find the place because her hand was shaking. It would be all right if they never touched, if he never got so close to her. She settled the fragile needle onto the spinning record.

When she moved away from him Luke had the impression of desertion. Her closeness had been dangerous intimacy. Now he was alone. Leigh lay down with her head on Paul's lap. They began to talk. Luke's heart was pounding hugely, as if it had doubled in size and his head felt light. *Headrush*, he thought, waiting for the slowing-down he had seen in other people, and to be able to laugh. It didn't hit him like that. The sudden unravelling of the many threads of his thoughts wasn't good. They were talking about the performances that night, Jack, and *The Penal Colony* – he couldn't follow it all but knew it was ludicrous, there was nothing to say. It was all over and the mess of it was abhorrent; the wreck of a future that was now the fallen past. He wanted to be able to join in but he couldn't find a place to say anything. He wasn't sure how long they'd been sitting there. He began to sweat.

Paul looked at him and said, 'You all right?'

Luke nodded, then he got up and left them.

As if he were stepping through a mirror he saw himself from a distance, going down the hallway and into his room.

He could feel the sweat on his neck and on his face and the cold air making him shiver but his room was quiet and at least he was on his own.

He went straight to the desk where a half-finished page stuck out of the typewriter, abandoned for rehearsals at Graft. He looked at it. It was a scene he'd been rewriting that he didn't think was working. He pulled it out and added it to the heaped manuscript on the desk.

Then he remembered the drafts that had come before on the floor behind.

He knelt down and pulled them out, laying them out around him on the carpet. His heart was still pounding but his type-written words drew him in. He began to look through the drafts; sorting the scenes, the pages, handwritten, typewritten, and the many scrawled messages to himself. There were box files under the bed, papers under the bedside table and in the cupboards; the notebooks he had brought with him to London years before.

He got them all out and spread them chronologically round him in a spiral. His mind was playing lines from *The Penal Colony*, *Macbeth*, *Cartwright* – and things Jack had said in insistent, repetitive sentences.

They had done mediocre work and he had let them do it.

Intently, he tore blank paper into strips to join the notebooks and manuscripts into a pattern. Then he started on sub-divisions, splitting the chronological into the thematic. He made new piles of what failed and what succeeded; the things he had hopes for and others he needed to abandon. Paul came to the door, on his way to the bathroom and said, 'Fuck. What are you doing?'

'Sorting some things out,' said Luke, not looking up. Paul stood over him, watching. It was irritating. 'Can you not stand there?'

'This is nuts,' said Paul. 'It's after two.' And he left.

Luke could hear whispering somewhere in the room. It wasn't Paul or Leigh, it was someone else, someone with him in the room. He stopped, suddenly, and thought it was strange that there was someone whispering in the room with him, and wanting them to stop. He sat back to listen, holding a sheaf of papers in his hand and trying to hear the separate words. And then he remembered his mother. He remembered very clearly how as a child, a teenager, he had observed her searching compulsively through the pages of a book, or rifling through her sewing basket, or the drawers of her room and whispering her plan to unseen companions. He remembered her arguments and counter-arguments with people only she could hear. And recalled his discomfort and pity, not knowing whether to play along or try to stop her. He remembered and he thought that he had seen enough madness in his life to know what it looked like.

He looked down at the pages he was holding. His hands were like another person's hands. He realised that he couldn't remember exactly what was written on them. The whispering grew louder and then louder again, as if a volume knob were being turned, and now the words were clear.

*You have greatly sinned*, said the voice. *In your thoughts and in your words, in what you have done and in what you have failed to do, through your fault, through your fault, through your most grievous fault.*

*Shit*, thought Luke, *that's funny*, but the voice continued. He wondered if so many mad people heard God communicating with them because religion was Man's essential delusion. *I'll look into that tomorrow*, he thought. Then he got to his feet.

In the sitting room, music was playing and Paul and Leigh were reading at either ends of the sofa. They looked up when Luke came and stood in the doorway.

'Can you help me?' he said. 'Please. I really need to go to sleep and I can't. It's important.'

Paul was sitting on the floor in Luke's room near the door and Luke – eyes open, fifteen milligrams of Valium and two shots of Bell's down – was in bed in his clothes. Leigh, also dressed, was on the bed too, with her body around him and her chin resting on the top of his head. It was half past four. Paul was rolling cigarettes in the dim light, drinking tea and trying to stay awake.

'You said it every night before sleeping?' she asked.

'Yes,' said Luke. 'Hypnotic.'

'Tell me it again,' said Leigh. 'The words are nice.'

'*Zdrowaś Maryjo, łaski pełna . . .*' said Luke.

'English this time,' said Leigh.

Luke moved his head back an inch, into the space under her chin, and his shoulders pressed against her chest. He closed his eyes.

'*Hail Mary, full of grace*,' he said. '*Our Lord is with thee. Blessed art thou among women, and blessed is the fruit of thy womb, Jesus. Holy Mary, Mother of God, pray for us sinners, now and at the hour of our death.'*

'I'm Jewish,' said Leigh.

'Yeah, I know,' said Luke. 'And it's all just made-up spells to comfort idiots.'

'Yes,' said Leigh.

'The whole concept of a messiah is infantile and flawed.'

'I know,' said Leigh. 'That's not the point. Tell me it again.'

'Although, as it happens, I was thinking; the *Word*. *In the beginning was the word*. That's good, isn't it? What else could there be but the word? In the beginning, I mean.'

'*Shh* – yes.'

'The very first thing, the *word*—'

'*Shh*.'

'Sorry.'

'Go on.'

'. . . *Hail Mary, full of grace*,' Luke murmured, and Leigh closed her eyes and took deep slow breaths along with him. Luke closed his eyes, too. '. . . *Our Lord is with thee. Blessed art thou among women . . .*'

When he woke the next day his bed felt half the size it normally did. Leigh and Paul were both sleeping on it with him; Paul lying across the bottom like a giant hound and Leigh, who had moved away from Luke in the night, alongside him. Luke sat up, examining his mind as if he were feeling out a bad tooth, but there was no danger. He just felt cloudy from the Valium. Daylight. All the usual components of reality and nothing added. The day before returned to him and that Graft was over.

Neither Leigh nor Paul stirred. Paul's arm was over his face, Leigh's head half-covered by a pillow. They must have fallen asleep holding onto one another because their two left hands lay open side by side like an interlocking symbol. He was a trespasser on their gentleness. His only experience of such joining was the quick fusion of sex. Maybe it was the same thing, he thought, just different ways of escaping lifelong mortal loneliness. He remembered Nina Jacobs looking at him over her shoulder as she walked away. The image of her had not faded, and it surprised him. He often saw her in his mind. He knew his feeling for her was not reality, just a phantom he had conjured to fill the cutout gaps within himself – but still, the certain instinct of his heart had not surrendered her. The way she looked at him as she walked away. It was no good thinking about Nina Jacobs. He'd been doing that all week.

He got up – carefully – so as not to wake the others and was confronted by what had not been visible from the bed; the floor was entirely carpeted with paper. Years of work spilled out like guts. Remembering the state of himself the night before he seriously doubted there was any magical order to it.

And yet. He stood there gazing down on the floor made of paper. He surveyed the sea of black on white, and like the clearest church bell ringing out the hour he knew the time had come. He could no longer keep himself from judgement. The safe experiment of other people's work was gone; there was only his own.

\*

Later that day, when Leigh had gone out, Paul was shaving – to the Stones, very loud, singing 'You Can't Always Get What You Want'. With the music deafening him, Luke cleared the floor and found the latest draft of his play from the mess of the night.

. . . *You can't always get . . .*

He picked it up, and some other shorter ones – the better ones – and took them into the sitting room.

. . . *You get what you need . . .*

He put the manuscripts on the table, biting his lip and the side of his nail as he stood over them. Paul came into the doorway, drying his face with the threadbare towel. He turned the music down.

'What's all this?' he said.

'I want you to read something,' Luke said, bright with fear and conviction. 'If that's okay. I want you to tell me how shitty it is or isn't.'

'Well . . . Finally.'

Paul went over to the table in his jeans and bare feet, drying off his neck and chest, behind his ears, scanning the piles of work.

'That one,' said Luke.

'This one?' Paul picked up the manuscript. Luke clasped his hands behind his head and rocked to stop himself snatching it from him. Paul looked down at the others.

'Cor, there's enough of them.'

'Yeah,' said Luke.

'What are they mainly?'

Luke laughed. 'Plays, Paul. It's plays, mainly.' He walked up and down. 'There aren't as many as it looks.'

'Why not stories? Or a novel?'

'Or a handsaw.'

'Yes, hilarious.'

Paul flicked through the pages of the play; close, handwritten lines, held together with elastic bands. Luke stared around the room, rubbed his hair, scratched his calf with his foot, squinted at the ceiling, shook off an imaginary shiver – and looked back at Paul.

'It's not typed,' said Paul. 'You type a lot.'

'The last draft was at night. I didn't want to keep you and Leigh awake.'

Paul was unexpectedly touched by this. He eased the elastic band off the manuscript, looking down at the top page.

'*Paper Pieces* by Luke Last. Who's Luke Last?'

Luke did not answer.

Paul adopted high camp. 'Sorry, love, but *Luke Last*? Sounds like a pop singer. *Coming in at number 15, "Ooh Yeah", by Luke Last.*'

'Yes. Fuck off. Thanks. It's just better,' said Luke.

'Better than what?'

'For a name. *Lucasz Kanowski.*' He said it very Polish, swallowing the sounds.

'Yeah,' said Paul, 'Kanowski. And?' Paul waited, counting his friend's cost.

'I'm not ashamed.'

'Why would you be?'

'It's my father's name,' Luke said. 'It's bad enough that . . .' He ran out of words. 'I don't want my father's name.'

Paul watched him and saw that it was as much as he could do to stay in the room. He was a high-wire act with vertigo, he thought. He wasn't going to be the one to make him look down. He left it alone.

'*Paper Pieces?*' he asked.

Luke cheered up, instantly. 'Yeah. Well. It was called *A Piece of Paper*. Then I wrote some more. For a long time it was *Seven Pieces of Paper*, then it was *Twenty-two* . . .'

'Yeah, okay, I get the idea. You might want to reconsider that.'

'*Three Acts and Some Words?*'

'Now we're cooking,' said Paul, enjoying himself. 'What's it about?'

'Some people. They talk, and walk about.'

'Super.'

Paul put the notebooks on the sofa next to him and rooted in his pockets for roll-ups, matches . . .

'So are you going to piss off so I can read it?' he said.

Luke could not stay inside. He walked. He felt as though he were being skinned, slowly, and in public, and could not take himself seriously enough even to calm down. He stopped by the Brompton Cemetery and went inside, walking the paths among the graves.

Winter wind shifted the trees. Clouds rolled helplessly above the tombs. There was nothing he could do. It didn't matter if his play was bad. It probably was. He had others. He could rewrite. He walked for an hour and a half and then, unable to stay away, started back.

Paul had come out to find him and they met with the timing of trapeze artists in the street near the flat. It was a moment they both would always remember, knowing even as it happened that it was a rare collision.

'It's good!' called Paul, catching sight of him. He was smiling solidity and belief itself. 'It's *very* funny, Luke!'

'Yes. It's a comedy.'

'But it's *properly* funny. And strange. Did you hear me laughing?'

'No, I was,' Luke gestured, blank with nerves, 'in the graveyard.'

'Of course you were.'

———————

Nina and Tony were married at the Chelsea registry office in late September that same year, immediately the run of *In Custody* had finished. They stood on the steps, photographed, fitting together; Nina in her cream silk trouser suit, Tony with his girlishly soft looks, androgynous, meeting halfway between their genders, *au point*. Their guests filled the broad King's Road pavement, bringing a party to the weekday street. Men's hair curling over their collars, women in gauze scarves, droopy-brimmed hats; high shoes and paisley. And Tony, with his cool, empty expression, delighting in it, as confetti and flash-bulb pops rained down. Shoppers and teenagers stopped to stare, policemen held out their arms to encircle the wedding party and wave the staring cars past, music floating from their open windows, T-Rex, Kiki Dee.

Aunt Mat, solid and suburban in her sensible heels and brand-new suit, stood apart with her handbag on her arm. She searched for Marianne in the crowd but her sister-in-law had deserted her as they left the Town Hall. Aunt Mat clutched her fistful of confetti and found she could not throw it, but let it fall, clumping, onto the pavement. She had invited Tony and Nina to tea when she heard the news of their wedding, but Nina had cancelled at the last moment. She had tried, but had seen her niece only rarely in the seven years since she had moved out and she felt the rejection very keenly. She had shared Nina's erstwhile favourite, the Victoria sponge, with the ancient cat, now gaunt, and the neighbours from across the road.

The wedding party was held at Meridiana, with champagne and profiteroles, chicken Kiev and cocaine, actors, musicians and models, shouting laughter and the newly-weds clinging together in the centre of it all, Nina's eyes shining, her bunch of autumn roses, overblown, scattered across the table at her side. In the evening they went to Tramp, with Tony having changed into black on black, and Nina in a white suede mini-dress, her insect-long legs in platform boots. She felt her bare thighs printed by Tony's occasional pressing fingers, high on the attention and short-sighted, anxious dreams.

They went to Corsica for their wedding holiday. A short week on hot, windy beaches; Tony, languorous and unexpectedly boyish in cotton trousers and T-shirts, a sudden, briefly natural breath of honest relaxation.

The hotel was basic but Nina had never been abroad before and everything was new to her. She felt released, escaping the drudgery of her mother's judgement. They drank Negronis in the morning and white wine at lunch. They ate clams and gambas with sharp vinegar-laden salads and dipped their dry bread crusts into the juice. They sunbathed in the last of the heat, fading into autumn with each day that passed. Strong wind whipped sand around their ankles. In the afternoons they slept in the sun on the rocks by the crashing sea and woke with dry mouths, and then, with Nina in long silk scarves wrapped around her small naked breasts, they walked back across the spiky volcanic rocks to the bar.

And the nights. When they were not making love they did not hold one another. He liked her to face away from him when he fucked her, and often put his hands over her eyes, or closed them gently about her throat. The lack of intimacy was dangerous-safe. She was content to feel that he was attracted enough to want her in the first place. He didn't like to come inside her, and sometimes she didn't think he came at all, or if he did, he kept that moment hidden, as if it were too personal to show her. She couldn't see, or feel it, and didn't know what he did. One night, overcome by the need to know him, she turned around to face him when he was too deeply into his pleasure to stop. She lifted her long leg up and over his head and swivelled to face him, wrapping herself around him, a loving prison, bravely putting her hands on his shoulders to look into his eyes.

'Don't,' he said, 'don't.' But then he came, and immediately, as if in pain, his face crumpled into tears, like a baby.

'Bitch. Bitch. Don't look at me, I'm horrible, I'm sorry,' he said.

He climbed off her and rolled into a ball, sharp shoulder blades and the knobbled fossil curve of his spine protecting himself from her.

'Don't cry,' she said, 'don't cry . . .'

'I'm sorry,' he murmured, with his face hidden. 'I'm sorry.'

Nina pulled the sheet over herself and sat up in the dark.

Her hair fell down around her, she was undone. The two of them were alone with the hours of night-time. The bright, low moon shone into their room.

'I don't know anything about you,' she said.

'Yes, you do, you know everything.' He sounded bored.

'You've never told me anything about your parents,' she said, adding in her mind, *nothing true*.

'There's nothing to tell.'

Tony turned onto his back and stretched, and reached for a cigarette. She took one too, and lit them both. He stayed flat on his back, smoking.

She waited for revelation, confession – a clue to him – but he did not speak.

She watched his profile and wondered what she had done in marrying him and what awaited her.

'Tony,' she said, 'will we be all right?'

'We'll be marvellous,' he said. 'Look at us,' he waved his cigarette in a generous arc, '*killing*.'

'It's just – I want to make you happy.'

'How quaint. Darling,' he looked across at her and smiled with warm, ironic charm, 'I hope you're not going to buy an apron and start messing about with coq au vin.'

He'd done it. He had made her fears sound funny. She loved him.

'Fondue set,' she said.

'Chicken brick.'

And they laughed loudly in that moonlit night, hoping someone would hear them and be disturbed.

In the morning they swam in the chilly sea, thick with salt on their tanned bodies, and fought through the choppy waves to shore.

They got back to London as the leaves were turning and Nina went straight into a short week of rehearsals and tech runs for the transfer of *In Custody* from the Nag's Head to the Duke of York's.

Tony's wife was starring in the West End in a play that he had produced; he moved the *Wot, Not Married?!* poster to the downstairs loo, where everyone would see it but no one could say he didn't know its place. The revue was still coasting along, making him money while he slept, and he was free to raise his standards, to travel the regionals looking for another play, and read the stack of submissions he had neglected.

---

The upstairs room at the Lord Grafton was vacated and the flaps, cyc and lighting rig flogged off to other companies; nothing left but a little money in the bank.

Leigh and Paul looked for work, calling friends and circling ads in the back of *The Stage*, but for now, unemployed, they had their evenings free. It was luxurious. They lived on savings and Luke's wages and ate out of tins, and Leigh went to Biba with girlfriends in the middle of the day to try on hats and drank coffee not just to keep awake. The grief for their lost company faded more easily than they had imagined, replaced by Paul's enthusiasm for Luke's work and the struggle to find him an agent, anyone who would read him and take notice of his talent.

The three of them went to all the plays they'd been missing, saving money by sitting up in the gods or seats where they had to crane their necks around columns to see the stage, then met up in the interval to talk. They went to parties; early ones, where everyone else was looking for work in theatre too, and late-night ones for those whose shows had just come out. They drank Rioja and smoked hash — except for Luke — and argued and laughed. They went to shared houses in unknown streets and sat on beanbags with burn-holes in them, spilling foam, or rickety kitchen chairs wobbling on terracotta kitchen floors. They listened to music for hours at a time and lay in bed until late in the morning because there were no rehearsals to go to.

Leigh was the first to find a job. It was the best she could have hoped for.

'We can eat,' she announced, flushed with pride and confidence, returning from the interview.

It was the first cold day of the year, wind whipping the tainted leaves from the trees before the stems were weak enough to drop them, gritty dust flying up from the pavements.

'Bloody brilliant!' said Paul, and hugged her.

'Call me the last-minute-girl,' said Leigh, taking a bow. 'Up for ASM at the Strand, right? But then the stage manager who interviewed me, who was really nice, sent me over to the Duke of York's, because the SM there has chicken pox and they used the excuse to fire her too because she couldn't –' she laughed '– manage! The whole place is a *mess*, I'm going to have to sort *everything* out.'

'Stage manager? At the Duke of York's? Fuck. Brilliant.' Paul hugged her.

Luke grinned. He patted her shoulder, smiling. 'Well done,' he said.

Leigh blushed and went back into the safety of Paul's arms. 'They were really nice,' she said. 'I don't know why me.'

'Why not?' said Luke. 'You held Graft together with string and glue.'

'I'm probably carrying all the fired-one's chicken pox germs. She was there to hand-over and she was stumbling around like a plague victim.'

'What's the play?' asked Paul.

'*In Custody*. Same cast. Nina Jacobs and Henry Fidele. They're opening a week on Wednesday.'

Luke stood up, quickly. 'Cool,' he said. 'Monday, then?'

'Monday.'

They went out to the Fulham Road to celebrate; pizza and red wine, and got home late, Paul and Leigh quite drunk and kissing their way to the sitting-room floor and laughing as they kissed.

'Goodnight . . .'

'Night.' And Luke went to his room alone.

He lay in bed to the sounds of records being played and their voices through the wall. He saw Nina Jacobs kneeling before him. He felt her very close to him; the imprisoned girl and the closing-in of cell doors accompanying him through the night.

———————

When Nina was playing the part of Elena in custody, she visited the heart of herself. It was the only time in her career that she had felt such honesty. It was entirely personal and yet released her. She existed only as the work dictated, within the moment. She had no nerves. In rehearsals, she could be businesslike, holding back, walking through the new blocking, taking her part in the machine of the production growing about her easily and with confidence. But on the stage, in performance, she lost herself in focused truth. Between shows, afterwards, getting ready to go on, even then, she savoured the knowledge of her talent, and her present success. She felt it with exquisite nostalgia because she knew how precious it was, that she might never find such joy in her work again. It was not in keeping with the rest of her existence. And it did not in any way represent the reality of her marriage with Tony. In that, she lived the perpetual insecurity of pretence.

Their house was not her home. Tony dictated the redecoration and the entertaining. Tony decided the food and the colours and who they would see. Once it was up and running he lost interest in *In Custody* as he had in *Not Married*. He hardly ever came to the theatre and had no sympathy for Nina's growing exhaustion as the weeks of the run went by. He was proud of her triumph and of having found the play for her and expected her to be consumed by it but he didn't want to hear about how it had gone that night, or if the director had been in. Marianne gratefully filled the gaps. She telephoned her daughter every morning at ten — *Darling, you'll never guess* — while Nina was still in bed with the papers and Tony across the landing in his study writing his column — yapping at the world about Ayckbourn or Olivier — up and down the stairs to collect people at the door for meetings, shouting down to Mrs Wills for coffee, or playing the piano in the living room. The walls were jungle green, with shiny potted plants in the corners and the furniture on deep-piled rugs. When *In Custody* was nominated for an Evening Standard Award, and Nina as its leading actress, Tony had bought the gloss-white piano to celebrate. When he was bored, or angry, the sound of thundering, bouncing chords would fill the house, along with his high voice, singing along a little sharp, like a rattling Noël Coward.

His Sunday-night parties had grown with his success, not aspiring any longer, but buzzing, happening and desired. Nina often dreaded them, they stole her one night off, but when she looked around at their guests and saw the living face of their achievement she warmed herself with it, grateful not to be alone with her husband.

Tony took a lot of cocaine, chopping the lines with a razorblade on a mirror on his desk or the glass coffee table in the sitting room. She dreaded his taking it at night because it made him impersonal – more impersonal – in bed with her. Strung out, numb, he took delight in games that discomfited her; the subtle manipulation of her body and heart. His controlling her like that triggered adrenalin that occasionally excited her but more often sickened her. Just the way he held her arm, or pressed her neck, or trailed a thing she could not see across her body when her face was pressed into the pillow coloured the nature of their sex. When he was working, he took coke to focus and when he was hosting his parties or out with Nina and entertaining he took it for fun and to quell his appetite. He didn't want to put on weight. Like her mother, he watched Nina's figure. *Careful* – he would murmur, warningly, if hungry from her night's work, she absent-mindedly broke off pieces of bread and ate them before her steak and salad arrived. Occasionally she had them both together – *careful, naughty-naughty* – one on one side, one on the other, winking at each other and poking her taut waist to check for a spare tyre.

Nina did not communicate much with the backstage crew. She was polite but very much the star. She had learned from her mother's example that she didn't have to be best friends with everybody to do the job. Tony had bought her a fur coat. She took pleasure in wearing it to the theatre over jeans, hair tied back roughly but sweeping through the dusty warren of corridors to her dressing room protected by its richness. She found she did form friendships of a kind with the men, but hardly at all with the women, taught by her mother as she had been that they were jealous, and would not like her.

Leigh developed a minor fascination with Nina. The play was demanding, harrowing in places, and Nina was consistently good in it. Even as the audiences got more responsive, anticipating the high notes because the play had become widely known, she never show-boated, never broke out of the human scale of her performance. Leigh liked her best when she saw her getting her breath and gathering herself between scenes in the darkened wings; quite alone against the backdrop of expectant silence from the auditorium, ignoring the whispered activity of the scene change. At those times Leigh saw the artist in her, and what it cost her to do it. Apart from that, recognising her charisma, she was confused by Nina's conflicting sides, that she was at once timidly childlike and cool. If she warmed to you, you had no choice but to like her, and Leigh experienced it for herself when, six weeks into the run, passing by her one day between the matinée and evening performance, Nina stopped to speak to her. She had a cold and looked pale; shadows under her eyes and a tremendously long woollen scarf wrapped around her neck, trapping her hair. Leigh was heaving a box from her office to wardrobe as they passed on the concrete stair.

'Oh,' said Nina, turning like Pierrot on the step to look down at her, 'it's my birthday on Wednesday.'

'Happy birthday for Wednesday,' said Leigh under the weight of the box.

'We're having a party at the house on Sunday night. Tony wanted – would you let everyone know? We're not doing invites, but everyone is invited. Put the word out.'

Leigh nodded.

'Great,' she said, and bumped the box up from sliding down her thigh, feeling like a carthorse.

Nina seemed to notice the box for the first time.

'Would you like a hand?' she said, unexpectedly.

'I'm fine – thanks, though.'

'Really, here,' said Nina, and took half of the weight from her. 'Where are we going?'

'Up,' said Leigh, and they carried it together.

'You work so hard,' said Nina.

'We all do, don't we?'

When they reached the door of wardrobe they put the box down.

'Thanks,' said Leigh. 'And thanks for Sunday – would it be all right to bring my boyfriend?'

'Bring whoever you like. The more the merrier.'

Nina smiled at her, but her smile looked sad. It was wistful. Leigh found she was examining Nina's expression. Actresses' faces like dancers' bodies were trained to express themselves. Nina's seemed to do it without her meaning it to – but Leigh couldn't tell, perhaps she wanted to be asked.

'Are you all right?'

'It's just this cold,' said Nina bleakly. 'I can't seem to get rid of it.'

'We've all had it. And it must be tiring giving so much of yourself every night.'

'It is.' She smiled at Leigh as if she had said something especially perceptive.

'You should take vitamin C. Orange juice,' said Leigh, but Nina had drawn down her blinds and lost interest.

'Thanks, darling, I will,' she said. 'See you later. I'm half-dead.'

And she was gone.

'Completely bloody super bloody news,' said Paul, coming into the flat. Luke was lying on the sofa with a pad and pen on his stomach, his arm over his face and his feet up.

'What?' he said. 'I'm working.'

'Oi, *Luke Last*,' said Paul, '*Kanowski*. I've got not just a *bit* of bloody super bloody amazing news; *two* bits. One, John Wisdom who runs Archery is going off to do a season at the Oxford Playhouse from January and he wants to meet you to talk about *Pieces*, and the other is Lou Farthing is interested in talking to you about a new play.'

Luke sat up.

'Christ,' he said.

'Yes,' said Paul, 'that's what I said. Are we going to this party, then?'

'What party?'

'BBC fella. Nice.'

The party was in a big, tatty house in Shepherd's Bush which belonged to a man Paul knew slightly called Jonathan, who was a director at the BBC. His sister was married to a theatrical producer. Paul didn't know Jonathan well, the BBC fella, but he had decided Luke should make contacts and was determinedly pushing him. He had given some sketches and another short play to the BBC but had had no response. Luke dreaded the rejection and was pretending he wasn't waiting to hear. He was writing a new play he wouldn't show to Paul yet, or talk about, but while Leigh was at the theatre the two of them worked on sketches and one-act plays – old and new – shaping them and testing them on one another.

BBC Jonathan's house was cold, filled with books and the smell of pipe tobacco, and everyone there was older than Paul and Luke – or felt it. There were actors and one or two television writers, ignoring one another. A large pot of something to do with aubergines, or chicken, was lazily bubbling in the small back-kitchen, while Jonathan's wife Jessica wandered about in a kaftan with a wooden spoon. They didn't want to leave before they could get something to eat, even though Paul felt more than usually out of place.

Luke wandered off around the house and got talking to the woman's au pair who was a seventeen-year-old French convent girl. They met, passing on the stairs as she went to check on the baby. She was so relieved to be speaking French she burst into tears on the landing. Luke put his arms around her small weeping body and pressed her into the corner, protecting her from view and smelling her hair, which was not altogether clean.

'I am homesick,' she told him, in Inspector Clouseau-accented English.

He kissed her. She gulped, kissing him back and crying. Luke wondered how long she had been out of her convent school and decided it must have been quite a while because she was unsurprised at being kissed and practically pulled him backwards into a bedroom.

'Is the baby in here?' he asked, peering round.

'No, it is lying on the other floor,' she answered. Luke wondered vaguely about her commitment to her job as they stumbled onto the bed.

'Don't do it, be careful,' she said. She had forgotten about crying.

Her wiry arms were around his neck. She was wearing thick ribbed tights under a corduroy skirt and, kissing her, he pressed the flat of his hand hard up between her legs, closing the undesirable gap between the stretched wool and her body. His mind was hushed as if covered by a blanket of snow. The clamour in his brain stilled by her breath in his ear, her ribs and hip-bones pushed up against his weight and his thoughts were reduced gratefully to the heated maths of getting inside her clothes, taking up all of him in blessed focus.

'*Merde*,' she said, digging her nails into the back of his neck. Definitely well out of the convent then, and he dragged her skirt up around her waist, hauled down the tights and knelt down between her wide-open legs.

'So I told Jonathan about *Pieces*,' said Paul as they left, walking down the wet street in the mist that had come down after the rain.

'Who's Jonathan?'

'Where were you? The chap with the glasses.'

'Yep.'

'He wasn't interested.'

'Why would he be interested?'

'Jesus Christ. I don't know if I'm a producer or a pimp,' said Paul. 'Because he's directing Tony Menzies' thing for BBC2 . . .'

Luke paused. 'Producer?' he repeated.

It was the first time it had been mentioned between them.

'Well, what the fuck do you think we've been doing?' he said. 'If *Pieces* gets picked up I'm not saying goodbye to it.'

'Of course not,' said Luke. 'It's not going anywhere without you.'

*

It was one o'clock when they let themselves in. Leigh was under a blanket on the sofa reading, with a glass of wine and Jacqueline du Pré's cello playing Bach in the background.

'Hello, boys,' she said.

Paul jumped onto the sofa, two legged, feet up. 'Hello, gorgeous,' he said.

Luke went to the fridge.

'Have you eaten?' asked Leigh.

'I have; Luke was busy.'

Luke began to make himself a white bread sandwich with margarine, slathering it on and sprinkling it with salt.

'How was the show?' he heard Paul ask.

'Nina invited me to her birthday party at the weekend,' said Leigh. 'Us, I mean.'

'Me and you?' said Paul.

'Yes, or all of us. She said whoever I liked. She was really nice about it.'

Luke came to the door of the sitting room, holding his sandwich.

'Crikey. The great Tony Moore,' said Paul. 'We're going up in the world. You'd better come along, Luke, and behave yourself, she's a married woman now.'

———————

Tony sat cross-legged on the sofa, ribbed cashmere pleasingly snug across his chest. The room was almost full. He noted with pleasure that they were a better class of person since *In Custody* and reminded himself that his snobbishness was not frivolous, but to do with quality. His nursery slopes may have been a little tawdry but he was fighting upward to ever more rarefied air.

There were people on the stairs. People in the kitchen. People pushing to get past other people; pleasant laughter. He had rented some staff for the night, a couple of queers who worked for a pittance in wardrobe at the Opera House or somewhere. Champagne cocktails were served from the drinks trolley. Vodka and tonic. Whisky and soda. And Martinis — because Nina liked them. The ice buckets kept running out. Elaine Cross, fresh from Hollywood, was enthroned in the wicker chair, alone. Her enormous blonde hair floated against the upright fretted-fan, apparently arrested in wind-tousled movement. *Halted by the powers of Elnette*, he thought. It had rather more personality than she did; he felt he should offer it a drink. Perhaps she was wearing a fall; did people still do that? His fringe slipped down from its side-parting and obscured his vision for a moment. He swept it up with a fingertip, blinking. Julian was chatting to Bill Levinson — Tony could hear snatches, something about rehearsal space — actor-whining; Anthony Upton and Diana Long's conversation looked earnest. He was a marvellous director but she was a bore. She wasn't managing that part at the Old Vic. She probably knew it. A fortnight into a twelve-week run and she must know she stank; on stage every night, the weak link in a stellar cast, stinking up the first three rows. Tony suppressed a snort. She should go home and have some more children.

Across the room Nina was putting on a record, holding the sleeve at an angle as she lowered the needle; he couldn't make out what it was. He really should talk to Elaine Cross and not leave her there but she had no substance. Fame was no protection against sitting like a stick at a party if you were boring as hell. He would talk to her for a moment and indulge his intellect elsewhere. He examined Nina's rear-view as she bent over the record player and the song began. Roberta Flack, gospel voices, piano and harmonies . . . Nina was wearing peach palazzo pants and a white silk shirt, slashed to the waist. No bra, she didn't need one. He could see the line of her knickers. She should wear French knickers. Or no knickers. There was a revue title to conjure with – *Wot, No Knickers?!* Nina straightened and turned to him – catching the smile as it left his face. She looked questioning, worried. There was nobody else in the room for her, she always looked at him.

'A little too loud,' he murmured, with no hope of being heard.

*What?* she mouthed.

*Too loud*, he mouthed back, waving a hand somewhere near his ear. She looked uncertain.

'Oh!' She turned back to the record player and lowered the volume. He wouldn't reassure her. He moved towards Elaine's wicker chair before Nina turned again, and leaned down.

'May I kneel at your feet?' he said.

Leigh, Paul and Luke drove to the party in Leigh's new car, a five-year-old VW Beetle she called Janis. Luke half-lay across the back seat with one leg up and two bottles of Rioja rolling around next to him. Leigh drove, leaning the little car into her corners.

'Brands Hatch,' said Paul.

'You drive like the Queen,' said Leigh.

She turned into Tite Street and she and Paul wound down their windows, trying to read the numbers. Luke, in the back, was assaulted by the cold fresh air.

'Sixteen, eighteen . . .' said Leigh.

'Seventeen . . . twenty-three . . . This is nice. No dog shit.'

'Rich dogs shit. You just can't see it in the dark,' said Luke.

Leigh swung the car suddenly into a long space, braking too late. The Beetle's bumper met the one in front, harder than a kiss but not violently enough to hook underneath.

'Bugger,' she said.

'Anyone see?'

'Don't think so.'

She reversed noisily and switched off the engine. It began to rain, a veil falling over the car. She and Paul wound up their windows.

'It's probably Tony Moore's Daimler,' said Luke.

'Not yet,' said Leigh. 'He drives a Peugeot. Navy blue.' She hauled her tapestry bag from beneath the seat and dropped the keys into it. 'Are we getting out?'

They stood by the car in the chill night with a film of water beading their hair and the collar of Paul's sheepskin jacket, street lights shining off the roof of the Beetle and the sounds of a police car from the King's Road.

'Do I look all right?'

Both men looked. She didn't normally ask. She was beautiful. Rain dewed her cheek. She was wearing some sort of dress, they hadn't noticed before she put her coat over it but they could glimpse cleavage.

'Gorgeous,' said Paul.

'Cleopatra's cheekbones,' said Luke, wanting to kiss her. He always wanted to kiss her, he was used to it.

She smiled.

'Good teeth, too,' said Paul.

'Piss off,' said Leigh. 'Let's leave the bottles in the car – I've a feeling it's not that sort of party.'

Leigh took Paul's hand and they went on ahead.

'Everything smells wonderful,' said Luke to the night-time air, taking joy from each second as it came.


Nina was standing with her back to the window in the sitting room when Luke came in.

The party was in full swing, a roar of noise and a couple dancing in the corner by a potted palm, hands resting on one another's hips.

Nina had been talking to her director, Malcolm Dewberry. She happened to look across the room just as Luke walked through the door.

And it was, to her, as if the many people between them had fallen away and formed a space for her to see him. He had dark hair, messy, and a grey-blue cotton shirt. He was quite tall and his shoulders, or the way his shirtsleeves were rolled up to the elbow – no, it wasn't that. He was with two other people but they were out of focus to her; his energy took the light from the space around. He looked restless, head half-inclined to hear what the man next to him was saying but distracted, and then he caught sight of her – his head jerked up minutely and he looked.

They looked at one another across the room for perhaps two seconds. And then he put his hand up quickly and turned away – a movement that was half a head rub, half-flinching, hiding his face from her. With his back to her she saw his hand go to the back of his neck and then a group of people stepped between them, and she couldn't see him any more.

Time jolted back to speed; she was out of breath. She felt

herself blush and she looked guiltily around. Malcolm had gone. She put her drink down clumsily on the window ledge, looking for some occupation, fumbling for cigarettes. And then as thoughts returned to her she wondered who he was.

She looked up again. He wasn't by the door – just other people, frustrating and faceless, in and out. She looked quickly about, both dreading and hoping to see him. There, ten feet away, through the crowd, the arm of his shirt. The thrill of the sight of it was acute – she leaned to the left to see who he was with. A dark girl, with extraordinary eyes – it was the stage manager, Leigh – perhaps it was make-up or nerves lighting her; she didn't look the same as she usually did. Jealously, Nina remembered her asking to bring her boyfriend, but she and the man looked more like brother and sister than—

'Nina!'

Chrissie Southey. Drunk. Good. She could talk to Chrissie and still keep looking at him.

'Chrissie, darling, have you got a drink?'

Chrissie held up her glass and jiggled the ice in it.

'An adorable boy keeps topping me up. Looks rather like Petula Clark.'

Nina laughed. 'He's one of Tony's.'

'How do you know?' Chrissie leaned in, eyes wide, amber hair tousled and falling.

'Know what?'

'The *boy* . . .'

'No, Chrissie, Tony found him – and his friend. To serve.'

'How Jean Genet of him.'

'Yes . . .'

Nina glanced over Chrissie's shoulder, she couldn't see the grey-blue shirt any longer. She looked the other way, to her right, past Chrissie's upheld glass, and she saw him leave the room – his back – disappearing into the shadow of the hallway.

'All *play* and no fun makes Jill – you know the expression,' said Chrissie. 'I've turned down three – no, four – tellies recently just because why graft, graft, graft?'

'I thought you were waiting to hear about that film that went to Judy Geeson,' said Nina, forgetting to be tactful, looking over her shoulder.

'Not really. There's so much *else* to do. Alexander says he loves one and one loves him, of course – but the movie scene is a drag.'

She carried on talking. Nina didn't listen.

'And does one want to have a baby?' said Chrissie, leaning in to her.

'What?' said Nina. Perhaps he'd left. Perhaps he'd been there for hours, in the kitchen, without her knowing, and now he was leaving.

'Sorry, darling,' she said, 'just a minute . . .'

She left Chrissie and pushed through the crowd towards the door, and for a second she was aware of Tony watching her from the sofa.

The landing had some people leaning over the banister as if they were in a box at the theatre and laughing uproariously. Nina almost ran past them and down the stairs. The front door was open. He wasn't there. In the hall she looked into the dining room but it was empty. The tiny room at the back that was supposed to be hers was empty too. She went to the top of the kitchen stairs. A troop of people were coming up. She was forced to wait, leaning back on her hands, smiling automatically as each of them went by.

'Nina.'

'Nina, darling.'

'Happy birthday, darling.'

She pretended pleasure, desperate, waiting for them to go.

And then, suddenly, there he was. She was face to face with him at the top of the stairs, inches apart. He had been coming up behind the others, hidden, and now he was in front of her.

He was younger than she'd thought. Younger than Tony. Perhaps even her age. He didn't look English. He was staring at her.

'I'm Nina,' she said, but she couldn't smile.

'I know,' he said.

Then he took a step backwards, winced and shook his head once, as if he was having a conversation with himself, and bumped into a woman coming along the landing to go down.

'Sorry,' he said, and moved back out of the way of the stairs.

'Funny how people always walk about at parties.' She rushed the words. 'Always looking for the best bit.'

'I'm Luke,' he said.

She stared at him again. He was staring back. People passed them by and she had the sensation everybody could tell what she felt, that the air between them was different from everywhere else.

'Come over here,' he said, and he went to the window at the back of the hall.

She followed.

They stood a safe distance apart, on either side of the window facing one another as the party carried on above and below and people paraded past with glasses and cigarettes held aloft, from hall to kitchen to sitting room, up and down.

Her wrists were very narrow. She was lightly tanned and wearing a silver bracelet.

His hands – one resting on the window ledge, one by his side – were quite bony, big, and had prominent veins on them like hands in a life-study, then his wrists went into slim fore-arms and up, to the roll of his shirtsleeve.

She had a flame-coloured silk scarf tied in her straight brown hair; leaving her hairline and her forehead bare, like something innocent revealed.

His belt was a little too big for him and sat on his hips quite low. His shirt was wrinkled and limp, making creases over his body, half-tucked into his trousers, catching the light; his body was a secret beneath it.

Her smooth skin was exposed straight down between her breasts like an arrow, dipped in to the small crescent of her breastbone then went to shadow.

His cheek was shaved cleanly. The tendon of his neck went down to the horizontal of his collarbone, she could sense the life beneath the skin, vital.

He was still looking at her.

They felt, both of them, that until that point they had only been waiting.

'I don't know what to say to you,' he said.

'I don't either,' said Nina.

He looked into her eyes – not at some indistinct point – directly.

'Are you . . . all right?'

'What do you mean?' she asked.

'Is everything – fine?'

She looked up at him, clearly. 'No,' she said, raw with danger. 'It's not.'

Luke nodded, slowly, and he looked down. 'All right,' he said. 'I see.'

A woman passed by, her glance caught them and moved on.

'Sorry — have we met before?' Nina asked him.

Luke looked away, down the hall across the people. She had the feeling he wanted to get away.

'I saw you in the play, *In Custody*, when it was at the pub. You walked past me afterwards. You wouldn't remember.'

'Oh. I do. I think.'

'You were very good,' he said.

'Thank you.'

He took a step, as if to leave, and then stopped and turned back, frowning at her. 'What's wrong?' he said. 'Why aren't you happy?'

'Why do you ask?'

'I just want to know.'

'I don't know why,' said Nina, cornered. 'I don't know why I'm not.'

She looked helpless. 'It will be all right,' he said. 'I promise.'

Then he turned and left the house, stopping sideways to pass the people in the hall, as if he couldn't get away from her fast enough.

---

When Luke left, when she was quite sure he had gone, Nina started upstairs. She went up away from everybody, straight ahead into Tony's study, and closed the door behind her. She turned the key in the lock. There was no lock on the bedroom door. She could hear the noise of music and raised voices below her. She sat in her husband's chair behind his desk. She smelled the tooled leather, turned her head to look at his pictures on the wall. She had never been in the room and not felt subsumed. Now it was an empty space, just a place for her to be. She closed her eyes and saw Luke. She imagined him and there he was, standing in front of her.

*It will be all right. I promise.*

She waited a long time before she went back to her party.


It was after three o'clock in the morning. The trains had stopped, the cars had gone, the houses about them up and down the road slept. Soon the milkmen would be out on their rounds – and still there were people in her house.

Nina wandered through the wreckage and quiet music, unaware, for once, of where Tony might be.

The sitting room was a sea of strewn cushions, three people were lounging with a joint on the rug by the fireplace. She didn't know them. They looked like students. She had no idea who they had come with. The girl looked about sixteen. They were listening to Elton John singing 'Yellow Brick Road' and she thought if she turned it off they would leave, so she did. They dragged themselves giggling to their feet, uncomplaining, wandered past her as if she weren't there and down the stairs.

Nina picked up a half-empty bottle of champagne that someone had abandoned to get warm and poured herself a glass. Alone, she held it up to the empty room – and to Luke, wherever he might be.

'Happy birthday,' she said. 'It will be all right.' She drank all of it to the last small drop.

The last stragglers were down by the door saying goodbye. Nina started down, unnoticed. Before reaching the bottom she sat and watched them through the banisters. Chrissie

Southey was leaving with Alexander Talbot holding her up. He was as good-looking and as drunk as she was, yelling out for the taxi they had kept waiting in the street for an hour. They were a perfect couple. Nina sat on the stairs, drowsy with her secret, fond of them in their babyish small-hours passion as they snipped and squabbled. They caught sight of her.

'*Sorry* – bye, darling –'

'Sorry –'

'Lovely –'

Kisses goodbye. Hugs. Farewells. Chrissie was drawling, sprawling drunk; Alexander was no better, and the people with them – Eleanor, Willy Lansbury, Jack – all trying to organise themselves into different cars with different people.

'No, no, you said you thought it, and now, *now*, you're lying. Why do you *lie* to me?'

'Oh, shut up—'

'You're *lying*—'

'God, you're boring. Boring, boring, boring.'

'Goodbye, goodbye, Nina darling . . .'

And Nina, through the banisters, uncaring, looked past them to the street with the idea that somehow Luke was waiting for her and would appear, and take her with him. *I must be drunk, too*, she thought. *I'm as drunk as they are.*

And then silence. No movement that she could hear in the house. *Tomorrow*, she thought, *thank God there's no matinée. I'll sleep all day. I'll sleep until four.* But she felt she might never sleep again. She got up, trailed down the rest of the stairs, and as she closed the door, at last, heard movement in the house behind her. She was chilled with exhaustion. She hoped Tony would leave her alone. Had he gone to bed already? There, a noise again. She tiptoed to the top of the kitchen stairs and hung her head down to listen. No. It was definitely upstairs, in the small back room. Her room. She went up in her stockinged feet, silent and thinking of nothing but what had happened to her and how it had made her feel and, reaching the landing, she pushed the door of her little room open.

Tony was lying back on the small chaise they had bought together on Lots Road with his trousers round his ankles. One of the waiter boys, with his silver-blond curls bobbing, was kneeling between his legs – and Tony's head tipped back, his hand on the back of the boy's head. The other boy was in the corner, with his trousers open and his white cock hanging limply out like raw dough, leaning over a mirror on the mantelpiece and snorting a line of coke. He jerked upright, hand slamming to cover himself as he registered her presence, while her husband and the boy continued, oblivious. Nina stood frozen with embarrassment at bursting in on them. She had trespassed. Then shock and fierce revulsion broke coldly over her, her throat closing as if something were being forced down it – as if Tony were forcing himself down it. She heard herself say something – a word, a noise – muffled. And as she backed out into the hallway, she saw Tony raise his head and see her, while the boy's head continued to bob up and down.

Turning, she headed down the stairs, but with sudden vertigo, tripped at the top – saved herself – and then ran on, leaning on the banister. Down as far as she could get.

The kitchen was empty, wrecked, strewn, half-eaten cheeses scattered over the table. Nina halted, drenched with sudden sweat, as if her skin had been violently altered, her pores gaped. She got to the cloakroom door, onto her knees on the hard tiles, grabbing the seat just in time to get the lid up and vomited up champagne, vodka, olives, pieces of bread – gobs of the contents of her stomach splashing into the water, heaving agony in her throat. Her eyes streamed tears. When she was completely empty she sat back on her heels and wiped her eyes and her face with the backs of her hands. Her throat burned. She spat into the toilet bowl, coughed, spat again. And shakily stood up.

She turned on the taps, washed her face, rinsed her mouth. And then she sat down on the closed toilet. She stared at the *Wot, Not Married?!* poster and thought she might laugh but instead began to cry. She cried for a few minutes, trying not to make too much noise, thinking clear, shocked, childish thoughts – *My husband is queer – Why would he do this to me? – Does everyone know but me?* – dully aware all the time that this moment would be the easiest, cleanest part of the whole affair. *No, I'm not all right*, she had said to Luke and hadn't known the truth of it. She could not think of Luke. The picture of him, that had been so clear, dissolved. But she had finished crying.

She dried her eyes. And now it came into her mind that she would have to get up, and leave the safety of the damp cloakroom. She would have to face him. They were married, after all. But she could not get up. She had no idea where she could go. She wanted her mother. She began to cry again, weak, but was stopped by the front door slamming above her.

She sat still and silent, holding her breath.

She waited. She waited long enough to get colder and uncomfortable, and listened stiffly to the house creaking around her and then she heard Tony's voice, distantly calling her name. She shut her eyes.

She heard him coming down the stairs above her head like footsteps in a game of hide-and-seek.

'Nina, darling?'

There was a gentle tap on the door. She stood up and after a moment opened the door.

He was very neat and it looked as if he had combed his hair. He held out his hand and smiled, ruefully.

'Darling, you can't stay in there all night.'

She shook her head.

'Shall we go upstairs?' he said. 'It's awfully late, I should think you're exhausted.'

She looked at him, dazed.

'I don't know what came over me,' he said. Then his composure crumpled. 'I'm sorry.' Childlike tears brimmed. 'In our house. I'm so sorry. You couldn't loathe me as much as I loathe myself. My darling.'

His face was melted, features blurring. She realised he had been crying before and must have cleaned himself up to come to her.

'I don't loathe you,' she said. He kept crying, his hands hanging helplessly at his side.

She reached out and took one of them.

Gripping her fingers, he knelt on the kitchen floor at her feet. He pressed her hand to his brow.

'I love you,' he said. 'It doesn't change how much I love you. Forgive me.'

Nina felt dizzy. She leaned her back against the toilet door, her husband kneeling at her feet.

'Get up,' she said. 'Come on, it's time for bed.'

He stood up and wiped his eyes. 'Yes,' he said, 'let's go on up.' There was a fresh red stain on the knees of his trousers where he had knelt in a puddle of red wine.

He took her hand and led her up the stairs. As they crossed

the landing and passed the back room, she glanced in, wonder-ingly, through the open door at the blameless *Nina's room* they had always said was hers.

'Shh,' he said. 'Come on. Don't be cross.'

And they went on up to bed. He spent longer in the bath-room than usual, and so did she.

―――――――――

Luke woke in the clean morning. The sunlight shone straight in onto his bed through the open curtains. He sat up, rubbed his face, looked out of the window at the blue sky over the rooftops and thought of Nina.

Leigh and Paul were not awake yet. He made some coffee and did two hours' work on the new play with sharp concen-tration and lovely peace. Then he bathed, rigorously, found clothes from the clean pile in his room – put last night's in the dirty – and took his keys and wallet. It was still too early, she wouldn't be at the theatre yet. He couldn't go to her house. She was married. He laughed at that, standing alone in his room, laughing at the idea she was married. It wasn't real. She wasn't anybody's.

It was still only twelve o'clock. He thought he would try to do some more work but the morning had got away from him so he took a paperback from the shelf, shoved it in his jacket pocket and started out, opening the front door just as Leigh came out of the bedroom in one of Paul's shirts.

'Morning,' she said, croakily. 'Is there coffee?'

'No milk,' said Luke, who didn't take it but knew she did.

'Are you going to the shops?'

'If you like.'

He thundered down the stairs into the street. It was mild. It didn't feel like November, it felt earlier in the year.

He walked to the corner shop and bought milk, eggs, a newspaper and some sliced bread and chocolate and went back up to the flat. Leigh was lying on the sofa with her legs stretching out from beneath Paul's shirt and a cushion over her face.

'I hate wine,' she said. 'Why? Why?'

Luke put down the shopping, took the bar of Cadbury's from the bag, and went over to the sofa. He knelt and slit the wrapper with his thumb. Leigh turned her head beneath the cushion. He lifted the corner, gently, and broke off a square of chocolate.

'You smell of shaving,' she said, with her eyes closed.

She opened her mouth and he put a square of chocolate inside it. She put the cushion over her face again. He looked at her bare, long white legs, crossed at the ankle over the sofa arm and the shirt tails barely covering the top of her thighs.

Leigh held out her hand. He stopped looking at her legs and gave her some more chocolate. She took the cushion off her head and turned to look at him. When she woke she always had make-up smudged round her eyes like a 1920s film star and her lips were full – from sleeping or the dreams she'd had.

'So?' she said.

He was embarrassed and proud at the same time. 'It was good. Nina . . .' Saying her name out loud was strange, like giving everything away. 'That Nina Jacobs,' he said, 'she's a nice girl.'

Leigh knew what he meant. She always knew what he meant.

'That's one way of describing her,' she said. 'Married girl is another. Not that that would make any difference to you.'

Luke shrugged. Got up quickly. 'I'll put the kettle on,' he said, and did. 'See you later.'

And then he left.

Leigh sat up.

'See you later,' she said to the closed door, hugging her knees to her chest tightly for protection as Paul slept on in their bedroom.


Luke walked to the King's Road and along it, past the Chelsea mothers with their neatly dressed children and other people, long hair and platforms, hats, patterns, like a different species. He went to the top of Tite Street and stood about on the corner, scanning the faces that passed by, absurdly happy and thinking he might see Nina.

He sat on a bench in Sloane Square and watched the people going in and out of the tube, teenagers meeting and laughing by the *Standard* seller on the pavement, and the closed Royal Court, tattered posters, litter. Pigeons hopped and scrabbled about his feet, sidling up to a tramp on the next bench and pecking around his string-tied boots. A man in a pinstripe suit with a kipper tie came and sat nearby, taking sandwiches in Tupperware out of his briefcase then closing it to use as a table. The pigeons moved in on him and the tramp did, too, shuffling over to ask for change, reaching out his blackened hands, but the kipper-tie man turned away and pretended he was alone.

The Court was showing Arnold Wesker's *The Old Ones*. Luke had seen it three times, partly to further the argument with Jack Payne, Graft's director, whose voice in Luke's head, even in his absence, still fought its laboured corner. Jack had thought the

Court a soap manufacturer – called it that – a fairytale machine for a lazy society to pass cud through its seven stomachs, a funeral party for socialism. Even now he had gone, and Graft gone with him, Luke mentally fenced with Jack's absolutism, even now he was exasperated at being dictated to. He checked his watch. One o'clock. No matinée. She wouldn't even be out of bed yet.

Nina had woken very early, her stomach screwed up with emptiness and bile, coming immediately to consciousness as if she hadn't slept. When Tony got up he didn't go to his study but went out without acknowledging her, and when the house was quiet she sat up against the pillows. Mrs Wills came in at ten. Nina ran a bath, lying for a long time in the pine-scented bubbles, and let the telephone ring. It would be her mother. She had arrived early the night before and not spoken to Nina before she left. She would want to talk about the party. Nina didn't know what she might say to her, she had no face to present to the world. She lifted her wet legs and arms from beneath the water, shining and female, and examined them coldly. She washed her hair, dried it. She took a Valium. She dressed. The phone rang all morning, and Nina ignored it.

She slipped quietly out of the house at two and walked down to the Embankment, staring at the slow-moving brown river and wondering at the world she now inhabited. Then, earlier than she needed to, she went to the theatre. It was the only safe place.

Luke stood in the alleyway by the stage door remembering Leigh would come into the theatre too, not just Nina, and he didn't want her to see him waiting there. It had begun to feel like winter now as night came on, sharp and tinged with frost and smoke. The day had been a half-hour, a blink, a bright, clean, ready intake of breath for the moment she would arrive. If Tony Moore was with her he would go home — he could back out of sight easily — disappear. It was like a happy game, for all its importance.

The purring rumble of a black cab. The squeak of brakes and the *for hire* sign switched back on. The door opening. Nina.

She was alone. She paid the cab driver, then turned — and stopped when she saw him.

She was pale. Guarded. He didn't know if it meant guarded from him. Suddenly he felt scared — of her, or for her — scared of himself.

'Hello,' he said.

She didn't answer him, she just shook her head.

'Can we go somewhere?' He felt foolish. 'Can we talk or something?'

She began to walk — but not towards him, past him, looking down.

'Wait.' He put his hand on her arm, halting her, but withdrew it immediately. 'I'm sorry,' he said. 'Last night—' Then he stopped because if she didn't remember the same thing he did then there was nothing to say.

But then she looked up at him and he saw she was desolate. He had to keep himself from reaching out to hold her.

'I have to get inside,' she said. And she went past him to the stage door, rapping on it urgently.

He didn't follow her. It wasn't right to pursue somebody who was already hunted.

'Tomorrow?' he said as loss erased the gilded notions of his dreaming day.

She paused, as if alerted to the reality of him for the first time. And before she went inside she nodded.

Luke queued for a standby in the upper circle and sat in darkness as the prison doors closed. This time it wasn't Seston's captivity, or even his own, but only Nina's. The cold light came up on the stage. She entered, blind; she knelt, she bowed her head and Luke hurt with the need to free her. He sat in his seat with all the other strangers and watched her subjugation, her fight, and her defeat.

The rest of the week was the same. In the mornings he worked on the new play, staying as long as he could in the controllable, rigorous world inside his head, and then he would surrender, and go to the theatre and wait for Nina. She would get out of the taxi, acknowledge him, perhaps smile, and he found that each day he waited he could do it more quietly and was more passive, that he entered the held framework she imposed, as if that in itself was being with her.

————————

'You can't go wherever it is that you go today,' said Paul. 'We've got to meet John Wisdom in his office and then Lou Farthing.'
    'Where's the first one?'
    'Floral Street.'
    'All right.'
    They were eating eggs that Luke had fried at lunchtime in the kitchen at the flat. Leigh had finished and was washing up.
    'Will you bring the new play?' asked Paul.
    '*Diversion*? It's not done.'

'Can you talk about it, then? He'll want to know what you're doing.'

'Yeah. I can try.'

'This could be good.'

Luke nodded, head down, eating. 'Yeah.'

Leigh turned round, drying her hands on a tea towel. 'Do you care, Luke?' she said suddenly. 'If you sell your play?' Her voice was hard.

Luke looked at her. 'I haven't thought about it.'

'Well, why do you do it?' She was blazing, angry with him for some reason.

'Why do I do what? Write?' He was confused, surprised that Leigh, of all people, would ask him that.

'Yes, what's it *for*?'

'It's for – I just have to do it. I don't know. It's what I do.'

'Well, you're not a baby – you must have a plan.'

Paul turned around. 'What's up?'

'Nothing. I just think – Paul is doing everything, running around for months, trying to get something done for you, trying to get things together.'

'I know that,' said Luke. 'I know he is.'

'Well, aren't you *grateful*? Are you ambitious?'

'Ambitious?' The word didn't mean anything. He had hopes, and love, but not that.

'What is it that you want, Luke?' she pushed.

'Leigh . . .' said Paul.

*I want Nina*, thought Luke, and didn't say.

'Well?' said Leigh. 'Well?'

'I don't think about what might happen,' said Luke. 'I just write. It's all I can do. I try to do it well.' There was silence. 'I am grateful,' he said.

Paul looked away. 'Nah—'

'For God's sake! Just forget about it,' said Leigh, and left them alone.

Paul exchanged a *women* look with Luke.

'It's all right,' he said. 'You do your thing, I do mine.'

'Yeah. I know,' said Luke.

Paul got up to go after her. She had gone into their bedroom and started to make the bed, furiously.

'You know he spends every afternoon at the theatre,' she said, not looking round, 'trying to chat up Nina Jacobs? And then he stays and watches the bloody play most nights.'

'I didn't know that,' said Paul, watching her violently tucking in sheets. 'He's weird about girls. Does it matter?'

'I don't *mind* all the stupid girls.' Her voice was very harsh. 'I'm just so scared he's wrecking himself over her when he's worked so hard and you're trying to get his work seen and I hate it. We all used to be *different*,' she said, stopping and standing with her back to him, spiky. He went to her and put his arms round her from behind.

'It's all right,' he said, 'it's okay.'

She turned and buried her head in his shoulder. 'I'm sorry,' she said. 'I don't know why I'm being such a bitch.'

'You're not,' said Paul, 'you never are.' And he stroked her hair and her back, soothing her, resolute, and not asking himself the questions he already knew the answers to.


John Wisdom's office was up three shabby flights, the walls covered in posters and the floors and desk with piles of plays. He was a small, wrinkled man of fifty who smoked cigars and didn't empty his ashtrays. Paul waited in a coffee shop across the street while Luke went up alone.

Seeing *Paper Pieces* on the desk between them put him at a disadvantage and the chair he was in was half-broken so the swivel seat wobbled, adding to his insecurity. But John Wisdom had met a million writers and took Luke's nerves for granted. Most of them couldn't string a sentence together in conversation.

'How old are you, Luke?' he said immediately.

'Twenty-five.'

'You've had nothing produced yet?'

'No.'

'You were at Graft? I saw *Cartwright's Army* — one or two other things. Paul Driscoll was the artistic director there, Jack Payne — what about you?'

'I read. Bit of design. Helped out. I did some editing — with the writers. We all worked together.'

'George Myers hasn't had any more success since *Cartwright*. I've read his latest play. *Cartwright's Army* is the best by a very long chalk. Was that you?'

'No,' said Luke, 'it was all George. I didn't have that much to do with it — except defending it. I learned a lot at Graft. What works, you know. Me and Paul worked in rep for about four years before that. I read for The Majority when Layton Lewis was artistic director. Stage crew. Bit of everything. And small parts here and there.'

'An actor?'

'I'm not an actor, but it was helpful to put someone else's dialogue in my mouth—'

'Then?' John interrupted him.

'I mean I'm a terrible actor,' Luke went on, looking out of the window, round the room. 'I'm not an actor-writer. Not like Pinter, I mean really God-awful.' It had always amused him what a bad actor he had been. He knew he should stop talking. He fixed his eyes on John Wisdom's desk for focus. 'Then, after The Majority I worked with Tom Leeson as a reader, in Sheffield.'

'It's the only way to learn. Being at the sharp end.'

'Yes. And working.'

*Paper Pieces* sat between them, waiting its turn. Luke glanced at it. John Wisdom shoved his cigar in his mouth and picked up the manuscript. He flicked through the pages, squinting. Luke wanted to tell him not to touch it and began to bounce in his wobbly chair, biting his lip, hitching up his ankle, rubbing it.

'I fucking love this play,' said John, and set it on the desk, patting it. 'It's fucking marvellous. I woke up my wife laughing.'

'Good,' said Luke. But it wasn't enough. 'Why?' he said. 'Why do you like it, anyway? What is it you liked about it? I mean, did you laugh at them for being so blind or did you see Eric didn't want to be like he was?' He stopped himself.

John Wisdom stared at him.

'You know it better than I do. What do you want me to tell you? You can tell me something, though. You're twenty-five, Luke. It's your first play. Where are you from?'

Luke thought of Seston – and that Luke Last wasn't from there.

'What do you mean?'

'I mean, how did you do it? Where did it come from?'

'Well, it took a while, didn't it? And it's not my first. I've written a lot. It's the best so far. I don't like it that much any more. I'm writing another. *Pieces* isn't like a play, even, it's just long sketches and needs tying together but I never know how to do it. And it's dead derivative. Too much bloody Kafka or Stoppard or Buñuel flicks or something. I need to get under the bonnet, it's not finished.'

'Luke, I want to take it to Oxford, try not to talk me out of it.'

'All right,' said Luke, biting the side of his nail, 'and Archery will co-produce with Paul?'

John looked at him sharply. 'He and I talked about it.'

'Good. That's important,' said Luke. 'But the play needs work.'

'We'll have to get on with casting before the end of the month. What do you think it needs?'

Paul was on his third coffee when Luke came in; he was lit up and couldn't sit still, so they walked.

'Fuck,' said Luke. 'Fuck. Fuck. He wants to take *Pieces* to Oxford. He thinks we should triple cast. Partly for money, partly because the sections work best like that. I never saw it, but it's so obvious – they're all the same person!'

'Good idea.'

'He said he'd call you.'

'Good.'

They talked and walked, not seeing where they were going, just the future rolling out in front of them like the wide-open sea. They were nearly late for Lou Farthing and had to hurry back, pacing along Long Acre with Paul smoking and talking at speed and Luke even faster.

At Farthing's office they stopped and Luke said, 'Paul Driscoll Management, mate. *You bloody did it.* I hope you've still got the writing paper.' And Paul grinned at him.

'Jesus,' he said, and they hugged, unembarrassed, delighted with themselves, then broke apart and laughed, hitting one another's shoulders and getting in the way of the people trying to pass them.

'Shit,' said Luke. 'Shit. Oxford.'

'I knew it,' said Paul. 'You're a fucking genius,' and then, 'Now we can find you an agent. The recalcitrant bastards — they'll all want you now. And I'd better find another play, too. Most of the stuff I read is bollocks.'

Luke went into the hotel to meet Lou Farthing. Lou was in his seventies, had a secretary, a hand-made suit and ran on power. He was flattering and patronising and said he wanted to read Luke's new play when it was done. Luke told him he'd get Paul to send it and went away with his smile stuck on his face like a wild, untroubled inmate at Seston Asylum, delighted by the possibility his life had given him. He bought a postcard with a picture of the Queen on it for his mother and wrote his day out, all through — fast, in tiny writing — in the pub while he and Paul had a drink to celebrate. They parted on the street in the late afternoon.

'You not coming back, then?' said Paul, remembering what Leigh had said.

'No, I'm meeting someone,' said Luke.

'Well, be good. See you later.' And left him there.

This time, when Nina got out of her taxi — and when he was quite sure she was alone — he went to her and took both her arms, feeling the thinness of them under her coat.

'I think you're lovely,' he said, and he kissed her mouth.

The kiss was very short and just as he had known it would be. She pulled back and looked around, panicking.

'What are you doing!' she said. Then seeing his smile she laughed. 'What is it?'

They hurried past the stage door into a shadowed archway that smelled strongly of piss; fire-doors, over-spilling cardboard boxes.

'I want to see you; this is stupid,' said Luke.

She went into his arms as if it was what she always did. He folded himself around her and held her there. They stood in elemental joy with their feet in the filth and then she went into the theatre to work. That night he didn't watch the play because he didn't need to.

---

Chrissie Southey and Alexander Talbot were getting married at the Brompton Oratory that Sunday. The wedding was at eleven, then the party, just for close friends, was to begin at lunchtime at Alexander's house in the Boltons. His ex-wife had been a rich woman, an American heiress, and with her money and his film career he had kept the house after she had gone back to Los Angeles to stop drinking and live with her new lover. Alexander hadn't stopped drinking, he'd found Chrissie to drink with him instead.

Nina had promised to leave the party early and meet Luke. She couldn't tell him what time, only that she would be in a pub over the river in Battersea, where neither of them knew anyone, as soon as she could.

Tony and she got out of the taxi on the Brompton Road and went into the vast, crowded church, decked with waxy, hothouse flowers, photographers – invited and uninvited – mixing with the guests. The organ underscored the laughter with solemn discord.

Tony held Nina's hand tightly as they found their places. He had been busily generous towards her since the night of her birthday, and not touched her at all in bed or out of it since. Now he sensed something in her that alarmed him. She did not seem as unhappy as she had done. That pleased him — he didn't like her unhappiness — but there was a barrier to his observation of her heart. She had something on her mind that was not him; she gleamed with youth and secrecy.

'What fun,' he whispered in her ear, 'Chrissie Southey in a white dress. Whatever next?'

Nina smiled. 'She never had boyfriends at drama school,' she said. 'Not real ones.'

'Well, Alexander's been rogering her silly for two years.'

'It doesn't count if you're engaged,' said Nina, vaguely, looking around at their friends and the glowering artistry of the vaulted ceiling. Her chin was so delicate, her throat so fine and naked.

'Darling,' he said, 'can you forgive your silly husband?'

'For what?' she said, facing him. Her expression was unreadable. He felt a chill.

'Good,' he said. 'I hope you know you're the only important creature in my life.'

She did not answer and he felt panic so stifling that he had to swallow not to reveal it to her, bending down to fiddle with the laces on his narrow leather shoes.

Alexander Talbot, broad and smiling, stood before the altar, turning to wink at friends as he waited for the wedding to begin, his famously blue eyes blurred only slightly around their crinkled edges with drink and his fortieth year approaching.

'Here comes the bride,' sang Tony in an undertone as the organ surged. '*She's all dressed in white, drunk in a taxi, fell out the other side . . .*'

Nina ignored him.

Cars queued around the Boltons dropping people at the door. It had started to snow and nobody wanted to walk the last few yards and get their shoes wet so the party was slow to begin. Waitresses with trays of champagne shivered by the door, gas-fires roared inside in peace. Nina had hurried Tony along because she wanted to get it over with. She checked her watch. It was half past two. Chrissie and Alexander hadn't arrived yet, or changed into their party clothes. She drank two glasses of champagne and went to the bathroom upstairs to take a Valium because she was shaking with nerves and couldn't stand the thought of Tony noticing it. He was very alert because the party was full of people he wanted to cultivate. The house filled. Voices rose. Diana Martin was persuaded to sing, accompanied by the pianist on the baby grand. She sang Sondheim, holding her glass up to them all, a stage legend, charging the room with febrile charisma. Nina stopped on the landing to look at Alexander's film posters in their splendid parade along the snow-white walls.

Luke. Luke.

The piano and Diana Martin's cracked, trembling voice came up the stairs. *Don't you love farce? My fault, I fear.*

Nina knew too many people to leave while so many of them were sober. She would wait until Tony was absorbed in conversation and didn't seem to be wondering what she was up to.

*And where are the clowns — quick, send in the clowns.*

It was no good. The toasts. The canapés. She waited. She

waited. The snow stopped in the pitch-black night outside. She found Tony.

'I'm going home,' she said. 'I have a headache.'

'You never have headaches,' he said sharply.

'I've got one now.'

'Do whatever you want,' he snapped, and she turned and left. It was the first time she had not appeased him.

Running down the icy steps in her coat she felt delight. She caught a taxi on the Old Brompton Road.

'Battersea,' she said, 'Latchmere Road,' and slammed the door.

She ate three Polos to sweeten her breath and checked her face in her compact mirror, terrified of what she was doing and the reckless delight in it.

It was half past six. Luke had been there since three and was sure she wasn't coming. He had been watching the people at the bar and in the corner playing darts; all men, regulars. He would wait until last orders, whatever happened. And then Nina walked in — absurdly glamorous, incongruous gold and beige. She looked frightened. Saw him. He stood up. She came over.

They didn't kiss or touch. He was at a corner table and they both sat down — Nina backed into the corner and him next to her, half-turned from the room.

'Do you want to play some darts?' he said.

She didn't smile.

'I'm sorry. I couldn't get away.'

'How was it?'

'Pretty ghastly,' said Nina quickly. Her voice was constrained in her throat. 'I was at drama school with Chrissie. She's practically my oldest friend but I don't really know her at all.

Alexander and she met filming in France. She had a bit part and there was no air-conditioning for the extras so he let them into his trailer or onto his bus or something and probably slept with most of them and one of them was Chrissie. I'm so sorry I was late.'

'It's fine,' said Luke, studying her. 'It's all right. Do you want a drink?'

'I've had lots.'

She looked around the room self-consciously but the men at the bar weren't taking much notice of them. Luke put his hand on top of hers on the seat and she pulled away.

'What are we doing?' she said, rigidly.

'People do this all the time. Are you leaving him?' said Luke.

'*Tony?*' said Nina, in comical surprise. 'Did you just ask if I'm leaving him?'

Luke nodded. She was jittery but he felt calm. He was focused only on her.

'Do you love him?' he asked.

Again she was surprised, as if it wasn't his place to ask.

'I don't, I can't . . .' She looked down. 'Can we not talk about this?'

'Well, what is it that you want?' he said, frowning.

'What is it that *you* want?' she asked back, quick as a flash. There was a silence.

'I'm sorry,' he said evenly. 'I didn't mean to upset you.'

Neither of them spoke. There was only discomfort and the painful spoiling of delight.

'You didn't upset me,' she said. 'I think . . . I'm not used to —' She stopped, because she wasn't sure what it was she wasn't used to; Luke, the danger he presented, or the honesty.

He took a breath. Sat up straight.

'Right. Let's do it like this then: my name's Luke Kanowski. My father was a Polish fighter pilot and my mother is from France. I grew up in Lincolnshire. I went to grammar school and then worked for a while before starting to work in theatre. I've just sold my first play, which is why I came and kissed you yesterday, because I was – happy – and you didn't run away.'

She said, 'I didn't know you were a writer.'

'Well, I work for the council part time,' he told her, not wanting to misrepresent himself. 'And I live with my friend Paul and his girlfriend. I want to just write but I'm not sure how it will all turn out.'

He let out a short laugh at this easy understatement of his shrouded future, but Nina didn't see the joke.

'What do you do for the council?' she asked politely.

'I'm a dustman.'

At that, Nina yelped with laughter. There was a brief pause and she began to giggle.

'Are you really?' she said.

He nodded, smiling at her. All he could think was how sweet she was when she giggled.

'Your turn,' he said.

'Leigh isn't your girlfriend, then?'

'Leigh? No. Why? I've told you.'

Nina didn't say anything else.

'Go on,' said Luke. 'Who are you?'

'Oh. Yes. My name is Nina Jacobs. I went to LAMDA and until I was married I lived with my mother – who's French, too. My first professional job was Worthing Rep. I got my Equity Card in TIE in Cardiff during my second summer at drama school.'

'That's it?'

'I'm sorry, I'm dull.'

'No. You're not dull.'

And then, just then, in that second, for no reason at all – except perhaps his honest reassurance – the mood shifted. They looked at one another and didn't notice anything else. It felt as if they had moved closer but neither was aware of having done so. They spoke more quietly, taking in one another's features closely, intent with unspoken need.

'What's your play about?' she murmured.

'Which one?'

'The one you've just sold.'

'It's about people being stupid to each other and telling lies.'

'Adultery lies?'

'Among others.'

'Are you a liar, then?' she asked, lightly.

Luke thought about it.

'Only to myself,' he answered.

Nina hadn't had any expectation he would answer truthfully.

'Don't you lie to yourself?' asked Luke, not noticing her shock. 'How else are you married to that man if you don't love him?'

Nina didn't move. They were very close, held in stillness.

'Or *do* you love him?'

She couldn't answer, broken into by his directness. She wanted him to kiss her. Wanted him to kiss her and make love to her, and he knew. He put his hand lightly to the back of her head and, very carefully – did.

They kissed as if they were alone – softly – and then harder.

Small, close breath and secret, just-open mouths — the inti-mate, quick heat of need. She leaned back into the corner, Luke's body shielded her from the humorous glances of the men at the bar and she forgot about them. Hidden, she put her hands inside his coat and felt his blood-warmth. They kept on kissing. She wanted him so badly she couldn't keep herself still and so she pushed him away.

'Stop it.'

They both tried to breathe steadily. He smiled at her and at what they would be. She wanted him too much to smile, and looked away from him. He took her hand and there was no other thought in either of their heads.

'We have to get out of here,' he said. 'Come to—' He thought of Paul and Leigh. 'Where can we go?'

'I have to go home,' she whispered, not meaning it.

'A hotel. Let's go to a hotel.'

'We can't.'

'I want you.'

Hearing it made her hurt. Jolts that went through her so she couldn't think.

'God, please don't,' she said.

He hooked his finger underneath the thin gold chain around her neck. The minute touching of the chain against her skin, the feeling of his hand so close to her —

'When?' he said.

'Tomorrow. Think of something. Phone me.'

And then the taxi back, the scribbled numbers on torn scraps in biro, her body pressed against him in the dark. He didn't dare do what he would have with another girl in another taxi. He wanted to make her come and to know how she felt to him when she did, but he couldn't. With other girls he could feel the rush of their release and then let them go free and forget. He couldn't bear to do that to Nina and then leave her weak and alone and not be able to take her home with him.

———————

Tony was in his study when the phone rang the next day at nine o'clock. When he picked it up there was silence and then whoever had called put the phone down. He listened to the dialling tone for a second and then there was another click, the extension going down in the bedroom. He had a hangover, and was drinking black coffee and cleaning his nails with an orange stick, an Alka-Seltzer fizzing in a glass beside the telephone. Half an hour later the phone rang again and when he picked it up the same thing happened. The next time it rang, at ten, it was Marianne and although Nina had answered it, he listened to their *hellos* before replacing the receiver. An hour later, Nina left.

She put her head around the door and said, 'Just popping out.' She hadn't bathed.

Nina went to the pay phone at the river end of the street and dialled Luke's number. Her hands were shaking. A woman answered. Nina recognised Leigh's voice.

'Hello,' she said. 'May I speak to Luke, please?'

There was a pause.

'Hold on,' said Leigh. Nina couldn't tell if she had recognised her or not. She swallowed, nervous, dry mouthed. She heard, 'Luke . . .' and footsteps, and then Luke, his voice familiar, close, inside her head as if they hadn't slept apart.

'Is that you?'

'Yes. Tony picked up the phone before. I'm in a phone box.'

'Sorry. Can we meet?'

'I — my mother is out. She'll be out today from — I don't know — twelve. She won't come back until later. I'll meet you at her flat at one.'

The pips went and she shoved in another 2p.

'Hello?' she said.

'Yes. Where is it?'

She gave the address. Marianne, on Nina and Tony's money, had moved to a serviced one-bedroom flat off Bayswater, which she insisted on calling *the wrong side of the park.*

'I'll be there. *One?*'

'One. But wait until you see me. Don't ring the bell.'

'I won't. I'll wait for you.'

Neither of them could say goodbye. Silence. The hiss of the phone line.

'I'll see you later then,' she said.

'Yes.' He put down the phone.

Nina went and bought some cigarettes and walked back to the house. As she went up the stairs she looked at the closed door of Tony's study, clutching the solid packet of fresh cigarettes, preparing her alibi, but he didn't come out.

She bathed and dressed. Tony was still in his study. She went to the door and knocked.

'Darling?' she said. 'I'm just off shopping with Chrissie.' She knew she shouldn't elaborate but she couldn't help it. 'She needs honeymoon things — they're off to the Bahamas on Boxing Day.'

Silence.

'I know,' he said, unseen. Nothing else.


She went to Peter Jones and bought a sheet and towel from

the solid middle-aged ladies on the ground floor, then she took a taxi to her mother's. She had a key. She passed the porter on the door clutching the Peter Jones bag, feeling sure he would know what was inside and why she was there. She took the caged lift to the third floor.

'Mummy?' She knocked. Silence.

Marianne had said she was lunching with friends in Knightsbridge and then she had a doctor's appointment. They were safe, but Nina felt far from it, desperate with anxiety. She knocked again and then let herself into the flat. The sitting room was at the front with the kitchen and bathroom between it and the bedroom, down a short corridor at the back. The thick carpets were pale green, freshly hoovered, and there were flowers in a vase on the window ledge that boxed in the radiator along the curved 1930s window that ran the length of the room. Nina slipped off her shoes and quickly went to look out. She could see Luke standing on the street corner in his coat, nervous even from a distance. She ripped the sheet from its tissue paper, threw the towel into the bathroom, and ran back into the bedroom. She hauled the bedclothes from the bed and scrambled over the mattress on all fours, tucking in the sheet, hair messing over her face, sweating with haste. She stood up. Looked around. Shoved the tissue paper back into the bag and pushed it under the dressing table with her foot. The telephone rang – so loud it shocked her into breathlessness. She almost answered it, let it ring, and as she did so, realised with a quietness that crept over her in smooth delight, that the telephone was ringing in an empty flat. She wasn't really there. Nobody knew she was there.

She walked over to the window, opened it and leaned out into the wintry day. Luke looked up immediately and she waved. He crossed the road to her, dodging the traffic.

They didn't speak. He came in, and after glancing around for a moment, moving close almost without looking at her, he kissed her. Then there was no restraint, no uncertainty, just pushing past clothes, crushing, hurting and gentle. He was inside her before they were properly undressed; blind force, helpless.

Then they undressed. They stayed in bed all afternoon until they were sore and dizzy from each other, slick with sex and sweat. The room became darker. They didn't put on the light, or stop. He couldn't stay out of her, she couldn't hold him close enough.

'What will we do?' he asked, when she was quiet in his arms.

She hid her face. 'I don't know.'

'It can't stay like this.'

'I'm married.'

'Not for long.'

She laughed. 'You're so—' She stopped.

'I'm so what?'

'Sure. Are you really?'

'Aren't you?' he asked her.

She looked up at him, their faces inches away.

'I don't know why you like me,' she said. 'And I'm – I'm just . . .' She summoned her courage. 'I'm just so frightened.'

He didn't answer that, but kissed her temple and her forehead, and held her more tightly. He thought of what he had been like with other girls and that of course she couldn't know she could be sure of him.

'It's all right,' he said, kissing her. 'I'll wait for you.'

They stayed there, as long as they could, for as long as they felt safe and apart from the world, and then they took turns to wash and put everything back as it was, and laughed over her going to Peter Jones to buy an adultery sheet, and her fear.

They caught a taxi to the theatre and Nina dropped the crumpled worn-out sheet into a rubbish bin in the street.

They kissed goodbye in the shadow of the alleyway where they had kissed the first time.

'I can't stand it,' she said, and he shook his head and crushed his cheek against hers and his mouth into her neck, holding her tightly, because he couldn't either and thought he would cry. Then she went inside.


For three weeks Marianne had no other lunches to go to, no reliably lengthy shopping outings to send her from her house. Tony didn't leave London and wasn't planning to. No shows in the provinces, just home all day. Nina and Luke met for snatched, discomfiting moments – a frustrating hour near the theatre, coffee shops and pubs, and Archery began casting *Paper Pieces*.

They were auditioning the actors in the American Church on Tottenham Court Road. John Wisdom had hired a director called Richard Scott-Mathieson, of daunting reputation. It was already the end of November and the play was set to go into rehearsal at the beginning of January. Tense, hasty meetings with the designer, the producers, rewrites, readings. Luke was grateful to be given any place in the making of this brave new world. He had lived his life with need and hunger driving him to unknown consummation – the seeking of his heart's home – but nothing touched this. He fixed the play as well as he could and watched its first tentative realisation, scared of everything until Nina's voice made him forget everything but her. They spoke on the phone. She in the phone box at the end of her road, Luke sitting against the door in his room because the wire would only stretch that far. They made plans and she had to break them and he railed against what felt to him the false constriction of her marriage. He was halfway mad. It was a delicious disorder.

Leigh was getting ready to leave the theatre after the evening performance when Nina came and found her. It was after eleven. The actors usually left long before the crew; off stage and out of costume in ten minutes flat, and Leigh was often the last to go. Now Nina stood in the doorway to Leigh's windowless office and smiled with timid conspiracy.

'You live with Luke, don't you?' she asked.

'Yes.' Leigh was unwilling to be drawn.

'Would you give him this?' Nina held out an envelope, sealed, with no writing on it.

Leigh took it, feeling the weight of the paper inside. She saw the light in Nina's eyes, heard it in her voice as she said, 'Thank you, Leigh. I hope you don't mind?' She had never looked so beautiful, or perhaps she had never looked beautiful at all until now, and suddenly Leigh felt scared for her, trusting all her fragility to Luke's thoughtless appetite. She shook her head and could not answer.

'Goodnight,' Nina said, gave her a smile like Christmas morning, and left her.

When she got home the flat was dark. She took off her coat and Nina's envelope from its pocket and went to Luke's door.

She bent, slid it underneath and stood to go — but he opened the door, dressed, holding it.

'Don't you ever sleep?' she said.

'Sometimes,' he said. 'What's this?'

'Nina gave it to me for you,' said Leigh, trying not to watch his reaction as he took it. He smiled at her. She wished it didn't hurt her — Paul was sleeping in their bedroom, just there, next door.

'Night,' she said.

'Is it all right?' asked Luke, generous in his happiness.

'What?'

He gestured the letter. 'If we do this.'

'Of course. If you like.'

He leaned forward and pressed his mouth to her temple.

'Night.' He closed the door.

It had been so unexpected.

Leigh undressed quietly in the dark bedroom, hoping not to wake Paul as she slipped under the covers and lay down next to him, but he reached out for her.

'Hi,' he said, sleepy and pleased.

He pulled her into his arms.

'I'm so tired,' she said, and waited for him to go back to sleep, unwanted tears slowly sliding from beneath her closed lids.

The next morning there was an envelope from Luke on top of her bag, waiting. She took it to Nina's dressing room just after they called the half, and knocked.

'Yes!'

Nina was at the mirror, which was stuck all over with telegrams and postcards, some flowers dying in a vase on the cracked ledge underneath it and her costume hanging nearby on a metal rail. Leigh held out the envelope. Nina took it, delight coming off her like heat.

Leigh indicated the dead flowers. 'I'll take these for you, shall I?'

'Thanks.' Nina was bent over the envelope.

Leigh picked up the vase and turned to go.

'Oh, Leigh . . .'

Leigh turned.

'I've asked – Luke –' she faltered over the name, 'if he'll come to my house on Sunday.'

Leigh was speechless. Nina had invited Luke to go to her house where, presumably, her husband would be. She couldn't decide if she was desperate or corrupt; she had shown no signs of being either before she had met him.

'I would ask you and . . . ?'

'Paul.'

'Sorry, Paul. But Tony only wants people who are more—' She stopped, corrected herself. 'It might look strange, if you all come.'

'Just Luke, then?' said Leigh, coolly.

'Well, Tony likes – I mean, Luke is a writer, isn't he?' asked Nina.

It wasn't a rhetorical question, she didn't seem sure if he was or not. Leigh wondered whether they had talked at all or if Luke just fucked her, or if she had bothered to ask Luke anything about himself, or just fucked him.

'Yes, Luke is a writer,' she said, 'and we had a company that did quite well. And Paul – my boyfriend – is working with Archery producing Luke's first play, now, actually. In Oxford.'

Nina looked as if Leigh had slapped her.

'Yes,' she said quietly, 'he told me.'

'Right,' said Leigh brightly, 'but he does also work as a dustman for money. Did he mention that?'

'Yes,' said Nina again, shrinking, so that Leigh took no pleasure in making her uncomfortable.

'I hope you're not offended,' she almost whispered. 'It's just if I don't see him on Sunday I won't see him until after Christmas.'

It was as if this catastrophe explained everything, excused anything. Leigh wondered if Nina had any idea how to manage herself, if she had forgotten completely what was normal behaviour because of Luke. Because of him.

'But I'm sorry not to ask you,' Nina said again. 'And you won't say anything to anybody about us?'

'Why would I?'

'Promise?'

'Of course.'

'Thank you,' said Nina. And she smiled like the sun coming out. 'Thank you.'

Leigh left the dressing room holding the vase of dead flowers. She wasn't sure just what had happened, but she knew she had been beaten.

When she got home she scrawled a message on a piece of paper torn from her notebook and pushed it under Luke's door – *No More Letters Please*.

---

They were hemmed in by impossibility.

Sunday, 22 December. Then Monday's show. Then two days of Christmas and back to work. Luke was leaving London for Oxford to start rehearsals before New Year.

This desperate act of inviting him to her house — Nina sat at her dressing table on Sunday night, trying to keep calm.

He would be there and they wouldn't be able to touch. But she would see him.

She opened the drawer, took a Valium from the packet and swallowed it without a drink. She spat into the block of mascara in the narrow tin and rubbed the brush into it. Layering on the black, she wondered where he was. If he'd left his house yet. How long it would be until he arrived. Voices down in the street. Tony's feet on the stair . . .

'Darling? Come down.'

'I'm on my way.'

The evening was rowdier than usual. Tony played Christmas carols on the piano, fitting dirty words into them. Only their closer friends were there: Eleanor Scott, Willy Lansbury — people Tony called the widows and orphans who were free every Sunday and seldom away. It wasn't anyone important.

Nina sat on the sofa pretending languor, but imagining Luke walking in hit her like sickening stage-fright. And she must pretend not to know him. She shocked herself. It was mad. She couldn't imagine it, not really, only a dream-version, of him coming into the house and telling everything, striding up the stairs and confronting Tony with the bare-brave truth of it, and taking her hand. Taking her away.

But he didn't come.

It was after nine and he still hadn't. The gas-log fire made the room stifling, burning all the air away. He wasn't coming. He didn't love her. She got up and went to the window, forgetting what she looked like, not caring. She held her hands up to the sides of her face, trying to see down into the street. She couldn't see much — just the reflected room, the vague houses opposite and the tops of bare trees against an orange sky. There was a shout of laughter behind her at something Tony had said. She turned back, heat prickling beneath her dress.

Eleanor was curled in the wicker chair like an elf. She was a dancer and now, recently, a mother, and missing Broadway. She would never go back, everyone knew but her.

'Nina,' she said, smiling up at her, 'I expect you're dying for us to leave.'

'Don't be silly, you and John have to stay. It's Christmas,' said Nina and left the room.

They mustn't go; Luke hadn't come yet. She went across the landing to the window. She felt tears, painful – he wasn't going to come. She was making a fool of herself. He had loved her in a clever play and now it was fading. She wasn't good enough to keep him. She should have known. She would call him. She could call from the kitchen——

'Nina?'

Tony was on the landing, the people behind him oblivious to the two of them. He walked to her, pale and bright-eyed with chemical sharpness. Nina had the feeling he knew everything – that even before she knew it, he knew it. She kept her face blank.

'Enjoying yourself?' he asked, looking into her eyes.

'It's so hot,' said Nina. 'I was going to get ice.'

'Let's open the window,' said Tony. He unlatched the sash and lifted it. The cold wind blew in. He touched her shoulders and turned her to it. 'Better?'

Outside was the free night. She pretended he wasn't observing her. The hard air went straight through her clothes to her skin. She shivered. Tony took her wrist with the thumb and forefinger of one hand and ran the fingertips of the other down her chest then lightly across her nipples.

'Don't do that,' she said. She stepped back quickly and slipped her wrist from his grasp. She closed the window.

'It wasn't that bad,' she said. 'I'm freezing now.'

She left him and went back into the sitting room, holding her arms up across her breasts. She went straight over to the drinks cabinet and, with her back to her guests, sloshed vodka into a glass and knocked it back as though it would clean her out.

Luke, waiting on the pavement, kept well out of the glow of the street light. They had arranged that he would just ring the bell but she had said not to mention her name – just pretend an apparent taking-up of the open-house Tony was known for. But the phoniness grated. He had been standing in the cold for an hour and a half, arguing with himself.

He walked up and down, leaned a foot against the wall, shook his head, fought the rushing of his blood at the thought of her nearby, trying to drag reason from the dangerous state of himself. Normally you'd at least go along with a friend. It would look as if he was after a job. He might be a burglar; hitting the whisky and slipping ashtrays into his pockets. There was no professional reason Tony Moore would be interested in anything about him. He might even turn him out. To be taken down in front of Nina would be humiliating. He wasn't proud but – that. *Paper Pieces* hadn't even opened yet. It could fall through. Plays folded all the time without ever seeing a first night.

He watched the lighted windows of the house, locked out like a stray cat. Sniffing round her. Unentitled. Undesirable.

Poor. He didn't care about that – he didn't care about Tony Moore or his acolytes or backers or whoever it was that hung out there, but he couldn't walk in and stare at Nina all night and pretend he wasn't, hold out a begging bowl to that great luminary of West End theatre the producer of *Wot, Not Married*?! – he ignored the fact he was also responsible for *In Custody*.

There she was.

Luke watched as she stood in the first-floor window, looking out. Looking for him. She was almost silhouetted, impossibly slight. She turned her back to him.

He would not walk into her house and lie to her husband in a room full of strangers. And not be able to touch her. It wasn't right.


Three o'clock in the morning. Nina lay wide awake next to Tony. She couldn't tell if he was sleeping. She slipped out of bed, not daring to breathe, and tiptoed from the room. The telephone rang in the flat like a fire alarm in the silence. Luke sprang up to answer and reached it just as Paul opened his door – shut it again.

She was whispering. She sounded as if she had been, or was, crying.

'Where were you?' she said.

'I couldn't do it.'

'I'm in the kitchen. He's in bed . . .' He heard her breath shudder.

'I'm sorry. I just couldn't.'

'Never mind.'

'Never mind?' he said. She didn't answer. 'Nina, it was all wrong. Are you all right?'

There was a silence, then, 'I can't stand it here,' she whispered. 'I hate it here.'

'Well, leave. Whenever you want. Tomorrow. Now.'

'Don't be silly.'

'Why is it silly?'

She didn't answer.

'You don't know me,' he said. 'I can – care for you. You'll see.'

He heard himself make promises he had never thought of before, commitment coming to him fully formed, a sureness he had never felt.

'Nina?'

'It's not that,' she said.

'What, then?'

'He—' She stopped. He wasn't sure if she'd said something.

'What? What did you say?'

'Nothing. I can't talk. I have to go,' she said.

'No. Don't go—' There. Now he was desperate.

'But when shall I see you?' she said, and it felt like a reward.

He felt weak. He sat down on the floor, getting his breath.

'Luke,' she said, urgently, 'come to the theatre at six thirty. Come back – I'll be there.'

And Luke lay down on the floor in the dark with the phone pressed to his ear and loved her.

'Are you mad?' he said quietly. 'What could we do in half an hour?'

\*

Nina put down the phone. Upstairs in their bedroom Tony drowsily heard the *ting* at his bedside as the extension went down and he opened his eyes.

The next evening Nina went in to the theatre early, passed Leigh in the corridor with a smile and went to her dressing room. She waited, standing, facing the door.

The moments passed. Her heart beat fast. His knock, and quietly, 'Nina?'

'Yes.'

He opened the door, came in. 'Nice,' he said at this new place for them to be in.

She was disorientated by the sight of him, couldn't move.

He took off his coat and laid it down on the floor, took the cloth that covered her broken armchair, a shawl, a dressing gown. They lay down on the hard floor just covered, without a word, and he made love to her. He pushed up her skirt, pulled her underwear to the side and went hard into her, no waiting. She wrapped her arms around him tightly, his cheek pressed against hers, her lips next to his ear. She pushed up to meet him as he went deeper. They stayed like that, holding the deepest, longest moment still, as if they could stop time passing, breathing softly. Then when he moved in her again she whispered to him and her voice was in his ear as he came. He went down on her almost before he'd finished. The taste of her pleasure, holding her hands.

They lay quietly together and trembling, knowing time was taking them away from one other. Unwillingness. The increasing sensation of loss. She kissed his neck delicately; closer, close, privileged and soft.

'Why does it feel so perfect?' she said.

'I don't know. I don't know why it does.'

Then the strange clumsiness of cleaning up with tissues, getting dressed in the hazy disoriented fall from height; slipping reluctantly into the chill of separation.

By the still-closed door she hid inside his arms and he said, 'Be careful. Be clever. Don't feel sad about anything. I won't really be gone. I'll write to you.'

'Do you write poems?'

'I can try it if you want. But you're prose. And I won't be able to match you.'

'Just send me postcards then.'

And at that Luke felt the collision of his worlds, like the unstoppable glide of the planets' rule.

'Just one line, so I know you're there,' she said. It was as if she knew his past and secrets, knew them all. 'Every day, one line. What would it be?'

'I love you,' he said, automatically.

*Good evening, ladies and gents, this is your half-hour call*, said the speaker above their heads. *Thirty minutes to curtain up. Thank you.*

They tried to smile. He should leave.

'What will your Christmas be like?' he asked, not letting her go.

'We'll visit my aunt. Just drinks – deadly.'

'Does . . .' he couldn't say Tony's name 'he have family?'

She shrugged. 'He's a closed book. We'll have lunch out – widows and orphans.'

'You won't let him touch you?'

'I'll try not to.'

'Please.'

'I don't know what will happen. There's nothing I can do.'

Luke was amazed at his flat-out sickened jealousy. And how much it hurt.

'You?' she said, not seeing what she did to him.

'Me what?'

'Your Christmas.'

'I go home,' said Luke flatly.

'That's nice.'

*Nice.* He didn't answer.

Footsteps outside. Voices. He had to go. He held her face. He kissed her forehead. He tried to take in all of her but each second made it worse and he couldn't.

'Goodbye,' she said.

'Goodbye.'

'Goodbye.'

———————

Luke took the two trains to Seston on Christmas Eve morning. He took food with him because there would be nothing open, feeling like a strange, unimaginative Father Christmas with a holdall full of raw meat and vegetables. He brought light bulbs with him too this year, because his father let them go out one by one, and when Luke had been there last Christmas the house was all but unlit. He hauled the bag onto the train at King's Cross and off again at Lincoln. By the time he was on the small train to Seston his life in London had drawn back into shadow.

Entering the familiar, alien house he paused, gauging the atmosphere. The year before, his father had forgotten what day it was and they had cleaned the kitchen together; mould on the plates, stacks of chip paper, empty bottles, squalor that had disturbed even Luke who thought he had long since stopped being shocked by his father's incapacity. But this year there was no need for the light bulbs, the lights worked, and Tomasz had put tinsel along the mantelpiece in the kitchen, even though the fireplace contained only the boiler. Luke smiled at the pathos, holding his father in a firm embrace, as if he could transfer his strength to him, and the fat red tinsel shone, looped against the neglected wall. Tomasz, in his sixties, was still a big man, but Luke was taller and each year stronger in comparison as his father's body shrunk onto his bones.

Luke fried pork chops for their tea, flashing fat flames from the pan, and kept a galloping monologue going, wanting to talk about Nina but fearing what this place would do to her name if she was spoken of here; his father at the table with his bottle and the dented bins in the yard by the outside toilet. Nina. Her fragile name would diminish and fade, or he would find the house even more stupidly disastrous than it was already.

'How's my mother? Have you seen her?' he asked, knowing his father had not.

He always asked because it was important Tomasz knew that it would be the right thing to do to see her.

'We'll walk there in the morning, Dad. We should leave at eleven,' he said.

There wasn't a bus to the hospital on Christmas Day; it was a four-mile annual pilgrimage they made on foot.

He managed to ignore his father even while talking to him, just as he had done in childhood, and when he went to bed he stood in his room, alone at last, and thought doggedly, *Tonight, tomorrow night, and away again.*

Each year it was the same, but this one made both better and worse, because of Nina and *Paper Pieces*. He said his rosary, thanked Leigh for it as he always did – without even noticing – Leigh and the God he didn't believe in at all, and then he worked on *Diversion* until he fell asleep; small notes, comforting himself with minutiae. The bed had been too small for him as long as he could remember. He went onto his side to fit into it, curved around an imaginary Nina to keep her safe, and closed his eyes.

Leigh's mother had come from New York for Christmas and was staying in a friend's flat in Knightsbridge. On Christmas Eve she and Leigh wandered around Harrods – the cashmere, the scent, the book department.

Erica was a long-legged woman with glossy black hair and a matt, highly coloured complexion, Leigh's bone structure but rail-thin. She was a privileged New Yorker who had met Leigh's father at the Sorbonne. He was a post-graduate European historian, who would teach and planned to publish; he would not leave London again. Erica was absorbed into the exotica of North London's liberal elite until two children later, endangered to the soul by her husband's various blinkered infidelities, she left him. *Your father was a progressive socialist who wanted his wife barefoot and pregnant in the kitchen,* she would say. Leigh saw him only rarely. As a little girl she had craved his attention but her overriding memories were of his closed study door, awareness of the force of his intellect, its dominance in the house. She was fourteen and her brother seventeen when her parents separated and they moved into a flat on Prince of Wales Drive, the furthest point in Erica's London from Hampstead. It was Leigh – her brother having fled to university – who listened to her mother crying in the next bedroom, or playing records at two o'clock in the morning; who lived with her burning supper or forgetting to buy any at all, slamming the front door as she went out into her erratic newborn life; the loneliness and fresh experimentation of her solitude. Leigh went to Sheffield to university and her mother, liberated further, moved to Manhattan – and into therapy. She acquired a degree in Psychology and a zealot's passion for women's liberation. Leigh registered Erica's triumphs proudly and chose not to see her departure as another infidelity in the succession that had made up her life. She had never visited her mother in New York, Erica preferring to spend her money coming to see her daughter and catch up with old friends.

They were standing in the book department among the Christmas decorations.

'And Paul?' Erica asked her daughter, staring eagle-eyed from the soap-box standpoint of her self-realisation. 'You omit him from your letters.' She turned pages, drifting through Brancusi, Kandinsky . . .

'Do I?' said Leigh.

'Does he oppress you?'

'Don't be silly.'

'And the other one?'

'Luke.'

'Luke . . . ?'

'Kanowski.'

'Is he Jewish?' Her mother's sophistication did not stretch to neglecting this question about every man Leigh associated with.

'No.'

'My daughter – keeping house for two men. Are you writing?'

'Erica, I don't keep house. Luke does nearly all the cooking. And he's the writer. He—'

She saw Luke in her mind; preoccupation, conversation, working at the typewriter in the corner; frying fish for dinner; breakfast when they were up late. The sound of the door as he left for work at four. Came in at seven. His footsteps in the hall. His restless movement, laughing.

'Beware the worship of the great male brain,' said her mother.

'Shut up.'

'So *are* you writing?'

'Not just now.'

'When did you stop?'

'Ages ago. I work.'

'Wasted talent.'

'I'm not a writer.'

'That's what all the writers say. Except your father. Honey, you know I'm proud of you, but how many men do your job? You're a glorified maid.'

Leigh thought of all the cups of tea she made for people at the Duke of York's, changing Nina's dead flowers. 'Come and see *In Custody*,' she said.

'If it's any good they should bring it over.'

'It's too political for Broadway.'

'No pinko subsidies to pay for it,' said Erica, with heavy irony; she considered herself a virtual communist. She turned to Leigh beneath the bright shop-lights, examining her face.

Leigh shrank from the scrutiny. 'Can we get out of here?' she said. 'You know I hate shopping.'

'I shouldn't get a gift for Paul's mother? What kind of a woman is she? Christmas. My *God*. Are they religious?'

'Of course not, they're English.'

They trailed past gold bottles of scent and diamonds behind glass.

'I don't know how you stand this city,' said Erica, and they went to the Food Hall with all the other tourists, where Erica bought marrons glacés, a ten-year-old port and a gift basket of marzipan fruits.


On Christmas morning Paul and Leigh drove Janis the Beetle into Knightsbridge to collect Erica from the borrowed flat. Leigh got into the back to let her mother have the passenger seat and Paul drove because he couldn't fit in the back as easily – although, Leigh thought, Luke did it all the time. Looking at the back of her mother and Paul's heads, Leigh had the uncomfortable sensation she was watching her older self. It was easy to imagine. Here they were, in their forties, driving to his parents on Christmas Day. She looked out of the window, preferring deserted pavements to visions of the future. As they got out of the car in Stoke Newington, Paul turned to her.

'What's up?'

Erica was already striding towards the door, cape swinging.

'Christmas,' said Leigh, avoiding his eyes. 'Let's go in.'

Paul's family house was a modernist beginning; a Victorian terraced house knocked through to an engine shed next door and separated from the railway by twenty feet of brambles. It had been an ongoing project for twenty years. Christmas Day was chaotic – trestle tables that wobbled, all the food ready at different times. Paul's brother and his wife had two little girls and his younger brother had brought friends along. Paul fitted into the cranky family machine with unquestioning solidity, and Leigh and Erica were welcomed by his parents and then largely ignored.

'This is a zoo,' said Erica to Leigh, not very quietly. 'You know, I *like* these people.'

In Tite Street, Tony and Nina dressed up and went forth. Nina tried to shut Luke from her mind and play her part. Christmas drinks with friends for an hour in the morning and more friends for an hour before lunch. At two o'clock it was widows and orphans at the Dorchester; white tablecloths and obsequious waiters among the old ladies. Nina drank a lot. She gave up trying not to think of Luke. She surrendered. But telling herself she would see him soon, sometime, didn't help her sorrow. It didn't stop the longing for him. She wanted to talk about him, recklessly, caring less and less what might happen if she did, but something stopped her. His heart, she thought, was too good for the company.

Lunch was a long, many-coursed, drawn-out affair. Wines and brandies of every type and colour were passed around the table, spillages and stains marking the damask, layer on layer of debris. The ten of them, mismatched family-less acquaintances, grew louder and wilder as Christmas night fell outside.

'We're scaring the wildlife,' said Tony, glancing around at their fellow diners.

Nina felt his hand under the table on her thigh. He didn't know that Luke had been there too, and more recently than he had. She wanted to laugh in his face.

There were several different Christmas lunches at Seston Asylum depending on which wing and which ward the patients and staff were in. Hélène, Luke and Tomasz were at the best and most public, the one Dr Herrick, the other consultants and even Seston's mayor would occasionally visit and praise. All twenty patients and their assorted, strained families were at table, looking their smartest, while the catering staff served them their special meal: sprouts sticking in a green mush to the bottoms of the brown and blue pottery bowls, roast potatoes that were leathery and evenly shaped, grey meat. Luke always leapt up and down to help because it was easier to be active than to be present – better than to feel, absorb, hurt – far, far better to have a job to do. Each of the other six years since leaving home he had found a nurse to flirt with – or more than flirt – but he didn't crave that particular anaesthetic now. The habitual medication of desire had dissolved into the air like ether. He had Nina at his shoulder, a different kind of spirit. The thought of her did not numb him but brought his too-sharp awareness of his parents' tragedy out into the glare.

Tomasz sat next to Hélène but rarely looked at her. She behaved herself immaculately, as if her outward appearance didn't condemn her before she moved a muscle. She had aged. No residual gleam of prettiness relieved her face of its situation. Luke saw how she would glance at her husband occasionally as if he had the power to transform her – there had been years he hadn't even been sure she recognised him. This year she was lucid. It was worse. She had the look of someone in unrelenting pain who would writhe or scream but knowing she could not escape, was quiet. His father had a way of staring into the middle foreground that was specifically his. He took his world with him like a carapace. He might have been anywhere. He did not partake. Luke, in perfunctory habit, talked to his mother as well as he could, told her things that had happened, reminded her of things he had said before, but as the hours scraped by, all the time his anger built against his father. He hadn't felt such outrage for a long time; growing up he had learned not to waste himself on it. It frightened him, dragging him back into his childhood.

His mother took him to her room to show him the postcards he had sent, as she always did, all in rubber bands, stacked in her cupboard and made her repeated reassurances that he was not to worry about her. They held hands as they returned to the dining room. He felt older than she, every year more separate and relieved to be. He pulled out her chair for her and they sat down again. Tomasz, heavy with self-obsession, bitter, did not even acknowledge their return.

After the farce that was pulling the crackers and before the travesty of the pudding ritual, Luke left the table again alone and stood in the blessedly empty staff toilets breathing his distress into submission. He thought of the small flat in Fulham – his and Leigh and Paul's things. Their books. Their records that meant home. He pictured the cover images one by one: the brand-new – black-and-white Lou Reed with his electric-outlined guitar – and the old – Bob Dylan and his girl in the winter Greenwich Village street arm in arm. With an effort, he reminded himself of his realities. *Paper Pieces*. His friendships. And Nina. Nina. He summoned the sense-memory of her, the scent of neck beneath her hair, the particular sweetness of her skin.

But it was no good. As he and his father walked home his resolve faltered, his perspective failed. Perhaps it was the absence of visual reference points in the obliterating country dark. Just the two of them in their pitch-black disablement. He was holding the torch in one hand and his father's arm with the other, keeping the yellow beam on the road ahead. Winter frost was falling down around them, cracking and splintering the night. He heard himself saying, 'You should visit her. It's wrong not to. You should know that.' His voice low and angry.

He never said it. Not since he was a child and had imagined he could change things. Tomasz did not answer but slowed his pace. His breath was heavy.

'You didn't even speak to her,' Luke said. 'She's just a – she's ill, and you should visit her.'

No answer and so he kept talking, not knowing if he was confessing or accusing. There was too great, too painful an accumulation of fault.

'She couldn't help leaving you. There's no one for her now. She doesn't have anybody.'

Still no answer from his father at his side, arm hard-braced beneath Luke's young man's hand. The yellow torch beam lit their way. Luke kept his eyes on it as he spoke.

'She wouldn't have left you if she could have stayed,' he said. He couldn't see his father's face but he knew it. He knew his feeble, badly shaved chin, cut from shaking hands; his weakness, his empty lumpen failure to give battle—

'You fought a war, didn't you?' he said viciously, and with a sudden formless shout Tomasz wrenched his arm away, pushing Luke sideways so that the road disappeared, the torch beam swinging into the empty air. His father hurried ahead of him into the dark. He heard his running footsteps stumble, and he fell.

An exhalation of breath, scuffling shoes – quiet. Luke stopped. He pointed the torch at the old man slumped on the road. He went to him and knelt.

'Are you all right?' he whispered. 'I'm sorry.' He touched his father's arm.

Tomasz pulled away, cursing him in Polish, incoherent, and Luke couldn't help but smile because all he could clearly make out was that he wanted his vodka and his home.

Tomasz, enraged, clambered to his knees and walked stubbornly on alone with Luke, accepting, faithfully lighting his way, and ready to catch him should he fall again.

By morning his father was his sodden affectionate self. All was forgiven – or forgotten. Boxing Day. The trains would be few and the journeys broken, but Luke was leaving. He hugged his father at the door.

'Write to me, Luke,' said Tomasz. 'I like to read the news and stories.'

'I will.'

Luke's letters to his father were rare and perfunctory. Tomasz did not write back as his mother did, and Luke did not feel he owed him anything, least of all revelation.

'Did you know your grandfather was a poet?'

'No,' said Luke, 'I didn't.'

His father eyed him with calculated sentiment. 'You are not alone,' he said.

He put his hands on Luke's cheeks and smiled.

'Such hope. Such optimism. But remember you are a man, now, eh? Forget your mother.' He spoke with perverse delight. 'She's gone, for a long time.'

Luke turned from him to the welcoming cold. 'Goodbye,' he said. 'You do what you can.'

The train was crowded on the way home. Most of the travellers were young, heading for the city and away from the bonds of their history. Luke felt a grateful part of the collective relief; Christmas escapees coming back to life. He looked out of the window. With heightened clarity, he remembered his mother smiling at him on the bus as he took her away from the hospital to London, so long ago, and felt again the thrill of rescue. He thought of Nina crying on the telephone, and the taste of her release against his tongue. Who would not free a caged creature? Who would not help the wounded?

———————————

Paul's younger brother and his friends ate, drank and left, able in their youth to play with Christmas. In the kitchen Paul, his father and elder brother washed up the pans and plates, scratching off the cold grease. Leigh and Erica and Paul's mother, Joan, sat around the fire; heaped coalite and ash, glowing like a furnace in the concrete sitting room, and watched Paul's brother's wife chase after the two baby girls; one tottering, the other crawling and reaching with tireless acquisitiveness.

The television in the corner played endless Christmas Specials; song and dance men in wobbly sets with studio Christmas trees covered with blue tinsel.

Joan was settled comfortably, sherry and Milk Tray by her side.

'Erica, tell me about your psychiatric practice,' she said.

'No, Joan, as I said, I'm a Jungian therapist. A psychiatrist is a medical doctor.'

'Americans pay so much more attention to themselves,' said Joan. 'I'm sure it's very good for you.'

Politely, they sized one another up, like matriarchs in a historical court. Leigh watched the eldest child tipping matches out of a box and putting them back in again with finger and thumb, concentrating earnestly, as if she were catching up on homework.

'That child is playing with matches!' cried Erica suddenly.

'It's all right,' said Joan, 'she can't strike them.'

In the kitchen Paul's brother swept the floor as their father, head of washing-up, handed the dripping baking trays to Paul to dry.

'So you've stopped with this theatre company and it's an *independent producer* now, is it?' he asked.

'Working on it,' said Paul, envying his brother, safe from interrogation with his teaching job and exemplary young family.

'I see,' said his father, Yorkshire vowels flattening his tone into irony. 'And apart from this *play* your friend has written . . .'

'Luke.'

'Right. Apart from that, Paul, how's business?'

This had been the tenor of Paul's day. His elder brother's success, his younger brother's entertaining antics and his own assumed failure. He did not see how in his father's eyes he would ever be anything else.

'And what about Leigh?'

'What about her?'

'She's gorgeous,' said his brother, sweeping.

'Are you going to make an honest woman of her?'

'She's an honest woman already.'

'We used to call it living in sin. Can you support her?'

'She supports me just now,' said Paul, sick of it. He handed back a roasting tin in childish revenge. 'Still dirty.'

By the time they went home Paul was weighed down by his father's disapproval and couldn't remember ever having felt differently. Neither he nor Leigh spoke in the car.

Erica rattled through her impressions of the day. They were 'good people', his mother could cook, could she do anything else?

'She's been a teacher for thirty years,' said Leigh. 'You didn't bother to ask.'

'*Jesus Christ bloody hell!*' she shouted when they had dropped Erica off and she was back in the passenger seat.

Paul gave a laugh, grim. 'Bloody Christmas,' he said.

The moment they had let themselves into the flat Paul took Leigh in his arms and kissed her.

'Leigh,' he said, 'shall we get married?'

Leigh, caught off guard, recoiled. She tried to arrange her face into something he would want to see, but it was too late.

'Right,' he said. 'That answers that, then.' And he walked into the kitchen.

She stood by the front door and shook. She had not known she would feel like this.

She thought of Paul's nieces tottering around, their mother following in patient compromise. She thought of registry offices and love songs; her father and the shadow-memory of abandonment he'd left. The picture her mother painted of all the years of deception; late-night waiting, the smell of other women, drudgery and the constant knowledge of his appetites. She thought of Luke and Nina, endangered by their passion and Luke's restless hunger, the used-up girls left behind. Marriage.

She took off her coat and went into the kitchen. Paul was standing with his back to her. He wasn't putting on the kettle or opening the fridge – his back, his hands by his side, were action enough. They were not used to crisis.

'You know I'm going to Oxford tomorrow with Luke,' he said.

'I know,' she answered.

'Will you miss us?'

Us. Not me. Us.

'Of course I will,' she said automatically, trying to read him from the way his shoulders were set, the angle of his head.

He turned to her. He looked straight at her. And he said it. 'Who will you miss most?'

Leigh's heart began to thump uncomfortably. She couldn't look away because his hurt eyes met hers in brave challenge.

'What do you mean?' she asked, hearing in her voice the falsest liar, the weakest creature on earth. She faced his courage with denial. He wouldn't ask her again. She could see he couldn't make himself. *I've got away with it*, she thought, with self-disgust.

But still. And yet. She knew that she loved him. Beyond him was the precipice.

'It's kind of funny, when you think about it,' she said.

'What is?' Paul didn't raise his head.

'That your father thinks you're some kind of a drop-out when you're the steadiest person in the world.'

Paul looked up. 'Yes. I'm Mr Reliable,' he said, hurt and doubting.

She smiled. She didn't know how she did it. 'Just what he wants his son to be. If he could only see it.'

'What about what you want?' he asked.

There, again, his courage; more than she could imagine.

'I want you,' she said. She meant it.

Late at night, after supper and some wine, after music and a joint, when normality had given them enough safe distance, they made love. But even in the heart of it – when he was lost in her and helpless – she could not forget herself, and in the safety of his arms a cool voice within her took inventory of her pleasure and the qualities in him upon which she relied. Early in the morning, as she rose from the depth of sleep, her first thought was, *Luke is coming back today*. And before denial of it, before the unwelcome image of Nina and even before she registered Paul's closeness in their bed, all she felt was joy.

It was early afternoon at King's Cross when Luke got off the train. He would go home to the flat to wash Seston off himself and then straight to the theatre to see Nina, and not think about having to leave her the next day.

He came in just as Leigh was setting off for work; coat and bag trailing, startled by his sudden close proximity at the opening of the door.

He put his arms around her and hugged her, burying his face in her.

'I'm home,' he said. 'Happy fucking Christmas.'

Leigh extricated herself and smiled. 'How was it?'

'Yours all right?' he asked, instead of answering. 'Your mum still here?'

'I'm meeting her now. Paul's in the bath.'

'Paul!' shouted Luke. 'I'm back from the city of death!'

Paul shouted something they couldn't hear that might have been 'ahoy –'.

'See you later,' said Leigh, and left.

She slammed the door behind her.

Luke, blasted by blissful gratitude to have a home to come to, put his hands to his face and grinned. He shook off the last three days and exalted. Then, recovered, he stood in stillness, and resolution. He would not live in silly dark and lying. He would not have himself defined by infidelity. Nina would have to steel herself, and choose. But anyway, he thought, he did not care, he did not care; so soon, that day, in hours, almost now, he'd see her – and there wasn't anything else at all but that.

Then, after the longing and the loss and the pained breath-held waiting, the half-hour at the theatre that she gave him was not enough. Not happy. Not private. They had to stay outside in the cold because she hadn't been able to get away from Tony, and there was nothing to talk about that meant anything. They just stood unhappily and searched for common ground.

He did not feel connected to her, just distaste and dissatisfaction. The separation had begun before they were even parted. The loneliness to come subdued them.

'Was it all right, your Christmas?' he asked and she shrugged, expressionless.

He had nothing to tell her about his either and didn't press her.

'You'll forget me,' she said, which seemed to him so ridiculous it made him doubt she felt the same as he did about anything.

He wanted to be in bed with her, or else –

'Let's forget it. I'm going,' he said abruptly.

'Right now?' She was bereft.

'I hate this. I'll ring you.'

He kissed her head and went, without properly looking at her. He had almost reached the street before he heard her call.

'Luke!'

He turned.

'Postcards,' she said.

There it was – with her smile the feeling came back; it

filled the twenty yards of space between them, miraculously living in the empty air. Happiness.

He nodded. 'I promise,' he said.

'Oxford isn't far.' She was as hopeful as a child, as though he could make her better. 'Will you visit?'

She was shivering inside her coat. She shouldn't be outside.

Luke tried to arm himself. He shook his head.

'I'll be working. I mean, maybe while I'm gone you can decide if—' He stopped. Realised he didn't dare go on.

He gestured the narrow gap between the buildings, the service doors and dirt.

'We aren't just this,' he said. 'It will be a new year.'

'I know,' she said, and smiled, but he saw her face, uncertain, as he went.

It was cleaner to be away altogether, just for now.

He and Paul made the journey to Oxford the next day with three drafts of *Paper Pieces* and Luke's typewriter, a bag each of jeans, socks, pants, shirts. Books.

The unknown.

Paul stood on the pavement outside Oxford station, frowning down at his map, trying to find the street with their boarding house on it, while Luke bought twenty postcards – the Bodleian Library, some dreaming spires – and shoved them into his back pocket. Now he had two women to send postcards to; news to his mother, love to his girl.

'Hope it's not a dump,' he said as he came out.

'I think I stayed there before once, when you were up north with The Majority. It's all right. Good breakfasts.'

'We're all right, then,' said Luke, and they set off.

They shared a room, twin beds, because Paul wouldn't be there all the time.

'Eric and Ernie,' said Luke, cheerily, slinging his stuff onto the floor and pushing aside the net curtain at the window to look out at the houses, the dripping trees. Paul had been quiet all day. Luke was making up for it with jokes, trying to draw him out, or just throwing chance remarks into the silence hoping something would interest or irritate him into talking. He got his radio from one of the bags and put it on the floor, pulling up the aerial.

'Radio bloody Oxford, probably,' he said, switching it on and spinning the dial through the static. 'Hi Ho Silver Lining' came dimly through the noise. Then Jimmy Osmond. He turned it off.

'Wanna get something to eat?'

Paul gave him a flat look. 'We're meeting them all in town, Luke. John, Scott-Mathieson . . .'

Luke twitched through one of his imaginary shudders.

'Is he going to be dead grand and difficult?' he asked.

'No idea. Suppose we'll find out.'

'Well, I'll go for a walkabout, then.'

Paul didn't look up.

Luke hesitated. 'I can't sit round here going mad, I'll . . .' He gestured the door.

'Yeah. Go on.'

Something in the way he said it was angry. Luke turned to ask, thought better of it, and left.

He walked into town along the Woodstock Road and went to Blackwell's. He kept nearly being hit by bicycles  they were so quiet. It felt like a cheap television costume drama because the students wore gowns and then had flared jeans sticking out underneath – or brightly coloured tights, clogs. He wrote his first postcard to Nina, addressed it to the theatre and posted it. *In Oxford. Wish me luck.* He hadn't meant to write about himself, rather something clever and pretty about her, but suddenly he felt quite alone.

He walked to the Playhouse; different to the times he'd visited as audience with his ticket bought and paid for; now *he* was bought and paid for. The scruffy canopy showed Alan Gifford in *The Dame of Sark*, and fresh vertical posters to the side announced Archery Theatre's arrival and new season. Luke did a massive double-take – his name. Not his real name. But his name. Luke Last. Orange and yellow geometric design and the leads: *Jennifer Ellis, Jonathan Yates in Paper Pieces by Luke Last* – as if it belonged. Then *Twelfth Night* in March. Then something by F. Scott Fitzgerald – he hadn't known Fitzgerald had written any plays, was momentarily distracted; he'd see if he could find it. Then he looked again: *Paper Pieces by Luke Last*. He laughed and looked round to see if anyone else was watching. There it was: *From 21 January – Paper Pieces*. His strong feeling of joy was replaced by a clear presentiment of disaster. Empty seats and silence. Dismissive reviews. No – worse – vicious ones. Luke Last. Why did he choose that name? He should have taken Joe Furst's name, the unknown bastard with the winning name would never have noticed.

'Fuck,' he said.


'Hey! Shit! Paul!' Luke burst into their room.

Paul was where he'd left him, on the bed with his arms behind his head.

'At the Playhouse,' said Luke. 'The poster for *Paper Pieces*!

You have to come and see, man. It's fucking mental. Shakespeare, Fitzgerald and me: God, the Son and the unholy upstart. Shit. And David Bowie's going to be playing at the New. No one's going to come.'

Paul grinned despite himself. 'Don't worry, not your audience.'

Luke hovered in the doorway, hopefully, but Paul didn't get up.

'I didn't know Fitzgerald wrote any plays,' he said.

'That's what I thought!' said Luke. 'So you coming or what?'

'I'll see it tomorrow.'

———————

Three weeks later, 20 January 1973 at the Duke of York's, Nina stood barefoot on the warm stage facing the living darkness of the auditorium. For the last time her interrogator came onto the stage carrying the wooden chair and placed it next to her. For the last time, she turned to him, held out her hand and smiled at him as he took it.

'Thank you,' she said.

He gently helped her to the chair and she sat, and kept holding his hand as he put her other one to the gun on his hip. The lights went to black. One, two seconds, and the applause began as the curtain fell, with the heavy, soft movement of air around them. Exhale. Pause. The two actors hugged and quickly stood. The curtain lifted again and they stepped forward in bright light.

*It's finished*, she celebrated. *It's over.* Her mind dancing with release as the applause grew louder.

Even as she took her bows she imagined herself gone. She

thought of Luke in Oxford, that just as she was freed from the long run of her play, his was about to open. She had been held in this relentless commitment for so long. As the house-lights slowly came up she seemed to see her future in the rows upon rows of people standing to applaud her leaving.

Backstage, Tony heard the outbreak of applause from the audi-torium as he climbed the stairs to Nina's dressing room. In the corridor he pushed open her door. He glanced at the disarray. She hadn't yet cleared out her things or taken the pictures from the mirror, it was just as it had been for the months of the show's run.

He went in and ran a finger along the Formica shelf beneath the mirror, looking at her make-up, magazines, pens and paper, and a biography she was reading for a possible job. Beneath it there was a shadow. The book was resting on something smaller than itself. Tony lifted the book, the distant applause still surging, subsiding, surging again. *That's good*, he thought, *that's a minute and a half, at least.* He picked up the stack of postcards. They were all from Oxford. Colleges, churches . . . there were more than twenty. He turned them over.

A biro scrawl: *In Oxford. Wish me luck.*

He read them, one after another:

*I think that you are with me all the time.*

*No poem yet. Sorry. Rewriting.*

*My play, not the poem. We spoke. I love you.*

*The moon I see here shines on you, but prettily.*

The sound of applause faded and stopped.

Tony carefully replaced the postcards and turned towards the door, arranging himself. Then her running feet, pattering like a child, and there she was in the doorway, hair loose, elated. She stopped, momentarily shocked at seeing him.

'Oh, Tony! I don't know what to feel.'

'Nor do I,' he said and then waited for a moment. 'Be quick, I'm starving and we must get to the wake.'

Henry Fidele strode past behind her in his heavy boots on the way to his dressing room, smacking Nina's bottom with a grin.

'Free at last,' he said. 'Champagne's waiting.'

At dinner Nina's feeling of heady release cooled. She looked around the table at the faces, and at her husband by her side. They drank toasts. Toasts to her, the absent Hector Romero, the director, and Henry — who had shaved off his PFA moustache in two minutes flat in the dressing room and, transformed, kept stroking his clean upper lip and laughing. He was off to Stratford in a few days. Nina had nowhere to go. She could pack her bag and find Luke in Oxford if she wanted and she almost laughed out loud. Such faith was absurd. *You coward*, she thought, *you coward*.

'To Tony!' they toasted, and Nina lifted her glass too, and drank. Her hand was shaking.

Tony met her eye.

'You look tired,' he said. 'Let's go.'

All the way home she rehearsed the line in her head. *I'm leaving you. I'm leaving.* But she did not say it.

'Come along,' said Tony as he led her up the stairs.

They had made love since her affair with Luke started; not often but too much. They had done it what he called *the usual way* — facing her, and simple. If Luke asked if he had touched her, Nina thought, she would lie about it, because she did not feel he had. Sex with Tony did not have any connection with what she and Luke were like. He wouldn't understand that. How could he? He wasn't married, he could luxuriate in purity. She didn't have that liberty.

She undressed in the bathroom and put on her long silk nightdress, staring at herself in the mirror all the time she did it. *I'm leaving you. I'm leaving you.* Tony was waiting for her.

Pausing in the bedroom doorway she saw he expected her to go to him and so she did. He slipped the thin straps from her shoulders.

'Nina,' he said, 'is there something you wanted to tell me?'

Of all the things she expected from him it wasn't this. She started like a frightened animal. His expression was unreadable. She remembered how he had looked when she found him in her dressing room, the tiny tugging notion he had changed. He didn't say anything else at all but just waited, with his expectant eyes upon her. She could not have uttered a word and yet in her head she repeated the sentence, *I'm in love with somebody else; I want to leave you.* It span and replayed, demanding to be said. Unsaid. *I'm in love with someone else.* Tony was still watching her.

'Nina?' he said.

She shook her head.

'Are we sure?'

She nodded.

'I'm very glad to hear it. Get onto the bed now,' he said, 'darling.'


Nina lay naked on her front on top of the sheets. Tony stood at the foot of the bed holding a pair of her tights loosely in his hand and looking at her body. He got onto his knees on the edge of the mattress.

'Put your hands behind you,' he said.

She did.

'Here, no, like this,' said Tony, taking her hands and pushing them together. He tied them, with a figure of eight, and made a knot. She began to breathe more quickly. The elastic material was tight enough to fill her fingers with blood so that they throbbed slightly.

He leaned forward close to her ear and whispered, 'I thought you might miss being in custody.'

She did not answer. He took off the scarf he was wearing, tied as a cravat, and put it over her eyes. She did not speak. He put a leg on either side of her body and like that, on hands and knees, he lowered himself down to speak to her again.

'You have your friends. I have mine,' he said quietly.

He began to kiss her neck. 'You are not to make a public fool out of me,' he said. 'Open your legs.'

She did. He stroked the back of her leg from the ankle to the inside of her thigh. He pinched her wrists and waggled the two hands pressed together at the small of her back. Her shoulders were drawn back but her chest and throat pressed close into the soft mattress.

'Are you uncomfortable?' he asked.

Nina had no words. Her mind was limited by sensation and misty panic.

'Are you uncomfortable?' he asked again, and then, because she did not answer him, continued.

She had become familiar with being tethered or blindfolded, but this was different. This was the first time he took the next step, and put himself into the virgin part of her that truly fascinated him; the shock and the pain of it made her scream.

'Relax,' he said, 'you'll like it better.'

She tried to do as he said, and concentrated on freeing her mouth from the pillow to breathe.

When he had finished he went to the bathroom. Nina found she could get her hands free quite easily and turn over.

When they were both in bed, and clean, he kissed her. Before turning the lights out she took two Valium, but they didn't distance her from distress enough; she cried herself into a deep sleep, sobbing as Tony patted her hand in the dark.


The next morning she called Marianne. They met in a Chelsea restaurant. Nina wore dark glasses because her eyes were so swollen she looked freakish. She needed comfort. She would have done anything for it.

'It's raining, you look ridiculous,' said Marianne, and so Nina took her glasses off.

'Oh. You've been crying. You're not pregnant?'

Nina shook her head. The waiter brought their wine and poured it. Nina tried to hide from him, chin down, and when he went away she raised a glass to her mother.

'To marriage,' she said.

'Oh,' said Marianne, 'has Tony been naughty? So soon?'

Nina's eyes began to cry again, despite herself. Marianne took her hand.

'Darling,' she said warmly, the voice Nina loved more than anything. '*Tell me*.'

'It was stupid of me to come out.'

The waiter returned and stood over them, expectantly. '*Mesdames?*'

Nina looked down while Marianne ordered.

'And for you?' said the waiter, and when Nina kept her face turned away Marianne ordered for her, too.

'Ridiculous man,' said Marianne as he went. 'You're quite right. If you were in such a state you shouldn't have come.'

'I couldn't stay there.' Nina spoke so quietly that Marianne had to lean forward to hear. She took her hand and held it.

'Mummy, he's − not −' She made several false starts.

'It's all right, darling. Go on.'

'I think that he hates me. He hates women. He hates sex but he does it anyway to − I don't know − to make me low or hurt me.'

At the outright mention of sex Marianne stiffened.

'Darling, this is hardly the place.'

'I'm sorry. I know.'

'But I have to tell you that wasn't *my* experience of him at all.'

Nina had forgotten her mother's affair with Tony, neither of them had spoken of it since. She was appalled at the mention of it now, and the insinuation that it was not Tony who was at fault, but she. Had her mother not inspired this sadism in him? Was it only she who invited it?

'Is it very horrible? Very often?'

'No.'

'Well,' she said briskly, 'perhaps you're making a bit of a fuss. It's not exactly a huge surprise if he's unusual in that department. He is Tony Moore, after all. But I am sorry for you.' Marianne began to fidget with her bracelet. She had had enough of the conversation.

'It isn't normal, the way he is!' Nina's voice broke.

'Oh, stop it.'

Nina drank half her glass of wine, gritting her teeth to

swallow, trying to hold on to the outrage – that it was not all right what was happening to her. She tried again.

'I think,' she said steadily, 'I think that if I am this unhappy, if I *think* he's cruel. Isn't that enough?'

Her mother regarded her coolly. 'Are you thinking of leaving him?' she asked.

Nina wiped her eyes. She swallowed and took a breath. 'I have to.'

There was a pause. Marianne glanced around the restaurant and then at her daughter wiping the constant tears from her cheeks with her fingertips.

'Well, where on earth would you go?' she said, irritable. 'What's your next job? Does Jo have anything for you? I imagine Tony knows a great deal more than you what you should go onto, now the play is over.'

'I'm not sure.'

'If you stay in theatre you'll barely support yourself.'

Nina looked her mother in the eye. She knew all Marianne saw were her swollen lids, dark circles. Her gaze had always been an unflattering mirror. When Nina's eyes met Luke's she was a different person altogether.

'I've met somebody else,' she said.

'Oh, I see,' said Marianne, sitting back. 'Fast work. All becomes clear. You're *looking* for an excuse to leave your husband then.'

'No—'

'Who is he?'

Nina blushed and couldn't say his name. She didn't want to tell. He felt too real to make a show of. She wouldn't know what to say – and if she was honest, she didn't know how to make him sound acceptable to her mother.

Marianne watched her closely. 'Does this person really want you?'

'Is that so unlikely?'

'Don't be silly. You know what I mean. Is he serious?'

'I think so.'

'Is he rich?'

'No.'

'Is he in the business?'

'Yes.'

'Not an actor?'

'No.'

'Thank God for that.'

'Tony found out about him.' Immediately she regretted this further confidence; trust she knew even as she gave it would be abused.

'Oh, you *absolute* fool!' said her mother. 'Was he livid?'

Nina gave a short laugh. 'I would say,' she said slowly, 'I would say he's quite pleased.'

They sat in silence once more and their salads arrived. Marianne raised her eyebrows at hers and pushed it about with her fork. She ate a few mouthfuls.

Nina finished her wine. She was beginning to lose sight of her goal; she couldn't remember what had felt so urgent that she must rush to her mother and announce she must leave Tony. She could not now see that this day was any different to any other.

'Well, Nina,' said Marianne, and her voice was practical, her *we must face reality* voice, 'I honestly can't see you have a serious problem. It seems to me you are managing to have your cake and eat it, aren't you?'

'What do you mean?'

'Darling, if there aren't going to be any black eyes then Tony can have his friends, and you can have yours.'

Nina opened her eyes wide. 'That's just what he said.'

'Did he?' said Marianne, and smiled. 'He's absolutely shocking, that man.'

There was silence. Her mother continued picking over her salad for morsels.

'He is,' said Nina, her own voice surprising her.

'What?' Marianne glanced up.

'He is shocking.' The need to explain herself had left her. She pushed her chair back from the table with both hands.

'He is shocking. And so are you,' she said loudly, her tears had started again. Even in rebellion she was feeble.

'*Just be quiet!*' whispered Marianne with urgent embarrassment.

'I *can't!* I can't—'

She stood up quickly and left, pulling her bag from the chair but forgetting her dark glasses by her plate – finding her way somehow, clumsily, observed by all – out into the open air of the street.

———————

Six hours later the curtain would go up on the first night of *Paper Pieces* in Oxford.

The first few days of rehearsals had been a disjointed, low-energy scraping together of actors disgruntled to leave London between Christmas and New Year, then happier, but hungover, as January began. The script settled into solid shape and they moved from read-throughs to blocking it out in the freezing-cold rehearsal rooms with tape on the floor for walls, doors and marks, and rows of chairs for furniture.

The second week had been a five-day run of extended delight; startling and unlikely. Luke would remember it all his life; his interior world made solid, the voices that had been for so long in his head ringing out physical and real. The laughter. The actors and Scott-Mathieson, the crew, the SM, even the producers, if they were in, were all pushed into laughter – big, real laughter at the play; nobody could get through a scene without corpsing. They were filled with confidence and the feeling of the united company moving towards performance – more than he ever anticipated, more than he had known at Graft or almost anywhere. The piece – the three pieces – were linked, one-act plays; two before the interval, one after. The characters were taut sketches of fragile people, clinging to the slippery hand-holds of status. They were the paper pieces fluttering in Luke's dialogue, mocked; absurd yet pitiful.

Then, with days to opening night, the laughs drained out of it. Luke fiddled with the scenes and dialogue while Scott-Mathieson kept his cool, not always showing the changes to the actors; sometimes surrendering to Luke's late-night panics, sometimes letting the phone in his room ring. Once, memorably, with three days until they opened, Luke turned up at his hotel out of a rainstorm at midnight, an entire page-one rewrite in his head and ready to burn the script and start over. Scott came down to the lobby in his dressing gown and told him to shut up, have a whisky and go to bed – or back to London. When he had gone, Luke sat in the hotel bar and cried – really cried – into his cheap and useless whisky.

'It's not any good and it's not funny,' he said to Scott the next morning, trying not to look crazed. 'It's in the structure of it — the foundations are poor.'

'Don't be such a fucking old queen,' said Scott. 'It's not *funny* any more because there's only so many times you can laugh at the Christmas fairy giving marvellous head — only the vanity of a writer would expect a joke to be laughed at three hundred times. The actors are crapping-it, you're crapping-it. Just don't be so bloody wet.'

He was a public schoolboy to his core, smooth hair combed back and thick sideburns. Luke suspected he had been an officer during his National Service and absorbed the persona permanently.

'All right,' he said. 'All right.'

'Good,' said Scott-Mathieson. 'Now shut up and bugger off.'

After that Luke sat in the corner of the rehearsal room, hid his face and tried to smile at the actors if they looked at him, which they did less and less.

Over that weekend they moved into the theatre, vacated late on Saturday night by the last show. The old set was struck immediately and the new one, moved in overnight and put up early on Sunday morning, took all day, with hasty carpentry and a succession of unforeseen practical failures. On Monday the actors drifted in and made homes of their dressing rooms as best they could with photographs of children, cushions, bottles of booze, and in the afternoon was the tech run, a grindingly boring, tense event that ran four times the length of the play, late into the night, studded with explosions of rage or terror from everyone. Everyone except Luke, who for some reason had descend upon him a mood of extreme bliss, like a drug, wrapping him in the pleasure of his play being produced and taking from him all fear.

Throughout rehearsals Paul had come and gone on Archery business, or his own; a couple of days in Oxford, then meetings in London, not always saying where he was going or when he would return. Relying on Paul's constancy as he did, Luke registered something had altered between them, but respecting his privacy he kept quiet, waiting for the return of their mutual sympathy. Then, on the day they opened, he saw that Paul was setting off for the station.

'I'll see you at the theatre tonight, then?' he asked, unable to hide his wounded surprise.

'Yeah, I'll see you before the show. Around half six.'

'Leigh should be here,' said Luke. 'I wish she was.'

'What?' said Paul abruptly, pausing in the doorway.

'Leigh should be here,' said Luke again.

'Do you? She would if she could,' said Paul with a tight smile and left.

They hadn't finished the tech until midnight the night before and were powered by nerves and coffee for the dress rehearsal; everything as it would be, but no audience. The mock performance played like a silent film with stone-cold gaps where the jokes landed in emptiness; a monotonous dumb-show too mediocre to be called disastrous. They finished at half past four, and then the strange lull before the evening, the first public performance; paying audience, the press and all of Archery – with wives and girlfriends along for the ride.

They were meeting in the bar beforehand; Scott and Luke, John Wisdom and one or two of the others.

At six Luke went to the theatre and paced the silent foyer. He checked the box office, searching the front-of-house manager's face for clues or omens, finding none. The house would be almost two-thirds full. It could be worse.

Time had stopped; it would never be half past seven. He went to the empty bar, just opening, and had a drink looking at the framed pictures of past shows – Taylor and Burton in *Dr Faustus*, Gielgud, Ian McKellen. Fear weighed on him as though he walked through thicker air. He went up to the lobby. It was the emptiest thing he had ever seen. He thought of the actors in their dressing rooms, the activity even now behind the silent front of house.

He went out into the street, looking for Paul. Unused to terror he didn't know what to do with it. He checked his watch, twenty-five past six.

He decided to walk to the corner and come back. On the pavement he saw a group of four people approaching the theatre and ducked out of the way as they went up the steps.

'Let's get a drink, we've got ages,' said one of the two women.

*Have large ones*, thought Luke. *Have three.*

He turned away – and saw Nina.

She had just got out of a taxi.

As it drove away she looked straight at him. He thought it couldn't be her, that he had arranged some stranger's features into hers. He did that every day. But she came towards him.

'. . . there you are.' Her words were carried on a trembling exhalation, as if at the end of a long sentence inside her head.

'Yes, of course,' he said. She looked desperate. 'What?'

*She's left him*, he thought. She went into his arms and he held her very tightly.

'You came.' He thought he might crush the life out of her with his gratitude.

'Can you take me somewhere?' she said.

He kissed the side of her head. She was shaking. 'What's happened?'

'I just had to see you. Do you mind?'

'Mind?' He wanted to pick her up, spin her round, cover her with kisses and laugh like a madman, but he just kept smiling at her. 'You look gorgeous.'

'Where can we go?' she asked.

'Go? We're here.' He looked up at the theatre, *Paper Pieces* in bright orange and black across the top, the silhouetted characters of the ensemble and *Luke Last* beneath. In darker, brown-orange it said, *Directed by Richard Scott-Mathieson*, Scott's name larger than Luke's. *A new play*, proclaimed writing below the posters, on a banner. A new play.

Nina looked around her vaguely and up at the theatre.

'Your play . . .' she said.

'Yes.'

'First night,' she stated, recalling it.

'Yep,' he said and felt his throat constrict.

'Oh my God. I'd forgotten,' she said flatly, not in false apology but realising it and sad. 'I was just going in to ask them where I might find you.'

Luke's brain tipped in adjustment that not everybody's world contained only this moment, and then again, because the curtain went up in less than an hour.

'Christ, I'm a cow,' she said. 'I'm sorry. I just had to get away.'

He noticed more people stopping outside the theatre, going in. It had started. Time was not frozen now but rushing away, and his feelings were quickening too, assaulting him.

'Everything's all right,' he said calmly. 'I'll get you a drink. Will you watch it with me?'

'Of course.' She was subdued.

He took her hand and led her away, calculating the time it would take to get to the pub, get served, get back, and be in his seat in the stalls with the others when the curtain rose. Nina nestled into his shoulder, seemed almost blind as they walked.

'Luke!' He heard a shout behind him and turned. Paul.

'What's going on?' He was in the centre of the pavement, out of breath and legs planted apart.

'Hello,' he said to Nina, shortly.

'This is Nina,' said Luke.

'I know,' said Paul. 'Luke, it's almost seven.'

'We're going for a drink, we'll be back in a minute.'

Paul didn't say anything, then some people crossed the pavement between them, and when they had passed he was gone.

They went into the nearest pub. Luke counted out the exact change for her drink to save time, hands shaking with haste. She had a vodka and soda with ice. He didn't want anything but handed it to her and looked for a quiet place to take her. She stood in the corner and sipped her drink. Luke tried to take in everything about her – what was wrong and what she needed; tried to suppress his joy and subjugate his nerves, and he lost himself in the examination of her face; numbed by her presence.

'Every day I see you about fifty times,' he said.

She finished her drink and put it down on a table.

'That's better,' she said. She looked up and into his face. 'Hello,' she said, and smiled. 'Are you nervous?'

'Not any more,' said Luke. 'But we should get back.'

'Of course. I'm so sorry. Let's run.'

They did run, all the way back up to the theatre, and

laughing, and when they got there the two-minute bell was ringing. Paul was nowhere to be seen.

'He must have gone in,' said Luke.

They went past the ushers – spotty teenagers in striped waistcoats too big for them. One of them – who Luke had got talking to a few times about how he had escaped Eastbourne to come to Oxford – winked at Luke and said, 'Good luck, mate.'

Luke nodded his thanks and they went inside.

They went along the back row sideways, holding their coats close to their bodies and trying not to be noticed by the people in front. John Wisdom lifted a hand in greeting, holding a half-smoked extinguished cigar.

'Not a bad turnout from the press,' he said, gimlet eyed. 'Bastards could have let it bed in a bit. Cubitt. Kurtz, Jesus – He's not here. He may as well be.'

John looked away. There was nothing to say. At the end of the row Luke could see others from Archery, John's partner, a financier, two more. He couldn't look at them. He was solely responsible for all of it. He wanted to stop it and send everyone home. Sitting in between the producers and John Wisdom was Scott-Mathieson, immaculate hair curling over the collar of his loud pinstripe and wearing a broad tie and an expression of rigid coolness. He barely acknowledged them.

'I know him,' hissed Nina in Luke's ear. She ducked behind his shoulder and pulled him into a seat before they reached the others.

They eased down the squeaky red velvet seats, holding their breath.

People were still coming in, checking their tickets, talking. There were empty seats on the ends of the rows, most of the front, and even a few, terrifyingly, in the middle. Luke knew the back five rows of the circle were empty too. The spaces in the audience made it gap-toothed, there was no sureness – wobbly.

'Are you all right?' whispered Nina.

Luke nodded, nauseous, and saw Paul come in just as the house-lights dimmed.

'I waited for you in the bar,' he hissed, sitting next to Nina, on the corner of her coat, which she pulled out from under him, but before Luke could answer the curtain went up.

————————

For the first ten minutes of the play Nina didn't look at Luke, but when she did she saw that he was covering his face with his hands, not watching, even through his fingers. She looked back at the stage and for a while did nothing but wonder at the fact of seeing his work, which she had not considered a reality until that moment. The set was a collapsing works-yard or factory; non-existent walls and irregular perspective. The three men revealed as the curtain opened were arguing as they waited for somebody to arrive. She knew all three actors; had been at drama school with one and worked with another. Two were playing long-haired anti-establishment characters with no sense of humour, and the third a disgruntled private soldier fresh from an unspecified conflict. They were involved in a vicious argument and blaming one another for past mistakes and misdemeanours. Their words fell into an abyss. The actors were looking for their lines, helping one another out and the audience was completely silent. For fifteen minutes, longer, with Luke at her side vibrating with horror, it was as if there was nobody watching the actors at all, as if they were playing to an empty theatre. She glanced down the row of house seats.

Everyone had the same expression of rigid waiting. The play was like nothing she had ever seen. Perhaps that accounted for the silence. There was something of Beckett in it, something of Nicholls, but a fresh, bizarre reality that was all Luke. And then the first laugh; a scattered, surprised sort of laugh, moving from the front of the audience to the back as if it were asking permission, and not quite reaching them. She looked at Luke again. He had dug his face further into his hands, hunched down in his seat. Then there was another laugh – this one quick and shocked – quite loud and from the whole theatre together.

It was as if the audience had decided as one how they felt, from then on there was a batting back and forth between the actors and the watchers, like percussion: beat, line, laugh, line, line, laugh, beat – and the play came to life. Nina's body relaxed. She settled into her seat. Until now she had no reaction to the performance, only its reception. She was present now, even forgetting Luke beside her. The next time she remembered him she saw he was looking about the audience, wondering and tentative; up to the people at the sides of the balcony, and ahead, trying to catch the expression of their profiles. She took his hand. He squeezed hers tightly. *It's all right*, she sent him the thought. *It's good. They like it.*

In the brief pause between the first and second piece, under cover of hesitant applause, the back row whispered to one another; reassurances and relief, urgent criticism. Luke turned to her, self-doubt put aside for a smile that was for her.

'You're brilliant,' she said, and realised just then that it was true.

In the interval, before the curtain had finished falling, Luke, Scott and John got up for the bar, hurrying.

Nina said, 'I'll go to the loo. See you back here.'

She slipped out past Paul without speaking to him and locked herself into a cubicle for the whole fifteen minutes, terrified of seeing someone she knew. She sat and read the *now wash your hands* sign over and over.

The second half. A falter, a trip in the flow of it, some mess-ups with the lines but then, again, it was off and away – and laughter, precious laughter, took it to the end.

In the crush of leaving, when the audience, loud and talkative, were funnelling through the doors and out, Nina followed the others down the long row, one after the other, with Paul behind her and Scott at the head of the charge, signalling like a flag-bearer, a shout of—

'Come along!' as they went.

'Well done,' she kept whispering, holding Luke's hand where no one could see.

He was distracted and alight, with her and not with her. The others, whispering, glanced around to catch sight of the critics' departure, then hurried down the sloping side aisle towards the stage. Nina stopped, tugging at Luke's hand. Luke turned as Paul pushed past them.

'Come on!' said Luke, pulling her.

'No, I can't! I know half of them,' she whispered in his ear.

'Luke!' Paul called from the end of the row.

Luke didn't move. He said to Paul, 'You go on.' And then to Nina, 'I'll come with you. I don't have to be there.'

She saw Paul staring, shocked.

'Are you mad?' she said.

'Luke!' snapped Paul, and a gesture, exasperated.

'I'll go to the pub,' she said. 'I'll wait. I don't mind.'

'Then you're staying?' Luke asked. 'Good, right, we can find a hotel and—' His words were falling over themselves.

'We'll talk afterwards. Go!'

Like an animal released he was gone.

She put her collar up like a spy and went the other way out of the theatre and into the street quickly, elated, delighted with it all.

The theatre was almost empty as Paul and Luke hurried down the aisle.

'Has she left him, then?' said Paul.

'I don't know. I hope so.'

They went up the few steps on to the stage and crossed it.

Paul, in front, went off into the wings but Luke stopped, held by the charged air. All day, time had been out of step, racing away from him or falling behind. Now it came into sync. He looked out at the auditorium; the quiet rows of seats, repeating in their shallow arcs as they went back. Above, the gilded balcony and the big black lamps suspended, extinguished, cooling.

He stood behind the imaginary wall looking out at the world, and he felt he had come home.

Everyone was in and out of the dressing rooms, bottles opening, flattery and flirting, stupid relief instead of analysis, then into the bar – the dozen or so from Archery and the actors, one after the other. As the barmen cleared up and turned the lights up they took over the place. Luke couldn't stop questioning, praising, pushing for absolutes, fast-running ecstasy outpacing order. Paul stayed close, occasionally resting his hand on Luke's shoulder as if to keep him from disappearing.

They all said goodbye on the pavement beneath the dark canopy. Scott patted Luke's back, winked, and left him without another word.

Luke and Paul were left alone.

'It's started,' said Paul.

'Critics,' said Luke, suddenly cold. 'Leonard Cubitt. Bloody hell, Kurtz.'

Paul shrugged. 'No point thinking about it.' He looked at his watch. 'What are you doing now?'

'Going to meet Nina.'

'Want me to move out?'

'We'll find a hotel.'

'Big spender now,' said Paul.

Luke laughed. 'I'll sell my typewriter.'

'No,' said Paul, with sudden seriousness, 'don't do that. See you tomorrow. Be good.'

Luke turned and ran, the fastest he could run, jumping out into the street to avoid slamming into people – between the gutter and the night sky – street lights streaming in his vision.

Nina had found a hotel while she waited for Luke, standing with a drink by the pay phone with the Yellow Pages in the corner at the back of the pub. Last orders had been called before he came in.

He stood in the door and looked for her but she did not wave. She watched him, breathing hard in the doorway and looking round. She revelled in the secret observation of his face, alive with searching for her. As she watched, his expression changed, anxiety replacing joy. She couldn't help it. She waited still, until she saw fear. Then, only then—

'Luke.'

When he smiled, she smiled. He joined her.

'I thought you'd gone.'

'Did you? Look, I've found somewhere.'

He looked down at the phone book as if he'd never seen one.

'I've called them. It's called the Tower House. It looks nice. Small. I booked a room.'

'The Tower House?'

'Rapunzel, Rapunzel . . .' she said.

'What does that make me?'

'Oh, the prince, I should think. Don't get conceited.'

'Doesn't he get blinded in that one?'

'By rose thorns.'

He looked down at the advertisement. 'Well, I won't – no roses in Ship Street,' he said. 'Are you hungry?'

'I'll watch you eat.'

'Don't want to,' he said. 'Let's go.'


The man who gave them the room was in his dressing gown, nicotine stained and disapproving.

'The lady said you'd be here before ten,' he said. 'It's after eleven.'

'Sorry,' said Nina and she and Luke tried not to laugh and couldn't look at each other.

He *shh'd* them as he led them up the creaking stairs and opened the door to their room.

'Theatre people, are you?'

'Yes,' said Luke, revelling.

The man tapped the radiators, grumbled when they said it was cold, and told them breakfast finished at half past nine, as if people like them weren't expected to make it out of bed at a decent hour.

'There's no tower,' said Luke, to annoy him.

The man gave him a sour look. 'You can see it from the window,' he said.

When he had shut the door behind him they were alone.

'He's like someone out of your play,' said Nina. 'Your wonderful play, I mean.'

He smiled at her. 'You don't have to keep saying it.'

'I do.' She looked around at the chintzy bedspread, wardrobe and dressing table. 'Well, it doesn't smell,' she said.

'Are you tired?' asked Luke, who felt he'd never sleep again.

'No,' said Nina, shivering.

He ran her a bath. She was shy and kept the door shut while she washed and Luke pulled back the bedspread and tried to see out of the window. The dressing table looked a good place to put his typewriter. He would be happy living here with her. He washed after her, getting warm too, and when he came out in a towel she was in bed, blankets to her chin, looking at him.

'I feel a bit stupid,' he said.

He got into bed. With all the hours ahead and no panic they were both intimidated, as if they had never been together alone before.

'Will you put the light out?' she asked.

'Seriously?'

She nodded. He put out the light. Now they were both blind, just the two of them together in the dark. He kissed her. There was time for everything now, time to please her, time to wait, and hold her, and be in every second of the feel of her hair against his face, slim arms around him; time to run his hand slowly down the naked length of her and sense each quiet, heating moment of her gradual wanting. She opened her legs for him.

'Don't wait,' she said. 'Now.'

There was luxury inside her. Held in her warmth he could stop, and stay, just kiss her and feel her moving up to him, and around him, both of them breathing quietly and close, pressing the moment to its perfect tension – then further, finding what she wanted with all the strength and sweetness celebrated, until she trembled, and her soft breath became like weeping and she was broken apart for him.

And Nina, when Luke at last surrendered, felt a strange possessive joy, as if she had brought him down with her. She put her hand on the back of his neck as he drifted, his mind slipping into the quiet pause, waiting for the return to life that followed.

He was leaning on her shoulder and it hurt her arm.

'Get off,' she said, because she had no proper words to make sentences.

He went to the side and they resettled. He began to play with strands of her hair over her face, twisting them in his fingers and annoying her with them. She laughed. They held each other.

'So have you left him?' he asked, unconsciously echoing Paul.

'No,' said Nina.

'When will you tell him?'

There was silence. Her mouth was near his chest, he could feel her breath stop-starting as she thought.

'He knows,' she said.

Several thoughts occurred to Luke, several feelings – relief, panic – then he said, 'How did he find out?'

'I think he found your postcards.'

'Where?'

'In my dressing room.'

His mind raced. It was getting difficult for him to keep still.

'Cigarette,' she said.

He sat up gratefully and not wanting to put on the light felt around in the dark for her bag on the floor. He had to get out of bed, then fell over, was forced to switch on the light. She hid her head from the glare under the pillow while he found the cigarettes and an ashtray and began to get cold again before jumping back into bed and returning them to darkness.

'Okay,' he said. 'Safe,' and she removed the pillow, put it behind her and sat up.

He felt his way to giving her a cigarette and watched her face illuminated as she lit it.

'I'd say you look like an oil painting but you're lighting a fag,' he said. 'It's the light and dark. Chiaroscuro, love. It's like a Rembrandt.'

'Big nose and bad teeth?' she said.

'Leonardo then. *Madonna and Child. Madonna and Fag.*'

'Divine.'

'You are. So if he knows . . .' He couldn't finish. He tried again: 'Well, if he knows, what did he say?'

Nina smoked in the dark, and was silent.

Luke sat up so that he was next to her, burnt by jealousy, extreme pain that he had not asked for and could not explain. He didn't think he had the right to demand anything but felt still all the rage and distress of the betrayed.

'You aren't going to tell me what he said?' he waited. 'Nina, what did you tell him about me?'

Nina heard his honest hurt and again, she was surprised by him. He wasn't even trying to hide it from her, he laid himself open and defenceless.

'Was he angry?' he said. 'Was he – upset?'

She thought of Tony, and what had happened between them that night – his tastes and his persuasions. It was disgusting to even have it in her mind while she was there with Luke, but at the same time it was almost as if it had happened to somebody else.

'Tony seems to think it's all right,' she said, hating the words, almost a whisper.

'*Seems to think it's all right?*'

She heard his shock. She felt older than him not younger; older and full of shame.

'What's *all right* about it?' he said loudly. 'How can he think—'

'Luke – please, can we not? I don't want to talk about it.'

'Right. Okay. Except – no. Because I don't understand. I don't understand what you're doing here then. He knows; you're here. It was my . . .' He gestured in the dark towards the window, as if he were going to say something about the play but then, with too many things in his mind to articulate them, stopped.

After a moment he said, 'Nina, what the fuck is going on?'

And then he stood up, quickly, just to get away from her, and turned on the light in the bathroom.

She put out her cigarette with fumbling fingers, watching him as he washed his face, turning the taps on full and splashing handfuls, vigorously, then the towel – all over his face and neck. Even knowing he was angry – upset – she loved watching him.

He came back and sat on the edge of the bed, pulling the covers across to protect his nakedness. The light from the bathroom fell across them.

'It's fucking freezing in here,' he said.

'Get back into bed.' She touched his shoulder but he pulled away. 'Please?'

He turned to look at her directly but it wasn't the anger she expected, it was truth. She had hurt him. She was hurting him. She hated it – but also, somewhere deeper, she felt delight that she could matter so much, and was ashamed.

'What are you doing here with me?' he said. 'What is this?'

Nina was silent.

'I'm not here for fun,' he said urgently. 'I've done that. I've . . . girls, I mean. I don't know what *you* think we're doing, but I'm not here to mess around. I want you.'

She looked away, wishing he'd stop, hugging herself with her arms, but he didn't.

'I know I haven't got a place of my own,' he said. 'I haven't got any money—'

'Luke—'

'But I'm not broke or anything. I've got my advance and—' He gave a quick laugh, mocking himself. 'I binned the bins.' She looked away, uncomfortably. 'But I don't know how the play is going to do, so I can't make any – promises about the future.'

'Stop it, I don't want you to,' she said harshly.

He was silent. She started to cry. At first the tears just came fast, and fell, but then the pain in her chest made her sob, and she hid her face. She couldn't tell him how the corrupt bargain with Tony had been struck; she had not admitted to herself until now that she had agreed to it.

Everything was spoiled. What had been perfect was wrong and bad, and it was she who had done it. She had run from Tony, from him and from her mother, into Luke's sanctuary, thoughtlessly. *She was to have her friends and he was to have his.* She didn't want it like that. She wanted to be clean and to be able to give to him. She cried and found she was rocking, breathing hard and rocking, her head light, and misty hysteria blurring the edges of her misery.

'Don't,' he said. 'Don't do that.'

She couldn't stop. High sounds from her throat, growing panic. He moved across to her, put his arms around her rigid body.

'Nina . . .'

He hushed her, and wiped at her tears as if she were a broken toy he was trying to put back together.

'Don't do that,' he said. 'I'm sorry.'

'I don't know how to do anything,' said Nina. 'I can't do anything right.'

He pulled the covers round her to hug her so that she was wrapped up and she went gratefully into the warm place he made. He stroked her head and eased back against the headboard so he could better support her as she folded herself into him. She had never known such forgiveness.

They held each other like people taking shelter.

His skin was wet with her tears. There was quiet.

'You should be happy,' he said. 'You're not.'

'I'm happy with you,' she said quietly.

'Then you have to—'

'Please.' She heard her weak, small voice, and didn't know

if the weakness was real or if it had come to save her from the spotlight of confrontation. 'I can't talk about it now.'

She waited. She could feel him thinking next to her, his pain and confusion. She rested on his shoulder. He didn't move or say anything. *If I touch him*, she thought, *he'll forget all about it. That's what men are like.* And she couldn't help despising him, just a little bit, for being taken in and hurt, for falling for her and being weak.

She pressed her cheek against his chest, and then slipped down the bed next to him. She moved down, feeling his stomach contract as her trailing hair and breath touched his skin, kissing him and knowing that she had won; he wasn't thinking about anything now. She took him in her mouth.

In the wet heat of her mouth, her lips enclosing, taking him in, his thoughts were obliterated in the glare, starbursts in his head, and all he knew was gratitude for the blessing of her and, as she had meant him to, he lost himself.

Nina didn't eat breakfast, so Luke went down alone and had eggs and bacon and coffee at one of the small yellow-clothed tables, staring at the doily under the cruets and making maths and faces out of the shapes cut into it. It was difficult to concentrate knowing Nina was lying naked upstairs under the bedcovers so he ate very quickly, trying not to think about her body. Then he went up, taking coffee for her, watched by the shy and curious young waitress as he went. They made love, while the clock-radio on the bedside table flicked through the minutes, filling them out with college bells and footsteps passing and time pushed into their bed, tightening the confines of their limited freedom.

When they left the hotel Luke wrote a cheque from his crumpled chequebook, the covers scoured with pencilled deductions. Nina stood outside on the pavement in her fur coat and looked the other way.

'Thank you, Mr . . . *Kanowski*,' said the hotel owner, his mouth clumsy around the word as if it were an unpleasant piece of foreign food.

They walked to the station slowly because of her heels on the uneven pavements and on the corner of George Street they stopped. A cold wind scattered specks of rain. He put his hand on her face and when she looked at him he felt still again. Calm.

'Do you know what I think?' he asked.

'What?' She smiled into the warm complication of his eyes.

'I think that you can't imagine what it's like to be free.'

She was transfixed, adoring him; strong.

'I don't want to do anything except –' the words faltered in daylight's scorn '– except to love you.'

'Me too,' she said and touched his mouth with her fingertips, his brow, his cheek, and kissed him. 'Me too.'

He had everything then. He was right to make her sure of him. She would be sure of him, and she would leave.

'I love you,' he said again.

'I don't deserve you,' she answered.

He saw her onto the train, endured the pain as it pulled her away from him, then went to the theatre. Four hours' sleep; burned and aching within and without from her imprint.

\*

*Paper Pieces* would run for three weeks in Oxford and then go on tour. Warwick Arts Centre, Harlow Playhouse, Swindon, Cambridge; it was done. Luke went back to London rejoicing in his tiny scale against the uncaring mass of the city.

'Fuck me, the bright lights of Fulham,' he said, as he came into the flat.

Paul was on the sofa. 'They didn't need you down there all the time anyway,' he said.

'Yeah, but I needed to be there,' said Luke, going into his room. He dumped his stuff on the floor, hauling out the important things: typewriter, books, pens.

Leigh was in her bedroom changing, a wake of steam and scent following her from the bathroom about the flat. The smell of her was home.

'You can come to this party with us if you want,' called Paul. 'Nag's Head fifth-year birthday do.'

'I've got work to do on *Diversion*,' said Luke, coming back into the living room.

'There are loads of people you should be meeting – there's interest in it, Luke, and you've been stuck down there.'

'My second act is like a car crash. Without the drama.'

'Ever heard of commissions? Revolutionary idea: you could get paid to fix it.'

Luke shrugged and changed the subject. 'Did you meet Michael Codron like you were going to?'

'Not yet.'

Luke went to the window and watched the taxi-lights passing by below.

'Front page of the *Standard* said, "Official: *total chaos* tonight," he told Paul happily. 'Thought they'd pressed the button. Turns out it's just the trains.'

'Yeah,' said Paul, 'business as usual.'

'Oxford is mental. They live in another world down there, and the chips are rubbish. Did you hear Ken Tynan talking to Morecambe and Wise on the radio? It was surreal. And he *admired* them – the high priest of culture dignifying the taste of the masses for a bit of publicity – *plus ça* fucking *change*.' He turned around. 'I thought I'd move out,' he said.

Paul was concentrating on his cigarettes, making a store for the evening. 'That's a good idea,' he said.

'Find myself somewhere Nina might want—'

Then Leigh came in, and Luke rushed her like a Labrador, picking her up and hugging her breathless. 'Hello!'

'Yes, hello, *drop* – I'm clean,' she said.

'I'm not dirty,' he said, putting her down, pushing her cheek with his finger and grinning at her.

'Congratulations, Luke,' she said. 'For the play. I'm so, *so* pleased for you.'

Luke was embarrassed, she was so formal about it.

Paul watched them, licking a Rizla edge before smoothing it down. 'O brave new world, that has such notices in it,' he said; 'Leigh's been scrapbooking.'

'Well, someone has to,' said Leigh.

'You look a bit of all right,' Paul said, looking at her dress and the curves of her body under it.

He stood up, tucked the cigarette into his shirt pocket, took her in his arms and kissed her. Luke put his hands in his pockets and looked away. It wasn't the sort of kiss they would perform alone, he thought; Paul had kissed her for him, and he wondered why.

'Now you're wearing my lipstick and I'm not,' she said. 'I'll be two minutes.' And she left them.

Paul dragged the back of his hand across his mouth. 'So, what's your plan?' he asked Luke.

'I need to find somewhere, I suppose.'

'You can afford to now,' said Paul.

'Yup.' Luke took in the familiar room and his heart hurt at the speed of change, and at the loss, but Paul had gone back to rolling his cigarettes. After a moment, Leigh came back in.

'Swine,' she said to Paul. 'You can't kiss me again until midnight—'

'Luke's moving out,' said Paul.

She paused, then, 'Oh, all right then,' she said, turning from him as if like Paul it meant nothing to her.

'Who'll do all the cooking?' said Luke.

'We manage fine without you,' she answered.


The Nag's Head party was in the pub itself and upstairs in the auditorium, with the theatre dark for the evening. Leigh, Paul and Luke left the car and walked towards the open doors. The crowd inside was noisy, blurred with light and smoke. As they forced their way into the crush Luke searched the faces for Nina, as if because she was in his mind she might magically appear.

'Drink?' said Paul.

'I'll see you in a minute,' Luke turned back towards the door. He couldn't stop himself.


Tony was in the bath when the phone rang.

Nina was getting dressed for the evening; she knew it was Luke immediately, and snatching up the receiver, craned her neck to check the bathroom door was closed.

'Hello?'

'*I'm at this party . . .*'

His voice transformed the moment, transformed her and made her smile.

'This thing at the Nag's Head,' he said. 'Will you come?'

'We were invited, but we're going somewhere else. Are you mad, calling now?'

'Just come—'

'Luke—'

'*Come*.'

'I'll try.'

'Who was that?' called Tony as she put down the phone. She crossed the landing to the bathroom and opened the door a crack.

'Terence Fowles. Wanted to know if we'd be there later,' she lied, easily. 'We should go.'

Terence was the artistic director at the Nag's Head, he'd called before about the party and she knew Tony wouldn't check. Still, her heart beat fast as he sighed and she heard bath water splashing.

'Of course we *should*. But I really must get to the Globe – you know I want to talk to Michael.'

Nina held her breath. She felt a sexual thrill at the adrenalin of waiting. She said, 'Let's – I'd like to, for *Custody*.'

'Fine. We'll stop by,' said Tony, unseen. She'd won.

As Luke came back into the pub he looked for Paul and Leigh—

'Jonathan!'

A man was standing in front of him. He had thick, forward-brushed dark hair, glasses and a moustache.

'Jonathan Bates? You were at my house in the summer.'

He stuck his hand out at Luke. BBC Jonathan. Shepherd's Bush. The au pair on the spare-room bed . . .

Luke smiled. 'Nice to see you. I'm Luke—'

'I know *exactly* who you are; I've heard wonderful things about your play.'

They started talking, and very soon more people joined them. Paul Ellis from the Shaftesbury. Michael Stanmore, who was starring in something on its way to Broadway from the West End, and was puffed up with relief and conceit; Paul Elliott, who Luke had worked with in Sheffield . . . People he had read about or knew; who in the past had no interest in him. He hadn't minded, had always been happy to observe and didn't care what they thought of him, but now the attention was uncomfortable. It made him want to get away, wriggling helplessly inside, like a beetle speared onto a card. This was what Paul had meant – about *Paper Pieces*, about people being interested. He could see that it was good – for his work, that had lived so long in a vacuum – but it felt nothing but strange and threatening to him to be noticed like this. He liked people but he had become used to being reacted to in a certain way, and now it had changed. It didn't interest him. It took him an hour to get to the bar, answering the same questions but not having a second to ask any, and then his drink was paid for by Lou Farthing – Lou Farthing who managed the Trafalgar, who had three hit plays on the go and who, according to the papers, was helping Olivier with the National Theatre's agonising move to its new home at the South Bank – Lou Farthing, who put a hand on Luke's restless shoulder and said, 'I was talking to your friend Paul the other day. Says that second play we talked about is ready.'

'*Diversion*? It isn't,' said Luke.

'Six more under the bed, he says?' said Lou, peering up at him, sweat sheening his forehead, aftershave coming off him in waves. He handed him a drink. A signet ring dwarfed the stumpy little finger of his hand.

'Thanks,' said Luke. 'Most of them aren't any good.'

He couldn't keep his eyes on Lou's button-like ones and looked around, wondering if Nina had managed to get away and what she would have told Tony, trying to keep his need for her in check.

'Here, meet Johnny Marston – he's in a fix,' said Lou, reaching to put an arm around the shoulders of a skinny, tall man in a limp cheesecloth shirt. 'And come and meet me next week, Luke. It's great to see you.' He clinked glasses with Luke and melted away.

Johnny Marston was quite drunk. He was a television producer at the BBC and had a 'huge massive fucking hole' in his schedule.

Luke fidgeted as he told a long and rambling story about how it had happened and all the people who'd let him down and how it was an honour to meet a writer of Luke's calibre – although he hadn't caught *Pieces* in Oxford yet. Luke felt sorry for him and told him he didn't know how to write for television, but he had some radio material he'd been working on and Johnny introduced him to somebody else, who worked in radio. Then someone bumped into him – and he looked down to see Leigh.

'Hello,' he said.

'I thought you'd gone.' Her eyes were sleepy, her hair tumbling over one eye.

'Sorry,' said Luke, turning from the radio man whose name he hadn't caught. He put his hand on Leigh's arm. 'No, I'm here. Are you all right?'

She didn't answer, just pushed away from him through the

people. Without knowing why, he felt concern for her and was going to follow, but then forgot because there in the doorway, across the dense crowd as if she were spotlit, was Nina. She was with Tony.

The radio man next to Luke said, 'Tony and Nina Moore,' like a footman announcing arrivals at a ball. 'Listen, come in to Broadcasting House next week, I've—'

Luke hadn't seen them together since the very first time he'd seen her at all, in Islington, and here it was, vicious proof of her marriage. Tony's hand on her elbow instead of his own.

She hadn't seen him yet. The crowd thickened with each moment; Luke, still and watching in the centre of it. They began to move in to the room, greeting people, smiling. Tony slipped Nina's coat from her shoulders and gave her a cigarette.

Luke waited; he waited and watched and finally, her eyes drifted across the faces that surrounded her, and she met his gaze. She barely smiled. Her expression was cool. Luke nodded towards the back of the pub – the corridor to the toilets and the stairs up to the theatre – and, imperceptibly, she agreed. He was punched in the gut by desire and tried to stop it; her husband was at her side. That couldn't be a thrill to him. But she was. She was.

He pushed his way across the pub and when he reached the scruffy vestibule and corridor – stuck with posters and half-filled with another little crowd – he stopped. Some women were waiting for the toilet and talking about the government, unemployment, foreign crises . . . He stood by the bottom of the stairs and waited.

He saw Nina go from one person to the next. It was like a chess game: Tony following her; her separating herself, carefully; Tony introducing her to someone; her moving away again, closer and closer to Luke until he could see the details of her – her lashes, the silk of her hair tucked behind her ears. But it was Tony who caught his eye and smiled, Tony who reached him first.

He held out his hand rather high to shake Luke's. His eyes were pale, Luke noticed, never having been as close to him before.

'You're Luke Last,' he said. 'I'm Tony Moore. Congratulations.'

Luke had nothing to say. He wanted to hit him. He'd never wanted to hit anyone in his life before and part of him was calmly interested by this atavistic maleness surging up through the unremembered centuries.

'Ken Tynan thinks you're a genius,' said Tony.

'I'm not.'

Tony laughed. 'Dearest, if Tynan says you are you may as well surrender. You know my wife, Nina, of course?' He turned to Nina.

She wanted to pretend she hadn't noticed but Tony was in her eye-line. She came over to them. Luke, in the grip of unaccustomed rage, couldn't move.

'What a terrible crush,' said Tony.

'Hello,' said Nina. 'We've met, I think.' And the bland way she said it made Luke almost believe he didn't know the feel of her skin, the things they had done.

'Yes, Luke Last,' said Tony. 'What would you rather be, Luke? *Enfant terrible* or great white hope?'

'I'm twenty-five,' said Luke, feeling silly. 'Hope for what?'

'Theatre, my dear—'

'It's done all right without me for two thousand years,' said Luke.

'Better with you, I hear. It's a comedy, your play.' He didn't ask, he told him.

'Yes,' said Luke.

'Light as a feather.'

Luke couldn't work out if he was insulting him. Tony laughed.

'I wouldn't call it lightweight,' said Luke, thinking of his play and what it had cost him to get it right.

'I've nothing against lightweight,' said Tony; 'I'm married to Nina.'

'What do you mean?' Luke heard himself say and felt a warning from her though she wasn't looking at him. 'How was *In Custody* light?'

'You saw it?' said Tony.

'Yes. A few times,' said Luke and Nina stared quickly at him, then abruptly down to the floor.

'How flattering, darling,' said Tony to her. 'You've got a fan. I'll leave you two together.'

And with that, he was gone.

'Why did you *say* that?' hissed Nina close to his ear, her mask falling away all at once.

Luke was too angry to speak.

'Do you think he knows it's you?' she was saying, panicking.

'I don't care,' said Luke. 'He's a prick.'

'Shh – stop it – don't. Oh, for God's sake! Here.'

She put her hand on his stomach and pushed him backwards until they were by the stairs. The women by the toilets glanced at them.

There was another door, behind him, and Nina shoved him through it into a dark space, a cupboard or storeroom, he couldn't tell. His back was to a wall. She kissed him. Her soft, lip-gloss mouth pressed against his. He sensed her excitement was fuelled by Tony in the crowd so near them, and the lovely thrill of her was corrupted. Carefully, he pushed her away from him.

'What?' she said, tearful, excited, half-laughing. 'You wanted us to come, didn't you?'

She came close and lifted her face to him.

'Not him,' he said.

The room smelled of bleach. They were inches apart in the shadows. Nina reached out and opened the door a little. The light came in so she could see his face clearly.

'I just needed you,' he said. 'I shouldn't have called. I'm sorry.'

'Oh,' she said bitterly, 'just like that.'

Luke frowned at the quickness of the change in her, the hardness in her.

'I suppose it's enough for you,' she said. 'You called; I came.'

'Do you want me to reassure you? What do you want me to say?'

'Nothing. I don't want anything.'

Without another word, giving him no chance to defend himself, she left. Luke stood alone – ridiculous – shaking at being misunderstood so completely.

Shutting the door he felt for the light switch. It was a storeroom, he saw now, not a cupboard. The single bulb lit toilet-roll, cleaning fluid, collapsing cardboard boxes of ragged costumes. The gritty walls were damp and cobwebbed. She had gone. He came back to himself. The thought struck him that even as he stood there, debased, six actors were performing *Paper Pieces* on the Playhouse stage with a thousand people watching.

Luke knocked the naked bulb with his finger. It swung back

and forth so that the shadows leapt and everything violently tip-tilted. He waited as the changing perspective settled.

———————

Tony and Nina left very soon. The party didn't stop. Speeches were made. Glasses were raised to Terence Fowles, the artistic director, to Victor Calgary who had raised finance, to the writers – listed, applauded – whose stories had found homes on the stage upstairs; the directors, actors, transferred shows; the work, the fight, the commitment that had kept the place alive for five years. They drank to five years more. In-house politics were made light of, conflicts dusted down and celebrated.

The close group of fifty or so who belonged and the fifty more who knew or loved them stayed. A man and a woman started to play guitars, and people grouped around to listen. Leigh had not been with Paul all evening. She found him in a corner talking to a producer called Maggie O'Hanlan, a skinny, redheaded divorcee in a rag-tag velvet coat, drinking whisky and telling stories about her time on Broadway with her ex-husband. The three men listening were either enraptured or alarmed by her, or both.

Paul didn't look up at Leigh at all. They were smoking a joint and Leigh took it, and some of Paul's whisky, which went down a little oddly on top of the wine and beer she'd drunk earlier. The grass was very strong and settling though, and she forgot to give the joint back, enjoying the burning wet Scotch and the hot dry smoke taking turns going into her. She leaned her forehead on Paul's shoulder so she could enjoy the swoops and dives her head was taking without trying to stay sensible-looking.

'. . . and take his money, and, for Christ's sake, *my* money from *Glitter*,' Maggie was saying, 'and do something that isn't bloody Eugene O'Neill, bloody Arthur Miller. Christ, I'm tired of those *great – big – heavy* – American – trudging-along plays . . .'

Paul moved his arm away so Leigh's head dropped down and knocked on the top edge of the chair.

'Ow,' she said, not really feeling it.

'Sorry,' said Paul but didn't look round.

Leigh stood up slowly, going more sideways than she'd meant. She pressed her cheek against Paul's head as she righted herself. Still he ignored her. She walked away carefully. The heating – if there had been any – had long since been turned off and Leigh was shivering with the slow-blood, late-night beginnings of a hangover. She still had the joint. She finished it, and held the smoke in her lungs for as long as she could because it was the last of it, thinking she might find the loo. She saw the doorway and went to it.

Luke was sitting in his coat, alone on the bottom stair in the deserted vestibule. Leigh stopped in the doorway on seeing him. He had his head down in his hands. She could not see his face. Leigh noticed she was swaying. She tried to decide whether to go past him to the loo, or leave. She didn't want to talk to him but she felt, she realised, a little slow on the uptake, and didn't manage to move her feet before he looked up and saw her.

'Hello,' he said.

His face made her smile; automatic happiness she couldn't summon or deny.

'Hello,' she said. 'I was . . .' She gestured the toilet door and then back into the pub and forgot what she had been going to say. The tiny cardboard end of the joint was stuck between her fingers. Her mouth felt horrible.

'You wouldn't want any of this,' she said.

'Any of what?' said Luke.

Leigh held up her hand, but the roach wasn't there. 'That's weird,' she said.

'Here,' said Luke, moving along the bottom step, 'sit down.'

She went and sat next to him, crossing her arms against the cold. He took off his coat and put it round her. She put it on, getting in a muddle with the sleeves and he helped her. The coat was big and olive-green, warm from his body.

Luke put his arm around her, as if that were all right, and normal. She didn't want to remember why it wasn't; she leaned into him.

'Better?' he said.

She nodded. 'This isn't your old one.'

'The old one went.'

'It was nice.'

'It was my father's.'

'Greatcoat.'

'Yep.'

'Great. Coat,' said Leigh. She giggled a bit. 'It was a great coat,' she said.

'Yeah, I get it.'

'Did he fly in it?'

'Jacket.'

'Mm. It would probably tangle up the pedals. Do Spitfires have pedals?'

'I don't know, Leigh.' He sounded kind.

She closed her eyes. He was very warm. He was always

293

warm, she thought, always warm and never wore sweaters. Always moving. Never there.

'Where's your girlfriend?' she asked, through the safety of closed eyes.

'With her husband,' said Luke.

'Oh,' she said. 'Yes.'

Leigh allowed the weight of her body to take her closer to him and felt his other arm go around her. He hugged her quite tightly. Her face was against his shirt, one of the buttons pressing on her temple.

'I was feeling much worse before,' she said.

'Me too,' said Luke.

'What worse about?'

'My girlfriend,' he said. 'Because she isn't.'

Leigh looked up at him when he said that because she knew him very well, and that he was in pain.

Looking up from the position her head was in their faces were close, as if they were lovers and they were going to kiss. His mouth was close to hers. The cold air touched her neck below her lifted chin.

'What?' he asked.

'You don't protect yourself from her. Or anything. Aren't you scared she'll hurt you?'

'She does hurt me,' said Luke.

They were both murmuring because they were so close.

'You shouldn't let her.'

'She doesn't mean to.'

'Maybe she does,' said Leigh.

Luke smiled. But he wasn't smiling at Leigh, he was smiling because he was thinking about Nina. It was as if Leigh weren't there.

'No,' he said. 'She just needs something. If I can give it to her, she'll——'

'Be your girlfriend? Leave Tony Moore?'

He nodded, not smiling any longer, and closed his eyes for a second. Leigh began to hurt just from looking at him.

'She doesn't trust me yet,' he said.

'Why would she?'

'What do you mean?' He was unafraid, wanting to know her thoughts.

'Do you think you'd be faithful to her?'

Luke frowned. 'There aren't any other girls any more,' he said.

'In the world?'

'In the world. Except you, of course.'

'Can you not?' she said.

'Not what?'

'Not say stupid charm things like that.'

'Sorry. It was just because we're like this.'

'You noticed?'

He smiled.

'I noticed,' he said. 'And there *are* girls. There are beautiful girls.' He said it not because he meant it, but to be comforting.

'You're only saying it to be polite, and that's just rude,' she whispered.

Then he stroked her cheek. Leigh closed her eyes. He stroked her cheek with the back of his hand, then a finger — two fingers — along her eyebrow, and her temple.

'It's just that I don't want them. I love her,' he said.

'I know that you do,' she answered him.

'What the fuck is going on?'

Paul was standing in the doorway. Leigh jerked away,

overcome by shame as if they had kissed, all the things that were in her mind.

'What are you doing?' said Paul. He was speaking to Luke, not to her. 'What the fuck are you doing?'

'Nothing,' said Luke — sweet and not defensive at all.

'Paul! God's sake,' started Leigh, trying to get up, but he turned on her.

'You're completely pissed.' Paul was angry, unlike himself.

'Paul,' said Luke, and he got up. 'We were just sitting there.'

'You were about to—'

'No. We weren't.' Luke stepped towards him, pacifying.

Paul rushed him. He shoved him backwards into the wall. 'What is your problem? Can't you leave *anyone* alone? Are the rest of us too small to bother with?'

She'd never known violence in Paul, never sensed it. He was trembling with rage. Luke didn't move, just stayed against the wall. Leigh was behind Paul, the too-big coat falling down over her hands.

'Take that off,' said Paul, over his shoulder.

Leigh took off the heavy coat and held it out, past him, to Luke, who took it, holding the other hand up to Paul, palm facing.

'There's nothing going on,' he said.

Leigh noticed people in the pub watching. She saw how they must look — a bar brawl, ludicrous.

'Paul,' she said, 'we should go.'

'*We?* Really, Leigh?' His voice was breaking. 'You and me?'

The three of them made a triangle in the small space, as far as they could be from one another.

Paul was halfway to the car, walking fast with his shoulders hunched.

'Paul!' Leigh caught up. 'Paul!'

He reached the car. He looked in his pockets, realised she had the keys and he couldn't get away from her.

'For God's sake!' she said. 'Me and Luke? You're mad.'

'Don't do that! Don't you tell me I'm making it up.'

'I love *you*.'

He stopped moving suddenly and stood against the car, covering his face. She didn't know if he was crying or not, feeling the tearing between them.

'We're *us*,' she said, terrified of being parted from him.

'Shut up.'

Paul wiped his eyes, sniffed, and put his hands in his pockets. He looked away, down the street, recovering some learned projection of masculinity – for her benefit, or his own.

Leigh watched his profile. She felt very clear, her thoughts were sharp and controlled.

'Paul. Listen to me. Luke is in love with Nina—'

Paul laughed, disdainful.

'Yes,' she said, 'I know, but listen. He was saying that he's unhappy and then he gave me his coat. He didn't *do* anything else. He was talking about *her*. I know that you think I . . .'

Paul listened, head up, alert to her.

She gathered her courage. 'I know you think I'm in love with him,' she said.

He looked at her then and she had nowhere to hide.

'Paul, I'm not.'

He didn't say anything, but his look –

She took a breath, and said the unsayable. If she didn't, it would always be there between them.

'There was — something.' She saw him flinch. 'But it's not real. I promise you.'

She went over to him, put her hand on his hand and held it.

'When I was little . . . my father and his girlfriends,' she said, 'you know it all, I've told you.'

Paul nodded.

'Every single day was like a lie or a justification of one. It was like brainwashing. It was like the bloody *Manchurian Candidate*.'

Paul laughed. He tried not to.

'No trust. None. That's not what I want. I'm not stupid. I can choose. It's not him, Paul. It's *you*. I'm not one of those girls destroying herself for . . .'

And she thought of Luke; the brightness of him, the too many sides to feel safe with any of them.

'For nothing,' she finished, and she felt a burden that had weighed her down lift. She'd tried her hardest. Honesty. Honesty and strength, she had nothing else to give him.

Then Paul put his arms round her and held her. He hugged her tightly. She was filled with gratitude. It was done. They were safe. She was safe.

———————

The next morning Luke bought a newspaper and went to a phone box with a stack of coins. By the afternoon he had found himself a two-bedroom flat in Bayswater. After he had been to the letting agent's office to sign the lease he called Nina — put the phone down after two rings and then called back. She answered immediately.

'I knew it was you.'

'You should work for MI5,' said Luke. 'Meet me.'

'I'm so sorry,' she said. 'I'm so sorry about last night, Luke. I was—'

'Don't be silly. I'll wait for you on the corner.'

When they met she couldn't do anything but cry. They stood there by the brown river with the wind blowing hard against them, cold and insistent, and he held her against him.

'I've found us a flat,' he said. 'It's all right.'


She came home to find Tony in the hall. Pushing the door closed on the wind, she leaned against it, still in her mac, clutching her raw-cold fingers together. She knew she looked wild, fresh with love and crying, no excuse ready for where she had been. But Tony did not ask. He seemed unusually cheerful.

'Get your passport, darling,' he said; 'we're going to the provinces.'

'What?' She sounded like an idiot child, wrong-footed yet again and slow.

'There are a *million* plays to see,' he said, 'and I've been putting them off. Come on – you'll love it.'

'Where?'

'Manchester first.' He seemed to notice her appearance for the first time. 'Darling, you're freezing.'

Nina didn't answer. There was no coincidence in the timing of this sudden whim.

'Nina?'

And there it was; presented with the opportunity to refuse him she found she could not. She was bound to go, she was voiceless.

'Why don't you pack?' he prompted. 'You've left things at

the dry cleaner's, I was just off to collect them. Shall we get a move on?'

And Nina went past him up the stairs.

'I'll just run a bath,' she said.

Luke moved out of Paul's two days later. His typewriter, the bags he'd arrived with four years before, boxes of books and a record player — all found their new home in the first-floor rooms on Moscow Road. A new bed. New walls and window.

The telephone wasn't connected yet and so he had to go out to a phone box. Enjoying the playful transparency, he let it ring just twice again, then called back and waited, holding the coin against the slot, ready — but she did not answer.

He tried again an hour later but there was still no answer.

The next morning a woman he didn't recognise answered the phone.

'Mr and Mrs Moore have gone away,' she said.

'Away?'

'Who is it? I can take a message.'

'No. Thank you,' said Luke, and went back to the empty flat where the bags of food he had bought for them both sat on the kitchen counter where he had left them.

In the afternoon he tried to work, but could not, struggling to absorb the body-blow of her wilful desertion. He couldn't understand what might be in her head. He sat at his desk and got nothing done. The flat was unfamiliar and he was used to concentrating despite Paul and Leigh. Silence was too large a thing to fill without the wall of activity to enclose him.

She had gone away.

The next day he gave in and went to her house — even rang

the bell. When the daily opened the door he stood there, asking stupid, pushing questions, until she shut him out, suspicious of him. He didn't blame her. If half of what he felt showed he must have frightened her.

There were several plays to see in various cities. They stayed in hotels and in those anonymous beds Tony had more interest in her sexually than he did in their own. She thought he must have sensed the danger of her leaving him; his rituals were more overtly dominating. Protecting herself from pain she did not have the luxury of courage. Nina had been too ashamed to tell Luke before she and Tony went, whilst away she was too bound up with surviving.

He had not used her like a boy since the first time, after her birthday party – the night *In Custody* had closed – but now, freed from the responsibility of context, he forced himself into her that way again. The second night they were gone he told her to get up on her hands and knees. No preparation. No seduction. But this time Nina fought him. She had become accustomed to restraint but was helplessly frightened of the pain, and could not help it. She fought him, and Tony smacked her head and face – just twice – and did not stop shoving himself into her. The smacking was so unlike him, more shocking even than what he was doing to her, that she stopped fighting. She stayed still. She learned, as he required her to, to relax. It never took him long to finish. She would make her body go limp, absent herself, and achieve sometimes a dream-like state where fantasies of rescue would release her. While he abused her body she set her mind on other paths to safer places. She would lose herself in dream-visions of Luke saving her, and their escape together, until the very fact of one thing being done to her so invasively while her heart found safety in another became connected. Pain and freedom, linked by hard sensation, became one.

Washing afterwards, or in her seat in the theatre, fully dressed, she would reflect on what was happening to her and wonder at it. *This is just the same* – she would think, as she watched a play, or went backstage, or stood in the comfort of a theatre bar as Tony talked. *This is normal. It's not as if he wants me very often. My life hasn't changed a bit. I'm fine.*

When they came back to London two weeks later, when she was alone and feeling more herself, she called Luke.

'I didn't know where you were,' he said, and cried.

'I'm back now,' she said coolly. 'Can we forget about it?'

---

Nina's award sat on the mantelpiece in the living room. She was between jobs, and resting.

*Rest on your laurels if you like, Nina*, said her mother, *but you'll turn around and realise you're thirty. What then?*

Tony was producing a new play by David Ward for the Adelphi and in negotiation for the management of a West End theatre that he wouldn't talk about for fear of jinxing it. As he left the house excitedly, adjusting his clothes, calling for her to find things for him, see him off, wish him luck, she would wait until the door closed, and a full minute to pass, and then pick up the phone.

'He's gone,' she would say. 'Can I come now?'

And Luke always said yes. He always wanted her. His bed was clean. He cooked for her. He told her to come to him whenever she wanted to. At first she respected his working hours but she found such reassurance in keeping him from writing that she could not resist it. She alone could trump the ace of his creativity. She could make him forget everything but her.

And so their horizons narrowed; Luke waited for her, and she came to him. They stopped talking about the future but formed the sharp secrecy, the limited habits of an affair. When Luke made love to her it was a sweet counterpoint to the fearful rush of sex she was used to. He made it possible for her to live more happily with her husband.

And Luke, living alone, made few demands on her. He got up at seven and worked on *Diversion* until one and didn't bother cooking with nobody there to feed. Having cooked for his father since he was nine he'd never had that luxury — or lack — before. He ate sandwiches from the café on his street or soup from tins. If Nina said she could see him, then the afternoons were for her; if she could not he worked again until the evening. When he couldn't sleep he worked at night, too. The play saved him. There was nothing else when he was writing it. He wrote and he waited. He didn't believe she meant to harm him; she did not know his constant lack that he had been reduced to craving. He fought against it but he lost the fight. It was an extremis he'd adored, but now he could not stop, and he began to dread the febrile shadow left when she was gone. Sometimes, even when she was with him he felt it, even when she was in his arms, when he was inside her, it was as if he could not touch her, could never get deep enough into her to make her real.

He would have liked to rest, just a little bit, and feel at

home, as he had when he, Paul and Leigh were together. He missed Paul even though he saw him often. And he missed Leigh. He tried to understand that she did not need him, but it didn't make rightful sense because their intimacy was intact in his head, a steady dialogue that didn't fade. Sometimes it felt to him as though he were writing a postcard every day to everyone he had ever loved.

The new play – the second play, *Diversion* – had changed so often it was as if he had written three plays, with three plays' learning crammed into it. He had been determined to strap himself down to a full-length mature narrative, even as instinct carried him from the well-made shapes of the past. He wasn't Beckett, he knew, and he couldn't surrender the hard-won shapes of story on a whim. *If it was good enough for Shakespeare*, he had once said to a furious Jack Payne, *it's good enough for us*. But proper form was more easily read than done. If the play was political – and he felt it was – it would be politics truthfully discovered, not applied. And so he fought with it, putting in elements, taking them out – time sequences shuffled, dream sequences put in and discarded, put back in subtler tones; monologues slashed and built and slashed again.

    *Diversion* was about the conflict between a father and son. Instead of the old order replaced by the new – the revolution of the sixties that now seemed pitiful to Luke in its innocence – in *Diversion* it was the son who sought order; the younger man seeking to repair the damage of inheritance. It was not the son who was anarchic but the father. Luke thought of his play as he thought of life itself; as a tragedy with jokes. In it, the son's carefully built framework, his false home, was destroyed in the end by the chaos of his upbringing. As hard as he fought, the past had forged him a path and he could not leave it. The play was Luke's close companion and his bitter enemy. It was the very best that he could do. It must be better than he was. It was work to him; it was play and escape. He loved it, was as ashamed of its shortcomings as his own. Until one Wednesday afternoon, reluctantly, it was done.

He sat at his desk in the new silence of the moments that followed its end, the pages stacked and corrected in front of him. He ought to have felt happy but he did not. The first thought that came to him was that if it were produced he would be able to work on it again and delay the abandonment, this feeling that was like a death.

Paul and Leigh had known the play since its earliest, smallest life. Luke picked up the phone and dialled.

'Paul?'

'Luke.'

'Busy?'

'You might say.' This had become Paul's habitual tone with him now; guarded, cool.

'Would you read *Diversion*? It's done. Sort of.'


Paul had gone into partnership with Maggie O'Hanlan. They had met at the birthday party at the Nag's Head, and talked about forming a production company on and off since then. They shared a tiny office in Soho, a stone's throw from the Duke of York's, where Leigh was still stage manager. Maggie was a divorcee of thirty-five, setting up on her own having left both the partnership of her marriage and the company she shared in New York with her ex-husband. She had red hair and, like Paul, she chain-smoked — but hers were Gauloises and they only nicked cigarettes from one another in moments of crisis. Her ex-husband was a producer about whom the term *Broadway impresario* was increasingly used. Maggie's sensibilities suited London better. She felt there was too little innovation in New York, restricted as it was by commerce, what she called the 'low business of show business'. Maggie hated musicals and the brutal coin-flip of success or failure dictated by first-night reviews that saw plays open and close in a week. She had worked on one big-budget show that had such poor notices on opening night half the cast hadn't even bothered to come in the next day. In Britain — despite the fast-crumbling infrastructure, despite the tide of American pulp washing over the airways, despite the power failure of the tailspin economy — everyone talked about theatre. The death of the West End was announced regularly but still it had not died. In Britain theatre was not bread and circuses but a poke in the eye, a joker — a *play*. London. London, Maggie said, was theatre's beating heart. Why would she work anywhere else?

Maggie had *divorced well*, as she herself put it. Her passion was for the dangerous fragility of new work and she was unashamedly bankrolled by the fat returns of Broadway melodies and high-kicks. She bought a long lease on a warehouse below Covent Garden, saving it from demolition, and building work had already begun. With his slice of the producers' split with Archery from *Paper Pieces* and a loan Paul bought a portion of the building from Maggie. He called it his *Papercuts*. He would shout to Leigh as he left the flat — 'Off to Papercuts' — and never forgot that he wouldn't have been able to make his true start without it, or without Luke. The theatre would be ready to open with a new play in June – if they were lucky.

He and Leigh were working at opposite ends of the day; he office hours, she theatre. The new show at the Duke of York's was a bedroom farce; the light, fluffy opposite of its predecessor *In Custody*, uninteresting to Leigh in everything but that it was written by a woman. Given that, it was disappointing there was no alteration to the age-old tradition of men chasing reluctant women about the stage – except for the addition of a nymphomaniac, just to spice things up. It was like an upmarket *Not Married?!* and her feeling of treading old ground, revisiting old foes, was wearying.

'Sweetie, you should get the hell out of that theatre,' Maggie said, one Sunday when Paul had brought his work, and her, home with him. 'Move on. There are *amazing* things happening out there, my love . . .'

Leigh knew there were, but she and Paul needed the money. She didn't have Maggie's freedom to indulge in grand gestures. She said nothing.

She was cooking lunch while Paul and Maggie went over the contractor's invoices and argued about a proper name for their new theatre.

'We have to stop calling it Papercuts. It was the O'Hanlan until you showed up.'

'Thank God for me showing up. O'Hanlan sounds like a pub,' said Paul.

'We could call it the New.'

'Been done.'

'The Factory.'

'Andy Warhol. And not our ethos.'

Leigh made a heap of her potatoes, carrots, cabbage;

chopping calmly, soothing herself, trying not to interfere. She had too many opinions, she ought to leave them to it.

'It's getting ridiculous. The slab is laid,' said Maggie. 'Is the wine in the fridge?'

'Help yourself,' said Leigh.

'Thanks, love.'

'The Union,' said Paul.

'Awful.' Maggie poured her wine, and a glass for Leigh. 'The Directive.'

'Stalinesque,' said Paul.

'The Rose?'

'Pretentious.'

Leigh scooped a double handful of vegetables into the seething water on the stove and then she turned to face them.

'The Depot,' she said. 'It was a fruit and veg depot for Covent Garden. Call it the Depot.' And as she spoke, creating something even so very small as a name, she could feel herself light up.

Maggie and Paul looked at her.

'The Depot,' said Maggie. 'Genius.'

'That's my girl,' said Paul. 'Done.'

Leigh blushed and turned back to the stove. 'Paul,' she said, 'Gerry asked me to read some of the submissions at the theatre, and pass on the ones I like. He won't pay me. I said I would.'

But they hadn't heard.

Maggie lived in a house in Notting Hill. The back door was always open to the bramble-filled communal gardens and she had a child and a nanny, neither of whom she referred to by name. The Nanny. The Child. Everyone else was similarly *love* or *darling* or *sweetie* and she owned a St Bernard called Marigold — *the dog* — that Paul suspected she loved more than her daughter. The great wet-mouthed dog lay on the landing, or under her desk, and barked boomingly at the out-of-breath writers and directors who climbed the six flights for meetings. The important ones were met in the coffee bar downstairs, or at restaurants. The hungry and the hopeful made the climb.

Paul didn't know when he'd ever have even a veneer of the ballsy confidence Maggie displayed, and assumed she thought of him as a boy. He would hear her voice on the phone talking to prospective backers, sharp-carrying across the space between them, *Look, love, I'm not moving on this one.*

Maggie was deceptively kittenish in her looks, had a lewd turn of phrase and drank like a man. She scorned Paul's caution but he suspected she was more afraid than she looked.

'Are you going to post me the manuscript?' said Paul to Luke on the phone when he told him *Diversion* was finished, Maggie watching him shrewdly across the desk.

'Luke?' prompted Paul.

'I'll bring it in to you there, if that's okay,' said Luke. 'The post is rubbish.'

He couldn't let it leave his hands so easily.

He had never promised *Diversion* to Paul, but there had always been an assumption he would have first refusal. Now, with things the way they were between them, it was the one bond upon which they could rely.

'We could always talk about opening the Depot with it instead of the Denton,' said Maggie, when Paul had put the phone down. 'We haven't absolutely committed yet. The new Luke Last might be perfect. If it's any good.'

'It'll be good, Mags,' said Paul.

Archery Productions had gone into partnership with the Arts Theatre, and *Paper Pieces* was opening there in May.

'*Paper Pieces* with a West End transfer, Paul: all the more papercuts for you, you clever boy,' Maggie had said when they heard. 'I'll drink to that.'


Luke ran the six flights up to the Depot's offices with the manuscript tucked safe inside his jacket.

'Here,' he said, and put it on the desk in front of Paul, regretting the few bent corners it had suffered when he put it in the envelope.

'Will you stay for a bit? I can read it tonight,' said Paul.

'Hello,' said Maggie, eyeing Luke like a sailor on a dock watching prostitutes.

'Hi,' said Luke, with Marigold sniffing at his crotch.

'Coffee, then?' said Paul. 'We can go downstairs.'

'I've got to meet that Lou Farthing,' said Luke. 'But later?'

'What does my old mucker Mr Farthing want with you?' asked Maggie, getting up.

She hauled the dog off him and dragged her back to the desk, fondling her ears and kissing her.

'I don't know. He said to meet a while ago but I wasn't around,' said Luke.

'Watch out for him,' said Maggie, 'he bites.'

Paul picked up the play. 'Is this the only copy?'

'I made another down the road. It's at home.'

'All right. Well, then, shall I call you when I've finished?'

Luke hated to leave. He fidgeted about, glancing at it.

'Luke?' said Paul. 'I'll call when I've read it, okay?'

'Yeah, yeah,' said Luke. 'It needs work, though.'

He turned to Maggie. 'Nice to see you,' he said. 'How's the Depot coming?'

'We're getting there.' She looked at Paul. 'Aren't we, love? We're getting there.'

Paul nodded.

'Great,' said Luke with a last quick look at his play in Paul's hands. 'Let me know, then? . . . See ya.' And he went.

'Odd fish, your attractive friend, isn't he? Does he ever keep still?' said Maggie when he'd gone. 'Show me it immediately you've done, love.'

'If he lets me,' said Paul. 'Attractive?'

'Sweetie, everyone says it.'

Everyone did say it, but Paul didn't like to hear it from Maggie and didn't exactly know why. He didn't mind usually that she talked about men the same way men talked about girls, but her noticing Luke grated on him.

Luke walked the twenty minutes to Lou's office above the Trafalgar. He hadn't thought about the meeting and didn't much want to go, but he had said he would be there.

Lou Farthing liked to make an impression. Not for him the tatty posters and coffee rings, the shabby stairs and ashtrays. He had a vestibule to his office where his secretary sat at a walnut desk, and the whole place had something of the air of small-scale, nineteen-thirties Hollywood about it – including Lou himself, whose cravat and immaculate hair and nails spoke loudly of his success.

He made Luke wait. Luke had made him wait first, after all; it was the currency of power.

'My boy,' he said on greeting him, standing up and swelling to his full five feet five. 'What took you so long?'

'Work and things,' said Luke. 'How are you?'

Lou didn't tell people how he was. It didn't interest him.

They talked about the play. Lou was full of flattery. He said he had been excited to see how Luke would follow up *Paper Pieces* and he hoped he hadn't been seduced by television.

'No – I've been doing a bit of radio. But mainly finishing the play.'

'*Finishing* it? I wanted to talk to you about a commission. What is it? And, more to the point, who is it for? Luke Last's second play; I had hopes.'

'Of what?' asked Luke, thinking that when he was writing he never thought of his work as *for* anyone, and wondering if that made it worse.

Lou smiled. 'Have a drink,' he said. He took a bottle from the cabinet behind him. 'Melanie!' he barked. 'Ice!'

Luke heard a mewing response from the vestibule. 'No, thanks,' he said, 'not for me.'

'Nonsense,' said Lou. 'Have a drink.'

So they drank Scotch and soda at four in the afternoon, and Luke told him about the play.

'*Diversion*,' said Lou, trying it out. '*Diversion* . . . Where will it land? Ben Greene's your agent, isn't he?' He looked as if he might call him then and there. He tapped his signet ring on the telephone next to him like a metronome, a habit he was known for when he scented a deal.

'Yes, but it's on Paul Driscoll's desk,' said Luke, trying to be clear but still not knowing what that meant exactly.

'For the Depot?' asked Lou. 'If they ever finish the build.

That's taking a punt, isn't it? Ben must have told you, you could take your pick.'

'I don't know. I'm not sure. I haven't spoken to Ben. I've only just done it.'

Lou's telephone rang. He answered it. It was a well-known director and Lou talked, in a leisurely fashion, for several minutes before he turned his attention back to Luke.

'So, Luke, tell me, you've *sold* this piece to the Depot? Have they optioned it?'

'I've just given it to Paul,' repeated Luke.

The telephone rang again. Lou covered the mouthpiece — *excuse me* — he mouthed.

Luke left him. He stood about outside the door with the secretary at her desk and read the framed, glassed-in posters on the walls. They were all hits — varying genres and uneven quality, but all hits. Melanie typed and glanced, typed and glanced, and eventually said, 'He won't be long. When Lord Olivier calls he likes his privacy.'

Luke nodded. He'd read about all of this; the jostling at the top, but from the inside it was just one person talking to another and interested him less than overheard conversation in the street, the weather changing in the sky.

'You wouldn't believe the gossip,' said Melanie.

'I would,' said Luke, and rocked back and forth on his heels for a while.

'My boy!' barked Lou from within and when Luke went back into his office he seemed to have grown two inches since his negotiation with greatness.

'Now this play,' he said, grinning, 'I'd like to see it, if I may.'

'Yeah, of course,' said Luke, beginning to wonder how soon he could leave.

'I'm booking the new season for the Trafalgar. What do you think?'

'Of the Trafalgar?'

Lou laughed, as if he were joking. 'I'm *interested*. Send it to me.'

They shook hands.

The next morning he ran off another copy of *Diversion* in the back of the undertaker's down the road, sent it off to Farthing's office and thought no more about it; Paul had called him at midnight and told him he loved his play and Luke had no other question in his mind about it than that.

———————

Nina had been out with Chrissie. She came into the house with shopping bags and hair done, running up to the living room to spread out her new things and drape them on the furniture. She poured a drink – vodka over ice, and a brief squirt of the soda siphon – and lit a cigarette standing by the mantelpiece, her arm resting close to her award. She surveyed all the prettiness of the colours laid out.

'Darling?' came Tony's voice from the study, 'Darling!'

She went to him and pushed the door open.

Tony was at his desk, a cigarette in a holder resting in the square glass ashtray, a manuscript in front of him. He leaned back in his chair.

'Good day?' he asked.

'Yes, lovely,' said Nina.

'With . . . ?'

'Chrissie.'

'. . . Chrissie,' said Tony, slowly.

He left a pause, in which she began to feel nervous, and then he pushed the manuscript across the desk towards her.

His name stood out as if swelling from the page: *Luke Last*. Black typescript, the name, and above it — *Diversion*. Nina didn't move; she didn't breathe.

'There might be a very nice part in this for you,' said Tony.

'Oh?' said Nina. 'Where did it come from?'

'You remember our friend, the writer, don't you?' said Tony.

Nina met his eye.

'Vaguely,' she said.

'He was rather memorable, I thought, in that Jewish way. Good-looking.'

In that Jewish way. Nina realised that Tony knew all about it. All about her. All about everything.

'I'd be very interested to know what you think of it,' he said. 'You know me, I don't give out praise cheaply. It's the best thing I've read in years. Absolutely riveting. And very sad.'

'Why does it matter what I think?' asked Nina.

'I told you, darling, there's a nice part in it—'

'You know I hate reading all the way through things and finding someone else is doing it, or it will never see the light of day,' said Nina.

'This will,' said Tony. 'Lou is thinking about it for the Trafalgar. I say *thinking* — he's madly in love with it. I think you will be, too.'

'All right,' said Nina, and she smiled at him, 'I'll take a look.' She turned away.

'Nina!'

She stopped.

He held the manuscript out across the desk towards her, and when she took it, watched her as she left the room. 'Good,' he said.

She sat on the wicker chair in the living room, trembling, steadying her breath, and with weak fingers she turned over the top page.

> Characters: Tom, a son (20s)
> Peter, a father (40s)
> Mary, a girl (20s)
> Elsa, her mother (50s) . . .

Through the confusion of her emotions two things presented themselves with clarity: that she had never once asked Luke about the play while he was working on it, and that she wanted – hungrily needed – to know if there was a part that would suit her. Shocked at her own voracious soul, she put down the innocent manuscript and covered her face.

The radio was on in the study, and faintly from across the landing, she heard a male announcer's voice. *You're listening to the six o'clock news. In a landmark decision in the United States, the Supreme Court has ruled that abortion is a private matter to be decided by mother and doctor in the first three months . . .*

*More loosening of the reins*, she thought dimly. If her own mother had such a choice she never would have been born. Tony switched the radio off.

Nina uncovered her face and looked up at all her new clothes strewn across the chair and sofa-back. She slipped off her shoes, tucked up her feet, picked up Luke's play and began to read.

*

The Depot was still a building site. Luke went with Maggie and Paul and walked the uneven floors beneath the hanging wires while they met the lighting designer and architect.

The stage was an apron; the steeply raked seating would be on three levels and three sides. Three hundred and fifty fold-down plastic seats; no velvet, no proscenium arch – and yet nothing like the pub theatre it had been born of. It was to be a modern, raw place, not pretending anything; a scaffold for the work it would present. The brick was to be left exposed, or naked plaster. Maggie and Paul were keen not to mask the origins of the building; to hide as little as possible but still have the possibility of ambitious, large-scale productions. It was a vision realised in part – to Paul's ambivalence and pride – by his father's engineering company sub-contracted at Paul's request by the architect. *This is a tiny job for us, we won't be doing you and this O'Hanlan bird any favours*, his father had said. Financially he was true to his word, but Paul found unaccustomed pleasure in working with his father. And he hadn't wanted favours.

Luke stood on the sectioned concrete slab that would soon carry the stage and looked into the high dark spaces; as yet no seats, no wings, no lighting rig – and yet it was a theatre. He stood among the ghosts of the future, risking themselves.

'What's he doing now?' said Maggie, picking her way, in her high boots and belted coat, and peering down at him from the top of the grid deck, holding Paul's arm for security.

'He's just waiting for us,' said Paul.

The builders had gone home, and the architect. Paul had the keys to lock up. He loved this time of day, the spring twilights when he would often come and walk the site, alone or with Maggie, picturing how it would be, trying to put away the day's dirt and fear, the scrabbling for money.

'Sweetie,' said Maggie, teetering on the metal gridwork, gripping Paul's arm and the low rail that separated them from the hundred-foot drop. '*Diversion?*'

'No. We can't commit until next week,' said Paul.

Her heel slipped on the metal and Paul caught her arm to steady her.

'He's your friend,' she said, pulling away, 'and we *want* it.'

'I know we do. But yes, he's my friend. What kind of a contract can we offer him if we don't know if we can even open this year?'

'We will. And you're too honourable.'

'I'm sorry.'

'Don't be. But he might give it to someone else,' she whispered.

'Luke isn't like that.'

They both looked down again at Luke, hands in pockets, his expression responding to his thoughts, looking up and around him as if in silent monologue to the empty space.

'Does he hear voices?' said Maggie.

Paul looked at her, sharply. 'He's all right,' he said.

In a week they would know if they were opening in May; if the money was there and the building work on schedule. Six months of headaches and administration, pulling strings and squeezing the reluctant udders of Maggie's alimony cash-cow. *I'm not letting go of my twenty-five per cent of Glitter*, she would say grimly of the show she and her ex-husband had fallen out over, still going strong on Broadway.

They had not applied for Arts Council funding. Paul called subsidies hush money — *Big Brother telling us what we can and can't put on* — but as Maggie was putting up the bulk of their finance she was understandably nervous. There was no turning back. No grant. No help. No council remit. And the Depot was hoping to survive against – compete with – the heavily subsidised National. *We're not a fringe theatre*, Paul often said, *we're a West End theatre*. But now, looking about the grim warehouse it was hard to imagine seating, let alone applause and box-office receipts. Neither of them had slept a full night for months.

Luke looked up at them, alight with enthusiasm and love for the endeavour that scared them both so much.

'Fuck,' he called up, 'this is spectacular. This is like the fucking Colosseum.'

'There's a thought,' said Paul. 'Let's have lions eating critics on a Saturday night – bring in the punters.'

'Pub,' said Maggie. 'Whisky.'

They went to the pub and crowded on cushioned stools around the tiny table with their drinks, Maggie and Paul smoking as if it were their last meal and Luke pretending he wasn't thinking about *Diversion*, that it wasn't what he was there for.

'Let's not bugger about,' said Maggie. 'We had planned to open with the new Denton as our first production—'

'What's it about?' said Luke, who admired Gerald Denton, and forgot about himself at hearing his name.

'Revolution,' said Paul. 'Totalitarianism.'

'Again?' said Luke.

'It's different – more human. It's really interesting. We had Michael Elder to direct but he's gone off to Broadway with *The Party Leadership*.'

'Anyway,' said Maggie, glancing at Paul, 'we're bringing in George Bean's *Hamlet* from Nottingham—'

'Bloody hell,' said Luke, impressed. 'How did you get it?'

'Long story,' said Paul.

'Yes, I only had to shag about sixteen people,' said Maggie, and Paul choked into his beer. Luke grinned at her.

'Nice one,' he said. 'That *Hamlet*. Fuck me. For once the critics aren't exaggerating. What George has done with it is—'

'Yes, I know,' said Maggie impatiently. 'But we don't want to open with it, it's identified with the Playhouse. We want a new play.'

'Yeah,' said Paul, 'we don't think it's risky enough to start up a new theatre, totally unknown, we want something no one's ever heard of, too.'

Luke laughed.

'Darling,' said Maggie, 'babes.' Both men looked at her. '*Diversion*.'

Luke looked down at the table, fearful even at the name.

'Luke, man,' said Paul, 'let's get this straight. I don't want you doing us any favours.'

Hearing himself he thought wryly of the osmosis of inheritance.

'What are you talking about?' said Luke, leaning forward. 'I owe you everything, you know that. Where else would it go?' He corrected himself, embarrassed: 'I mean, if you want it.'

There was a pause.

'Oddball,' said Maggie, 'we want it.'

'Then it's yours,' said Luke. 'Thank you. If you're sure. Thank you.'

'We're sure,' said Maggie.

Paul nodded. It felt as if they should shake hands — something — but they did not. Nobody said anything. Luke's new play would have its first performance at Paul's new theatre. Neither of them needed to say how it felt, or that all the years since they met had lit the way to this moment. The three of them acknowledged the promise silently, the courageous moment flaring like a comet. The glare faded.

'Oddball?' said Paul. 'New nickname?'

'He's stuck with it now,' said Maggie. 'Right, let's think about directors.' And she got out her big pad and a clutch of biros.

---

Luke was at his flat. His agent was negotiating with Maggie and Paul on the contracts and he had put *Diversion* and the notes for it and earlier drafts in the top cupboard of the kitchen, and sellotaped the doors shut so that he could try to begin thinking about other work.

He had ideas, old and new, on one handwritten page, and blank notebooks waiting for him to find the focus. The phone rang.

'Christ,' he said, and only picked it up because it might be Nina.

'Mr Last?' said a woman.

Luke always wanted to say 'wrong number' when people called him Mr Last.

'Hello.'

'It's Melanie in Lou Farthing's office, I have Mr Farthing for you, will you hold on?'

'Hello, Melanie. Yes, thanks.'

After a pause, Lou's voice: 'Luke, my boy, glad to find you in.'

Where else would he be? 'How are you?'

'I've booked us a table at the Garrick this afternoon. Let me buy you lunch.'

'Today?' Luke looked down at his desk, and the notebooks waiting.

'Around two?'

'I'd like to, but I'm working.'

'I want to talk to you about *Diversion*.'

'Oh.' Luke had forgotten all about sending it to him and was wrong-footed, not knowing how to tell him he had already given it to Paul.

'Hello, Luke? Is this a bad line?'

'No.' He thought for a second.

Part of him was relieved not to have to face the blank page. He should tell Lou in person he had already found a home for *Diversion*, it was only good manners. He would probably have to pay the bill at the Garrick to appease him.

'Yes, fine, good,' he said. 'Two o'clock.'

'Marvellous. See you later.' And the line went dead.

The doorman at the Garrick had to lend Luke a tie. With the stained, striped, borrowed absurdity around his neck he followed another ancient, liveried man through the silent panelled ante-room, past the paintings and funereal flower arrangements, the leather armchairs of old men, staring at him as he walked towards the muffled clink of china and cutlery in the dining room.

At a table by the window, laid for three, were Lou Farthing and Tony Moore. Luke stopped.

Both men stood up: the round, oiled figure of Lou; the

slender, stylish lines of Tony, with his gleaming side-parting and narrow-cut jacket.

'Welcome,' said Lou.

Luke took a step back, gesturing the exit as if he would leave.

'I was—'

Tony smiled. 'We must stop meeting like this, Luke,' he said. 'Or start.'

The old man who had accompanied Luke into the dining room stepped forward and pulled out his chair for him.

'Sir?'

And Luke did not leave, he sat – across the table from Nina's husband, a place he never wanted – his mind scrabbling to find an exit, failing.

'Are you all right?' said Tony, not taking his eyes from his face.

'Yes,' said Luke clearly. 'Are you?'

Lou waved for the wine list and the lunch began.

Compliments and small talk; assurances of quality and taste.

The conversation moved from the shocked whispers of Peter Hall's regicidal usurping of Olivier at the National and declining audiences at the Old Vic, to Shaffer's divisive *Equus*; from the technical crews threatening to strike and leave the West End dark to the money, the critics, the work, and all the time Luke felt Tony's eyes examining him, and battled too familiar revulsion at his role of thief and liar. *It would be better to be the cuckold than the coward*, he thought, wanting to speak out, but honesty was denied him. Nothing could be said in Lou's company; no duelling pistols produced; no gauntlet thrown down.

They were not stupid, these successful men, they were not

crass. It was too easy, when struggling to find a place in the tight hard world, to assume those at the top knew nothing. Luke saw that they loved theatre, and cared for the plays and helpless as he was in his hatred of Tony as Nina's jailor he could not help but admire his incisive mind. He had a talent; he knew what worked.

There were no women at the Garrick; they were safe to play soldiers in the no man's land of ideas beyond full humanity's reach, but it was no kind of relaxation. Lucasz Kanowski; foreign, unentitled, unsettled and groundless, he muddled through the cutlery as he did the conversation – not intellectually threatened but floundering still; impressed by the money despite himself, and fighting to retain his balance in this rarefied atmosphere of invisible forces. This world of power.

Then –

'Luke,' said Lou with a wave of his cigar, 'L. M. Farthing Productions and Tony Moore would be honoured to produce your play at the Trafalgar.'

He said it as if he were whipping a large, wrapped present from beneath the table and bestowing it upon Luke just as the waiter brought the coffee and brandies. Tony leaned forward and smiled, waiting for his reaction. Luke looked from one to the other.

'You and Tony?' he asked.

'You've probably heard whispers, it's an open secret now; Tony is joining the Trafalgar as our new Artistic Director. I'm taking a step back. Other commitments.' He smiled his Lord Olivier smile. 'Tony is committed to good work, I have tremendous faith in you, and we would all see to it that you're involved in every decision.'

Luke pushed back his chair and it caught on the carpet, unevenly – he almost stood. Didn't.

'That's nice,' he said at last. 'I didn't mean to waste your time. *Diversion* is opening at the Depot in June. I should have said.'

'OH!' Lou gave a shout, throwing both hands in the air, so that every man in the room turned to him.

Tony remained watching Luke with rapt attention.

'When did this happen?' said Lou, his eyeballs bulging, his upper lip achieving a layer of sweat. 'Luke . . .'

'Just recently,' said Luke.

'Big mistake. Big mistake. That *divorcee*?'

'Maggie O'Hanlan,' said Luke steadily, knowing that Lou knew her name perfectly well and was trying to unsettle him.

'She's a loose cannon, the lady producer. A hysteric. Her husband was the brains of the operation. That woman – the stories I heard in New York.'

'I like her,' said Luke. 'She's bright. She knows what she's doing. And Paul Driscoll is an old friend.'

Still Tony didn't speak.

'That old warehouse, way over there?' gestured Lou. 'The cement won't be dry in time.'

'There's no rush,' said Luke. 'I don't mind.'

Then, finally, Tony said lightly, 'Is there *anything* we can say to change your mind?'

Luke looked him in his pale, cool eyes and tried to force the thought of Nina from his mind but she wouldn't go. He felt her with him; his companion, his girl.

'Nothing,' he said. 'It's done.'


He left the Garrick and walked. Down to the Strand and along the Mall to St James's Park.

The daytime was always an unusual delight to him, living so much in darkness – theatres, pubs, rehearsal rooms – he took the night for granted. This day was golden; crocuses and cut grass and people who knew nothing of theatre, who had other lives, were walking. Teenagers lay on the grass around a radio on the ground beneath a tree; flared jeans and kissing. It was as though he were being given this sunlit day specially and he felt grateful for its prettiness. He had the breath of life with Nina and he had his work. If he kept to truthfulness, and courage, he would not lose them.

He opened the door to his flat and as he was putting down his keys saw Nina naked in his bed. Her head was resting on her hand as she waited for him, smiling. Her long hair lay upon his pillow. The afternoon light from the window made lovely patterns in the creases on the sheet draped over her.

She had surprised him like this before. He had given her a key hoping that she would. Sometimes it was in the middle of the night; sometimes she woke him with her visits, slipping into bed, entering his dreaming senses before he knew the gratitude of her reality.

'Hello,' he said.

'Tony's out at some lunch or other,' she said.

Luke went and sat on the edge of the bed and kissed her as she sat up to meet him.

'You don't mind?' she asked, naked through the sheet, and him in his clothes.

'I'd rather you were properly dressed and made an appointment,' he said.

Then he saw that she had something – half hidden under the sheet.

'I read your play,' she said shyly. 'Twice.'

She pulled the manuscript out to show him. Her eyes were shining as she waited for his response.

Luke sat back.

'I've just come from the Garrick with – Tony – and Lou Farthing,' he said. 'Some lunch or other was with me.'

'With you?' she said, her innocent eyes widening. He nodded.

She pulled her knees to her chest, the sheet across her breasts.

'Oh,' she said, the happiness draining from her as the weight of her other life returned.

'You didn't know?'

'I should have done,' she said tiredly. 'What's going to happen?'

'With him? Nothing. I've given it to Paul – him and Maggie. For the Depot.'

'Oh,' she said again, looking down.

She picked up the play and looked at it, holding it like a living thing.

'Luke,' she said, 'whatever happens, I love it.'

'You love it?'

'I love it, and I love you,' she said.

She put her arms around him, kissing him. She did not let go of the play. He could feel it resting on him as she held him.

'You're so clever,' she said, with her cheek to his. 'I didn't know you were so sad.'

'I'm not,' he answered. 'It's a play.'

'A genius's play.'

'Yeah, I'm a genius,' said Luke, his hand on her bare back.

'Don't give it to him,' said Nina.

'Who?'

'To Tony. Don't.'

'I told you, I haven't.'

Pulling the sheet with her she moved onto his lap; arms around his neck, kissing him, and filling him with light-hearted joy. She dropped the heavy stapled pages on the bed.

————————

And then the fun. From the first list of ten there were three directors they were seriously interested in. Howard Emerson and Jeffrey Knight were busy, but James Bridge was available. Then Emerson's project fell through and Bridge was attached to the new Osborne. Then the Osborne was delayed by artistic differences and Bridge came back in. The artistic differences had been that Osborne was a wanker, he told them, and they started to talk about actors. Eight roles to cast, and of those, six significant ones.

There were actors Bridge had worked with and others that Maggie or Paul or Luke suggested. Lists were made over coffee downstairs or, more usually, at Maggie's house in Ladbroke Gardens while her eight-year-old daughter, boyish-haired and barefooted, wandered in and out. Maggie sometimes left meetings to feed her or argue with her ex-husband or her lawyer on the telephone.

They were in the basement kitchen. They had eaten chicken casserole, Maggie handing out drumsticks to the child and flesh to the dog — *the child can have the bones, the dog will choke* — and were now drinking red wine and going through *Spotlight* for actresses as if they were shopping from the Littlewoods catalogue.

'Nina Jacobs,' said Luke when Paul was out of the room, because the night before Nina had lain in his arms and whispered, 'I want to play that part.' Just that. No preamble, no persuasion.

Luke never considered casting when he made characters, but even looking at Mary from this distance he did not see the spirit of Nina in her. It surprised him because Nina had been so much in his heart while he was writing it.

When she went home to her husband, in the cold aftermath that followed sex when she was gone from him, he thought about it, and that he believed if she wanted, she could play anything. If she wanted it he would mention her name. It couldn't hurt the play, he thought, just to ask.

'Maggie?' he said again. 'Nina Jacobs?'

Maggie looked up at him over her reading glasses, pencil poised, eyes narrowed.

'She's a name, but I don't think she's right for Mary,' she said.

'Why not?'

'I just feel it. Bridge? Nina Jacobs?'

James Bridge was what Maggie called a safe pair of hands for *Diversion*; a skinny, fair-haired man, he had the prestige of having directed a season at the RSC, and also the confidence to have left there to work with Peter Oliver and 'the queers and blacks' at the experimental Oval House. He had vision, knew everyone, and didn't have an axe to grind with writers, Maggie said. Her word was good enough for Luke.

'Sweetie? Nina Jacobs?' prompted Maggie when Bridge did not answer.

'. . . Mary is very womanly,' he said at last.

As Luke thought about this remark, and what Bridge – who had lived with his boyfriend Steven for ten years – might or might not think was womanly, or what Nina was or wasn't, Paul came back into the room doing up his flies.

'What did I miss?'

'Nina Jacobs,' said Bridge, pouring himself a whisky.

'Really?' said Paul, looking round as if Nina were hiding somewhere. 'For Mary?'

'I don't think so, love,' said Maggie. 'I know Oddball has a soft spot.'

'Why not?' said Luke.

Bridge shrugged. 'We can put her on the list. You're right, she's a name and she could play it.'

'We'll read her,' said Maggie. 'No harm in it.'

'All right,' said Luke and they moved on.

'Nanette Calgary?'

'No.'

'Chrissie Southey?'

'No. And pregnant.'

'Hannah Gold?'

'She might be perfect, but she's working in telly.'

'Mandy Turnbull?'

'Put her down.'

And on. From their long-list of ten for each of the roles they made short-lists of six, and Maggie and Paul called agents from the office the next morning.

Nina took *Diversion* about her house with her. She marked up the pages with notes and the lines played in her head as if Luke were speaking to her. Mary, the son's love.

Tony had nothing to do with it now but since it was he who had given it to her he couldn't possibly object. And yet he did. They were in the kitchen when the telephone rang.

'Your agent,' he said, holding out the receiver, straight-armed.

It was almost six o'clock. *Diversion* was on the kitchen table and Nina was getting a bottle of champagne from the fridge. She took the phone from Tony, who began, idly, to flick through the pages of the play as she talked.

'Jo.' She gestured for Tony to open the bottle but he ignored her.

Jo was calling about the audition to give her the address. Nina knew everything already, from Luke, but went through the motions because she wanted it to be fair. Clean.

'Twenty-two Maiden Lane,' she said. 'Got it. Thanks, darling, I'll let you know.'

She put down the phone. Tony was standing across the table from her as angry as she'd ever seen him.

'You're really doing this?' he said.

'What do you mean? It's an audition. They want to read me.'

'I *gave* you this play. *This play*. For me, and the Trafalgar.'

He was pale, his whole face working for control. The words *hissy fit* came into her mind. She knew he wouldn't hit her. They weren't in bed, after all. Anger rose up, steady as a flame, but cooler.

'And?' said Nina.

'Can you not see your error?'

'My error?' she said slowly. 'Darling, you can't have *all* the plays.'

'I'm going to ask you this,' he said, 'and I won't ask it again—'

331

'Oh, don't be ridiculous,' she broke in. 'You saw the part was for me when you gave it to me and yet now – you think you can stop me. I'm twenty-four years old. Tony, darling, you're being a bit silly.'

His voice rose to a reedy shout. 'I will not tolerate this! I will not have you humiliate me! *This was mine and you took it.*'

Nina raised her eyebrows as he went on. She took in the sight of him; thin lips straining, long fringe slipping forward. The stairs going up behind him, the posters on the wall, the door of the loo to his left – where she had taken refuge in her own house, vomited and wept at the sight of his cock being sucked by a waiter.

When he had stopped shouting she picked up Luke's play.

'You're being a baby,' she said, holding it to her chest. '*Nobody* will *know* about anything. If they offer it to me I'm going to take it. I would appreciate your—'

But she couldn't think what she would appreciate; she was so proud of herself she forgot words. She just laughed, rather stagily.

'Just forget it,' she said and left him there.


The temporary rehearsal room on Maiden Lane was on the top floor. Unaccustomed views of London's sooty heart were spread beneath a pale blue sky. Luke was there for all the Mary readings because he didn't want to be too obvious about Nina when she came. James Bridge didn't appreciate his presence much so he sat far back from the others, with a paperback in the corner, sometimes reading, sometimes watching, trying not to interfere. They saw three girls before Nina. Two were competent, one was more interesting.

Nina knocked, and put her head around the door. The floorboards were bare. Sun streamed in making broad criss-crossed rectangles on the floor and glaring off the varnished pine table behind which sat Paul, Maggie and Bridge, and the new stage manager, Win.

'Hello,' said Maggie. 'Nina.'

Paul and she kissed. Then she kissed Maggie who said, 'We've met before.'

'Yes, how are you?' said Nina. 'Oh my God, Jimmy Bridge!'

She and Bridge hugged.

'I think it's been three years,' she said.

'Many moons,' said Bridge.

She glanced at Luke in the corner, and then back to him.

'How's Steven?' she asked.

'Injured again, rather fat with no class to go to.'

'Give him my love.'

'I will. Tony?'

'Fine.'

She turned to Luke. He stood up and came over. They met, awkwardly, and he kissed her cheek. She was unmade-up, in jeans and a thin white sweater, hair off her face in a slide.

She shrugged. 'Here we are!' she said.

They all said *yes* and there was laughter, a few more remarks.

Luke went back to his corner. She looked young, he thought. Small. He felt very nervous.

Nina knelt and rummaged in her bag. She held up the script.

'Got it!' she said.

'We've been working from the scene with Tom from the first act,' said Maggie. 'Where he brings her home after the concert. It's a good way into it.'

'Great. Where d'you want me?' said Nina, shrugging her

shoulders to relax and looking around. The sun was shining into her face.

'Wherever you like. Paul's going to read in.'

Nina nodded, licking her lips and turning away, working her face to lose the tension.

'Good,' said Maggie, for them to begin.

Luke, twisted in his chair, kept his eyes on his book as she began.

She wasn't Mary. He knew it before she even opened her mouth. He kept telling himself not to think about it, and that of course anyone would seem wrong to him, even her – especially her. With all his nerves for her and his wanting it so badly, still he felt it; she just couldn't be the woman he had written.

Nina held the script in one hand, looking at Paul, vulnerable.

'*I'm sorry you saw my dad like that,*' Paul read.

'*Forewarned is forearmed,*' said Nina. '*It wasn't your fault.*'

And on. They read the scene through without stopping: the lines told of Tom's embarrassment, Mary's strength; the beginnings of their naïve pursuit of a home together. The lines told it, but it was not there.

Then there was silence.

'Thank you very much, Nina,' said Bridge. 'Great.'

Nina looked from one to the other. She glanced at Luke. He smiled at her, trying to transmit something – encouragement.

'I didn't feel very – it didn't feel right. I can do it without the script. I do know it. It might be better?'

'It was great.'

'Could we do it again?'

Maggie and Paul exchanged glances with Bridge.

334

'Of course, darling,' said Bridge. 'Let's go again. Are you all right with the scene?'

'No, it's wonderful,' said Nina. She looked at Luke again. 'It's not the scene. Sorry, the sun is shining right in my eyes, I can't see anything when I—' She turned her face towards the window to demonstrate her discomfort. 'Could we put the blind down?'

They did, with a lot of fumbling and arguing, while Nina apologised. They talked about the play a little, and then, in the warm shadows, she went again.

When she had left them there was a long uncomfortable silence as her footsteps receded down the stairs.

'That was – very nice,' said Bridge.

'Yes,' said Paul.

Maggie swivelled in her chair to look at Luke.

'Sorry, Oddball,' she said.

Luke shrugged it off. They were all looking at him as if he were meant to add the full stop to the sentence of her rejection. He shook his head. But he couldn't say anything, there was nothing to say. They began to talk amongst themselves about lunch and where to go.

Luke got up and left, running down the stairs to catch up with Nina in the street.

She hadn't gone far, she was waiting for him.

'And?' she said, eagerly. 'So?'

'Well done, fantastic,' he said.

People passed them by, slow in the sun, with the traffic a distant rumble.

'I don't think it went very well,' she said. 'What did Bridge think?'

'I just came down—'

'What did *you* think? Luke?'

Luke didn't know how to answer her. 'How did it feel?'

'How did it *feel*?' Her voice rose, taking refuge in hysteria. 'I had *you* pretending you didn't know me. Paul *hates* me. That *Maggie* woman—'

'Paul doesn't hate you.'

'Oh shit,' she said, starting to shake. 'Shit. They don't want me, do they?'

'They didn't say.'

'Why are you here? Why aren't you up there? Talk to them. Luke!'

'I'm just the writer,' he said, to make her smile, feeling useless truth fading.

'You think I'm no good!' she said. 'I hate readings. Some actresses audition well – I just don't. I never have. But there's so much more to find. Luke?'

'I'll see what they say,' he said. 'Nina, I don't *know* what they think. I'll call you.'

'No,' she said, wiping her tears, pulling away, hurt and challenging. 'There's no reason you should fight for me, is there?'

And he, of course, surrendered.

'Every reason,' he said. 'You know there is.'


Paul went to dinner with Maggie and Bridge. When he got home, after midnight, Leigh was in the sitting room with some girlfriends, four of them, and the room thick with hash smoke.

'Hello, girls,' he said, going into the kitchen.

'Paul! *Girls?* I'm thirty years old!' shouted Tania, a pale woman with a huge round perm, sitting cross-legged by the window.

'Christ,' muttered Paul and opened the fridge.

'There's wine in the fridge,' called Leigh.

'I know; I can see it,' said Paul to himself.

He heard a wave of female laughter in the other room. The butt of their jokes were often male but they were not laughing at him, they were oblivious to him; he wasn't sure if it was better or worse to be insignificant in their eyes. He poured himself a glass, left it on the counter and took the bottle back in, offering it around but it was taken from him. *Thanks*, they said. *Cheers*.

Paul left them to it and stood in the kitchen with his drink. Leigh came in.

'Sorry, they'll go soon.'

'Not on my account,' said Paul.

'Of course not. How are you?' she said.

'Yeah, fine,' said Paul. 'Nina came in to read for Mary today.'

'For Mary? She's all wrong for it,' said Leigh.

'I know. She wasn't *bad* – just wrong. Luke wanted it.'

Leigh let Luke's name fall unremarked upon between them.

'So have you found anyone?'

'Not yet. Karen Melrose tomorrow morning.'

'That could work.'

'Yes.'

They didn't hug. They didn't kiss, and Leigh stood awkwardly in the doorway as another wave of laughter from the sitting room broke over them.

When Leigh read *Diversion*, she had cried. Paul had read it first, of course, and left it for her, but she hadn't picked it up – hadn't touched it – for days. Seeing Luke himself was one thing, and the three of them together, not as they had been but a reminder, like hearing an old loved song. But reading his play felt dangerous. She resisted that close-up glimpse of him. She finally read it when Paul had gone one morning, before coffee, when her mind was open and vulnerable, before common sense could guard her. She read it and was filled with pride for Luke; that he had come so far and for the risks he was taking. She almost held her breath – had to remember to breathe. She read jealously, in self-damning recognition of his art. She read it and cried. She cried because she missed him. And because the play was so good. And because she did not know if she would ever have enough guts to make anything at all of her own.

She had carefully left Paul and Maggie alone with the play, and from her prosaic place at the Duke of York's found real delight in watching Paul do something so important, the thing that he had always wanted to do. She supported him from the background as though she felt she owed it to him.

---

The evening after her audition for the Depot, Tony found Nina curled up on the chaise in her little room at the back. She was crying. There was a nearly finished bottle of champagne and her small silver pillbox of Valium next to her on the table.

'Darling,' he said. 'Darling, what is it?'

He went and sat next to her. Her face was hidden.

'I won't get it,' she said. 'They don't want me for it.'

She kept crying. She was like an abandoned child, abject. He soothed her and stroked her hair.

'Darling,' he said. 'My poor darling girl. Look at me?'

She turned; reluctant, tear-stained and ugly.

'Are you sure?' he asked and she nodded.

'Why don't I run you a bath? Come along, up we go.'

He took her hand and helped her up the stairs. He ran a bath and laid out her night things on the bed. When she came out of the bathroom he unwrapped the towel from her damp body and held out her nightdress and robe for her, then he tucked her into their bed.

'Shall I bring you a nice glass of champers?' he asked.

She nodded.

'Don't worry,' he whispered, 'everything will be fine, I promise.'


And Nina did not call Luke.

Three days went by.

Four.

He tried to call her but she did not answer the telephone. He waited. There was nothing else. Just the waiting. Not work, not sleep. Just the gap she cut from him. The blank notebooks on his tidy desk remained. There was nothing to put down, nothing to say but that he needed her. He wrote her name just to fill up the pages, disgusted at the banality of his longing. He wrote her letters, pleading with her, prayers and promises – as if by writing he could summon her. He wrote in English, French and Polish to beg her with all of himself and then, scared by his own derangement, threw them all away.

On the fifth day the phone rang.

'Luke, Lou Farthing,' said Lou's voice – no Melanie putting him through, just him.

Luke adjusted. Caught up. Did not speak.

'Lou Farthing,' said Lou again. 'How are you, my boy?'

'Fine, thanks,' said Luke and right away he knew.

The last few days had been preparing him so that when the way out was offered him he'd take it gratefully, and be free.

'Good. This play of yours. Have you signed contracts with Maggie O'Hanlan?'

Luke was beaten before he answered. 'Not yet,' he said. 'They're going back and forth.'

'Lawyers and agents! My God.'

'Yes.'

'All right then. I won't ask again, Luke. I don't play games. For now — just now — my offer of the Trafalgar is still good. If you like, we can meet you with your agent to discuss it. Are you there?'

'Yes.'

'Just one proviso. We have some casting obligations.'

'I understand.'

'We think Nina Jacobs would be perfect in the role of the girl . . . the girlfriend?'

'Mary,' said Luke quietly.

There was a pause.

'Yes, Mary. You haven't signed anything yet, so we've got time. Let me know when you've made up your mind, eh?'

'No. You can have it.'

'What did you say? I beg your—'

'You can have the play.'

'That's marvellous. the Trafalgar is the best place for it. You've written a big play. We can do it justice. You should be pleased.'

'Yes.'

'A deal, then? Shall I call Ben?'

'A deal,' said Luke. 'No. I'll call him.'

Before Lou could say anything else he put the phone down.

He sat at the desk by the empty notebooks and tried to form the sentences he would say to his agent. His mind felt as if it were not his own.

In a very short time the telephone rang again.

'Luke?' Nina's voice was breathless. 'Darling?'

'Yes.'

'Is it all right?'

'Of course.' He felt far away.

'I'm sorry,' she said. 'I didn't ask them to, you do know that? I'm so *sorry*. Your lovely Paul and everything – it's horrible. Do you want me to turn it down?'

'Of course not.'

'You're sure? You sound strange. I should turn it down. I will.'

She was upset. She meant it. He stood up and began to pace, the long cord trailing after him, tugging, and her gentle voice in his ear.

'No. Don't,' he said, and then the lie, 'It's fine.' And again. 'It's fine. It's wonderful.'

'When can I come?' she said, alight. 'I can't be happy until I see you.'

'Come now.'

'I can't *now*,' she said immediately. 'Tony—'

Luke stopped pacing.

He sat down, bent forward around the telephone.

'Whenever you want,' he answered her quietly, bowed. 'I'm here.'

In the moments after he put down the telephone he realised he had to speak to Paul, before anyone knew, before the agent's call, the coldness of the battle that would follow.

He took his key, left the flat, and ran out into the street to find him and confess.

Maggie was speaking to Christopher Morgan's agent offering him the father's role and Paul was on the other phone talking to Bridge about set design and budget. His feet were up on the desk and he was sifting through index cards while reassuring him the Depot would be ready. When Maggie put down the phone it rang again, immediately.

Paul knew at once that something had happened. He tried to take in what Bridge was saying to him and listen to Maggie's conversation at the same time. He couldn't work out what was wrong.

'You are joking,' she said. 'Jesus fucking Christ, Ben, tell me you're taking the piss—'

Paul thought it must be Ben Ryan, the electrical engineer from his father's office, and wondered what new setback he must overcome now. He imagined sparking wires, deaths, falling rigs. Maggie gestured violently for him to get off the phone.

'Bridge, something's come up. I'll call you back,' he said. 'Sorry.'

He put down the phone as Maggie got to her feet, still speaking into the phone.

'All right,' she said shrilly and Paul pitied whoever it was on the other end. 'Well, I can imagine you are. It's appalling. Yes, do, you tell him. And you'll be hearing from my lawyer.'

She slammed the phone into the base, making the bell reverberate.

'What?' said Paul, laughing with nerves. 'For Christ's sake, what?'

'You're going to love this,' said Maggie. 'That was Luke's agent.'

'Ben Greene?' said Paul, slow-wittedly.

'Luke has *given the play* to L. M. Farthing—'

'What do you mean?'

'He's given *Diversion* to Farthing.'

'He can't have done.'

'Well, he fucking has.'

'But what—' Paul began and then stopped, wondering. As Maggie started to speak again they heard quick footsteps on the stairs, a knock at the door, and then, like a physical manifestation of betrayal, Luke came in.

He was hot and out of breath, looking from one to the other.

'What have you done?' said Maggie, immediately rounding on him as if he had been there all along, as if they were already arguing.

'What's going on?' said Paul. 'Luke?'

Paul waited for Luke to deny it or explain but Maggie exploded viciously.

'What's going *on* is that your *friend* has decided the Trafalgar is the best place to showcase his girlfriend's limited talents and, not having *signed a contract* yet, has spoken to Lou Farthing and given his word the play will go to him,' said Maggie. 'Oh, and by the way, *her husband* is running the Trafalgar now, right, Luke? So that's all *very* cosy. How lovely for you all.'

Maggie and Paul both stood, staring at Luke, waiting.

In the short pause before another word was spoken Paul had the incongruous thought occur that something was wrong with Luke, and that he needed his help, but it evaporated into nothing when Luke said only, 'I'm sorry.'

'Sorry?' said Paul.

'I wanted to tell you first,' said Luke. 'I'm sorry.'

Maggie sat down, pulling herself back from the conversation to observe the two of them coldly.

'Because of Nina?' said Paul quietly.

Luke nodded.

'Right,' said Paul. 'I get you. It's done, is it?'

'Yes,' said Luke. 'It's done.'

Paul didn't move. 'That's that, then,' he said. 'There's nothing more to be said, is there?'

Luke began to speak but Paul stopped him. 'No. No. I'll speak to your agent.'

'Paul—'

'I'll deal with Ben from now on. Understand?'

'Of course.'

Luke had the grace at least not to justify himself. It was Maggie who had the luxury of insults, and bile.

'You self-serving, sneaky little *shit*,' she said, and Luke nodded with a half-smile that was like agony, then looked up at her again. 'You absolute bastard, you shafted us – and your play. *Your play!*' she said.

And he stood quietly as her insults rained upon him, rightfully acknowledging them as his due.


When Luke had gone there was silence. Marigold went to Maggie and rested her wet muzzle on her lap. Maggie stroked her head. Then Paul said, 'I'm sorry.'

'You? Why?'

'I don't know, it's my fault, I should have – done something differently.'

She shook her head. 'That's crap, Paul.'

They didn't discuss it further. After a moment she said, 'Right.' She pushed Marigold away and swivelled her chair back to her desk. 'I'll call Gerald Denton's agent, shall I? I had a drink with David Aukin the other day and he said he and Denton might be putting something together – some co-operative – so we'd better move fast.'

Paul, not for the first time, marvelled at her strength.

'I'll do it if you like,' he said.

He thought he saw her quiver. She did not look up, but bit her lip, then sat straighter than ever.

'No. I'm fucking fine,' she said and picking up the phone began to flick through her index cards with the tip of her biro.


At home that night Paul sat and applied himself to getting very drunk. He stayed immobile on the sofa with a bottle, getting determinedly and uncomfortably pissed while Leigh stormed and ranted about the flat, slamming things down and shouting.

'Why aren't you angry?' she yelled at him once.

'I am,' he said and knew he should be, or would be, but couldn't feel it.

Misery pushed all the anger out of him. Maggie's straight-forward rage was easier, and even Leigh's, for all that it was complicated by history. He knew he was at the beginning of a fight; Maggie would call her lawyer and letters would be written, agents would threaten and bellow, but they would lose the play; he had already lost the play, and he had lost his closest friend. He surveyed the years of loyalty and unquantifiable debt, and couldn't explain it to Leigh. He had no words for it. He hated the stupid blunt pain. He had lost his friend.

Leigh went off into the other room, still shouting, and then came back in and picked up the phone.

'I'm calling him,' she said, 'the *fucking bastard*.'

'No, don't. Leave it,' said Paul. 'We'll sort something out. The Denton—'

'The *Denton*? What does it matter about the fucking Denton?'

'It matters. It's a good play. It's not *Diversion*—'

'What is *wrong* with you? He should know what he's done!' she railed. 'He should *know* what he's done – and that it's over.'

'He does,' said Paul.


The next day he was forced to leave Maggie in the office to break the news the play had fallen through, and to cancel rehearsals alone, while he spent the morning on site at an emergency meeting with the contractor and engineer. Paul's father had, unusually, left his office to join the meeting; it was insulting, as if he couldn't manage without him. For two hours they tried to restrict the costs, limit the time wasted; pored over damp, unrolled blueprints in the dim light.

'You didn't need to be here,' said Paul when the others had gone.

He and his father were standing in the dripping guts of the backstage area; no play, no plan, no guarantee of anything.

'I know that, Paul, your mother told me to.'

'Great, right, thanks,' said Paul, reaching into his pockets for tobacco and Rizla papers and thinking he should get back to the office and help Maggie.

'She sent these for you.'

He held out a tartan bag, plastic-coated canvas, that Paul

recognised from long service to his mother – shopping trips in the Morris Minor to the high street in his childhood.

'What's that?'

'Fish paste sandwiches and,' he peered inside, 'a Granny Smith.'

Paul smiled, but grudgingly, because he was exhausted and felt powerless.

'Dad, how old is that bloody bag?'

'About your age.'

Paul took it from him; he wasn't hungry. He looked around them both at what felt like a shipwreck, not a theatre, and waited for his father to leave so he could throw it away. Above them on ladders the electricians worked – no whistling, no chat, just dogged work.

But his father didn't leave, he stood with him.

'This was always a risk,' he said, as if Paul didn't know. 'Paul?'

Paul looked at his neat grey hair, the success written in every line of his face.

'Yes. Thanks, Dad.'

'You're not the only one.'

'What?'

'Every project I've ever worked on went like this, at some point. What you're doing, Paul, is *admirable*.'

Paul had armoured himself against criticism not kindness.

'You think theatre's for pansies,' he said.

His father didn't laugh. 'What's that got to do with it?' Then, with ironic awe, he intoned, '*The Post Office Tower* . . . It looks impressive now it's all over and went well. At the time it were nothing grand, just terrifying. the Depot is to you what that was to me.'

Paul nodded.

'You're going to have setbacks,' said his father. 'Not to worry. Well done.'

Paul nodded again, but couldn't speak.

'Your mother sends her love.'

He patted Paul's shoulder, and left. Paul watched him stepping with practised, middle-aged caution over the cables and at the door he turned.

'See you at the opening night – the fourteenth, isn't it? Save me a seat.'

'Hope so,' said Paul, and raised the hand that wasn't holding the tartan bag.

'What do they call them?' said his father.

'Call what?'

'The special seats.'

'House seats,' said Paul. 'They're house seats.'

'Well, save me one.'

'I will,' said Paul.


Paul went back to the office and sat on the battered armchair in the corner. Marigold came and lay at his feet, sighing and smelling of gutters. Maggie was bashing out a letter with two fingers. Her typing always sounded angry. He had a headache. The inked metal letters hitting the paper hurt his brain; the bell, the zip of the cylinder turning as she checked back. Paul just sat, knowing he had to get on with it, unable to do so. She stopped typing.

'Dear Leonard Cubitt, c/o *The Times*,' she pretended to read. 'As you will no doubt be carrying out a hatchet job on the Depot, I *urge* you to consider burying your axe in the head of Luke Last—'

'And his agent,' said Paul, not looking up.

'And his agent, Ben Greene.' She paused, and leaned back in her chair. 'You are so different from my ex-husband,' she said.

'I hope so.'

'You're a man, for starters.'

'Funny.'

'It wasn't.'

'How'd it go? Ringing round.'

'Oh – you know. I've delayed the rehearsal rooms – we won't lose too much money, then—' She stopped.

She got up, abruptly, and went to the window.

Paul realised with surprise that she was upset and tried to reconcile it with the Maggie who made New York lawyers quake. He imagined her morning: making call after call, having to tell people what Luke had done to them, and admit they had got as far as casting the whole play before the contracts were even signed. Amateurish, naïve trust.

Maggie had her back to him, looking out. He got up and went to stand a few inches behind her.

'Never mind, eh?' he said.

He couldn't see her face but he had a horrible feeling she was crying. Medusa to Little Bo Peep.

He wanted to comfort her, the urge to make her feel better was strong. Then she turned to him and tucked her face into his chest. He was surprised, but instinctively put his arms round her. He hadn't realised how small she was, how much shorter than Leigh. He thought of her always wearing high heels, even to visit their building site, presenting as big a version of herself as she could. Confused, he held her – and suddenly wondered if he ought not.

'Don't worry,' he said. 'You're all right.'

'I'm sorry. It's just too much,' she said. 'All of this, and Helen's not happy at school.'

Paul had no idea who Helen was. Then he remembered, the daughter, of course, with the boy's hair.

'I never say the right thing to her,' said Maggie.

Her head stayed resting on his chest, her grown-woman's problems laid out for him to mend.

'She'll be fine. And we'll sort this out.' He thought of his father. 'Nothing big ever went smoothly. You wait and see.'

He couldn't believe how easy it was. He may as well have said abracadabra and produced a dove from his sleeve – Maggie looked up, grateful and admiring.

'Do you know how nice you are?' she said.

He shook his head. 'I'm not.'

'. . . Does Leigh?'

She looked down when she said the name, so he could only see her lashes.

Leigh. Who never got at him, never criticised him, never cut him down. Whose love was like someone completing a task they had set themselves.

Maggie looked up again and he couldn't get over the strangeness of it; thinking about Leigh but Maggie's face so close.

'You are, Paul, you're a really – *wonderful* man. Don't make me say it, it's embarrassing.'

'I'm not. Don't,' said Paul, relishing this unaccustomed vision of himself.

'Please just kiss me,' said Maggie, so he did – thinking oddly that it would be rude not to. He didn't want to hurt her feelings.

Her kiss was surrendering and sweet. There was the first

touch of her lips, then the feeling of it; weakening. Then wanting more – and he stopped, guilt hitting him hard and leaving him cold. He didn't step away from her, he just stopped kissing her and she rested against his chest again.

'God. I've hoped you would do that for so long,' she said.

———————

*Diversion* went straight into rehearsals at the American Church. It had lost James Bridge, whose loyalty and another job – that wouldn't cost him friends and allies in the business – prevented him from accompanying it to its new home. Tony hired Malcolm Dewberry who had directed Nina in *Custody*, and they cast from scratch. After Luke's initial work with Malcolm on the script Nina kept him away.

'Please don't come in,' she begged him; 'it makes it so much worse.'

The dynamic in the cast was uncomfortable; the producer's wife in the show, and bringing it down, as well as the gossip she was also sleeping with the writer.

Luke wasn't working on anything new. His inner landscape was only *Diversion*'s arid, absent progression towards opening. *Paper Pieces* had been rehearsed at the American Church too, before going to Oxford, but Luke tried not to look back at that time that was so different to this, that had been so pure.

The two actors playing the father and son were good, and their chemistry right for the roles, but Nina, as Luke had known – as Maggie, Paul and Bridge had known – was wrong. Very soon she realised it too. The fault was beyond technique; it was elemental. Mary was earthed; Nina was of the air. Her attempts at strength seemed brittle; her passion insincere and Malcolm Dewberry, powerless and already resentful of the fait accompli of her presence, abandoned her to her struggles. Nina, increasingly isolated, suffered.

She became even thinner – her costume had to be taken in because of the weight she had lost since the first fitting – and Luke couldn't help thinking, with unwelcome detachment, that it made her less Mary even than before.

At his flat, during their scattered afternoons alone, he ran lines with her, discussed the part, comforted her and felt less and less connected to the work, more and more exclusively connected only to her.

'Mary feels so confident,' she said, 'so sure. It doesn't feel right to me to say that line to Tom.' And so Luke offered to rewrite, betraying the truth that had presented itself to him as if it were worthless, and seeking only Nina's truth instead.

'Maybe,' he said. 'I'll change it.'

Nina took Malcolm aside.

'Luke mentioned perhaps Mary might be a little less sure of herself in this scene – that it might work to have her more vulnerable,' she suggested.

Malcolm gave her an appraising look – appraisal tinged with contempt.

'This isn't Am-Dram, Nina; we're not a collective in some basement somewhere. If Luke has something to discuss with me he knows he only has to call.'

Tony insisted on dropping her off for rehearsal and collecting her at the end of each day. She stopped lunching with the rest of the cast because she felt uncomfortable in their presence. They were part of something she was not. Sometimes she asked her mother to come and take her for lunch, just for the company, or if not, it would be Tony and the two of them would sit in virtual silence until she went back to work.

In the second week Tony started to watch her rehearse, too, his new role at the Trafalgar giving him a legitimate pretext. He would offer criticism in an undertone in her ear in the breaks between her scenes, but had nothing but praise for the others.

'What did you expect?' he said, as they drove home one afternoon. 'You want everything your own way, like a child. You wanted your special friend, I overlooked it – rather generously, I thought. You wanted his play; I got it for you. You're a big girl. You've made your bed, my darling – we're all lying in it. Crowded and uncomfortable it may be, but there we are.' And he patted her knee.

He refused to allow her to stay at home when he went to parties, to La Terrazza or the Café Royal after shows to meet friends, where she was sharply aware of the gossip surrounding them and imagined – felt she knew – everyone was talking about her not managing the part she had caused such scandal to acquire. Tony seemed to lap it all up with brittle pleasure. He wanted sex from her more often – the proper way, straightforward, looking at her eyes. He would whisper that he loved her. She, less and less able to absent herself, strained harder and faster against the confines that surrounded her.

There was only one other woman in the cast, playing her mother. She was a character actress called Joan Meeks, who prided herself on turning up, doing the job, and knitting for various babies in the waiting hours in between. Their main scene together was key to the second act. It was one of Nina's happier dialogues, the scenes with the son, Tom, being more challenging. This afternoon, though, she was exhausted from not having eaten and Tony watching from the back and the other actors grouped together, Malcolm barely looking up from his notes and an early summer heatwave stifling them all. She stumbled over the lines. Her mind kept blanking out. Joan was considerate but bored, Malcolm increasingly irritated.

'We've been off book for over a week, Nina,' he said, with a sing-song intonation, casting his eyes to the ceiling.

'I'm sorry,' said Nina, 'I'm sorry.'

And she fainted.

Seeing her crumple to the floor, dead white, the others immediately sprang into life, forgetting their ungenerous thoughts for the drama.

Nina came to consciousness with a clammy sweat over her face. She had her head in Joan's lap. Malcolm was kneeling at her side and the other actors were standing over her like mourners at a grave.

'I think I'm going to be sick,' said Nina.

They all took a step back. Nina sat up and somebody handed her a glass of water. The stage manager was hovering behind Malcolm's shoulder, a mousy young man, called Joe.

'All right, love?' he said.

Behind his shoulder she could see Tony. His face was a mask of boredom. Nina closed her eyes. She felt better. She took some more sips of water.

'Did you eat lunch, dear?' asked Joan, patting her with dry, fat hands.

'Yes,' said Nina, who hadn't.

Then she heard the actor playing Tom – Tom who loved Mary and lost her to the chaos of his father's hand – whisper to his stage father, 'Pregnant . . . ?'

'But whose?' said John to him, and they laughed.

Nina turned over onto her hands and knees, determined to get up. Her head felt detached from her body. She thought she might have imagined they said it. She felt them all looking at her.

'You'd better go home,' said Malcolm. 'Go *home*, love, have a good night's sleep and forget all about it. We don't need you until Friday, do we, Joe?'

'Not till Friday,' echoed Joe.

Nina nodded. She got to her knees.

'I'm fine,' she said.

She saw Tony's hand come into her line of vision, his long white fingers. She took it. He helped her to her feet.

'I'm so sorry,' she said to them all. 'I'm so sorry.'

She sat quietly, staring out of the window of the taxi on the way home.

'I can't do this part,' she said.

'Don't be silly,' said Tony absently.

'Tony – I can't.'

He didn't speak to her again until they were at the house. Bright afternoon sun shone down and blackbirds sang as he opened the door to the dark hall.

'Luke wrote a different girl,' said Nina, 'and I can't play her.'

He turned to her. 'That's your problem, love, not mine,' he said.

'Is it what you wanted?'

'Me?' He was surprised.

'Did you know this would happen?'

'You give me far too much credit,' he said. 'How on earth could I know you'd humiliate yourself? And in *his* play?'

'You're pleased,' she said, wonderingly.

'No,' he said. He paused, and went to her, taking her hand. 'You don't understand, it is you who hurt me. I only want you to be happy. You're my wife.'

He let go of her hand and went to his study and Nina went up and to the back of the house, to the chaise in the tiny room, and sat.

She could still hear the blackbirds singing, and Tony's feet above her as he went about his room. She felt insubstantial, like balsa wood, a stick figure. She picked up the telephone and dialled Luke's number. As she dialled she heard Tony pick up the extension and the moment's sound of his breath before he covered the mouthpiece with his hand.

'Hello?'

'Luke?'

'Hello . . .'

In that one word she could hear the weariness, the fear for her — or of her — that she had weighed upon him. She thought of Tony waiting, listening, upstairs.

'Luke,' she said, 'I'm leaving him.'

'You're—' He stopped. Then, 'Really?' as if she would lie about a thing like that, as if he didn't think that she loved him.

'I'm leaving him now. Will you be there?'

'Yes,' he said. 'Yes.'

When she had put down the phone she went to the hall. There was no sound from above. She climbed the stairs. Tony's study door was closed. She went to her room and filled a suitcase – underwear, a few changes of clothes, make-up – the long habit of years of rep and packing quickly on tour made it easy.

When she left her room with the suitcase she knocked on the door of the study. There was no answer.

'I'm going now,' she said to the blank door, and she left.


She felt nothing as she walked the sunlit street towards the King's Road and caught a taxi, nothing as she watched the streets that separated her from Luke go by. The taxi took her up through Knightsbridge and across the Park to Bayswater and the ease of it amazed her. It was just a drive away.

They turned into Moscow Road. He was standing on the pavement outside.

'Just there,' she said to the cab driver. 'Where that man is standing.'

The taxi stopped. She got out and Luke paid the driver, fumbling for coins and dropping them in the gutter while she stood in the warm, bright sunshine by her case. Then he turned to her. He didn't say anything, he just put his arms round her.

'Thank you,' he said. 'Thank you.' He picked her up, like a bride. 'You need to eat more,' he said.

———————

'Absolutely fabulous gossip! Unbelievable,' cried the actress, throwing her arms out to the crowd at the table.

'Nina Jacobs has run off with Luke Last!'

With happy consternation, exclamations, guesses and

rumours, the group fell upon the news like lions tearing the hide of a gentle zebra on the African plains.

'She's been having an affair with him for *months*,' said the actor to the other actor, and the director next to him said, 'And Last's play? What will happen with the play?'

'God knows – he left Maggie O'Hanlan and Paul Driscoll high and dry.'

'Or maybe they left him – it might not be up to much, who knows?'

The food was abandoned for this new feast; the papers they had been poring over for friends' reviews, the first night they had been at earlier, everything was forgotten but this.

'I always thought she was a bitch.'

'Mind you, Tony's been up every rent-boy in town for years.'

'He must be hell.'

'She's hell, too.'

'Oh, I think she's sweet.'

'And Luke Last is a genius – and so attractive.'

'Genius, really? There's a word to conjure with.'

'Didn't you laugh in *Paper Pieces*? So *clever*.'

'Laugh? I cried.'

'Well, he must be deeply neurotic, of course.'

'Apparently. Nina Jacobs? My God.'

'I know!'

And so it went on. The only people in London not talking about it were any who happened to be in Tony's company; then the conversation was assiduously respectful. And the scandal was not just in the air, it was on the page – clotted lines of news print in the *Standard*, the *Mail* – photographs of Nina and Tony leaving theatres, their wedding, Luke circled in white in the middle of a crowd. It was good enough to eat. It was a full meal.

Before Nina awoke the first morning after she left Tony, Luke was up and out, hurrying, buying food and flowers for her, blinkered by delight and anxiety.

When he got back she was sitting up in bed and on the telephone.

'Goodbye,' she was saying, shakily, to someone, 'and thank you, darling, I'm so sorry . . . But I am. Bye.'

She put down the phone and smiled at him, pale with dried tears.

'That was Jo. I've asked her to see if she can get me out of this play,' she said.

This play. His play. *Diversion.*

Luke put down the shopping bags and took her the flowers. He sat on the bed.

'I can't believe I've done it,' she said.

'They've got nearly two weeks. They'll recast. He can say you aren't well.'

Nina nodded bleakly.

'My name will be mud in this town,' she said, with a rather poor American accent. He smiled anyway.

'No,' he shrugged, 'you'll be all right. Girl like you?'

'Better than wrecking your play.' She stopped and looked down. 'I wish we could get away.'

'Then we will,' he said and kissed her.

Later, they walked in the park, slowly, and then went for lunch. It was a blank. The quiet before or after battle. In the afternoon he left her alone and did not say where he was going. She tried to read and then watched television —

children's programmes because that was all there was; quite comforting, with nanny-like presenters in stripy jumpers and talking animals, until she was distracted by the honking of a car outside in the street. It did not stop. She got up and went to the window.

Luke was standing by a maroon and white Triumph convertible. It had the roof down. He gave a small bow and Nina stood at the window, like Juliet, and laughed.

Chrissie Southey was in bed when Nina called her.

'Darling – where could you be?' Chrissie rolled over and cradled the phone, the hot weight of her pregnancy dragging at the ruined muscles of her waist.

'I'm at Luke's. Could you do me the most enormous favour? Are you using Trapps?'

'Not for months – we've been so busy, darling, and I'm afraid it's a tip.'

'Luke will come by for the key, is that all right?'

'Any time, I'm holed up like a fat hedgehog and Alexander is filming, the bastard.'

They left London that afternoon, cold-boxes and cases in the back, and bottles of wine, steaks in bags with ice, bread and cheese, and Nina in a hat to keep her hair from the wind.

'I'm sorry I ruined your play,' she said, while they were sitting at lights, the three-year-old engine of the Triumph steadily growling. Luke was trying to get used to the gearbox, and putting the lever through the gears one by one, with his foot on the clutch. He glanced up at her when she said it.

'You haven't ruined it,' he said. 'It's just a play. They'll sort it out.'

The way he said it – *just a play* – she didn't see a glimmer, hear a note of anything more. He dismissed his play and she believed him. Her fear receded, he did not hate her; he had chosen her above all things.

A woman in a short, bright-yellow dress with white flowers printed on it, a pram festooned with string bags and two children hanging onto her heaved herself across the road in front of them.

But still –

'I shouldn't have . . . forced that part,' she pressed. 'She wasn't me.'

'You're an actress.'

'But, Luke, who was she? Mary.'

The lights changed.

'Who was she? She wasn't anybody. I made her up. And Tom isn't me,' he said, reading her mind. 'I bloody well hope not, poor bastard.'

They crawled in steady progress south, towards the suburbs.

'It's all right, the car, isn't it?' he said.

'It's lovely. I've never seen you drive.'

'Got my licence up north with Paul. We shared the Transit. Never driven in London, though. Leigh always liked to drive Janis the Beetle.'

'Janis for Janis Joplin?'

Luke smiled. Laughed – thinking of some part of his life that she didn't know about.

'What?' she said.

'Yeah, Janis Joplin – she was like that.'

'Who, Leigh?'

'Yes,' said Luke, smiling again, remembering. 'Silly names for things.'

Nina tried to stop it but she hated that smile; it was so easy, he seemed so light when he thought of other girls, not her.

'The first time I saw you I thought she was your girlfriend,' she said.

'Leigh?' He was surprised.

'And then I thought she must be your sister. You look so alike.'

He frowned at this. 'Never thought of it,' he said.

'You do.'

Then the traffic moved and he changed gears up, and up again, as they left the city for a wider view.

Trapps was Chrissie's bolt-hole in the Sussex downs. It had been the scene of many drunken silly weekends with Tony and she and then, once or twice, with Alexander too; a tumble-down cottage at the end of a muddy track with four bedrooms, no central heating, wood stoves and fields and woods all around the small post-and-railed garden. The track was not muddy now, but overgrown with nettles that brushed the bottom of the low car as they approached and budding cow-parsley trailing and bumping at their sides. Nina held her hands out of the car and touched it, the smell of grass on the cool air, fresh and lively as she breathed it in.

'This house is always so *dark*,' she said, as she unlocked the cottage door. 'It's a good thing we brought sheets, Chrissie doesn't keep them here because of the damp.'

The stone-floored hall was a jumble of mismatched welling-tons, spiders scuttled.

'I love it,' said Luke. 'I'll get some logs.'

There was a wood-pile, covered, in the garden and Nina

unpacked the car while Luke carried logs in and lit fires in both the downstairs rooms and the stove in the kitchen. Only in the height of blazing summer was the cottage warm enough to do without.

'I've just realised the most wonderful thing!' called Nina from the car, pulling bags from the open boot. 'No telephone! We'll have to go into the village! Oh dear, how *ghastly*, we won't be able to speak to our very cross agents.'

---

And in London, in the mess they had left behind: the Depot, Paul, Maggie, the cast, director and producers of *Diversion* all waded in the debris, finding ways to fix the chaos. After forty-eight hours of wrangling, Nina's agent, Jo, implacable in her loyal assertion Nina was unwell, and the rest of the cast quite openly relieved to be rid of her, Hannah Gold was cast as Mary. Tony ceased attending rehearsals, too, and nobody could say that he was missed.

Hannah Gold found Mary quite naturally, in the lines and within herself; she had a stoical, steady heart. Coming from three years in series television with her bosom crushed into a corset and dreadful scripts, she was happy to be returning to theatre, and had enough of a name to satisfy Lou and Tony. She didn't mention she'd worked with Luke before – and had slept with him, too, more than once over two happy months, some years before. They had found one another easy companions. She didn't think her nostalgic reminiscences would go down well with the company at the Trafalgar, so she kept her memories of him to herself; their laughs – the delight he had in the curves and shape and kindness of her. Hannah learned her lines fast, kept her fears to herself, and a week later they were in the theatre proper, for the dress-run.

The Depot had less luck. The Denton play had been neglected in deference to *Diversion*'s planned big opening. It needed work and Denton lived up to and beyond his reputation for collaboration. He invited other writers to contribute, throwing agents and contracts into disarray. It was a big moment for him, his third full-length play, and insecurity led him to distrust the directors Paul and Maggie offered, while those he wanted to work with were busy or out of the country. Paul and Maggie's philosophy for the Depot was set in stone; they were a writers' theatre and couldn't pull rank on him and overrule, however sorely they were tempted.

The play, *Hierarchy of Angels*, a fierce dissection of corrupted socialism in Eastern Europe, was being built and cobbled together with brilliance but not with ease, and the theatre itself was scarcely having better fortunes. The building was beset by problems; damp-proof courses that failed, botched electrics that needed re-doing. They had used to joke about the theatre not being ready but now the laughter had stopped. They were two weeks into rehearsals, the play was advertised, posters up and the box office open for business; their first night was in less than a fortnight and they still had no final draft of the script and no seats in the auditorium.

Paul and Maggie's days and nights bled into one another with no respite from tension but one another's company and belief in the place they had imagined so many months before.

Leigh offered to leave her job at the Duke of York's and come in to help but Paul wouldn't have it.

'We need your income – and one of us has to stay sane at least,' he said.

'*Fucking* Luke. Fucking, fucking, fucking Luke.'

It had become Leigh's reaction to every piece of bad news and there were enough of those to feed her rage indefinitely.

Beyond the anger, she found strange joy in his having betrayed them. Despite herself she had believed in him, but he was unfaithful – not just to girls, to friends too, everyone – and didn't care what he did to people. She cut him from her heart with equal pain and pleasure, and refused to grieve the loss. She closed the place inside herself where he had lived and waited for it to scar-over, and be gone.

Nina and Luke's days merged into one as well, but theirs in ignorance and blind pleasure. They walked into the village to buy food and Nina's cigarettes and went to the village pub for lunches and suppers sometimes, the other people there were like extras, the rustics in their love comedy. The landlord knew Nina, and that she was 'in show business', and they didn't mind the stares they drew from people they would never know or be beholden to. Luke always had whatever pie they were serving, because he loved it even though it was inferior southern pie, but Nina had the soup if there was any and bemoaned the lack of salad as they sat at their table near the leaded window.

'We should make a vegetable garden,' she said. 'You still haven't written me that poem.'

'I'm working on it.'

'You didn't bring your typewriter.'

'I forgot it.'

'I don't believe you,' she said, jealous as she was, even of the thing he did not have, but once had loved.

'I have nothing to write,' said Luke and quickly looked down at his plate. She saw that he was frightened.

They had no books either, apart from the few at Trapps. No paper, no pens except to write cheques at the pub. When Luke said he didn't miss those things at all she was almost taken in. She had all his focus when they were together, he was intent only on her, but once, from the open cottage door, she saw him standing on the grass. He was on his way somewhere, but stopped and did not know that she was watching him.

'Luke.'

Turning, 'There you are,' he said. And smiled as if it had been she he was looking for, but it had not.

He crossed the grass and leaned against the wall next to her. The fading sun was on his face, hers looking up at him from shadow. They were close together but she did not feel it.

'What are you, if you don't write?' she asked. The unwanted question coming fully formed.

'What do you mean?'

'I mean, what are you without it?'

'I'm not without it.'

'But you're not writing,' she said, not wanting to go on, not able to stop.

He frowned. 'I will.'

'What if you don't? What if because of me you don't?'

'Are you the artist's curse?' he said, teasing, 'The anti-muse?'

366

'I might be,' she said. 'For you.'

He looked at her and she looked back. She saw what she had never seen in him before. Darkness. Doubt. So easily she had turned the two of them to something bad. She thought it must be a knack she had, to do that.

'I want to inspire you.' She said, bereft.

He smiled at her then, as if she were the most innocent thing on earth.

'It doesn't really work like that,' he said, and kissed her. She remembered, suddenly, as they kissed, the first sight of him at her birthday party. How complete he was before he knew her. How happy he had seemed, and sure.

The date of *Diversion*'s first night crept up day by day, not spoken of. Its presence was a shadow. The day of the opening, he was very quiet and Nina, nervous, dared offer,

'You should go . . .'

But he shook his head. She couldn't imagine what it must be like, to miss it, she did not want to know. The next day he walked to the village alone while she was sleeping and when he came back he just said, 'Saw the papers. It seems to have gone off all right.'

'Really?' she said, as happily as she could.

He flashed a smile back; young, delighted, another sharp reminder of the Luke she did not own.

'I told you — you can go up if you want,' she said, hearing the grudge in her voice that she could not hide.

'No. It really doesn't matter.'

And nothing more was said.

They made love in the deep, soft mattress that had no springs in it and in the fields in the sunshine on damp grass. May had become June and they hadn't noticed, but for the long blue twilights and the singing birds. The hours of darkness were few. Their love-making was at first fuelled by escape, and the particular passion it produced, but then Nina wanted – and he gladly gave it – sex that was fast and sudden, hard, then harder, quickly forced. Not for her his offered hours of closeness, the slow examining wonder. She did not like the length and hours of pleasure that he did, but more the spark of something other that he felt she searched for but could not voice.

In bed, in darkness, once, she held her arms up high above her head and knotted her hands together as if restricted. She was passive beneath him, a mute object for his invasion. He wanted only to please her, and held her that way, bound, while he did it to her, he wanted nothing other than to free her.

Then the dark, the moon, the whispering trees were all around them in the quiet that followed, just outside the open window.

'I'll have to go back to London,' she said.

'What for?'

They could not see one another.

'I ought to get more pills.'

He could not think what she meant for a moment.

'Birth control,' she prompted.

'Oh. There must be a chemist – a doctor we could find,' he said. 'When will they run out?'

'They're finished.'

Her period, he remembered, had ended days before. The blood hadn't stopped their sex. He didn't care for politeness and didn't want to be neat. He had loved the mineral taste, loved the mess, the bright proof of her. But that was nearly a week—

'So we're being dangerous, then?' he said.

'A little.'

'Shall I be careful?'

'I suppose.' There was a long pause. And then she said, 'Or . . .' And she turned over and away from the warm place of them together and onto her front.

He ran the flat of his hand down her spine, moved his hand up to her hair, and gathered it in a gentle fist. Her voice came out of darkness.

'Do it like this,' she said.

The sound of her asking for him was delight; he turned and covered her with his body. She shivered and pressed upwards. He kissed the back of her neck and then – again – she put her arms above her head and held them together, out of reach, raising herself to him.

Hard for her and loving, he opened up her legs with his and began to enter her—

'No,' she said, a whisper hidden in the pillow, and he put his head down close to hear her say, close and frightened, 'the other way.'

Still he didn't know.

'Hurt me,' she said. 'Hurt me.'

Luke felt a halting, stopping fear that mixed with his need for her – but did not stop it. He reached up and took both her knotted, twisted hands in his one and held them. He eased the tight fingers from one another as if untying her.

He didn't do as she had asked. Freeing her, he moved deeper into her. But then – her hands did not relax into his, they pulled away. She yanked her hips down and off him, cold, away; rejecting.

'Do it,' she said fiercely. 'Please.'

She lifted herself up beneath him. He waited. Aching. Suspicious. He would do it if she wanted it, but—

'Is that what he does to you?' he said.

Her body stiffened.

'This is what he does,' said Luke. Sickened sadness.

And she began to cry – hoarsely. He moved off and turned her – fought her reluctantly until she faced him – pulling her close to him; heart to truthful heart of what he felt. But Nina cringed in his arms, and hid from him.

'I like it,' she cried. 'I think I like it when he does. I'm used to it.'

He held her closely but he could not say anything else.

Slowly, she pushed herself away. They lay facing. She saw just his outline, the suggestion of his features. He could not speak. He was failed.

'It's too late,' she said.

They lay in their spoiled bed, and waited.


There was no morning, none to recognise. The sun rose and lit the day, but like a mortal thing the love between them had tipped over and decayed.

'Let's leave today,' she said.

He tried to find words – he who could always find words. He wanted to make her promises, tell her he could save her, and wouldn't give up, but he couldn't find any faith to offer. He only felt alone.

'Don't you want me?' he said at last, like a child.

All her weakness called out to him, but she found beyond it – just this once and gratefully – something better.

'No,' she said. 'I don't want you. You'd better take me back.'

An image came into her mind's eye, glossy and complete, of a counter and a till, some spoiled purchase held in gloved female hands, to be returned with the receipt; forgotten and replaced.

They packed up the car and left that afternoon.

On Holland Park Avenue he turned the Triumph into the side of the road beneath the dusty summer trees and stopped.

'Where are we going?' he asked.

They looked at the blank future, the impossibility of the doors she had closed, that he had closed with her.

'I'm not going to my mother's,' she said harshly.

'Stay in my flat. I'll work something out,' said Luke.

'That's mad.'

'What else will you do?'

'Well, you can't be there.'

'*I know that* — I'll take you to my flat,' he was resolute, 'and you'll have time to think.'

They held one another, leaning across the gearbox; parked on the yellow line at lunchtime in their anomalous distress. Luke gripped her hands in his with his head bowed, murmuring close to her neck, her ear, like somebody praying.

'Please, please, let's try, we'll make it better, don't do this, please stay, please let me try.'

She didn't move.

'We have to say goodbye,' she said.

'I can't.'

'You can' she said, 'because you need to.'

And tears. And aching loss. Defeat.

\*

He drove her to Bayswater, unpacked her things and saw her up, and left her there. He drove away thinking of nothing else but that he was leaving her, turned into the park and then with nowhere to go, he stopped.

He switched off the engine. It ticked gratefully into silence, it seemed to sigh, and rest. She could have the flat. Whatever she needed she could have, it didn't matter. He stayed sitting there in the romantic, foolish car and watched the children playing around him, and searched for some truth to salvage from the wreck that he had made.

Nina and he. It had seemed so clear, so familiar; as if the path were chosen just for them by fate. He had brought the sword of stupid love; St George to slay the dragon and save the maiden, but he had failed. He had lost himself and everything he loved, gracelessly, to the mirage of salvation. The vision had evaporated. There wasn't anything. She was not that maiden; he was not that saint. She did not want to be saved.

And Nina sat on the floor in Luke's flat and cried and thought it was the only heroic thing she had ever done or was ever likely to do, not to go after him, and take him back, and ruin him.

————————

Paul and Maggie had a party for the Depot in an Italian restaurant near to the theatre.

Paul was too busy so Leigh organised it – the guest list, the menu – and Maggie paid from her personal account, not the Depot's, which might not see a profit for years. They weren't gloomy about it. They felt triumphant; up and running, legitimate.

Maggie and Leigh were in the restaurant early, sharing a bottle of wine and talking plays and profiteroles.

'You do *everything*,' said Maggie. 'You've kept him in stew and clean shirts for months as it is.'

'We're not like that,' said Leigh.

'Aren't you?' Maggie smiled. 'I've said that before.'

The waiters stuck candles in bottles around them, clattering and shouts came from the kitchen like a discordant opera behind.

'You know how it's been,' said Leigh.

'God, yes,' said Maggie.

Given *how it had been*, the party was a riot of relief and celebration. They all drank too much. Denton, the director and cast of *Hierarchy*, the architect, the contractors, Paul's family, old friends and new; backers and backstage crew, stars and stage management and Maggie's daughter, Helen, traipsing round with friends between the tables.

Leigh, who had heard more of the Depot than she had seen, saw them all through Paul's eyes and felt the sentiment and joy of it on his behalf. Smilingly she watched him, as he stood with his arm around people, as much to keep himself up as with affection.

She worked all night, making sure the waiters were doing their jobs and not just smoking in the kitchen, filling herself with reflected glory and glasses with wine. She wallowed. She thought she probably loved it even more than Maggie did, or Paul, who were more closely connected, because she had safe distance and a measure of their success. After midnight she sat, and put her feet onto a chair. Two women were earnestly talking nearby about a collective they were forming, an all-women's theatre to tour the country, new plays, experimental. She had met one of them before, who was going out with someone at the Duke of York's, and liked her.

Across the room a group of actors were shouting to be heard, topping one another with ever sillier accents, worse disasters they had faced in New York . . . Sheffield . . . television . . . but the women near Leigh drew her in with dangerous whispered plans of risk – they had a grant, they had a play, they were hoping to be ready.

'You still SM at the Duke of York's?' said one to Leigh, who had almost forgotten she was physically present, so absorbed was she in her role of onlooker.

'For a while,' she said.

'Chuck it in,' said the woman, huge serious eyes over her glass. 'We need someone like you.'

'I might,' said Leigh, thinking of Graft and how happy they had been.

She realised how it scared her, the idea of leaving the security of her limiting job.

She remembered she had used to be braver.

She smiled and got up. She took some plates as she passed a table, tucking her glass between her forearm and the edges, precarious. On her way to the kitchen a waiter bumped into her, and the red wine tipped and spilled onto her front, the wet fabric smell of it rising up immediately as it spread.

The waiter began to apologise but could not speak English. He was very skinny, long-haired, and looked as if he ought to be on a Vespa in Italy somewhere, not like a waiter at all.

'It's fine,' she said, knowing the stain would never lift. 'Don't worry.'

They both mopped at her dress and she saw, as she looked up, past him, Paul and Maggie at a table in the corner. They were about three feet apart. They were not touching, but sat almost unnecessarily distant from one another. They were talking intently, and there was something in it – something in the way they faced one another, the atmosphere around them – that made Leigh halt.

She gave the plates and glasses to the waiter, hardly looking at him, and went over as they both looked up as if she were interrupting them.

'Hello,' said Paul. 'What's that?'

She had forgotten about the wine stain down her front.

'You look as if you've been stabbed,' said Paul.

'Here, sit,' said Maggie, and pulled out the chair between them.

Leigh turned away from the suspicion in her mind, dismissing the moment's perception.

'Good idea,' she said.

She saw Paul look at her – check her expression – as she sat, but again she put it from her mind.

She turned to him and he put both his hands on either side of her face and kissed her mouth.

'Missed you,' he said.

She leaned against him, closed her eyes and drew the safe-keeping fabric of her life around her like a cloak. Paul was her own, and steady. It was nothing he had done, only her own fugitive heart, always alert to danger. She must remember she had conquered it. She opened her eyes.

'You two have been to hell and back,' she said, with slightly drunken sincerity. 'No wonder you are so close.'

At home she went about the process of undressing and washing like a mechanical toy winding down. All she wanted was bed. It took her several minutes to realise that Paul was not doing the same. Usually they moved around one another at bedtime like a well-rehearsed stage crew between scenes; silent, not bumping into one another in the dim light as they undressed, washed, climbed into bed. But Paul was not there. She took a blanket, wrapped herself in it, and went into the sitting room. He was on the sofa in the dark.

'Too tired to sleep?'

'I have to tell you now or else I never will,' he said.

Leigh stopped in the doorway. Knowing but not accepting. Waiting.

'I'm sorry, Leigh. I've been — Maggie and me are seeing each other.'

Leigh stood wrapped in her clumsy blanket and all she felt was the humiliating comedy of not having realised. He had looked at her each night after being with Maggie all day and she hadn't known. She had been foolish. The words kept coming at her. Foolish. Stupid. Pitiable. Idiotically happy while her boyfriend was seeing someone else.

'How long?' she said.

'Long enough.'

'How long?'

'A month. Bit more.'

She stood in silence, taking it in. Then the pain started. She didn't have anger, only this embarrassing, ugly pain that she, ridiculously, had felt safe. It felt as though she had been kicked.

'Leigh—'

She shook her head and went into the bedroom, her breath and body out of kilter with her mind, sick. She sat on her side of the bed and then got up again. Sitting was too vulnerable.

Paul came into the room. She was not going to show him anything. She would not.

'I want you to go; I can't talk to you about it,' she said.

'All right,' said Paul, recognising her right to tell him how this should be, because he had wronged her. She must be given her way.

'Are you in love with her?' she said, despising the cliché and the victim tone of her voice but knowing it would matter later when she had to piece herself together.

'I don't know,' said Paul. 'She's really very—'

'No,' said Leigh, warningly, who could not hear what Maggie was.

She turned round.

'I'm sorry,' he said and she saw that he was wrecked by it. He'd had time to feel it, after all. He looked so sad. He looked as if he might cry, and she felt sorry for him because she loved him very much and she did not want him to suffer.

'Please can you go?' she said. She knew she was going to lose herself to grief or protest, and could not bear for him to see it.

He nodded, and he went. *He'll probably go to her*, Leigh thought, and she remembered her mother throwing her father out and into the arms of other women and herself, a child, watching from the top of the stairs.

*

Paul did not move out immediately and neither did she. There was all the mess of it to get through first. A week of helpless arguing, circular conversations, apologies and blame. Sometimes they decided they would stay together, as if nothing had gone wrong at all, and take refuge in familiarity, knowing there was nothing really left of the two of them. The habit of one another broke like bones. And her rage. Her rage. She indulged in elaborate revenge fantasies; confronting Maggie in rooms full of people, spilling food on her, sending her hate-filled letters that she wrote in her mind, and rewrote, and sometimes put down on paper, but never surrendered to sending. And she would say to him —

*What's it like with her?*

*How did it feel to lie to me, was it fun?*

*Where were you the first time?*

*In the office?*

*At her house?*

*Did you bring her here?*

*She's so old, Paul — for God's sake, a divorcee!*

*Does she like her younger man? Good for her vanity?*

And at her worst —

*You're just like my father, you fucking bastard, you shit . . .*

She hit him. He fended her off, gently. She cried. He wiped her tears. And he would say —

*I'm sorry, I'm sorry.*

*I didn't think of you.*

*It was selfish.*

*She's not a bitch — leave her alone.*

*She's nice. She wants me.*

*I didn't want to hurt you, Leigh.*

*Don't make me tell you.*

And once, when he was cornered, 'I went to her because you don't really love me,' so that Leigh laughed in the face of her pain and his.

'Now you want me to tell you I love you?'

'No. You always say it.'

'I mean it.'

'I know I'm not enough for you, Leigh. I've never felt safe,' he said.

'I did,' said Leigh. 'I did.'

She had prized safety above all things, had backed herself into a corner and found nothing but danger there.

She handed in her notice at the theatre; Paul put the flat up for sale, and they said goodbye.

'What are you going to do?' he asked.

She had offers from friends to sleep on their floors, rent their rooms, but London – her London, the theatre – had Paul in it, and she couldn't be there.

'I don't know,' she said.

He didn't ask her any more. She was not his to uncover. Such a very long short-time together, from that long-ago February of '72 to this July of '73, but her secrets were now not his to keep.

———————

*Diversion* was a stone-cold hit, smashing cracks in every other production of that season from the RSC's redefining *Antony and Cleopatra* to Alan Ayckbourn's *Norman Conquests*; *Diversion* made that year not just a good year for theatre but *the* year. The season. The play.

\*

It was three weeks before Luke went to see it. When he did, it was to stand at the back of the stalls, dazed by the surreal experience of the words being his but the design, cast, the production all new to him. It was like seeing a dream made flesh, but generations from the origin. The text had been altered slightly in places, and he could not be offended; Malcolm Dewberry couldn't have discussed the process with him if he had wanted to. Luke doubted he would have wanted to.

*Diversion*. The most loved, the most painful and — he did not mind the reductive judgement — the *best* piece of work of his life. Seeing it on stage, from a distance, he registered that having betrayed it, it was not now his, and could not now be loved.

Hannah Gold, playing Mary, was just right, he noted. She was warm and — as Bridge had said of the part — she was womanly. He remembered how sweet she had been when they were together. He left in the interval.

The week before, he had written Paul and Maggie a letter of apology, stilted and heartfelt, but had not heard back. His agent, Ben, was busy sticking plasters over the cuts and grazes Luke had inflicted on his professional relationships, but he was sanguine about it.

*Success causes amnesia, Luke, and Nigel Dempster's poisoned pen never harms the box office.*

Earlier that day Luke left his cramped, dirty hotel room in Bloomsbury and went to the matinée of *Hierarchy of Angels* at the Depot. Sitting in the top tier of the brand-new theatre he was overwhelmed with pride at what Paul had done. The foyer still smelled of paint. The play was very good. The agonisingly tight timing of its opening had lent urgency to the Depot's originality. Cubitt, in *The Times*, had sneered that the factory-like setting was *inconducive to the appreciation of art of any kind, even Denton's grating polemic*, but Kurtz in the *Observer* had fallen in love with the space and said that . . . *all thinking people welcome the Depot with an open mind and open heart; it is the future, and Denton its perfectly pitched voice.*

Luke hoped that Leigh was cutting out the notices for her scrapbook as he was for her, in his mind.

When he came out of the theatre, before he could lose his nerve, he went straight to the Depot's offices.

Paul looked up at him as he came in, and covered his surprise with blankness. Luke stood in the doorway, twitching with nerves and shifting from foot to foot, as the phone rang and Paul ignored it.

When it stopped Luke said, 'Come to say hello.' He noted Maggie's absence with relief.

'Hello,' said Paul.

'Did you get my letter?' said Luke.

'Yep,' said Paul.

'I just saw *Hierarchy*, it's a bloody – well, it's really good, Paul.'

'Nice of you to say so.'

Luke winced, knowing nothing good would come of this and yet unable to leave. He deserved the slings and arrows and couldn't back out a coward, too.

'What's next, then?' he asked.

'What?'

'For the Depot.'

'The *Hamlet*, you might remember?'

'Oh. Yes. Right. Good.'

'Listen, Luke, I'm busy.'

'Yes, I know, I just wanted to – how's Leigh?'

Paul did not answer and Luke felt frustration. This wasn't natural to him, this cool enmity, he would have talked if Paul would let him, tried to find some truth to close the distance. But then Paul asked, 'How's Nina?' and Luke didn't want to talk any longer, just get out of there.

'I don't know,' he answered, and found he couldn't say any more because it hurt too much.

'Don't you have to go and get interviewed by someone?' said Paul, and the funny part was, he did.

The *Observer Magazine* journalist was waiting on the pavement in Cartwright Gardens, outside his hotel; a bespectacled man of Luke's age, like an overgrown student. He had a photographer with him who took pictures of Luke as they talked, standing by the window in the tiny hotel room, because there wasn't a bar and nowhere to sit but the bed. They turned towards one another unnaturally with the *click-whirr* staccato of the camera punctuating the questions like a pulse.

*Does it surprise you to be compared with Arthur Miller? Peter Nicholls? Pinter? Beckett?*

*Is there any truth to the rumour Peter Hall has commissioned you to write a play for the new National?*

*Do you consider* Diversion *a tragedy? A comedy? A morality tale?*

*What about Kurtz's accusation you're 'reactionary'?*

*You're not English. Where are your parents?*

*Are you Jewish? Did your father change his name?*

*Does fame appeal to you?*

*Is 'madness' in your work a political preoccupation, or personal?*

'Do you think the real world is as nightmarish as the one you depict in your play?'

'Sometimes it is,' said Luke. 'Yes.'

When Nina had left his flat, the day he went back, he searched for clues of her. He went around carefully like a dog checking for any piece left behind. There were ghosts – the smell of her on the pillow, the sheets, a gold cigarette packet crumpled and dropped into the bin. Split-second relief from her absence. He pressed his face into the place on the bed where her body had been as if he could climb back into her. She had sent the key to his agent and a note saying 'Thank you', which made him angry for being so fatuous. He would rather no note at all. He wasn't angry with her, it was just the instinct to fight back against the pain, and nobody to fight with. He had felt the hit, the rush, the heat, the taste, the oblivion of being inside her. The wound she left didn't close. He forgot why he should want it to.

And still he had nothing to write. The limited world was in intolerable focus. All his life there had been so many other lives within him he had taken them for granted, even held them back. Now, when he looked, there was a void. He did not write. He could not conceive of writing. She had hollowed him out.

Then, in September, his mother died.

He knew it when he heard the doctor's voice as he answered the phone. The hospital only ever called in a crisis.

He put down the telephone thinking coolly, *This is what it feels like to hear news like that. It's all right. It doesn't hurt.* But then, over hours, it began to.

He drove to Seston. Death mixed the elemental and the base unflinchingly. Even for a poor woman like his mother, who had almost nothing, the authorities must be notified, forms filled in, in triplicate, coffin paid for; the details of her death examined and dismissed. He welcomed it all; it kept him from self-recrimination and being with his father. He had let his anger with Tomasz lie unexamined until it had iced over. His mother's death made it hot again. Tomasz cried, and railed, or else just stared, as if contemplating his myopic soul. Observing him, Luke choked on harsh judgement.

He could not stay at the house. He went to Seston's best hotel – grey net curtains and mauve-flowered valences on the beds – and on the second evening he called Paul.

'Paul, it's Luke.'

'Hello.'

'I'm in Seston.'

'Where?'

'*Bloody hell! Seston!*'

He had never shouted at Paul before, he could feel his shock down the line in the pause that followed.

'Sorry,' said Paul finally, in what Luke thought of as his *ay-up* voice, dry – impossible to be angry with.

'My mother died on Saturday,' said Luke. 'Heart attack. Two hundred and fifty volts going through her every week can't have helped.'

A brief silence. Then Paul said, 'Shall I come up there?'

Luke nodded, forgetting Paul couldn't see him.

'Luke?'

'Sorry. Yes. Thanks.'

'Just me. Leigh and I split up.'

'Someone told me.'

'Someone would. See you tomorrow, then?'

'I'm staying at The Pines.'

'It's seriously called that?' said Paul.

They laughed, didn't say anything more, and Luke put the phone down.


'He's just *sitting* . . .' Luke ran out of words to condemn his father's inertia.

He and Paul were driving to the asylum. Luke needed to go through his mother's room and hadn't been able to alone.

'He lacks moral courage,' he said.

'Hark at you,' said Paul.

'He does. That and a spine.'

'Think of him like an animal, or someone you don't know,' said Paul. 'That's what I used to do with my granddad when he peed himself.'

'Compassionate.'

'That's me.'

'You were how old?'

'Fifteen, about. He's dead now.'

'It's quite funny, though – I used to think of my mother as a zoo animal when I was a kid. When she got out of hand.'

'What kind?'

'One of the nice ones, a tiger – or something just jumpy and a bit mad, like a gazelle or a monkey.'

'Is that it?' Paul pointed ahead, through the windscreen, as they reached the brow of the hill and the hospital, roofs first, revealed itself to them.

'Yes,' said Luke.

They approached. He turned the Triumph between the high gates and up the drive towards the dark-red turreted asylum. Gun-metal rainclouds were banked up behind it and a weak sun glinted on the slates.

'Bloody hell,' said Paul.

Luke spent two hours carefully boxing up his mother's things. He couldn't easily throw them out but there was no place for them. He found the cardigan with the daisies she had worn the day they went to the National Gallery. He didn't know what to do with her hairbrush. All the postcards he had sent were arranged in groups, views of churches, town halls and parks from every place he'd ever worked. There were more than two hundred and fifty, in both French and English. Some only had one line, others closely written, all over and around the edges, tiny biro words right up to the corners of the stamp.

'Do you mind?' said Paul, gesturing them.

'Go ahead,' said Luke.

So Paul sat on the floor and looked at the cards, front and back, reading, trying to decipher the French, while Luke went through the room doggedly, stacking her books, almost not breathing.

'Good they let her keep them,' said Paul.

Luke shot him a look, defensive.

'They're nice.'

Paul nodded. 'I know,' he said, but the hospital terrified him.

It was worse than any horror film he had ever seen, and smelled as bad as it looked. When they arrived he had heard screaming from somewhere – he wasn't sure if Luke had even noticed. He tried hard to see it from his perspective – *a second home, childhood games in the corridors, homework* – forcing himself past immediate appearances to the relationships and the everyday life of the place, but he was appalled to his soul by it. This dead woman's sanctuary and his friend's beginning was Victorian bedlam directed by Roman Polanski. Luke seemed to think he had known a mother's love like other children, but any normality he had was learned. Paul thought of the reasoned framework of his own childhood, the well-meant oppression he had pushed against to grow into a man, and was immeasurably grateful for it.

Hélène's body was in the morgue and the asylum's chapel booked for her burial.

'We have to change it,' said Luke. His voice was expressionless with his excess feeling. 'I want her to be buried at St Saviour's. The Catholic church in town. I think it's better. Free. More free, I mean. For her. To be out. Better.'

'Yes, we'll sort that out,' said Paul. 'What?'

He asked, because Luke, who had been so busy, had stopped. Paul thought he might be going to cry. He didn't want to stay to find out.

'I'll leave you alone,' he said, halfway to the door.

'I think I must be much more stupid than I appear to be,' said Luke. 'Deluded. Naïve, or something.'

'Why?'

'Because I'm still surprised she died here. I think I meant to come and get her one day. Why do we carry on believing like that?'

'In what?'

'This nonsense fairytale of salvation.'

Paul thought about it, and had no useful answer to give him.

'We must like it,' he said at last.

'I don't,' said Luke, without turning. 'I don't like it. It's better to believe in nothing.'

Luke, Tomasz and Paul were at the service and graveside at St Saviour's, along with hospital staff, some retired, who had visited Hélène over the years, sixteen people in all.

'Nice funeral,' said Paul out of the side of his mouth to Luke as they stood in church.

Seeing Luke crossing himself before the altar had been another jolt, another piece in his jigsaw.

'Not a pauper's grave,' said Luke.

'No,' said Paul, knowing what he meant exactly. 'Out with a bang, man. Jumpin'.'

Luke and he had bought a black suit for his father. Getting him into it on the morning of the funeral his frailty and stubbornness were extreme, much worse than the Christmas before. It was a grotesque enough experience to be funny now that Paul was there. After the funeral they had thick brown tea and bridge rolls in the nearby pub. The landlord was familiar with the funeral set. The nurses were driven by kindness to say nice things about Hélène. Luke was reluctant to hear them. Even knowing their words were only platitudes and politeness, it was too painful.

'She was so proud of you, your mum.'

He hated the formal exposure of his unreconciled grief, the sorrow spilling out, rubbing his eyes with the heels of his hands trying to force it back.

'It's like a crucifixion,' he said to Paul. 'You're being flayed, and people stand about and talk to you about it.'

'Funerals are good in the end. It always works out,' said Paul, comfortably.

Behind the bar the landlord watched the small, disparate crowd and the dark-haired young man, obviously the only family member, crying as if he were surrounded by friends.

'Very sentimental these Catholics, as a rule,' he murmured to the barmaid filling the teapots. 'Not like us. The foreign ones are the worst for it.'

The last thing they did before leaving Seston was buy food for Tomasz, and some more vodka. Luke had no compassion left for him.

'With any luck, he'll drink himself to death quite soon,' he said.

His father was a worse cripple than his mother had ever been, and she had had the dignity to fight.

And on the drive back to London, heading south in the afternoon light that set gold into the air and patterns over the ordinary road, they talked about nothing but theatre; risky, comforting, blessed theatre – until Luke asked Paul, 'Do you know where Leigh is? Is she all right?'

'She's in America,' said Paul, 'last I heard.'

Bayswater. Moscow Road. There were two people kissing in the street below his flat as he got out of the car, and someone playing a piano in another house by an open window. It was the theme from *The Sting*, tripping, stop-starting. Luke got his case from the boot. The two people kissing and whispering to one other; the piano playing the same ragtime phrase over and over; the sunlight moving leaf shapes on the paving slabs. He let himself in and went upstairs.

His desk stood against the bare wall opposite the bed. The notebooks were as they had been. Pencils in the jar. The typewriter, with its sagging ribbon, red and black. He put down his case and sat at the desk. He picked up a pencil and wrote.

*Funerals are good, in the end.*

## Afterwards – New York – 1975

New York was not Luke's city and this was not his life. He sat in a chair facing the view through the window of the small, top-floor apartment at his hotel.

In an hour's time, the curtain would go up on *Diversion* at the Morosco Theater, a shabby, thousand-seat old dame, squashed into her place along W45th, the brightly lit triangular billboard jutting out over the street fighting for precedence.

*Luke Last's Diversion, original West End cast.*

When the London run finished there had been more than a year's break while the actors took other jobs if they were offered them and the deals were done with the New York managers. Then the Broadway transfer. A second chance. A rebirth. A new city, a new stage.

Luke let Ben deal with Lou Farthing over it and had nothing to do with Tony at all. Rehearsals in the rented studio in Midtown had been intimate, just the cast and Malcolm and Luke, working in safe anonymity. But now there was a gathering of power. A number of L. M. Farthing Productions as well as Lou, and Tony Moore, were all there in the city. The generals come to witness the foot-soldiers' unarmed foray into the line of New York fire. Tonight at half past seven the curtain would reveal them, ready or not.

He should get to the theatre.

He was dressed; black tie and a dinner jacket that was clean but crumpled because it had felt unlucky to unpack it before now. He should have hung it up in the bathroom. He should have called down to the lobby for someone to collect it. It was fine, he had matching socks.

It had been an idyll of sorts. Or if not that, at least a taste of the life *Diversion* had once promised to him in the long solitude of writing. In New York he had seen it rehearsed and played all the way through for the first time. He changed small things here and there with Malcolm's blessing, to put his mark on it.

Then, that morning at the dress –

'Thought you should know, love,' Malcolm said, 'Tony arrived in town last night. Bit sticky? He's staying at the Taft, apparently.'

'Nina?'

Luke had only been able to say the name on its own. He had no other words to go with it, still.

'I imagine she's with him.'


At the opening of his first play in Oxford she had held his hand.

He looked at his watch. Six. He should go to the theatre.

The telephone did not ring. He had been getting telegrams and calls all week from London but now there was silence. He got up and went over to it.

'Good evening, sir,' said the receptionist, sing-song, a trace of Brooklyn. 'May I help you?'

'Do you have a number for the Taft Hotel?'

'Certainly, sir, would you like me to connect you?'

Nina and Tony were staying on the fifteenth floor of the Taft with Chrissie and Alexander. Alexander was rehearsing for a comedy soon to open at the Astor. Accustomed to his screen career, it was his first stage appearance since the RSC in his twenties and he was frightened, which made him drink more. Chrissie drank along with him and often without. Their nanny and the two-year-old Natasha were left behind in London. Chrissie and Nina travelled in taxis and got out only to shop or go to restaurants, terrified of muggers and drug-dealers, blacks and pimps – all of New York that wasn't sheltered by money or the theatre. It seemed a lawless place. Nina was six months' pregnant and felt particularly vulnerable. Everything seemed dirty to her, she washed a great deal and covered herself with scent.

Now Chrissie and Alexander were arguing in the suite next door – muffled growls and screeches, furniture going over – and Nina was looking out at the skyscrapers. Tony was on the bed with a Martini, feet up and crossed at the ankle, jittery from the speed he had taken earlier and irritation at Nina's mood.

'Look, come with me to the bloody play if you want, darling, or don't,' he said. 'I couldn't be less interested.'

Nina turned from the window, lamplight furring the silhouette of her miniskirt, pregnancy, and glass of champagne.

'I don't want to go,' she said.

'You do,' said Tony, affecting boredom. 'It's your lover's play. You'll want to congratulate him. We can all sit at separate tables in Sardi's while we wait for the reviews and toss

392

bons mots at one another. It will be romantic. Very Noël Coward.'

Nina felt her baby kicking. It never failed to give her a frightened jolt that she could not bear to analyse.

The telephone rang. Tony picked it up. He raised his eyebrows.

'Yes, she's here, hold on.' He held out the telephone. '*Author-author* — for you.'

Nina did not know what he meant. Luke wouldn't call her —
'Hello?'

And his voice, close, in her ear after almost two years.

'You are here,' he said.

'Yes.'

'Are you going to the theatre tonight?'

'I haven't decided.'

Tony was watching her. She turned away so as not to see him.

'I really can't talk,' she said.

'No, of course not. That's all right. But the thing is, Nina, I just need to know—'

Nina put down the phone.

Tony regarded her, hungrily. 'What did he want?'

'I think he wanted to see me.'

'How rude,' said Tony. 'Darling, ring down for a taxi, we should get a move on. *For God's sake — stop screaming in there!*' he shouted to the wall, and banged his fist on it, but Chrissie and Alexander's muffled battle continued.

Nina sat on the bed, trembling. She felt terribly sad.

She did not want to cry. Crying never got her anywhere, she always felt better eventually. Better but no different. She sat there, defences broken by the sound of Luke's voice, like the reminder of a sin. If she cried she would have to do her eye make-up all over again.

'I wish he hadn't called,' she said, in all her loneliness. 'I just wish he hadn't.'

'Yes,' said Tony, getting up, 'it was in very poor taste.'

As Luke put down the telephone he found that he was smiling. It was not because he was happy, but because he was thinking that somebody up there didn't want him ever to see *Diversion* open, in either London or New York. Perhaps it would be revived and tour the provinces in a few years. He might see it then.

He took off his dinner jacket and unknotted the bow tie. He called down to the desk.

'Could you send some flowers and charge them to my room? Roses. Or something. To the Morosco Theater. Yes. Yes. Thanks. *To Malcolm, Tom, Hannah, Richard, Scot* — one T — *Joan and Henry. Good luck, faith and thanks. Luke. Faith.* Yes, that's it. Fine. What? Two dozen. Thank you.'

He put the phone down, changed into normal clothes and left the hotel.

Times Square in the late afternoon made his own Soho look like a village fete.

In Luke's first few days in New York he had walked and walked. Everyone loved to tell their street-crime anecdotes, and warn him off, but he wasn't frightened of cities. He went through the crowds and low-slung cars at traffic lights, disobeying the *walk-don't-walk* signs as the unforgiving grid made wind tunnels, carrying dirt from uptown to down, from gutter to doorway to subway, and he absorbed the filth with a foreigner's appetite. In New York he found for the first time a place with an energy that matched his.

Now, as night slowly came down, beneath the noise-cover of car radios and siren blares, he headed away from 45th Street, downtown. He left the billboards of musicals, high-kicks and top-Cs, big names in lights, and smiled at the quaint sight of Alan Ayckbourn's name among the others, like finding a Bakewell tart in a stack of donuts. He crossed Times Square, passing the theatres that had been converted to movie-theatres, the movie-theatres that were now porno cinemas and the porn-houses that had been turned into peepshows. Those that weren't porn were mostly musicals. The cacophony of decay had held a wildlife thrill for the first couple of days. Now it was just visual static. He didn't glance at the giant Coca-Cola sign flashing above his head.

Focused, he carried on south, down Broadway, block after block. Each step he took felt lighter, each yard that separated him from the Morosco, and from Nina, was a fresh distance, a pleasure.

He realised, with quick and childish delight, that he was looking for something. He was on a pilgrimage that was saving him, inconsequential though it was, from introspection and grief.

Walking fast, he crossed E 23rd Street, reached Union Square and turned right, heated by the pace and pleased it was such a simple city to be lost in – no maze of history to negotiate, just one clear refreshing plan. He knew the direction he wanted. He took the streetscape as his reference. He would know it when he found it.

Words of songs went around his head. He resisted singing them openly. He forgot about the play and, realising he had found diversion from *Diversion*, he laughed a little.

He was getting closer. An adolescent thrill took hold. As the buildings dropped in scale so it seemed did he. The young delight of first loves took him over; the records, films, books and album covers of his seeking youth. He knew it must be one of these streets, not far away. He scanned the pavements for familiar signs.

The evening sky glowed French blue against the American skyline. And the city changed, softened into the bohemian, the neighbourhood; messier and yet somehow calmer and more human. He saw roads that nearly took him there, but not quite. He felt as if he were seeking home.

He was about to turn off Lafayette when he saw the Public Theater – known to him, respected from afar for its serious work. It was showing something called *A Chorus Line*. Bowler hats and canes. *Even here*, he thought as he turned off, onto E4th, and walked on.

He was close, he could tell he was. There were brownstones and stoops, cafés and junk shops. A group of musicians were loading a drum kit into a battered VW van, fire escapes zigzagging the buildings behind them and parked cars on either side. Luke stopped in the middle of the street to watch – imagining it in winter – but a yellow cab honked him so he walked on. Washington Square; a flat, green space to break the verticals. And then, on Bleecker Street – he saw something, and he stopped.

A rounded awning on a tall, flat-fronted brownstone over the pavement and, beneath it, two sets of double doors – theatre doors. The name on the awning was the Apple Tree Theater, and the playbills on either side were freshly posted.

The Apple Tree Theater Presents
GONE
By
Leigh Radley, Tracey Hillman and Violet Todd
Starring
Tracey Hillman and Violet Todd
Directed by
Leigh Radley


It was not what he had been looking for but it was what he had found.

He stood and stared at the poster, forgetting everything – his silly mission. He went closer, shuddering at the strange magic. He turned, but Leigh was not there. Just her name. He checked it. Leigh Radley. He decided it was another Leigh Radley. But he knew it wasn't. He knew it was her.

*Directed by Leigh Radley.*

Luke stood there, proudly staring at the names on the poster and the locked doors. He went up and rattled them a bit. A thick chain was laced through the handles inside. And so he turned to leave.


Halfway across the street to the theatre, Leigh saw him. He had his back to her, fifty yards away, standing by the doors – she knew it was him at once. As she watched, he turned, and began to walk away.

'Luke.' She said his name without thinking. He couldn't have heard, but he turned round and scanned the street. He saw her.

'Fuck,' he said, the sound lost in the space between them, but the word very clear. Fuck.

*Yes*, she thought.

He began to come towards her. Just the same. A mess. Too bright to look at straight.

As he reached her, he smiled as if he would gobble her up and held out his arms. She backed away so he changed the movement into putting his hands in his pockets instead.

'Say something,' he said.

'Hello, Luke?'

'Jesus Christ.'

They were standing in the middle of the street – where she had stopped dead at the sight of him. A car nearly clipped them as it swerved past and they sidestepped onto the kerb.

As they reached the pavement he looked as if he would hug her again.

'Stop it,' she said. 'Aren't you supposed to be at your opening night?'

'How do you know? And what's going on here?' He jerked his head to the Apple Tree Theater behind.

'We open in two days,' she said angrily, knowing she sounded as though she were accusing him of something. She must remember she had the advantage; she had known he was in New York. She'd been avoiding the theatre district for two weeks to be sure that in a city of eight million people she wouldn't bump into him. But here he was.

'Two days,' he said. 'That's wonderful.'

'Yes.'

'What's the play? Are you busy? Can we talk?'

'You haven't changed at all,' she said, like a curse.

'Why do you say that?' he said. 'Everyone changes, don't they?'

'Why aren't you at the Morosco?'

'Don't want to be. *Leigh* – your play?'

'No, Luke.' She glanced down the road towards the bar she had been going to, the evening he had snatched away. 'I really have to go.'

'Really?' He seemed completely taken aback and innocent.

'Yes – I'm meeting some people.'

'*Seriously?* Why? Can't we . . .'

He looked around, pushing up his shirtsleeves.

'My hotel is horrible,' he said. 'It's like a Barbra Streisand comedy. Where's your flat? Are you living on your own?'

Leigh didn't answer.

She made him nervous, the way she was watching him – judgement and heat.

'Look,' she said, 'I'd better go. See you.'

And she walked away.

Luke watched her going away from him, as around her all the street lights were illuminated, changing their meeting from afternoon to night. She was lit from above.

Her dark hair, longer, was tied back in a loose plait, her flowered skirt; rounded bottom moving through her hips, so female and intriguing, without knowing it, unaware as she walked what she looked like. Who she looked like. She was something like the woman he had written. Mary. Or the woman he had written was something like Leigh. He didn't know what it meant. Or if it meant anything at all.

'Leigh!'

She turned.

'What?'

She was furious. He didn't know why she was so angry.

'We never made up,' he said, walking towards her.

'We never fell out.'

399

'Yes, we did.'

He reached her. It was important he tell the truth, even if he didn't know what it was yet.

Leigh was staring at him as if she were about to call the police.

'I've missed you so much,' he said.

'No, you haven't.'

'Have you not missed me? I miss you like . . .' He looked around, trying to keep her, confused and searching for something to hold on to. He always wanted to kiss her and he wanted to now. He thought if he did she would probably smack him.

He knew she was angry — rightly — about *Diversion* and letting Paul down, but it felt so long ago to him, and they were in a different place, and he couldn't believe she just wanted to leave when it was so precious that they had met like this. He had never thought of her as a vengeful sort of girl. He didn't believe she had really forgotten how happy they had been, before.

'Don't you miss us?' he said, trying to find out just what he meant by it. 'All of us?'

And then she lost her temper.

'Why do you *say* those things? Why do you just *say* those things you don't mean? You're like a . . .'

'What?' He couldn't help smiling at her, he was so pleased to see her.

'Just stop it! I have to go. This is stupid.'

She was pink, vibrating with anger or raw-edged feeling that he didn't understand.

'What is it that you think of me?' he asked.

'Seriously?'

'Seriously.'

'I think you're ravenous,' she said quickly, not coming any closer. 'I think you've got pieces missing, like an animal. You're stupid — your *heart* is stupid and it makes you cruel. You don't care for your friends. You don't care about me at all. And here you are, saying you *miss* me. It's completely ridiculous. You go through the world like a plague. Unfaithful. *Unfaithful*. You're a locust. You eat everything up. You're dangerous and you're—'

A couple walking past stared at them, enjoying the show. Leigh stopped as quickly as she had started. Her quiet voice that had dropped such accusation and had so much rage ceased.

She looked very pretty, Luke thought, for someone who had such cruel weapons. He wasn't interested in defending himself. If she thought that of him, there wasn't any point in saying it wasn't true. It was her truth. But it hurt.

'I thought we were friends,' he said and began to feel sad. She ignored him. 'I didn't realise.'

She was rummaging in her bag. He remembered she always did that when she wanted to hide. She should know by now there was no point hiding, it was something he had always known.

'My mother died,' he said, after a while.

She looked up.

'September before last. Paul came up and helped me.'

Leigh thought for a moment. 'It's just me that hates you now, then?' she said.

'You don't hate me,' he said. 'And I don't hate you.'

They stood there in the street, locked in their different battles as the evening chill cooled them. Then she shook her head and looked to the ground.

'That was horrible of me,' she said in a low voice. 'I'm so sorry.'

'I don't mind.'

'And I'm sorry about your mother.'

Luke shrugged. 'Don't say that. It makes it normal and small and then there's nothing I can say back that isn't banal or sentimental, or phony, or otherwise – you know.'

She seemed to soften.

It was a start.

'Can we at least get a drink?' he said, thinking she must have said all her worst things now. Hoping she hadn't meant them.

She looked at him appraisingly for a moment, then she turned and started to walk along the pavement. He went with her. She didn't tell him not to.

As they reached the corner three people came towards them, recognising Leigh and smiling. Luke took Leigh's hand – without thinking – and noticed with surprise that she didn't pull away.

They stopped as the people reached them, two women and a man, good friends; they kissed Leigh's cheeks, halfway through a conversation, and expecting her to join them.

'This is Luke Kanowski,' she said.

They said their *hellos* and *hi-s* and Luke nodded to them, taking them in, and trying to fill out his picture of Leigh's life. They could have been to do with the theatre, or artists – fringed jackets, longish hair.

'We'll see you in there?' they said, and when they went, and the two of them were alone again, Leigh looked down at Luke's hand holding hers.

'Don't chat up the stage management,' she said, and pulled her hand away.

'What?'

'That's what you said to me: *Don't chat up the stage management.*'

'Yes,' said Luke, 'in your flat. When you came to work at Graft.'

'You remember.' She seemed surprised.

'Of course I remember.'

'Why did you leave me that night?' She was not accusing him now, but asking.

'Well, there was this girl,' he said, 'the SM we had – I can't remember her name, and—' Then he stopped talking because that wasn't it.

Leigh was looking down, waiting. She glanced up when he stopped speaking and then down again at her hands, as if she were in a courtroom waiting to hear her sentence, separating herself from him.

So Luke removed himself too. He left them both on the corner of the New York street and he took himself back.

It was easy.

He saw Leigh's bedsit that night as though he were watching a film unspooling. He remembered sitting on the bed with her, as Paul slept, and – like a photograph – the Bob Dylan album under their knees; him and the girl in the Greenwich Village street in winter, the street that Luke, in escaping the adult discomfort of *Diversion*'s opening, had been seeking. He remembered his first impression of her eyes through the just-open window of the Mini, with the Seston rain falling down around them, and Paul shouting in the background. And how, at Paul's flat, when she was there he had felt at home, could sleep; could feel her presence and still be safe from her, because she was Paul's. He felt again the way she had felt to him that blackout night, the only time they had kissed, against the wall

403

in her tiny room. He remembered her honesty and the frightening weight of her humanity. How badly he had needed to get away.

And then he came back to the present and looked at her standing in front of him now and waiting to hear why it was that in that moment he had known what they might be, and he had left her. He was wrong; they had never been friends. The distance between them had never been cool.

She looked so sad he had to stop himself from trying to touch her, knowing how angry she would be.

'Was it because you didn't like me?' she asked; a small voice that was unlike herself.

'I think it was because I liked you too much,' he said.

She did look up then. She looked up and she – he looked closely at her expression – she sneered at him.

'Really? Honestly? *Bullshit* is a very good word for moments such as this. *I liked you too much?* For God's sake, Luke *Last*, can't you do a tiny bit better than that?'

'You should be arrested for assault,' he said. 'Actual bodily harm.'

'Good.'

'I just didn't think you were for me.'

'*Bloody hell*—'

'You're not *listening*. I'm trying to tell you—' He struggled. And stopped. And tried again.

Leigh saw him struggle and she lost the taste for goading him. She had forgotten, in making him her enemy, the truth of him. It was not fair to push him. It was not fair to test his strength, because he was not sound. But then, he came closer and looked into her eyes very seriously. She could not breathe. There wasn't anybody else who stopped her breathing by being so close. It didn't seem something a person should want. But she did.

'The thing is,' he said, 'I had no idea what to do with you.'

She reached for her anger but it had gone. It wasn't that he lied; he lacked. He lacked. She felt as sad for him as she had ever felt for anybody.

She had no choice. She said, 'And now?'

'Now I do. I think I do now,' he said.

She had seen the damage he could do. She would have no assurance. She could walk away from him, if she wanted to. It wouldn't make any difference. She put her hand lightly onto his shirt, just below his collarbone. He looked surprised – then stepped towards her. His heart beating under her hand. She felt shy. He bent his head down to reach her. And they kissed.

They kissed. Both smiled a little, then it was serious. He put his hand to her face to do it better. It felt very beautiful to him. There was the cliff. There was the abyss. There was the dark. There was the fall, just there, ahead of her.

And then the kiss was over.

They stood there with nothing to say for a moment. They did not look at one another, but he took her hand. The world came back slowly and they joined it. They began to walk along the pavement in the direction she had been going, but together. They didn't talk. They were next to one another. It did not feel meant. It did not feel fated. It had not been written.

I am tremendously grateful to my editor and publisher at Chatto and Windus, Clara Farmer.

Also at Chatto and Windus, and at Vintage, to: Rachel Cugnoni and Tom Drake-Lee; Lisa Gooding and Susannah Otter; Dan Franklin, Gail Rebuck and Richard Cable; Suzanne Dean and Lily Richards.

And many thanks to Caroline Wood.

In the States, I would very much like to thank my editor at HarperCollins, Terry Karten.

Also at Harper, Jane Beirn and Jonathan Burnham, and at the Gernert Company, Stephanie Cabot.

To Tim Boyd, Richard Gregson, Rebecca Harris, Anna Parker, Nat Parker, Evan Jones, Joanna Jones, Melissa Jones, Brian Phelan, Jeff Rawle, Nina Rawle, Jodi Shields, Jon Summerill and June Summerill — thank you. Any faults and failures are my own.

In writing *Fallout*, *Modern British Playwriting: the 1970s* by Chris Megson was an invaluable resource, as were, among others: *A Theatre for All Seasons: Nottingham Playhouse 1948–78* by John Bailey; *Stage Directions* by Michael Frayn, *Looking Back: Playwrights At The Royal Court* by Harriet Devine, and *Kenneth Tynan* by Dominic Shellard; also Tynan's diaries and writings themselves.

# About the Author

Sadie Jones is the author of four novels, including *The Outcast*, winner of the Costa First Novel Award in Great Britain and a finalist for the Orange Prize for Fiction and the Los Angeles Times Book Prize/Art Seidenbaum Award for First Fiction, *Small Wars*, and the bestselling *The Uninvited Guests*. She lives in London.

## About the author

**2** A Conversation with Sadie Jones

## About the book

**6** On Writing *Fallout*

## Read on

**10** Author Picks: Books and Plays
That Inspired *Fallout*

**11** Have You Read?
More by Sadie Jones

Insights,
Interviews
& More . . .

# A Conversation with Sadie Jones

*Can you tell us about your childhood, growing up as the daughter of a scriptwriter and an actress? Did it inspire your interest in the theater world?*

*Fallout*'s central characters are older than I am and younger than my parents which freed me from the sense of autobiography. That said, my earliest, vague, but deeply rooted memories are probably those closest to the world Luke, Leigh, Paul, and Nina inhabit. As a very young child, at the beginning of the seventies, I remember the people who used to visit my parents' house in World's End, Chelsea. The area is now very smart and somewhat sterile, but then it was still quite bohemian. The basement kitchen was often full of people; overlapping talk of failure and success, plays put on and films made or, more often, not made— all the reported dramas of the adult world. My godfather is Brian Phelan, a playwright and screenwriter, and his wife, Dorothy Bromley, an actress and founder member of Common Stock, a seminal community theater company. I remember, though not in detail, their stories, and those of my parents and others, and the atmosphere of Gitane smoke, the bottles and the smell of red wine and whiskey as they talked, while my sister and I sat on laps and listened or didn't listen, before being sent off to bed.

When I was writing *Fallout* I did not speak to my godfather or interview my parents or any of their friends. I approached the book as though it were any other world and not close to me. It was partly because I did not want to write an insider's story. Luke—most evidently—is an outsider, but so are Leigh, Paul, and Nina. Very few people feel like insiders—and I certainly am not one of them. I find, too, that when I consciously visit my own experience, the imagination is inhibited. Denying myself the easy resource of friends made the research for the book longer, and even unnecessarily complicated, but it forced me to be rigorous. I wanted my story to be grounded *in*, but not *by*, reality.

**You were initially interested in becoming an actress. How did you determine you wanted to do something else instead? When did you decide you wanted to be a writer, and what did you write first?**

I always wrote, and took it for granted. I think I wanted to act because I was attracted to the thrill of being part of a creative group, more sociable and romantic than writing alone, and there was probably an element of youthful egotism and vanity, too. It turned out I had almost no talent and was crippled by self-consciousness, which I found out—luckily—quite early on, and abandoned the idea. I would have hated it. I always saw writing as something that would still be there ▶

when the adventure of living was done with. My ambition as a writer, if you could call it that, came a little while later.

***Which of your characters was the most difficult to write, and why? Who was the easiest?***

They each had their challenges, but I suppose it was Nina, in a way, mainly because in her conception she was to be Luke's downfall. I had to empathize with both of them, often within a scene, and her behavior, more than his, was hard to admire. There was a degree of honesty in writing her weakness and her sadness that I found uncomfortable. She was painful to be with. Leigh was tough to write for the opposite reason, because she is so sympathetic, and I feared she would lack depth because of it, but once I knew her backstory and imagined her there in front of me, she was flesh and blood, and the dullness I had worried about dissolved. Luke was just Luke, and once he turned up he stayed very close. I am often surprised when he is described as difficult—everything he did seemed perfectly normal to me. That is the best way to feel about a character, and what I work to have: the feeling that I'm on the inside, forgetting judgment.

***Do you have a favorite character? A least favorite? How do you summon such empathy for less pleasant characters, like Tony?***

I liked Tony very much, and felt sorry for him. He is, of all of them, the most lost. He loves Nina, and he does not want to hurt her. The decision not to tell his backstory and to leave the pathways of his damage mysterious was deliberate, because he himself never tells, even to himself, but I knew him.

### What does a day of writing look like for you?

I'm very boring, I work office hours. I start around nine and work a minimum of five hours. At the beginning of a book, or when it's going badly, I do procrastinate and sometimes lose whole days to it— mainly because I'm scared of writing badly or reluctant to force myself out of the real world into a consuming other. But the fear of not writing is always worse than the fear of writing, and housework the worst fear of all, so I tend to be fairly disciplined.  ∾

# On Writing *Fallout*

EACH BOOK has its own particular starting place. *The Uninvited Guests* began with a dream that on waking I realized I had dreamed before— a house inhabited by different people in a different time. *The Outcast* began with the line in my head, *There's something wrong with him*. The resulting preoccupation with who "he" might be led me to find Lewis, a damaged young man coming out of prison and determined to redeem himself. *Small Wars* was sparked by the stories I was hearing of soldiers who were fighting in Iraq and Afghanistan, and the questions I had about preserving humanity when moral certainty is endangered. And *Fallout* began with love. I am not a reader of romances and I have not often found any book that captures love's power. Passion in others, in fiction or in life, can look either sickly-sweet or incomprehensible. Illogical. Hackneyed. For humanity's most celebrated universal feeling it can be pretty hard to relate to. I was fascinated for a long time by a line I heard once: *Romantic love is the meeting of two pathologies*. I find the notion of people being made for one another vaguely sinister. Despite that, or perhaps because of it, I wanted to write a love story, to tell it not as sentiment or romance, but as something that drives and can destroy us.

Each of my books has been almost impossible to write at some time in the process—sometimes more than one time. With *Fallout* that point was at the very beginning. I worked for well over a year before starting to write properly but once I did I had a first draft in about seven months, which is very fast. It was consuming. It had to be, if I was to get it right. I'm not sure words written in detachment can engender anything other than detachment in a reader.

In trying to find the story, the months of planning and exploration, I knew very early that the central line of the narrative was a love triangle and that the '70s was the right time to tell it. It was an era heady with freedom, but the young people then, like every generation before and since, were living in the fallout of those preceding them. The social blueprint of the past had been torn up but there was no map to follow. Sex, legal abortion, divorce without stigma were presented as freedoms without consequences to the first generation for whom the gratification of the self was paramount. In the 1950s, Love in popular culture was— broadly speaking—boy-meets-girl- innocence and the post-war return to conventionality, and the 1960s was the time when youth ecstatically overturned those precedents. But the early 1970s was the decade "love" grew up. When I was getting ready to write I listened to the music, read the plays, and watched the films of the time. From high to low culture: the songs of Paul Simon, the films of Woody Allen, the plays of Pinter, all, in their different ways tell of a complicated world in which, while ▶

sex and liberty are taken for granted, their repercussions are freshly examined.

Of the many love triangles of *Fallout*, the one that I began with was between the playwright, his work, and the woman he is in love with: Luke, writing and Nina. That Luke was writing plays and it must therefore be the 1970s were essential facts, tied to one another from the outset, because his work had to be fundamental—not only to him, but vital in itself. There is wonderful and important theater now, and great writing, but many thinking, reading, apparently cultured people happily admit to "never going to the theater." (And sadly, even to "never reading novels anymore.") At that time theater was essential part of life. A good play was headline news. It was not icing, or highbrow and rarefied, it was in schools, factories, universities, and pubs. There were hundreds of theater companies, touring everything from Shakespeare to political propaganda; repertory companies providing entertainment and taking risks, a culture that was powerful and essential. I needed my characters, who are so committed to their art and to their loves, to be in a world that reflected their intensity. Luke, Leigh, Nina, and Paul are struggling to forge their own paths in a landscape shaped by their pasts. Their destinies are determined by the post-war years into which they were born as well as their specific circumstances, but the years have carried on without them. In many ways their story is only partly told. The end of one story must be the beginning of another, if it works, but whether that new story should remain in the imagination is unclear. In a way, it's unimportant. *Fallout*'s characters continue through the years I have not yet told and that is reassuring to me, as well as unsettling, because it is a proof of their life. ∽

Read on

# Author Picks
## Books and Plays That
## Inspired *Fallout*

*The Real Thing*—Tom Stoppard

*Theatre*—Somerset Maugham

*Betrayal*—Harold Pinter

*The Diaries of Kenneth Tynan*—
Kenneth Tynan, John Lahr
(editor) ⟿

# Have You Read?
## More by Sadie Jones

### THE OUTCAST

In 1957 Lewis Aldridge, newly released from prison, returns home to Waterford, a suburban town outside London. He is nineteen years old. A decade earlier his father's homecoming at war's end was greeted with far less apprehension by the staid, tightly knit community—thanks to Gilbert Aldridge's easy acceptance of suburban ritual and routine. Nobody is surprised that Gilbert's wife counters convention, but the entire community is shocked when, after one of their jaunts, Lewis comes back without her.

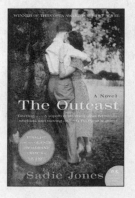

No one in Waterford wants Lewis back—except Kit, a young woman who sympathizes with his grief and burgeoning rage. But in her attempts to set them both free, Kit fails to foresee the painful and horrifying secrets that must first be forced into the open. The consequences for Lewis, his family, and the tightly knit community are devastating.

"Sharp and assured, a convincing illustration of the dangerous consequences of a muzzled society."
—*New York Times Book Review*

### SMALL WARS

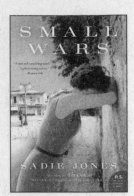

A major in the British Army, Hal Treherne is a dedicated soldier on the brink of a brilliant career. He is eager to lead his men into combat: his wife, Clara, however, is relieved when they are posted instead to seemingly peaceful sun-kissed Cyprus. But war erupts over unification with Greece, the island is consumed by violence—and Hal discovers that his military training cannot help him navigate the minefields of moral compromise that lie beneath every battle he fights. Clara grows fearful of her increasingly distant husband. When she needs him most, she finds the once-tender Hal a changed man— a betrayal that is only part of the shocking personal crisis to come.

"A taut and transfixing novel. . . . Jones is a gifted young author."   —*Boston Globe*

A grand old manor house deep in the English countryside will open its doors to reveal the story of an unexpectedly dramatic day in the life of one eccentric, rather dysfunctional, and entirely unforgettable family. Set in the early years of the twentieth century, award-winning author Sadie Jones's *The Uninvited Guests* is, in the words of Jacqueline Winspear, the *New York Times* bestselling author of the Maisie Dobbs mysteries *A Lesson in Secrets* and *Elegy for Eddie*, "a sinister tragi-comedy of errors, in which the dark underbelly of human nature is revealed in true Shakespearean fashion."

"Exhilaratingly strange and darkly funny. . . . *The Uninvited Guests* will haunt you—but happily." —*USA Today*